D0953561

Lady

Also by

THOMAS TRYON

The Other

Harvest Home

Lady

a novel by

THOMAS TRYON

Alfred A. Knopf   New York

THIS IS A BORZOI BOOK
PUBLISHED BY ALFRED A. KNOPF, INC.

Copyright © 1974 by Thomas Tryon

All rights reserved under International and Pan-American
Copyright Conventions. Published in the United States by
Alfred A. Knopf, Inc., New York, and simultaneously in
Canada by Random House of Canada Limited, Toronto.
Distributed by Random House, Inc., New York.

Manufactured in the United States of America

For Harry

"Here lies a most beautiful lady,
Light of step and heart was she."

Walter de la Mare,
"An Epitaph"

Contents

PART ONE   *Old Songs* 1

PART TWO   *New Songs* 69

PART THREE   *Sad Songs* 149

PART FOUR   *Last Songs* 211

PART FIVE   *Recollected Songs* 263

PART ONE

Old Songs

I

The wind sang old songs, as the tale went, and like the wind we too sang; sang "Good Night, Lady" at her doorway on Christmas Eve, but she would not come out. Why, I asked myself, why? Oh Lady, come out, we love you—*I* love you. Still, she would not. I couldn't understand then; no one could. I do now.

In small towns is there always a Lady Harleigh? I only know there was in ours. She lived in the handsomest house on the Green, a plaque by her front door identifying it as the "Josiah Webster House, Built 1702." A stranger inquiring who lived there would assuredly have been told there were three occupants only; that is, Lady herself, and her servants, the Griffins. But of course there were four, because the shade of Lady's dead husband also dwelt there.

No one but the mistress of the house was aware of Edward Harleigh's ghost, but so real was her apprehension, so evident her distress, that even I in time would glance up at a second-story window, almost expecting to see a half-realized presence brooding behind the curtain. But, of course, there were no ghosts in the house on the Green; only in Lady's heart.

During most of my boyhood I strove to know the heart of Adelaide Harleigh, to unravel the enigma that lingered in the corners of her mouth as her smile faded. For if she was everything to everybody, if she most often seemed joyful and content, her joy appeared to me something of a disguise. Still, she was Lady, ever Lady, and it is not of ghosts I write, but of love, for though I was only a boy of eight when I first knew her, and she well past forty, I came to love her, as she did me. She loved another also, if in a more comprehensible but less orthodox way; but I, unaware, had in those early years no cause for jealousy, because of all the children I was her favorite. It is not easy to learn much about love, but one thing I discovered, that Lady Harleigh taught me: it is not whom we love that is important, but only that we love.

Lady

The events I describe mainly concern a period of some fifteen years, from the early thirties until the end of the Second World War. Lady's house was opposite ours, on the west side of the Green, and we were in and out of it at all times and seasons during the years we were growing up. The Green was that locally renowned plot of New England earth that in Colonial times had been the village common, where our Pilgrim ancestors once skirmished with the Pequot Indians and where the Revolutionary militia shouldered squirrel rifles against the Redcoats of the tyrant George III. In my youth the Green was populated not only with strollers and game-players and children and dogs, but with the ancient elms that were the pride of Connecticut, one of them being the largest in America. Visitors would go out of their way to drive by and take pictures of it, and of Lady's house, and if they could, the automobile that went with the house, a custom-built Minerva landaulet—the talk of Pequot Landing.

I have a vivid picture in my mind of how the heavy doors of the carriage house would be swung open, and out would roll this peerless marvel. We would stand around in the driveway where the Negro houseman would observe us solemnly as he flicked a turkey duster along the gleaming hood, one guarded eye watching for Mrs. Harleigh's rippling reflection in the curve of a gleaming fender when she would come out of the house.

His darkly lustrous face freshly shaved, aromatic with bay rum and a generous dusting of talc, Jesse Griffin presented a spruce and natty figure, liveried in brass-buttoned gray, with a black-visored cap and puttees that had at least four buckles on each; but with nothing so much as a smile on his face when he handed his passenger up into the car and bore her off, as though he didn't know he was Mrs. Edward Harleigh's chauffeur and driving the only Minerva east of New York City.

Unlike its owner, the car was old-fashioned but, like her, it was sleek and shining and wonderful to behold, and we rejoiced in its magnificence. Gray within and without, it had coffin-tufted upholstery, with little silver-and-glass vases on the uprights behind the chauffeur's panel, and over the rear compartment a top which lay back for riding in fine weather.

And there would be our neighbor, Mrs. Harleigh, seated easily and gracefully against the soft upholstery, masses of flowers in her arms to take to the cemetery. I was sure that a word my sister, Ag, was always using must have been invented for her: exquisite. She

looked almost regal, always smiling, yet with sad dark places around
her eyes; always with a warm nod that made you feel important—
which is to say, happy (sometimes calling out to admire your Colonel Tim McCoy badge); always with a smart hat and spotted veil
tilted over her brow, her suavely gloved fingers describing friendly
feathery motions through the air, as though a bunch of knockabout
kids were the delight of her life; always calling "Hel-*lo*" in that
musical voice.

What impressed me most about Mrs. Harleigh in those days was
her laughter, gay, light, utterly feminine, like her step. (Her movement was only slightly affected by a bad fall she had suffered some
years earlier, and the injuries she sustained left her with the slightest
limp, which she never took notice of; nor did we.) She appeared to
enjoy life more than most, for all that she lacked a husband, and
that people talked about her under their breath and behind church
programs on Sunday. They said it was to cover the fact of her
tragedy (Mrs. Sparrow said Lady Harleigh was "pure *Pagliacci*"), a
scrim of laughter behind which she hid her broken heart. Mrs.
Sparrow, our next-door neighbor, spoke with such authority you
were compelled to believe her, but Mrs. Harleigh's laugh was so
real, so sincere, it rang with such "Ladylike" sparkle, you felt it came
from the depths of her being.

Everyone felt sorry for Adelaide Harleigh. This is not to say they
pitied her to her face—Yankees are not given to such signal displays
—but she had for years been the object of commiseration and
sympathetic if not downright tender looks as she ritually went to the
village cemetery to place flowers at the grave of her husband, Edward.

The fact most apparent to all was, of course, her widowhood and
her admirable constancy to the memory of her beloved, who had
succumbed to influenza in the thirteenth year of their marriage. We
understood her sorrow. She felt that her dead husband was *her*
dead, to take care of, to garden for, to reflect upon in her quiet moments, to remember, even to enshrine. But though she mourned him,
she was more interested in the living. In so many ways, large and
small, she allowed herself "the luxury of doing good," as Oliver
Goldsmith says. Perhaps her greatest trait was consideration for
others, and her ability to *feel* for people. She was compassionate,
generous, unselfish, and concerned. I never stumbled but she picked
me up and kissed the hurt place, never was despondent but she

tried to cheer me, never bored but she contrived some diversion; how nice she was, how kind and good.

Why wasn't Lady like our mothers? Why didn't she act like our mothers? Why was she always Lady?

I can still remember the stone marten furs—I believe Edward had given them to her—which lay about her neck so soft and glistening, with a silk tassel caught between the spring of the jaws, and the shiny yellow eyes, so lifelike you had to touch them to realize they were glass. Her hats were stylish, more so perhaps because in those days the women of Pequot Landing wore rather drab millinery, if they bothered with hats at all. And gloves; I used to sit fascinated, observing with what ceremony she would put them on, slipping the material over each finger in turn, with the merest upward shift of the brows as she managed the third left finger where she wore her gold wedding band, and doing up the pearl buttons at the cuff.

Best of all was her coat, sable or mink, I never knew which, but how wonderfully it became her, so fitting to both her person and character, with a rich luxurious smell to it. She liked to pin a bunch of flowers to the collar, violets or sometimes lily of the valley, whose scent, combined with that of her perfume, was like herself irresistible.

See her on Sunday: after entrancing the minister in the vestibule, down the steps she would float, with a few words for Mrs. Sparrow about last week's doings around the Green, a few for our mother (like Mrs. Harleigh, also a widow), another few for Colonel Blatchley, an airy wave for the rest, in an audacious hat, the net pulled up behind in a saucy bow; and Jesse Griffin, changed to his iron-black church suit, would hand her up into the open Minerva and off they would go, she in the back seat, talking into the speaking tube, he in front, listening and nodding, under the elms along Broad Street to the Green where Elthea Griffin would serve luncheon to her mistress and several invited friends.

See her in the evening, off and away to Bushnell Memorial Hall, to hear Lawrence Tibbett in *Rigoletto,* or to see the Lunts touring in *Reunion in Vienna,* on Colonel Blatchley's arm, dressed in satin or velvet, wearing diamonds or pearls, an evening cloak or her furs, wafted away like a Royal Personage—not in her elegant Minerva, but in the Colonel's more ordinary Studebaker, while not only Ruthie Sparrow but half the Green had its eyes trained on her, for indeed what else was there to look at or to talk of or to rejoice in?

The Green cherished its Lady Harleigh; to know her, people said, was to love her, and this was an absolute fact.

See her next day, the house windows thrown open, sunshine and air and all outdoors being let inside, she changed from velvet to cotton, from evening to house dress, the radio blaring while her daily routine of calisthenics is performed, then barelegged out into the garden to see to her flowers, to pick her cucumbers, to revel in her sprouting potatoes, then to fly back into the kitchen, becoming a whirlwind at stove and oven, always baking something for a poor person or an ill one (remembering, perhaps, her own illness, and how Edward had died), the wooden batter spoon in her hand, and when the baking was done, off would fly the apron and "Jesse, will you bring the auto out?" while she boxed a cake for one family, a pie for another, and down Broad Street would go the Minerva, Jesse beyond the glass in the chauffeur's seat, she in the rear with the pastries, administering her occasions about town through the little cloth-covered speaking tube.

But then, see her—altered. For, with no apparent reason, the gaiety would disappear, her behavior would become odd, she seemed scarcely to know if she saw you, and she seldom saw you, for invariably at these times she would shut herself away upstairs in the big house. Our neighbor Mrs. Sparrow called these periods "retirements" and said that Mrs. Harleigh "wasn't feeling herself." Whatever they represented, these manifestations of her malaise seemed to me unreasoning; but then it was not I, but Lady herself, who was living with a ghost.

2

What was Adelaide Harleigh really like? people sometimes ask. Who can say what anybody is really like? People are like what we see in them or remember of them. For me, she was like no other. The private and personal facts of her unhappy situation were frequently made public (and thus gained local currency) by Mrs. Sparrow. The Sparrows were gray little creatures like the birds themselves, he so innocuous that we seldom took notice of him, while she, on the other hand, was forever ensconced in her bay window observing proceedings around the Green and subsequently broadcasting them at random.

Wielding a pair of Seiss-Altag binoculars which Mr. Sparrow, an infantry sergeant in the First World War, had brought back from France, Mrs. Sparrow kept a weather eye out for any doings, scandalous or otherwise. In those days the Paramount Newsreel featured itself as "The Eyes and Ears of the World." Because she went Paramount one better, we called Ruthie Sparrow "The Eyes and Ears and Mouth of the World."

On the far side of the Green, open to her vigilant surveillance, was the Harleigh house, and the pertinent details of Edward Harleigh's wooing of Adelaide Strasser, their marriage, and its tragic conclusion were, during the period I write of, continually bandied about by Ruth Sparrow, and in consequence were commonly accepted knowledge throughout the town. I was privy to them because in addition to the sins of lying and stealing, I practice those of the habitual Peeping Tom and eavesdropper; and, being innately curious about my fellow-man, I relished it all. I would sit on our vine-screened porch entranced to overhear Mrs. Sparrow entertaining callers on her piazza, offering for their edification (and mine) the variously sad or comic histories of the neighborhood.

Hear Ruthie Sparrow:

"Oh, yes, Edward was a regular rake in those days. Folks said that money had spoiled him rotten. When he came back from Yale on holiday, was he ever to home? No, he was with his cronies in the taproom at the River House being sociable with that Elsie Thatcher, who was only too willing to serve those fellows whatever it was they wanted. Edward was a rip! But I *like* a rip, don't you? It just killed me, how that boy could cut up! But Lord, wasn't he handsome! And fascinating!" Even at my age it was plain that Mrs. Sparrow had been enamored of Edward Harleigh, and believed he could do no wrong.

"But, meeting Adelaide Strasser, didn't he change his tune? Oh, Lady . . ." (Here a tender sigh for the maiden Lady Harleigh, who had been Adelaide Strasser, the town's fairest beauty. Which, like many another of Ruthie Sparrow's notions, was not strictly accurate. Lady Harleigh could never have been considered a conventional beauty. Her nose had a bump in it just below the bridge, and several small moles marred the perfection of her features. Still, beauty being in the eye of the beholder, she was to me most beautiful, and I will concede to Mrs. Sparrow the fitness of the term.)

It is true that Edward's was one of the oldest and most esteemed families in Pequot Landing. The Harleigh bastion was over near the Center, where the awful Spragues now lived, and for generations there had always been a male member of the family on the Board of Selectmen or in the local governing hierarchy or among the Congregational deaconry. Not only powerful (old Mr. Harleigh had the whole town in the closed palm of his red and horny hand), these people were rich, their fortune having flowed in a steady stream from the Pequot Plow Company, manufacturers of plowshares and for years the only "smoking" industry around. When this firm was sold, the Harleighs, already speculating in onions during the Spanish-American War, wisely invested their capital in land along the Connecticut River. Through stock manipulations just preceding the Panic of 1907, greater awards accrued. To this long-accumulated wealth Edward was the sole heir, and since his father was already well advanced in years, every matron in Pequot Landing with a marriageable daughter had an eye cocked on the son.

Ruthie on her piazza again:

"Well, once Edward Harleigh saw Adelaide Strasser, there was never no question of his choice. Now, the Strassers had immigrated to this country from Germany back in the nineties. They lived over on Knobb Street, at the *wrong* end, just where the railroad tracks cross. Mrs. Strasser—her who got so high 'n' mighty later, living up there on the Valley Hill Road—back then she was nothing but a seamstress. Used to do her sewing for better-class ladies, and Edward's mother, being the sort of person *she* was, you know—awfully, *awfully*—she just had to have Mrs. Strasser down to cut some dresses. Seen 'em myself, pinning up brocades and bombazine by the yard in the front room; you could look in just by walkin' by the house. Anyways, Anna Strasser was plenty handy with a needle and she put in a good turn, sewing for Mrs. Harleigh.

"But don't think Anna Strasser didn't know what sort of daughter she had over there on Knobb Street, scrubbing the linoleum. So she arranges for Lady to come by the Harleigh house to bring her a pattern she 'forgot,' and it happened Edward was to home, this being over a holiday. He takes her for a sleigh ride, let me tell you, *lots* of sleigh rides. I seen 'em myself, whizzing around the Green here in that little one-horse sleigh Lady's got over there in her carriage house right now. Poor dear, she's sentimental about such things, like she can't bear to part with them. Can't bear to part with Edward's chifforobe, nor won't let anyone sit in Edward's armchair, nor won't get her hair cut, because Edward liked it long.

"Quick as a wink, there was an engagement at Christmastime

and Edward and Lady were married that spring. Mr. Strasser—he taught Greek up to the college—he never lived to see his daughter wed, and a sad thing that was.

"So off they went to Mexico on their honeymoon, right across the country in a Pullman drawing room. And don't think Lady was the only soul whose life changed by marrying the town prince—in no time Anna Strasser was moved out of that tacky house on Knobb Street and living in a new place down t' the end of Valley Hill Road near the golf club, and *she's* got someone doin' *her* sewin'.

"And there she was when Lady and Edward come home that summer, as beautiful a couple as you'd care to see. More tea, dear? 'Scuse me."

Here I would settle down on the porch, painting the wheels of my roller skates with Aggie's nail polish until Mrs. Sparrow returned with tea to continue the story. It had been late August when the bridal couple moved onto the Green, in the Josiah Webster House, Built 1702. A large brick house, with gleaming white-painted trim and rows of sunny windows between long shutters, the squares of glass twinkling in the light. Two splendid elms canopied the broad front lawn, and a flagstoned paving led from the street to its friendly sagging doorway where the stoop was laid charmingly askew, with two small panes of bull's-eye glass set in over the lintel. The slates angled steeply from the rooftree, where graceful wrought-iron rods served to ward off bolts of lightning that threatened the slender chimneys rising like sentinels over the gabled dormers.

Inside, generous furnishings, including a Sheraton dining table and eight chairs—one with arms, where Edward always sat when they entertained—to say nothing of Lady's expensive dressing table, and the walnut chifforobe with numerous drawers in which Edward kept his personal belongings.

And so the years went by, until, hostilities having broken out in Europe, and America about to go into the war, Lady discovered she was pregnant. The prospect of motherhood seemed to delight her and she spent hours selecting a layette. Lady's pleasure was matched by Edward's and, bon vivant that he was, he announced the coming event in church, then went home and had one or two too many at a celebration luncheon. He never *was* known among the country-club crowd as being able to hold his liquor well, and if he wasn't at the club, he'd be celebrating with Yonny Turpin and Al Yager, two unsavory local characters who hung out at the Noble Patriot, a café across from the Academy Hall, or at the nearby River House.

"There's your cup, dear. Did I mention Elsie Thatcher that used to wait table over there at River House, a saucy piece if ever there was, and all the boys in town chasing her? But when Edward was sober you'd see him and Lady making their rounds about the Green, for her health, dear. Oh, wasn't they the handsomest couple! I sat right there in my bay window and watched 'em, how Edward would encircle her waist and sort of lead her around; she was awfully weak then. Miss Berry from two doors down, she was a nurse—and a good one, let me say—and she was hired to look after Lady and the baby.

"Wasn't any baby, of course. About five months along, Lady slipped and fell, and was badly hurt. The baby miscarried; she never had another. Affected her brain somehow—couldn't talk at all, not a word, Lord." Here Mrs. Sparrow would roll her eyes to heaven as if seeking corroboration of the facts from her Maker.

"Next thing, Edward gets his commission and is off to France. We'd gone into the war that summer of '17, and even the fact that he had an invalid wife couldn't keep Edward Harleigh from his duty. He sailed in October—October, and he'd only live to see one more. Who was to know then they'd be happy for such a short time, and it'd all come to naught, with poor Lady living the rest of her life with a *ghost!*"

Mrs. Sparrow felt she had all the facts at hand concerning both halves of the separated couple on either side of the Atlantic. Lady's malady, hitherto undefined, was diagnosed by Ruthie as a *crise de nerfs*, a French term she had discovered in a *Liberty* magazine article called "Is American Womanhood in a State of Nerves?" (reading time: 2 minutes, 58 seconds). The implication being that Lady Harleigh had suffered a nervous breakdown following her miscarriage.

Between Miss Berry and the senior Harleighs, however, arrangements were made for the patient to be sent to a sanitarium outside of Washington, and by degrees, it was learned, Lady's responses showed a marked improvement.

But while Lady's affliction abated, so did Edward's fortunes. He was gassed in the Meuse-Argonne offensive late in September, and was hospitalized. The Armistice came in November, and when he recovered sufficiently, he was awarded a medal for distinguished service during the battle. The following spring, news reached the Green that he had been released from the hospital and was returning on the *Giuseppe Verdi*, an Italian ship out of Genoa.

Lady came back only weeks before Edward—a little anxiously, Mrs. Sparrow thought, watching her alight at the station. When

Edward arrived, he was given a hero's welcome, a parade, the First Selectman making a speech, and in newspaper photographs a pale but proud Lady was seen pinning a medal on the breast of her husband's tunic.

No sooner home than the couple left for Sea Island, Georgia, in an attempt to restore Edward's health. They were gone several months. Making their return, at Lady's whim they stopped in Washington, even though the city was locked in a torturous heat wave; there were Turners on exhibition at the National Gallery. And they resumed their married life on the Green and were, according to Mrs. Sparrow, the picture of domestic bliss, which is to say that, enjoying their fine house, they kept to it. It was during this period of their return to Pequot that both Edward's parents died, first Mrs. Harleigh, then, within three months, old Daddy Harleigh. Most of the family heirlooms found their way to the Green, and became part and parcel of that house. The heavy furniture Mother Harleigh had selected was sent to auction. "Lady still wasn't feeling too well, so Miss Berry continued looking after her. Nice as pie, Miss Berry, she gave Lady one of her little dogs to keep her comp'ny—one of them dear little whatyamacallits with the little beards? Then tragedy struck again. . . ."

The autumn had seen a cruel epidemic of Spanish influenza, and when Lady came down with it Edward moved from their bedchamber to another room to avoid infection. Attended by Miss Berry, Lady battled a dangerously high temperature, crying out in torment of her fever, and for a time it was thought she might not survive. But she recovered, now arising to help Miss Berry tend Edward, who meantime had fallen ill.

His lungs already impaired by the siege of gas, he lay wasted upon the pillow while Lady remained at his side, unwilling to leave for a moment, helping Miss Berry hold Edward over the inhaler, an apparatus used to produce vapors of friar's balsam to clear his congested lungs.

"Then," Mrs. Sparrow would continue dramatically, "just when it appeared certain he was getting well, he suffered a relapse. He contracted lobar pneumonia and went into a crisis no human soul could've recovered from. I remember that night so well, late October, it was—Halloween, as a matter of fact—and storming fit to beat the band. But storm or not, there wasn't nothing anybody could do, not Lady nor Miss Berry nor the doctor. I seen him come and I went over and held that poor shivering girl in my arms, and she frantic

as could be, crying for the priest, and Edward a good Protestant—
well, not so *good*, but we all have our faith, I expect.

"And who could keep Lady from blaming herself? All them weeks
she practically took on her own shoulders the nursing of that man,
not that Miss Berry wasn't a good nurse. But blame herself Lady
did, and bitterly. After the funeral, she went home and locked herself up. She closed them shutters and all that long winter wouldn't
see a soul. Not even Anna, her mother; wouldn't have her in the
house. She let the servants go, and only the priest come—Lady was
still Cath'lic then—almost every day for a time, and then he went
away and didn't come back no more. What a burden of woe he
must've been bearing—I seen his face through m'binoculars and that
poor man just looked tireder and more troubled every time he left.

"And nobody saw poor Lady for months. One day I went over
and peeked in a window. There she was, kneeling on the living-
room floor, her hands clasped before a picture of Edward and saying not a word. Utterly dumbstruck. The poor soul, I feared she'd
lost her speech again.

"By Saint Valentine's Day I was so worried I put on my best dress
and hat and took over a covered dish. I rung, and Lady herself come
to the door, was dressed in widow's weeds head to foot, and asked
me into the front room. I says to her she must come away, and she
sitting there in the wing chair as gracious as can be, but scarcely
hearing a word I'm saying, but only making polite chitchat about
was it going to be an early spring, and she hadn't put no bulbs in
that fall.

"And the parlor—you can't believe how dusty and frumpy it had
got, and her being such a particular housekeeper. But, with Edward gone, she just didn't seem to want to go on. She looked
*turri*ble, even though the black *was* becoming, and her hair was
neat as usual, and she'd taken his ring off, her hands were bare, and
I says, 'Lady, you're just incarcerating yourself in here, when you
should be out in the air. And where's your dear little dog that Miss
Berry gave you?'

" 'I don't care for the air,' says she, 'and the little dog is no longer
here.' Dog or not, I says, you'll never regain your health thisaway.
I tell you, she was willfully and deliberately destroying herself upon
the altar of her dead husband—why, it was practically a sut*tee!* Not
only that, she'd made a shrine! Right there in the living room on the
gate-leg table. Pictures of poor Edward in uniform under small
crossed flags, with his medal for bravery in a velvet-lined box and all

his citations and a framed copy of the speech the First Selectman made when Edward come home a hero. And the photo they took of the ceremony, with Edward smiling so's it'd break yore heart and Lady sort of looking off to the side, and that awful Anna Strasser positively lurking in the background.

"So I says, 'You've got happy memories, Lady, you must dwell on them, not the sad ones,' and she sort of smiles and says 'Yes.' And I says, 'You must start looking forward again,' and she says 'Yes' again. 'Yes, I shall.'

"Well, that gave me a feeling of hope, so I says, 'What you ought to do is get another little dog.' 'No,' she says, 'I will never have another dog.' And she opened the door, she threw her arms around me and cried and cried, Lord such bitter tears"—here another of Ruthie's celestial corroborations—"but it was a woman's heart that shed 'em and I told myself all the way back across the Green that now she's going to come out of it at last.

"And she did. Lovely, brave Lady, on the first day of spring she come to church, not her Cath'lic one, but Edward's, and she stood in the choir loft and sang 'The Lost Chord'—Lady has a beautiful voice. Then, come April, just before spring-cleaning time, I went over again, the forsythia was all in bloom and I took her some, and she told me the house was a mess—and it *was*, let me say—and it was time now to do something about it. My heart leaped in my bosom. But, I says, you can't do it by yourself. No, she wouldn't, she'd advertised for a couple to take over the entire running of the place. And there they came, Elthea and Jesse Griffin, all the way from Barbados in the West Indies, as clean and good-looking a couple as you could hope for, and not one whit shiftless like some of them colored couples can be. Well, they moved into the attic—up there where you see them two front gables—and *my!* didn't the dust fly around that house. Busy as bees, the pair of 'em, and in no time the house just shone."

And while they worked, Lady herself took an hour or two of sun each day, and by June was the picture of health. Her skin recovered its clear, natural tone; her hair (always one of her great charms, Mrs. Sparrow asserted, which was true; and she kept it unfashionably long as a tribute, even when half the ladies in town had had theirs cut or shingled) was glossy and shining; she purchased new clothes and linens, resumed wearing her wedding ring; and, Mrs. Sparrow declared, "Hearing Lady laugh, you knew for sure everything was going to be all right."

Her mother, Mrs. Strasser, died that summer, and after observing a discreet period of mourning, Lady began entertaining in the fall. The house having been completely refurbished by then, small choice groups came to and from her elegant board. The minister, some of the selectmen, Colonel Blatchley, members of the country-club crowd (but never Porter Sprague or his wife). Elthea Griffin, an excellent cook, introduced to Pequot Landing a number of Caribbean dishes hitherto unfamiliar, and before long the whole town seemed bent on serving calaloo soup and creole crab. It was all people could do to remove themselves from table, so interesting was the talk, so merry the laughter, with Jesse in his white coat silently passing coffee and dessert and afterward brandy and cigars for the men while Colonel Blatchley told stories.

And everyone present always pretended not to notice that the place at the head of the table was kept empty, or that their hostess would never permit anyone to occupy the Sheraton armchair where the dead Edward had sat.

3

My earliest recollection of Lady Harleigh stems from events that occurred not in Pequot Landing but in another place entirely. The picture of these events is spun out of the threads of dimmest memory, but they served, in later years, to shed a clearer light on what had been until then an inexplicable mystery. It involved Lady herself, a wire-haired fox terrier, a dish of tapioca, and a moonlight walk in a rose garden.

There used to be, and perhaps still is, a many-roomed seashore hotel of white clapboards and green shutters and wide verandas, perched atop a bluff overlooking Long Island Sound. People of moderate means would go there to pass part of the summer away from the heat. Women, especially the older ones, often wore long white afternoon dresses then, with wide-brimmed hats, and they still carried parasols. They would sit on the veranda fussily sipping iced tea and fanning themselves with oval fans of dyed palmetto, and conversing while they regarded the view of the Sound—never interesting—and the men, also in white, with jaunty bow ties, would play tennis behind the hotel or go off with golf bags to the nearby links.

The summer our father died, his parents were spending that August at the hotel, which was called the Manor House Inn, and, grieving over Pa's death, Ma was invited to bring us all for a week-end.

It was there that I first saw the Minerva landaulet, and its owner. We were in the bathhouses behind the hotel, which were attached to it by a long latticed breezeway grown over with some kind of vine—morning-glories, probably. Ma had helped me into my scratchy wool swimsuit and my feet were shod in tight bathing shoes of flesh-colored crêpe rubber. As we came through the breezeway, the great car drove in, circling the arbor and birdbath, and pulling up at the side porch. The liveried chauffeur got out and opened the rear door and helped two passengers alight. One appeared ordinary enough —I noticed the frisky wire-haired fox terrier she had on a leash, never dreaming that the dog would soon be ours, our Patsy. But the second woman! Coming up behind me, my sister, Aggie, said that she looked like a movie star. She wore a large hat with the light coming through the brim, and there was a red cloth flower pinned at her bosom, and she was laughing. I thought her the most exciting and splendid-looking person I had ever seen.

We had moved to Pequot Landing only that spring, and I had no idea who she was, or that she lived across the Green, but, "Why, there's Mrs. Harleigh," Ma said, recognizing our neighbor, and, leaving me with Aggie, she went to greet the new arrivals. A maid— even I could tell it was a maid—got out and began helping the chauffeur with the luggage while Ma and the two ladies strolled up the walk where Mr. and Mrs. Stevenson, the owners, came to greet them.

"Isn't she the loveliest?" Ag whispered, peeking through the shadowy lattice. I knew, of course, which person she was speaking of. She became the focus of my interest for the remainder of our stay, and I went out of my way to spy on her, or to try to contrive an encounter of some sort, but this I never seemed able to manage. Covertly I observed her strolling alone among the roses, nodding to the other guests or pausing for a brief word, but not really becoming socially involved. She never gathered with the ladies on the porch, only arriving for meals at the last minute, which she took with her friend at a corner table where she would talk quietly and stare out at the view. I wondered why the two Negroes didn't eat with them, and my brother, Lew, told me not to be dumb; servants didn't eat in the dining room. Neither, I noted, did the dog.

We did meet, finally, this marvelous-looking lady and I. Below the steep cliff the hotel was built on, there was a trio of large rocks, called The Three Sisters, where we would go climbing, or inspecting the tidal pools for starfish, snails, and other sea treasures. Playing among these rocks alone one afternoon, I had pulled off my bathing shoes, which were always uncomfortable, and was watching a hermit crab scuttle about with someone else's shell on its back. I happened to look up and saw above me the laughing lady. But she was not laughing then. Unaware, she was lost in thought as she gazed out to sea, the black silk of a parasol framing her face against the blue sky. Something bright caught the light beside her nose, and she touched it away with her fingertip, then used her handkerchief. She was crying, and some inexplicable but immediate rush of feeling rose in me—I wanted to run to her and comfort her.

Instead, I felt a sharp pinch on my toe, and I jumped up, yelping. A large crab had attached itself to me, and was holding on with might and main. I pranced around, yelling and crying, while Mrs. Harleigh hurried down to me. Closing her parasol, she rapped the crab with it until it released me, then sat me down and inspected the damage to my toe, which was slight enough. But it was she who was now comforting me, speaking soothing words, binding my injury with her handkerchief, and joking that "that bad old crab had better watch his steps." She kissed me on the top of my head, murmuring something about my being the little boy across the Green, then went away, along the sand toward the deserted end of the beach.

Thus my brief but memorable first meeting with Lady Harleigh. Later that night, there was another occurrence which in itself seemed in no way remarkable, but which had a certain bearing on my eventual comprehension of matters.

In the evening the hotel guests would gather in the front parlor, around the radio, listening to—I suppose—the A. & P. Gypsies or a talk on sound investments, the usual popular fare of the time. My two older brothers, Lew and Harry, had become friendly with the dog, Patsy, and this caused her owner, a Mrs. Hooper, to have a conversation with her friend Mrs. Harleigh and our mother. Just before dinner, the two ladies came out on the veranda where we were sitting watching Lew make Patsy do tricks on the raffia runner. After Mrs. Hooper gave her a little nod, Ma said to Lew, "How would you like to take Patsy home with you?"

Mrs. Hooper was giving up her house to live in a New York apartment where pets were not allowed, and she was looking for a good home for the dog. Lew, being the eldest, established immediate sovereignty over Patsy, while I, tears brimming, sneaked down the steps and off behind the hotel. Wouldn't that damn Lew get a dog to keep? I refused to eat dinner, and Ma, saying I'd gotten too much sun, put me to bed (up in one of the attic rooms where the children always slept).

The woman called Mrs. Harleigh gave me a long, sorrowful look of commiseration as I was led up to bed, eloquent with sympathy in the matter of the dog; she knew just how I felt, I could tell. Later, when the hotel was asleep, I awoke hungry. Somewhere I could hear low voices from another room on the same floor. I fought my hunger pangs as long as I could, and when the voices fell silent I crept downstairs to the kitchen. In the large refrigerator I found a bowl of tapioca, some of which I spooned into a green-banded white dish and carried it with me out behind the bathhouses where the dog was kept. Putting the half-eaten tapioca aside, I spent perhaps half an hour petting and talking to Patsy, the fox terrier, and hating Lew because it was to be "his" dog. I was coming through the latticed breezeway, finishing the tapioca, when I saw a figure in white walking along the moonlit gravel path in the rose garden. It was Mrs. Harleigh. I wanted to bring her to see the dog, but was frustrated in this action by another figure, who approached her from the veranda: Mr. Stevenson, the hotel owner, and as he came up to her, I crouched in the shadows and tried to listen. He spoke rapidly, in a low tone I couldn't understand, but I heard Mrs. Harleigh's laugh well enough.

"Of course, Mr. Stevenson, if that is your wish. In any case, I don't suppose the salt air is helping my complexion. We'll leave in the morning, if that will be convenient." With another low laugh, she went along the path to the veranda, and disappeared inside. I returned my empty tapioca dish to the kitchen and crept back to bed. Next day, Mrs. Harleigh and her servants left in the great car, while Mrs. Hooper stayed on. There was a flurry of conjecture among the other guests at the hasty departure, and when queried, Mrs. Hooper seemed as mystified as anyone else.

Returning to Pequot Landing, I stationed myself at various vantage points to glimpse our newly discovered neighbor, but there was no Mrs. Harleigh to be seen. While Lew and Harry were away with their gang, setting off firecrackers hoarded from last Fourth of July, or popping their BB guns down in Hubbard's woods, or wherever they went that I wasn't allowed to go, I kept a vigilant watch on whatever occurred—little enough, to my lights—over the way. Mrs. Sparrow may have seen more through her Seiss-Altags than I with my Peeping Tom's eye, but to both of us things were nothing if not downright ordinary.

I did not know it then, but this was one of Lady's "retirements," always distressing periods for her. Once I accidentally threw a rock through her window, and she came to the door and reprimanded me sharply. I didn't play around there for a while, but later, in speaking of her to Ma, I said, "Gee, Mrs. Harleigh sure is nice—except when you break her windows." The remark was repeated to her, and she came running out her door and across the Green to catch me on the way home from school and hug me, saying she was sorry she had scolded me. I think she liked me more after that.

But it was to be many years before I discovered why she had laughed when she swept out of the moonlit rose garden.

4

"Trees are God's most perfect race."

I recall Lady saying that to me once in one of her more dour moments when she was inclined to view God's race of men cynically. The trees are mostly gone now, but returning to the Green I still call up their images, they were so much a part of those times. And the Great Elm—what a tree was that! It grew halfway between our house and hers, one hundred feet high, the trunk almost forty feet in circumference, and must have been something short of two centuries old when it died of the Dutch blight. But while it lived, how grand it was. I think if anyone ever doubted God, one only had to look at that massive, lofty, natural creation to believe in Him again.

As in your small town, or anyone's, there was nothing much to do in ours back then, no place to go or anyone to see. In one geographical sense we were fortunate, for we lived "next door" to Hartford, the capital of the state, where you could make the five-mile trolley ride "upstreet," as it was called, and ride the escalators in the department stores. But Pequot Landing was a place whose today was unimportant and whose Colonial yesteryear, if historically remarkable, seemed, at fifth remove, dull and bookish; the town was only in our childhood emerging from the Icebox Age into that of the General Electric Refrigerator.

We lived on the less fashionable east side of the Green where the trolley tracks went by. For years our father, George Woodhouse, had worked at the old Jewett Belt Company out on Park Street in Hartford, saying that when he had saved enough money he would like to have a place in the country, just an old place he could fix up and where he could raise fruit trees and chickens in his back yard. And after moving our large family to Pequot Landing, the first thing he did was to plant the small but long-dreamed-of orchard behind the garage. He spaded out the holes, carried the trees himself, and one by one planted them—four cherry, four pear, four quince, four plum—and when he had tamped them down and watered them, he took a snapshot for posterity, came into the house, showered, and brought my mother to the bedroom, where he made love to her, suffered a heart attack, and died.

The old place never got fixed up.

Pa hadn't left much insurance, but Ma, a dauntless woman, found employment at the Sunbeam Laundry on the southern edge of the city, fifteen minutes away by car. Because she'd had to sell the family Auburn for funeral costs, she spent forty-five minutes each way on the trolley. Things were never easy for Ma. She was away from the house more often than she was there, and when she came home she was tired and sometimes cross, and she brought all her laundry problems with her. She seemed often bewildered by the brood our father's death had left her in charge of, but she tried hard to bring us up decently and intelligently. A simple woman, she never attained to the chic or "quality" of the country-club wives, nor did she have Lady's color and elegance, but she had her own style and humor. She hated being poor. I think it was her humor that most often saved her, for she never got over Pa's death, and until the day that she herself died his military brushes rested on the lace runner on the bureau.

The house was ample and ramshackle and tired, with tan printed paper on most of the walls, a furnace that clanked heroically but never sent up much heat, a kitchen that was barely adequate, with an intransigent stove and a balky sink, and crayoned yardstick marks on the door jamb which recorded our heights at every stage. The other rooms were small and chopped-up and the large pieces of furniture were catty-cornered everywhere. It seemed you were always meeting yourself coming and going; if not yourself, then Nonnie or Lew or Harry or Aggie or Kerney, or Patsy, the dog.

It became our mother's constant refrain that if she must live "in the country," she was just as glad it was Pequot Landing, which she thought was having the best of both worlds, urban and rural. Just south of us, where the elms stopped and the macadam became a dirt road, lay some of the richest agricultural land in the Connecticut Valley. Much of it Harleigh holdings, it was dotted with farms, with red barns and hayricks, corncribs and silos. A patchwork quilting of cornfields and truck-garden plots spread either side of the road, and there were wide pastures where cows and horses grazed. Even in the backyards on our street, barns and chicken houses were not uncommon, and though to us city people it seemed strange at first, for the old-timers it was no surprise at all to find a cow housed in a shed beside the car in the garage, as next door at Mrs. Flagler's. Nonnie immediately put herself to saving household money so we could have our own cow, but she was never able to save enough, and our milk came to the back door, pasteurized and in Smith's Dairy bottles ("A Quarter of a Century of Dependable Service").

With Ma working five full days and half a Saturday at the Sunbeam, it fell to our eldest sister, Nonnie, sixteen, to look after us and the house. Nonnie was a thoughtful, serious girl who took her motherly duties to heart. Old beyond her years, she tried to see to it that our arctics were buckled when it snowed, that our mittens were threaded on strings through the sleeves of our windbreakers, that we didn't hide our uneaten salad lettuce in the china tureen, that our rooms were straightened, that we didn't fight. Hopeless tasks, all.

My two older brothers, Lew and Harry, were twelve and ten when I was eight, and I didn't see them much, except at mealtimes. They had a gang of their own, and while they were allowed off on one of the islands in the river, where they could pitch a tent and stay out all night, I, too young, was left alone in the sleeping porch where we had bunk beds, and there I would lie, wondering when I would be old enough to sneak Lucky Strikes and swear and sleep on the island.

There was Aggie, of course, but though I loved her I didn't want to be with her all that often. Ag came between Harry and me in age and was "a walking romance" as Ma called her, because she spent so much time holed up in her room, getting gingersnap crumbs in her sheets as she read mushy stories in the *Woman's Home Companion* or the *Delineator*. True, Ag *was* romantic, soft, and sweet, with big surprised eyes that teared up for almost no reason, and long unmanageable legs whose bony knees she tried in vain to hide under her skirt. No doubt of it, she was shy, she blushed all the time, and was almost self-effacing, as if she were afraid someone might discover that she was living on this planet. But Ag had ideals and principles; she believed in things, passionately, profoundly, energetically.

Kerney was only three, and everyone fussed over him. It made me mad that just being the youngest could produce such attention, and I wanted to holler with frustration as they all stepped over me to see what Kerney wanted, or to assure him that he was "the *best* little boy in the world."

I would go to my bunk and hang my chin on the railing, looking over to the Harleigh place, hating our house and wondering what it must be like to live in *that* house, so grave and still and solitary at night, and secretly scheming how I might one day storm the castle across the Green.

As we came to know her better, the two sides of our new neighbor's personality were made clearer to all of us. She was gay and bewitching, both interesting and interested; she charmed where she went, reproached no one, offered no argument, never connived or gossiped—nor would tolerate it in others—helped where she might, lived her life generously and nicely, and was, we all felt, lonely.

Lonely, and—strange. We talked about it among ourselves, and wondered, and worried, too. When at last we were made at home in her house, it was often difficult to ignore the furtive looks, the murmurs aloud, the absently contracted fists which she, becoming suddenly aware, would turn into a feigned examination of her manicure, the tension in the throat cords as though to swallow were difficult, the abstracted lapses succeeded by a sudden waking as from a dream, the fugitive pain that came and went behind her eyes.

But all of this became disclosed to me by gradual degrees, for at that time she was still merely "the lady across the Green," and really all I knew about her was that she was nice, and had lost her husband, as our mother had. It was only after the first visit of Mr. Ott, the mysterious man with red hair, that I realized how deeply troubled she was.

He appeared one evening early in January two years after Franklin Roosevelt became President, when I was about to turn eleven. Only the day before, the forlorn Christmas trees lay with the ashcans in front of all the houses around the Green.

It had snowed briskly all morning, but had stopped by the time school let out. When we arrived home, Lew and Harry started arguing about who was to have the lucrative task of shoveling Mrs. Harleigh's walks, because whoever didn't would shovel ours for nothing or Gert Flagler's for not much more.

A board fence enclosed our property at the two sides, and over this fence to the right were the Sparrows, and to the left the lady companions, Miss Berry and Mrs. Gertrude Flagler. They had pets aplenty—a dozen small dogs and a canary—but not a man in sight. Miss Berry's first name was Mary, but she was too nice for us to make use of the obvious euphony of her names. Some of the guys from the feed store would walk by hollering, "Mary Berry's got beriberi," or, "Mary Berry loves Harry Carey," but Miss Berry, whose hearing might have been better, would only nod and smile. She always saved us empty boxes so we could send the tops away for radio premiums: Quaker Oats for Bobby Benson, Cocomalt for Buck Rogers, Ovaltine for Little Orphan Annie, Wheaties for Jack Armstrong. And there were wooden codfish boxes just right for keeping things in. Miss Berry, formerly a private nurse, was practically an institution in the town. People said that she had been beautiful when she was young, but with her plain, gray, wrinkled face, her steel-rimmed glasses, her collars edged with lace and a little velvet bow at the neck, and voluminous skirts whose hemlines far exceeded the dictates of either modesty or fashion, who would have taken her for anything but a perennial spinster?

Gertrude Flagler, on the other hand, favored tailored suits of seat-sprung tweed. She chopped her salt-and-pepper hair off at the ears and squeaked around in heavy brogans when she went out selling Spencer foundation garments, lugging a gigantic merchandise catalogue door-to-door. It took little to put her into a state of rage, and she was the large and constant target of our inventive deviltry when we were feeling prankish. (There had been a Mr. Flagler somewhere, but that was in the long ago, and no one ever seemed to know what had become of him.)

She got around in a secondhand Chevy, and as a driver she was a menace. Seldom did she maneuver the car from the garage without hitting the clothes reel; seldom did she get back to the garage without scraping the telephone pole or the fence, over which we could often hear her deep, rumbling voice, swearing like a sailor.

"God damn it, Mary, someone must have moved that fence—look at that car door!" "God damn it, Mary, what's wrong with raw milk?

You want pasteurized, you pay for it, but I'm not getting rid of Bossy." "God damn it, Mary, who left the rake in the driveway, the handle dented my fender!" Miss Berry endured these tirades by possessing herself in silence, and never offered argument. Miss Berry was noted for her stoicism; still it could never have been easy, living with the perpetually wrought-up Gert Flagler. And if, in a sense, Miss Berry was like a rock, she refused to be the flint from which her steely friend might strike sparks.

It was said of Gert Flagler that she could pinch a penny till the Indian said "How." Consequently, we always avoided the opportunity of obliging her with our slave labor. Not so with Mrs. Harleigh, who paid generously. Lew and Harry had come to fists and punches, until finally Lew swore and said the hell with it, he didn't care who shoveled Mrs. Harleigh out. He kicked over the kitchen chair and slammed down into the cellar. Harry's nose was bloody, and he said he didn't care, either, so I got to do the job.

I took a snow shovel from the back porch, and walked in the plowed roadway around the Green, heading for Mrs. Harleigh's. Glancing back, I saw Miss Berry, in her sun parlor, watering the sansevieria plant she kept in the window in a blue pot. That plant had been there as long as I could remember, so had Miss Berry. When I came to the Harleigh house, I began at the front door and worked my way down the flagstone paving to the street. I was sweating under my mackinaw and goggled leather aviator's helmet when the Griffins, Elthea and Jesse, came out the door to catch the streetcar. They usually took Thursday and Sunday afternoons and evenings off—generally the case with household help in Pequot Landing—and they often went upstreet for dinner and the movies. Shoveling a path for them, I whistled at Elthea, who looked like a flapper with her bell-shaped hat, the muskrat coat Mrs. Harleigh had given her, and her open galoshes whose metal fasteners clicked and clattered as she came down the walk at Jesse's side.

She laughed and did a little sashay, arm in arm with Jesse along the roadway to the streetcar stop. I waved them off when the trolley came, and as they climbed aboard I saw Blue Ferguson, the Pilgrim Market delivery boy, pulling his truck into the Piersons' next-door drive. Falling back in a drift, I snapped up my frosted celluloid goggles and sucked the snow from my mitten fingers while catching my breath. There was a snowball fight in progress out on the Green, and I ignored the calls to join the battle, reminding myself that my chore was not to be taken lightly. I had never shoveled Mrs. Harleigh out before and I wanted to prove my mettle.

Mr. Marachek, the postman, came along the roadway wearing earmuffs and tooting his whistle for the afternoon mail. Mr. Marachek, an emigrant from Czechoslovakia, was our friend; he always saved us the stamps on letters from his family in the old country. Tooting me a couple of whistles, he waved and went around to the far side of the Green.

Pretty soon, here came Rabbit Hornaday, with a rusty, beatup snow shovel. He watched the fight but wasn't asked to join, and after a while he trudged across and hung about at the end of the drive, peering at me through his thick glasses, which had practically steamed over.

What can I say about Rabbit Hornaday, except that he was a jerk? Nobody liked him much, and we all tried to avoid him, which was difficult because somehow he was always there. I didn't like him watching me, blowing steam through his puckered-up lips, so I suggested that if he wanted to make a lot of money, he should go over and shovel out Gert Flagler. He blinked, licked the run from his nose, and silently trudged over to Mrs. Flagler's, where he fell to work with a will.

I took up my own shovel again, and worked my way up the drive. By the time I had cleared the path to the kitchen, I was puffing hard. Suddenly the window flew up and a voice I recognized said, "Woody?"

I felt a pang of joy, hearing Mrs. Harleigh speak my name. Though I was the third son, I had inherited my father's nickname of "Woody" Woodhouse, and, as he had seldom been called George, I was seldom called Frederick, or even Fred. There were other, more important Woodhouses in town, members of the venerable Old Guard, and we were merely latecomers of no importance in the local social scheme—still I was pleased that Mrs. Harleigh knew exactly "which one" I was.

"Darling, you must be thirsty." She leaned over the sink, extending to me a glass of bubbling ginger ale, and as I stood on a milk box to take it she broke off the icicles fringing the windowsill and plinked them in my glass.

"Swizzle sticks," she said gaily. "You can pretend it's a highball. Don't get overheated, though."

It took another hour to complete the rest of the drive, the little walk from there to the kitchen door, a path to the bird feeder, another to the birdbath, and the wider sweep up to the carriage house. I shoveled in front of the doors, then pulled both pairs wide to be sure they would open all the way. Finished, I banged my shovel to remove the excess snow and was beating my mittens furiously before applying for my wages when I looked behind me. It was snowing again! Big wet flakes were already obscuring the path of my labors.

Tired, I tramped over to the dusty, cobwebbed sleigh I had discovered sitting opposite the Minerva, and flopped down in it to get the snow out of the tops of my arctics. At my feet I found a heap of sleigh bells; I picked them up and untangled the harness. The brass bells were tarnished, but they rang, and I sat shaking them in my two hands as if they were reins, looking at the Minerva landaulet and pretending I was engaged in a race; if I'd had a horse between the shafts, no car on earth—

"It's better in July."

I dropped the bells and turned at the sound of Mrs. Harleigh's voice. Wrapped in fur, she stood in the doorway, and I had the idea she had been watching me for some time.

"What's better?"

"A sleigh ride. You know, 'sleigh ride in July'?" She offered me her hand and I helped her up, making room on the seat beside me.

"How about a sleigh ride in January," I hinted, "it's snowing again."

"I *know*. All your work. Are you cold?" She put her hand to my forehead. "No, you're hot. It's too big a job for you. You must let Lew or Harry do it next time." Her arm slipped around me and she drew me close. The feel of her fur sleeve against my cheek was an inexpressible thrill.

"I can find other things for you to do if you want to earn some money," she continued. "This darn place is just too much for Jesse to look after. Gosh, isn't this seat *sprung*?" She bounced several times and her laugh reminded me of a young girl's. I picked up the bells again and jingled them. The sound must have disturbed her, for, her mirth fading, she reached and stilled them. As I let the bells fall in my lap, her fingers sought mine and she gently laced them together. I put my head against her fur coat and we sat this way for some time, without speaking, watching the wet snow come down beyond the open doors.

Out on the street, Blue Ferguson sped by in the Pilgrim Market

truck, its tire chains chattering and throwing up a wet spume under
the tail exhaust: the spell was broken.

"Modern times," Mrs. Harleigh murmured, lifting her arm from
around me. As she moved to step down, I looked up at her face. Her
eyes were moist and she quickly turned away, but her tone was gay
as she said, "Come along, let's make some hot cocoa."

She waited while I closed the carriage house and as we hurried to
the kitchen door she gave me half her coat to wrap in; the silk
lining had an embroidered monogram, a curly, curvy "A.H." *AH*,
I thought, Adelaide Harleigh. I was in heaven, and knew it.

"Brr! It's chilly!" she said when we had stamped our feet on the
mat and come through the back entryway. She touched the radiator.
"I think Jesse might have forgotten the furnace." She shed her coat
and tossed it carelessly on a chair. "Take off your things and I'll go
down and put some coal on."

"I'll do it."

"Can you?"

Could I? The coal I shoveled at home! When I had shaken up the
fire and returned to the kitchen, there was a pan of milk simmering
on the stove, and Mrs. Harleigh was bringing cups and saucers from
the cupboard. "You look like a chimney sweep! Here—wash your
hands." That was like her, ignoring the black coal dust I had tracked
across her floor and worrying only about my hands. While I took off
my mackinaw and washed with the cake of Bon Ami on the sink-
board, she used a broom to erase my anthracited footprints.

"I was going to put out cookies for us," she said, setting the broom
behind the door and spooning cocoa into the cups, "but I have a better idea. Do you think your mother could spare you on a snowy
Thursday evening?"

"Sure." Ma could spare any of us anytime she got the chance.

"I wondered if perhaps you might join me for a little supper of
veal cutlets."

It remains the most elegant invitation I have ever received, and
after phoning home I accepted it with alacrity. Then, the room
growing warmer, the cocoa steaming in the cups, and Mrs. Harleigh
humming as she brought things from the Frigidaire, I realized I had
stormed the castle at last.

The "little supper of veal cutlets" was a feast. In all the years I
knew her, I never saw Lady Harleigh achieve anything close to a

"simple" meal; it was not her way. To begin with, while she prepared the rest of the things and set the table, there were smoked oysters and anchovies and a deliciously decomposed block of cheese which she explained was Liederkranz, which meant "song collection." It was gooey and smelled awful and tasted delicious; I decided the songs must have been collected by angels on high. Then there were the veal cutlets, breaded and spiced, with scalloped potatoes and Harvard beets and pickled crab apples and thick slices of dill bread she herself had baked, and for dessert a cold chocolate dish in fluted gold cups: she called it a mousse.

I remember the evening well, in each of its particulars. We ate in the dining room at the big mahogany table, seated in its elegant Sheraton chairs with the heart-shaped backs and needlepoint seats. The armchair at the head of the table remained empty and Mrs. Harleigh placed me on her right because, she said, I must be the guest of honor. She liked, she told me, a little wine with dinner, and I was allowed some too. We clinked glasses, and she said, "To present company and absent friends." I thought that was a very handsome toast. I sipped my wine between mouthfuls, and meanwhile looked around. Never had I been in such a room, so rich and lustrous and romantic. At home we had an oak table and a bureau against the wall and none of the chairs matched, and we dined by electric sconces on the walls, with the window shades up, and Mrs. Sparrow always knew what we had for dinner.

Here the shades were discreetly drawn, and there were lighted candlesticks which made the waxed wainscoting shimmer. A bunch of winter cherries, looking like small Chinese paper lanterns, were arranged in an Oriental bowl. There were more of the same Oriental pieces in corner cupboards at the end of the room. On one wall was an antique gilt-framed mirror whose murky glass allowed me to see most of the room in its wobbly surface. Over the sideboard hung twin oval portraits, also in gold frames: one a man, his forbidding countenance frowning down, seemingly at the empty armchair. Smiling over her mousse, Mrs. Harleigh said, "Don't pay any attention to him, the old rapscallion."

Rapscallion! There was a word! She went on to explain that the baleful-eyed gentleman, Edward's father—whom she called Daddy Harleigh—had swindled half the town in stock manuevers before the Panic of 1907. The imposing woman in the other oval was Edward's mother. I recalled Mrs. Sparrow's description of Mrs. Harleigh, and how she would sweep grandly into church for Easter services, hair piled high with combs under a large and imposing hat, a velvet choker around her neck, glasses on a ribbon resting on her important-looking bosom.

"Let us eat our mousse in peace, darling," she admonished, waving her silver spoon at Mr. Harleigh's glowering face.

"Was that his sleigh in the carriage house?" I asked.

"Why—yes, I suppose it was." She had been bright and animated all evening, filled with questions and any manner of jokes, but now she spoke in short halting phrases, and her light voice suddenly took on a soberer tone. "We—I used to ride in it. When I was a girl. Edward would come. All the way to Knobb Street and we'd sleigh down here and go round and round the Green. . . ." Her voice trailed off for a moment and she murmured a few words I could not make out. Then she went on as though suddenly capturing a long-lost memory. "I remember one Christmas Eve. We went sleighing. Afterward there was a party at the old Harleigh house. The whole town was there, it seemed. Everyone was—waiting, you know. For my answer. I said, 'Yes, I will marry you, Edward.' But he already knew. He took me into the conservatory. Put a ring on my finger. He'd even arranged a surprise for the occasion. Carolers came to the door and sang to the party. The last song they sang was—"

She broke off, head down, staring at the gold band on her finger.

"'Silent Night'?" I suggested. We always heard Mme. Schumann-Heink sing "Silent Night" on Christmas Eve.

"No. It was 'Good Night, Ladies.' Only they changed it. They sang—'Good Night, Lady.' Extraordinary, I haven't thought of that song for—for years."

Surely it was a happy memory for her; and yet the way she spoke of it seemed tinged with sadness. It wasn't difficult to understand: she had loved Edward and she had lost him. Would she ever love another? Would she one day marry Colonel Blatchley, as Mrs. Sparrow was forever predicting? I watched her turn the ring on her finger, and the gold burned bright in the candlelight. I imagined her: young, in a hooded cloak, with Edward's arm around her, muffled in furs, behind a prancing horse, sleighing past a pine wood where foxes wintered.

The urge became irresistible and I asked, "Can we go for a sleigh ride sometime? You and me?"

"Oh-h . . ." She made a lovely face and leaned to press my hand and I could smell the scent of her perfume. "Oh, darling, who can sleigh anymore? The streets are plowed as fast as it snows. Besides, where would we find a horse?"

"Colonel Blatchley has horses," I ventured.

"I don't think the Colonel would consent to hitching one of his thoroughbreds to a sleigh."

"For you he would."

I saw her blush worse than Aggie ever did. It was very becoming. I said, "Mr. Welles has one."

"No-Relation's horse?" She began to laugh.

Mr. Welles was a farmer down in Talcottville who went about town selling horseradish from a horse-drawn cart. Because the Welleses of Pequot Landing were of ancient and estimable lineage, the horseradish man was constantly referred to as "No-Relation" Welles.

"And his horse—!" Mrs. Harleigh dissolved in mirth. "I don't think that poor creature could make it once around the Green at a trot. Sleigh rides are nice for children, though. On a 'Snow Queen' sort of night . . ."

" 'Snow Queen?' "

"Yes—have you never read it? Hans Christian Andersen? It's a fairy tale. 'And the wind sang old songs'—I always loved that line."

She looked at me thoughtfully as she served me coffee, in the Oriental china from the corner cupboard. Coffee was another first for me; at home we got Postum. As she poured cream from a three-legged silver pitcher, she made more inquiries. What did I do with my after-school time, who were my friends? I had the idea that she had observed me as closely as I had often observed her.

I shrugged and said I played mostly by myself. "I can't play with Lew or Harry," I added dolefully.

"Why?"

"They're older."

"I see."

"And they fight harder than I can."

"What sort of thing does Lew enjoy doing? And Harry?" she asked, leading me along. Well, I said, Lew was good at sports, and was in Boy Scouts, and was a good sketcher. Harry was sort of the inventor of the family, he could always engineer some clever mechanical device with the Erector set, he knew a lot about science and was good at magic. I never had been able to see much difference between Lew and Harry, they were simply my brothers.

"Lew is the athlete, Harry is mechanical and magical—now what of you?" She rested her eyes on me, in all their candor, and awaited a reply. I didn't know what to say. I had never given thought to what sort of person I was. I was just there, and felt myself lucky to get a crack at our one bathroom. I ventured to say that Ma always claimed me to be "the imaginative one."

"But of course you are!" Mrs. Harleigh exclaimed. "Anyone who sits in a sleigh and imagines he's out riding in it. That *is* what you were doing, wasn't it?

"Then your mother's right—you're the imaginative one, and that's as well. Imagination can often get people farther in life than bank accounts and good noses." She ran her slender fingertip along the bump on her nose. "Your mother's so pretty, isn't she?" she said warmly.

"Is she?"

She turned a surprised, almost indignant look on me. "Of *course* she is, can't you tell? She's *very* pretty. And *indefatigable!*" Another of those words. "I am in constant admiration of her, the way she works, going to the laundry every day, and then Saturday afternoon out scouring her stoop as if she lived in Holland. Your mother does not have things easy."

Ma was a worker all right. Her house was her house, and she saw to it that it was the best house she could make it, and with us assigned our daily chores—the week's washing on Mondays, the trash and ashes out on Wednesdays, painting, raking, mowing, shoveling coal, cleaning our rooms—we were like a troop of elves in thrall to her industrious broom. But we all knew, in spite of the fact that she worked the mangle at the Sunbeam and routed us out of bed in the morning with fierce cries and cold washcloths, that she loved us and exhausted herself providing for us. Though she had few of them, she enjoyed beautiful things, and she loved painting and music and poetry. I confided to Mrs. Harleigh that Ma's secret ambition had once been to go on the stage, that she had in fact entertained the soldiers in training-camp shows with monologues and recitations during the World War, when Pa was courting her.

As Mrs. Harleigh drew me out on the subject of my family, I found it was easier for me to voice things I would not ordinarily have disclosed; small private thoughts that I was sure must interest me alone, but all of which seemed to interest her, too.

"Tell me about school," she continued, and laughed when I made a face that summed up my opinion of schools in general and mine in particular. Well, I said, our teacher Miss Bessie was okay—we all really liked Miss Bessie—but Miss Grimes, our principal, was a pain. Nobody liked the dreaded and irascible Miss Grimes.

"Does she give you the strap?"

"Boy, does she!"

" 'Spoil the rod and spare the child,' I say. I suppose things haven't changed much. Miss Grimes was principal when I was a girl."

"Did you go to our school?"

"No, I went to school on Knobb Street. But we heard about Miss Grimes, even up there."

When I mentioned that Nonnie had wanted to be a teacher but had had to give up college for us all, it seemed to strike a chord. "Yes," she said, "I know how that is. Poor Nonnie, chained to a sink and stove. And Lew plays the banjo, you say?"

I said we all played an instrument of one kind or another; part of the money from the Sunbeam Laundry went weekly for music lessons; Ma was adamant.

"Do you play together?"

"No." We never did much of anything together.

She didn't say anything just then, but I knew what she was thinking. Then she said, "What kind of books?"

"Ma'am?"

"If you don't read Hans Christian Andersen, what kind of books do you read?"

I slunk down in my chair, wishing I had heeded Ma's eternal advice that we all should use books more. None of us did, except Aggie, and I hated my schoolbooks. "Well, I've read about Paul Revere's ride, and—"

"Yes?" She had a way of crinkling her eyebrows that was so funny, so filled with her own amusement. I wanted to tell her I'd read the whole history of the United States or the dictionary or something.

"*Famous Funnies,*" I replied weakly, dropping my eyes.

"Ah?"

"And—um—Big Little Books."

"Oh, *those.*" She made a funny, icky face. "Which are your favorites?"

Well, I said, I liked *Hairbreadth Harry,* and *Smilin' Jack,* and *Terry and the Pirates.* "And there's *Flash Gordon,* of course." Secretly I was aroused by the Witch Queen of Mongo, who wore slinky black dresses and was marvelously wicked. "And *Mickey Mouse* and the *Sky Pirates,* and *Tarzan.*" Tarzan was currently disguised in a crocodile skin and battling an Egyptian pharaoh.

My dinner companion said, "I used to read *The Dream of a Welsh Rarebit Fiend* when I was your age. I suppose the comics have changed a good deal. Although *The Katzenjammer Kids* haven't. I see them every Sunday. What else do you read?"

"We—um—listen to the radio a lot."

"Oh, the *radio*." She dismissed that invention with a wave of her hand. "Have you never read *Treasure Island?*"

"No, Ma'am."

"I see. Well, books perhaps cannot do for you what a piece of music does, or a painting, or a play on the stage, but they can perform their own kind of magic."

She lit a cigarette and streamed smoke through her nostrils. "What instrument do you play?"

I confessed I went to Mr. Auerbach up at Packard Lane every Tuesday afternoon, lugging a French horn, on which I was trying to learn the polka from *Schwanda, der Dudelsackpfeifer.*

"The French horn's a noble instrument!" Lady said enthusiastically.

I thought it was lousy. Ma had been swayed when the music teacher told her the set of my teeth was perfect for a brass instrument; the truth was the French-horn player had gone on to junior high. Lucky Harry got to play cornet.

"You have a musical family. We must have a musical evening one night soon."

"You mean it? I can come back? All of us can come?" I couldn't believe my ears.

"Of course, all of you," she said gaily. "Larks, my darling, we must have larks." Her smile vanished like a ghost and she looked at me with a grave expression. "It's been very nice, having you here. There have never been children in this house since I have lived in it. It's —as it should be."

"When can we come?"

"Well, let me see. I'm alone on Thursdays and Sundays. Perhaps a Sunday would be best."

Sunday was Jack Benny, but I didn't care.

"Let me consult with Jesse and Elthea and see what would be convenient," she concluded. She rolled her napkin, placed it in a silver ring—monogrammed: curly, curvy "A.H."—and rose from her chair. "Will you help me bring out the dishes? I don't want to leave them for Elthea." As we carried things back to the kitchen, she asked, "Do you know who Miss Shedd is?"

"No, Ma'am."

"She's our librarian. A remarkable old lady who loves children to come and take books out and read them. We must arrange for you to meet her one of these days."

She was at the dishpan, I was drying, when the doorbell rang.

"Darn, who can that be out in all this snow?" She took her hands from the water and flicked the suds.

"I can go."

"If it's Colonel Blatchley, invite him in and offer him a cigar."

I walked down the hall and peeked through the curtain of the window next to the door. Waiting on Mrs. Harleigh's stoop was a dark figure. The coat collar was turned up around the face, but I could tell it was not Colonel Blatchley. Nor was it anyone else I had ever seen before. Somehow I had the feeling I didn't like his looks. I put my hand on the brass handle and opened the door.

"Is Mrs. Harleigh at home?"

The voice was hoarse, and its owner seemed to be making an effort to keep it at a whisper.

"Yes. Do you want to come in?"

For a moment he looked uncertain. His mouth was clamped in a grim line, and his unblinking watery eyes shone in the gleam of the carriage lamp. His pale skin was splotched with pinkish freckles and his reddish, slightly curly hair was slicked back, wet with snow. He carried a leather briefcase, on whose battered flap was stamped the name "OTT." I immediately thought of Mel Ott, right-fielder for the Giants, whose picture Lew had in his bubble-gum card collection.

When I glanced at the flakes flying past me into the hall, the man finally spoke. "Tell Mrs. Harleigh someone would like a word with her, please."

"Yes, sir."

I left him on the stoop and let the door swing while I ran back down the hall to the kitchen.

"Is it the Colonel?" Mrs. Harleigh asked, rinsing a goblet.

"No'm. It's Mr. Ott."

"Ott? Ott? I don't know any—"

"He has red hair . . ."

The goblet crashed against the porcelain sink and shattered. She stared at the broken pieces, then, methodically wiping her hands on a dishtowel, she removed her apron, and quickly left the room.

While I gingerly picked the fragments of crystal out of the sink, the murmur of voices drifted up the hallway. It was all unintelligible to me; presently the conversation stopped and the door closed. I waited for Mrs. Harleigh to come back to the kitchen, but there was nothing but silence. I dropped the pieces of the goblet in the can under the sink and went into the hall. It was empty. Walking to the foot of the stairs, I looked up and as I placed my hand on the newel post I heard a low muffled moan. It came from the dining room.

She was standing in front of the mirror, staring at her wobbly reflection in the glass. She seemed unaware of me as I came in the room and walked to her side. I watched as long as I could in the mirror as a tear trickled down her cheek, then threw myself against her, holding her elbow in an awkward way, trying to squeeze her hand.

"Don't, please, Mrs. Harleigh, please!" I hugged her and tried to think how I could make her stop. It made me furious that a red-headed man in a snowstorm could cause such pain.

She was still staring at her reflection in the mirror. Her features looked distorted, narrowing and bulging with the imperfect glass. Then she wiped her eyes with my napkin in her hand, and as if to hide her image she hung the napkin on the mirror. Then she disengaged herself and removed the linen place mats from the table and put them away. "If we are truly to be friends," she said over her shoulder, carrying the saltcellars to the sideboard, "you must call me 'Lady.'"

Perhaps it should have been a thrill, her asking me to call her by the name all the grownups used, but I could think of nothing else but the man at the door, his bright glistening eyes, his tight, mean mouth, his snow-covered red hair. And not wearing a hat, on such a snowy evening. I could not then say "Lady," but "Please," I entreated her, "who was he—Mr. Ott?"

"Mr. Ott?" She gave a wry twist to the name as she repeated it. "Who was he?" She thought a moment, then smiled a strange, bitter smile and, without looking, removed the napkin from the mirror and put it in a napkin ring. "Mr. Ott," she murmured with a trace of amusement. She lifted from the table the Oriental bowl holding the winter cherries, but the single shake of her head told me she had no reply to my question.

5

I did not see her again for some time. No one did, and Mrs. Sparrow gave out the news that Mrs. Harleigh "wasn't herself," and was going through another of her "retirements." Each day I eagerly awaited a glimpse of furs and a veiled hat, to catch her going out in the Minerva landaulet, but in the brick house across the Green behind the drawn shades all was silence and I yearned in vain.

In school and out, I languished like a lover and, like a lover betrayed, I thought all the worst, the unkindest things, telling myself she wasn't worth a second glance. How cruel she was. How unfeeling after having led me on, promising me "Larks, my darling, we must have larks," and then not even so much as a sight of her. Shut herself up in the house and nary a wave or a hello, let alone a musical evening. What was wrong with people like that? Didn't they know they hurt people's feelings?

Still, it was only my feelings I was concerned with, not hers. I gave no thought to what might have occasioned her "retirement," or what she might be suffering in consequence. I thought only of the promised musical evening, and every Sunday when Jack Benny came on the radio and said "Jell-O again," I wished I was over at Mrs. Harleigh's. But I knew grownups had a habit of forgetting things they had promised, things important to children, and I decided she, for all her specialness, must be no different from the rest.

And she hadn't even paid me for doing her shoveling!

In addition to my weaselly thoughts regarding the lady across the Green, I was consumed by boyish curiosity about the red-haired man. Once, when the sun was going down and the tree trunks stretched long blue shadows across the snow, I saw a figure hurrying in the direction of the brick house: a man in an overcoat, the collar turned up, his hatless head bent against the wind. Sitting at the worktable in the sleeping porch where I was building an airplane model of Wiley Post's *Winnie Mae*, I decided it was the sinister Mr. Ott returning, but the man continued past the house and disappeared in the gloom beyond the streetlight.

Another evening I saw the carriage lamps come on. The door opened and someone slipped out. I recognized it at once: the fur coat, the little fur hat, and boots. Mrs. Harleigh came down the walk and stepped onto the roadway, her hands buried in her pockets. For half an hour I sat at the table, chin cupped in my hands, my plane model forgotten, watching her slow progress around the Green. Passing our house, she did not glance up at my window as I hoped she might, but continued her solitary circuit until who should come plopping along through the snow but Rabbit Hornaday. The Green-Eyed Monster dwelt in my breast as I saw her stop and talk, pulling his dirty little cap down over his ears and doing up the top button of his windbreaker. Me she wouldn't look at, but Rabbit Hornaday got a pat and a chuck under the chin and a wave before he plopped off through the snow again.

How I hated Rabbit Hornaday!

Hated her, as well. But then the time came when I almost stopped thinking of her, and of her mysterious visitor. I even stopped hating Rabbit Hornaday. The river was frozen and we couldn't think about anything except skating.

After school we would hurry home to get our skates from the back porch and make our way down through the snowy fields behind Mrs. Harleigh's house to the Cove. Out on the ice a hockey game would already be in progress and around it red and blue jacketed figures would speed by, scarves flying, sprays of ice shooting up from the tips of the flashing blades. And you could depend on it, there would be dumb four-eyes Rabbit Hornaday, sliding around on the soles of his shoes and cutting in everyone's way. Secretly I gloated that he didn't own skates.

Rabbit Hornaday was a curious case. He lived up by the railroad tracks near the Rose Rock soda-pop works. His sister Dora "wasn't all there," and she and Rabbit had come to town to stay with their aunt, after their mother, having fallen in with some reprehensible characters who involved her in an illicit bootlegging scheme, was sent to the women's correctional institution at Middlehaven. Rabbit showed off by eating worms, alive or dead, but that wasn't why he was called the Scourge of Pequot Landing. The very day he arrived, he spent the afternoon trampling down every flower bed along Main Street, unscrewing the plug on the fire hydrant in front of the Spragues' house, and opening Colonel Blatchley's rabbit hutch to commit mayhem on several of the Colonel's prize Belgian hares. It was not difficult to imagine how Harold Hornaday was instantly rechristened Rabbit, nor how he earned the undying contempt of every kid in that part of town.

On the riverbank there was always a fire burning, a great heap of scavenged rubber tires which sent up clouds of smelly black smoke, but whose warmth was comforting as the sun started to sink. When it got too dark to see, we would hang our skates over our shoulders and hike back up the windy hill to the Green, where Nonnie would have supper waiting to be put on the table by the time Ma got off the streetcar from the Sunbeam Laundry. Nonnie was always cranky and out of sorts these days. Her voice was shrill and mean, and she was forever carping at us for tracking in snow or leaving wet shoes under the radiator, which made their toes curl. Poor red-faced, angry Nonnie, who never sang anymore or played with Kerney or helped us zip our jackets up. I could tell that the whole trouble was her disappointment at not being able to go to college, and that the burden of looking after four brothers and a sister, and the house, was beginning to weigh on her.

Because she slammed pots and pans in the sink while we were all doing the washing up, Lew and Harry were glad to escape to the cellar and their newest project: a giant skating sail. While Ag stayed in her room reading magazines or pasting *Photoplay* movie stars in scrapbooks, they worked in the basement. I was allowed only to watch. They cut the canvas cloth themselves and because Nonnie complained she had too much work to do, they inveigled Ma into stitching it up on her sewing machine after work. The frame was a cross of bamboo, selected for its lightness; when it was assembled, the sail produced a kite shape eight feet across, and there were more than thirty square feet of canvas in it.

It was a grand success. One Saturday right after lunch I trailed along as Lew came bearing it down to the Cove. Naturally, he tried it out first. Holding the center staff against his back, one arm over his head, the other behind him, he turned his body so the sail caught the brisk wind, and off he shot across the ice to the far bank. To make his return he tacked the way a sailboat would.

Harry was next, and finally it came to me, and they both jeered because I couldn't manage it as easily as they. Gradually I found the hang of it, and discovered that when I got going too fast it required only a simple movement to toss the sail over my head, spilling the wind and slowing me down.

Then Lew took the sail away from me, and he and Harry spent the rest of the afternoon with it, in betweentimes selling rides to other kids for a dime. I got one last turn, then reluctantly handed the sail over to Lew. Skating back to shore under my own power, I looked up to Mrs. Harleigh's house on the crest of the hill. At a second-story window I could see that the shade was up and I was able to make out a face behind the glass.

Next day she came out. She wore a long flannel skirt and a little black fur jacket. Her hair was enclosed by the open end of a tasseled wool scarf. She had on dark stockings and, over these, white ankle socks. I watched from a distance as she sat and laced up her skates, white tops with shiny blades, and then—stepping on the points of the runners, daintily balanced like a ballet dancer—with graceful strokes she floated out onto the ice. A good skater, she turned easily and her ankles showed no signs of buckling. When she had cut several figures, as though testing her strength, she skated over to me.

"Isn't it glorious!" There was the familiar laugh, but no indication of remembering our last meeting. She looked pale and there were dark places under her eyes. I could feel her hand tremble as she took mine and we skated together, out of the way of the flying hockey puck, toward the opposite side of the Cove.

"You boys are having such fun with that sail," she said when we stopped to catch our breaths. "Where did you get it?" She was surprised when I said Lew and Harry had built it. "I must try it one of these days. First I'll have to get my sea legs back. It's been years since I skated."

She spun off a little way toward a clump of frozen reeds, the scarf twirling behind her head. She held her hands out to me and I skated to her. We clutched arms, laughing together, and as we met I lost my balance and we both sat down. When we struck the ice, there was an ominous crack.

"I remember," she said, helping me scramble up and drawing me away from the spot. "It's always thin there, where the bulrushes grow. It must have something to do with the current."

Before she left, she spoke with Rabbit Hornaday, who helped her off with her skates, then walked up the hill with her. She even took his hand! I was furious. More furious shortly thereafter, for the next time Rabbit appeared he had a brand-new pair of skates slung over his shoulders, the latest kind, and by no means cheap. I was sure I knew where he had gotten them, and when Lady came again to take a spin on the ice I joined the hockey game and pretended not to see her. She waved, then went skating off with Rabbit, and I got madder. But I couldn't hold out for long, and the minute Rabbit left her, I raced to her side.

She came often after that, sometimes skating alone, sometimes with Rabbit, but there would always be a quarter of an hour when she would suggest we skate together, sometimes hand in hand, returning red-faced and out of breath to the shore where she would remove her skates and go up the hill to supper behind the drawn shades of the dining room.

Though I waited for another invitation to the house, none came. Nor was any mention made of the "little veal-cutlet supper," or the promised musical evening, or of my shoveling money. It was as though she had forgotten the entire episode. Though friendly, she seemed nervous and edgy, rather brittle like the ice, if not as cold, but in no way inclined to further our friendship.

All this changed, however, one day later in the same month, when I suffered an accident which, had Lady not come to my rescue, might have ended my life. There had been a brief thaw, then another freeze. I had arrived home from my music lesson with Mr. Auerbach and, finding Lew and Harry out, I sneaked the bundled-up skate sail down to the Cove, where I planned on practicing alone. It was a bright breezy afternoon and, except for some younger kids scooting about near the shore, I had the river to myself. At the first gust of wind I lofted the sail, set it behind my back, and, leaning into the canvas, went flying across the ice. I worked my way upriver for a time, then let the force of nature return me on a free and easy tack, leaning back into the sail so it carried my weight along. The wind was blowing stronger. It bit my nose and I had to keep my mouth closed so it wouldn't hurt the fillings in my teeth.

After nearly an hour of sailing I was prepared to call it quits when I saw, some distance downriver, the familiar black-jacketed figure with its swirl of striped scarf. I waved but she didn't see me. I leaned into the sail at an angle calculated to drive me directly toward her, the wind catching the canvas, catapulting me along. I gripped the bamboo brace more tightly, and continued to gather speed, hollering to Mrs. Harleigh as I approached.

She raised her head and smiled when I sped past, about thirty feet away, planning at any moment to spill the wind and circle around her. But, thrilled by the speed at which I traveled, and wanting to show off for her, I refused to relinquish the wind and so failed to see the clump of bulrushes looming ahead.

When I heard the first fierce crack of ice, it was already too late to save myself. Mrs. Harleigh cried out. I let go the sail, which flew up in the air and landed with a plop behind me. Unable to check my path, I shot pell-mell along on my own power while the ice splin-

tered all around me. I toed my skates to force myself to a stop, trying at the same time to alter my direction. It was no good. The
frozen floor sagged under my weight, then gave way altogether.
Oozing cracks appeared all around me, the ice parted, broke, and I
sank into the river.

Grabbing the edge of the ice, I tried to pull myself up, only to
have it break under my chest, and I continued to flounder.

"Wait! Don't thrash about so!" I heard the voice ring out, and
looked to see Mrs. Harleigh skate up to a neat stop a safe distance
away. A space of eight or ten feet separated us. Another step and the
ice cracked again. Quickly she spun around and scooped up the sail.
She threw it in front of her, then lay flat on the ice and slid the bamboo so that by reaching I could grab the tip. Switching to a sitting
position, she dug the heels of her skate runners into the ice and held
fast to the kite while I pulled myself out. I flopped onto the sail and
in another moment she had dragged both it and me to safety.

When we got to the shore, my corduroy knickers were frozen stiff.
She helped me take off my skates, working calmly and swiftly to
undo the wet knotted laces. She pulled off my soaking windbreaker,
substituted her fur jacket, wrapped my head in her scarf, and, leaving the sail behind, hurried me up the hill.

Elthea must have seen my plight, for when we got to the kitchen
Jesse was down cellar stoking the furnace, the teakettle was singing
on the stove, there were Turkish towels and warm socks and a robe
waiting for me. When Jesse came upstairs, Elthea and Mrs. Harleigh
bustled around the room, toweling my hair and securing the wool
scarf more tightly around my neck, hanging my soaked clothes, and
pouring first one cup of tea past my chattering teeth and then another. Elthea said that the river should be posted for "No Skating"
and Mrs. Harleigh asked Jesse to bring the Minerva to the kitchen
door.

Wrapped in a blanket, my soaked things left with Elthea, I was
hustled home to bed in style.

The consequence of this damp adventure was twofold: first, on the
following day it was discovered I had contracted what was then
called the "grippe," and was confined to bed; second, and best, for
the term of my illness Mrs. Harleigh became my nurse, saying, "Larks
are what this boy needs when he gets well. And larks he shall have."
Though in fact they began even before my recovery. Every day, she

came across the Green to sit by my bedside while Ma was at the Sunbeam, freeing Nonnie to perform her usual household duties. It was a not unpleasant period for me, and because I did not feel particularly ill my sojourn under the bedcovers was a memorable time. Dosed with Vicks VapoRub and Argyrol drops which stung in my nostrils, with daily visits from Dr. Brainard, and my "nurse" in constant attendance, I recovered gradually. When I was fully up and around again, Ma said I surely must be as spoiled as an apple at the bottom of the barrel.

But during the two weeks I remained in bed my every wish was granted, accepted by Lady as the law of the land. Already I sensed a strong feeling between us, a power which we had over each other. Though I did not know what I could give her, I was selfishly aware of what she could give me, and how easily I could exercise my smallest tyranny on her. My slightest whim might be indulged. I could be read to or played games with, or listened to; my choice of menu was holy writ, and never since have I drunk so much ginger ale or eaten so many sugared crullers or dishes of tapioca.

I loved watching the way she used her hands around my room, as if examining it, the better to know me. The way she puffed up the pillows and smoothed down the sheet, turning the blanket with an exactly measured border, how she leafed the pages of a magazine, or rolled up my rumpled pajamas and dispatched them for Elthea to wash and return ironed—another first for me—or precisely aligned my slippers, just within reach if I wanted to go to the bathroom; her slender fingers with their loving touch. How nice it was to know those cool, capable hands feeling my forehead and chest, my pulse, though we both knew it was normal. How nice, and how painful, for—in my flannels, under the sheets, the thermometer in my mouth —I was falling in love all over again.

She was such a happy person, and delighted in making me—all of us—happy, making us laugh. She could be so comical. Sometimes for my amusement she would use a thick German accent like *The Katzenjammer Kids*—"Vot's der matter mitt dot?"—or like Jack Pearl, who did Baron Munchausen on the radio—"Vas you dere, Sholly?"— or, more often, it would be a phrase from *Krazy Kat*, whose antics she avidly followed, deriving great amusement in the triangle of Krazy, who loved Ignatz "the mice," and Offissa Pup, who was enamored of the Kat. She sorrowed for the Kat. "Poor, feckless Krazy," she said, "always getting beaned by one of Ignatz's bricks." (What did feckless mean? I asked. "Why—it means—without feck, I suppose. Come on, let's look it up." Out came the dictionary.) She appropriated much of *Krazy Kat*'s vocabulary to her own uses: things with her were often "grend," "magnifishint," and "wondafil." "Fa' goodnitz sakes!" they were. Or she would call me "Ignatz," and say that we were "boom compenions."

She had a collection of stories she enjoyed telling, which she called "The Dreams of a Welsh Rarebit Fiend," whose origins were one of the early Winsor McKay comic strips she'd read as a girl, involving the fanciful adventures of a child who had partaken too greedily of Welsh rarebit and suffered as a result from "extraordinary" dreams, as she called them. And, to tell the truth, you had the feeling that maybe her own dreams were in themselves extraordinary for their unsettling and disquieting nature.

Thus, through my childish demands on her love and her compliant ministering to them, because of my needs and her willing solicitude, we became bound together. All those things, careful, kind, and pleasing, which serve to make life enjoyable, became more vivid and intensified under Lady's loving hand. I had never known such indulgence, such benevolence, such lavish attention. And, watching her embroider in the chair by my bed, listening to her happy talk, how wonderful to settle back and take my pick of the bounty of amusements she had provided: Parcheesi or Chinese Checkers; a jigsaw puzzle of the Taj Mahal; a miniature loom or an Indian beading kit; a Kodak Brownie camera, with film; a soap-bubble set; a Winnie Winkle paintbook, in which, by the mere application of a dampened brush, the invisible colors of the Rinkydink gang, Spike, Spud, Chink, and Perry Winkle himself, were brought to life. It was during this period that I discovered the newest and most exciting thing of all: books; and through Lady Harleigh I found how easy it is to be taken out of oneself, to discover new vistas where nothing matters but the world that is on the printed page. Into this unexplored terrain I now ventured at length, traveling far and wide through a Wyeth-illustrated *King Arthur,* and *Treasure Island, The Arabian Nights,* Richard Halliburton's *Royal Road to Romance,* Hans Christian Andersen's fairy tales; and one called *East of the Sun and West of the Moon.*

There was poetry as well, and while I lay propped against the pillows with my knees drawn up, reading of Horatius at the bridge —brave Lars Porsena! Braver Horatius!—I could hear Mrs. Harleigh downstairs, making jokes with Nonnie while she prepared my lunch tray. Since our neighbor's advent in our house, my sister was no longer the Nonnie of the scowling countenance, the harsh voice, the pursed lips. Their earnest and steady conversation floated up the stairway, Mrs. Harleigh's questions bright and inquisitive, Nonnie's responses quiet and level, without the shrill, complaining tone we had become used to.

There came a time when there was no more "Mrs. Harleigh" at all, but only "Lady." On this particular day she had arrived with a large beribboned box which she placed beside me on the counterpane. I did not wait to guess what was in it, but greedily tore the wrappings apart to find a Roxy Radio Junior magic lantern. It was made of red-painted tin, with a telescope lens and a removable panel in back into which postcards, inserted upside down, could be projected onto a wall right side up. As I admired its elegant decoration of gold striping, I said, "Thank you, Mrs. Harleigh."

Ignoring my thanks, she gave a sudden puzzled look, "But don't you remember? You were going to call me 'Lady.' Surely you haven't forgotten?"

I said I hadn't, but thought she had. Her face clouded; pressing the tips of her fingers to her forehead, she said wonderingly, "Did I? I sometimes do forget." She gave a nervous laugh and continued: "No. I remember. Distinctly. Our little supper of veal cutlets. It had snowed. Jesse and Elthea had gone out. We ate in the dining room, alone."

She paused, as though to recollect the scene more clearly. "All that snow, and . . ."

And, I thought she must say, the man with the red hair came to the door. She gave a look of surprise and exclaimed, "I never paid you! Did I? Did I pay you?"

I confessed she had not. She scrunched up her eyebrows and made a mock-tragic face as though to apologize for her bad manners and, digging into her bag, pressed five dollars into my hand. And though she continued speaking of the evening of the "little veal-cutlet supper," never once did she mention Mr. Ott, or his mysterious errand, or how or why his visit had troubled her so painfully.

Before leaving, she sat on the side of the bed, while I snuggled down under the sheet, her hand brushing my hair down against my forehead.

"My hair goes the wrong way," I reflected glumly.

"It's because you're parting it on the wrong side. See, your crown is *here*"—pointing it out with her finger—"and I'll show you how to train it properly."

She left the room, calling to Nonnie for a stocking. Returning, she cut the bottom off, knotted it, and when she'd wet and combed my hair with a left-side part, she put the stocking cap over it to plaster it down.

"Now you sleep in that every night for a while, and pretty soon—no more cowlick."

"Lew'll laugh at me," I said; the cap looked ridiculous.

"Lew won't laugh," Lady asserted firmly, "and if he does, who cares?" She kissed me, then grew gravely silent. At last, with misty eyes, she said, "You're very good for me, Woody."

"I know," I answered simply.

She laughed then, and pulled me to her and held me in her arms. "I guess I'm better for you than Rabbit Hornaday," I ventured to add, nestled against her, and feeling her heart throb against my cheek. She murmured something, and I said, "Do you really like him?"

"Harold? Mm. Yes, I do. Things have not been easy for him."

"He killed Colonel Blatchley's rabbits."

"So he did. And is sorry for having done so. And since the Colonel has forgiven him, I think you all might do likewise. His mother is at Meadowland, you know, and then there's Dora for him to worry about."

Meadowland was the state women's home at Middlehaven where Rabbit's mother had been sent for rehabilitation. Dora, his sister, had been given into the care of the aged aunt they lived with, and was not permitted to attend school with others of her age. Though today she would have been called an "exceptional child," and helped accordingly, in those days she was left to get about by herself, and spent most of her time sitting on the baggage platform of the depot opposite the Rose Rock soda-pop works, throwing rocks at the freight trains.

"What d'you talk about with Rabbit?"

"Oh-h . . . he tells me what he's been doing, or how many trains pass his house during the day. . . ."

"That's dumb."

"Not if you like trains as much as Harold does. He's really a bright boy, but he doesn't want anybody to suspect it, so he pretends. Very hard, pretending. You ought to get to know him, all of you. He might just be smarter than you think."

"You gave Rabbit skates," I muttered in an injured tone. She sat me up with a surprised look.

"Yes, I did. He didn't have skates. And you do."

"His are better."

"Are they? Then perhaps that's why he skates better. You'll have to practice a lot to catch up with him, won't you? But I'm sure Rabbit won't be as ungrateful for his skates as some other people one might mention." There was more than a touch of asperity in her tone, and instantly I regretted my words. Here I sat amid all the wonderful things she'd brought me almost every day, and I was complaining about skates for Rabbit Hornaday.

"I'm sorry."

She kissed me, and oh, the fragrance of her perfume, the tiny surge of blue through a vein in her throat, and those beautiful brown eyes smiling down. Oh, how I loved her, and oh, how I hated her to leave. But tomorrow, she promised as she tiptoed out, tomorrow, what larks.

Lying on the pillows she had fluffed, under the counterpane she'd folded, warm and drowsy, and spoiled as an apple at the bottom of the barrel, I forgave her Rabbit Hornaday and resolved I would try to get to know him. Later, sorting again through the postcard views she had brought with the Roxy magic lantern, I thought what a very nice "lady" she was, and about how cruelly life had made her suffer, but knowing that she refused to be done in by it, and that she would content herself with the memory of Edward Harleigh. And it was from this period that I date the real beginning of our friendship, which lasted from that day, with one tragic interruption, until she died.

She continued coming every day, both mornings and afternoons. When Lew and Harry and Ag came home from school, they would hurry upstairs with their jam-and-peanut-butter sandwiches to the sleeping porch, drawn like nails to the magnet of Mrs. Harleigh, whom they also were now to call "Lady." With her in the house, Lew and Harry had never seemed less interested in their gang, or Aggie in her magazine stories, and when Nonnie came, trying to keep her eye on Kerney, but listening while Lady described the summerhouse she was planning to build that year, it seemed we were much more a family than we had been before.

Once, coming in while Lew had Harry down on the floor and was pummeling him and Harry was trying to twist Lew's leg from the socket, Lady went and pulled them apart. She listened to both sides of the argument, then hugged them together, telling them that they were brothers, and brothers didn't fight, they stuck up for each other. That was the end of internecine warfare in our house, and after that there was only good-natured roughhousing, and even Aggie didn't seem so shy and inclined to stay by herself.

Ma only shook her head, declaring helplessly that we were taking advantage of our neighbor. Once, on my way to the bathroom, I listened over the banister and heard them talking downstairs.

"Mrs. Harleigh, I think my family must be exhausting you—particularly that one. . . ." I knew who "that one" was.

"Nonsense—I'm enjoying every minute of it. If you don't mind sharing them . . ."

"Heavens to Betsy, no. I'm glad of the chance to get my shoes off."

"You have wonderful children."

"Do I? Really?" It sounded as if the thought hadn't occurred to Ma before. Now when she came home, she seemed to have left her problems at the Sunbeam and hurried right upstairs to join the circle around my bed—and around Lady. And in the evenings Lew and Harry would be at the worktable, putting together a crystal set, and talking to me over their shoulders, and for the first time I felt included instead of left out.

It snowed again, and I watched them all out under the Great Elm, making snowmen, half a dozen at least, and, bored with being sick, I wished I could join the fun.

"They're building a snow family out there, imagine!" Lady exclaimed when she came. She flung off her fur coat and I felt her cool cheek against my hot one as she kissed me. She had brought me clean pajamas from Elthea's laundry tubs, and when I had changed she rubbed my chest with Vicks and pinned on a clean flannel, watching the work out the window from time to time. Then she pulled up the chair and read to me, as she often did. Today it was the Hans Christian Andersen story, "The Snow Queen," appropriate for the weather, she said.

An expression I could not instantly decipher came over her face as she told of the goblin whose mirror turned everything it reflected into something ugly, where "the loveliest landscapes looked like boiled spinach, and the best people became hideous." She read it with distaste, as if there truly were such a mirror, and I remembered how she had stared into the wobbly glass in the dining room on the night the red-haired man had come.

The story continued. Even good thoughts passing through a per-

son's mind were reflected in the demon-mirror, and all the other
goblins said that was fine, for now it could be seen how ugly the
world truly was, and all the ugly people in it. The mirror was so evil
that in the face of heaven it shattered, and the fragments flew about,
some people even getting them into their hearts, which turned them
to ice.

Lady gave a little shudder, glancing at me for my reaction, then
went on to the part about Kay and Gerda and the Snow Queen. Her
features became more lively as the tale unfolded further. The Snow
Queen is formed out of a snowflake, "clothed in the finest white
gauze, put together of millions of starry flakes." She is beautiful, but
alas, made of ice, and as cold. At last she takes the boy Kay away
from Gerda, wrapping him in her furs and carrying him off in her
sleigh through the black clouds and the storm and "it seemed as
though the wind sang old songs."

I was thinking of the sleigh in the carriage house and, listening to
her voice, I thought of how it would be to go sleighing with this
Snow Queen, wrapped in her furs; she would not be cold as ice, but
warm and comforting.

Gerda searches far and wide for Kay, finding him at last a prisoner
in the palace of the Snow Queen, where there is yet another mirror.
This mirror is a great frozen lake, called the Mirror of Reason, which
had shattered into a thousand pieces, and the Snow Queen has
promised Kay his freedom, and the whole world, *and* a pair of
skates, if he can form from the pieces the word "Eternity." Poor Kay
cannot do it.

At last Gerda finds him, and of their own accord the ice pieces
spell the word, and he is released, and the roses bloom again.

"'There they both sat, grown up, and yet children—children in
heart; and it was summer—warm, delightful summer.'" She closed
the book and laid her head back, looking at the ceiling. "Odd, I
thought that story ended 'happily ever after.' But I suppose summer
is just as good."

I propped myself up on my elbows. "You didn't like the part about
the mirror, did you?"

"No, I didn't. And *you* didn't like the part about the skates, did
you?" Laughing, she laid the book aside and rose, saying she must
get home and dress; Colonel Blatchley was taking her to hear
Paderewski. "And anyway," she said, looking down at the Green,
"who could spell 'Eternity' out of the broken pieces of a mirror?

Aren't those snowmen marvelous!" She put on her fur coat, kissed me, and went away.

When Nonnie had brought up my supper, while Lew and Harry were on their beds listening to the crystal set, I put on my bathrobe and slippers and sat by the window. Down on the Green the snow-men stood gloriously appareled in hats and coats, gloves, and canes. Ag had explained that it was a family, there was a Mister and Missus, and the children, one for each of us; I was the one with the big ears.

After some time I saw Colonel Blatchley's Studebaker pull into Lady's drive. He was admitted by Jesse, and when he reappeared, with Lady on his arm, I glimpsed a shimmering sort of coat, and sparkly slippers as she came down the steps, and a white scarf around her head. She looked beautiful. Off they went to hear Ignace Paderewski, and while I waited by the window for them to return I thought of remarks I would make to Lady concerning the fact that my nickname was the same as the Christian name of the famous pianist.

Later, when the household had retired, Ma came in, surveyed the sleeping Lew and Harry, then whispered, "All right, young man, time for bed." She got the brush and parted my hair as Lady had done, and slipped the stocking cap on. I submitted to these ministrations, but asked if I could stay up a while longer.

"What on earth for?"

"Lady's coming home."

"I see." She seemed to understand. "She's a lovely person, isn't she?"

"Uh-huh."

"Lots nicer than your old ma."

"No, she isn't. She's just—different."

"Well, then, I won't be jealous." Her smile was wry as she turned to go. "Bless you." She glanced at Lew and Harry again. "Bless you all—you're your father's sons. Don't stay up too late."

She went to her room, and while Lew and Harry kicked the blankets about in their bunks, I alternated reading in bed with wait-ing at the window. It became a protracted vigil, and I wondered if Lady would ever return. The lamp in our room was off, and outside it was a bright moonlit night, bringing into clear focus the snowy Green, and the half-dozen snow figures. I looked up at the vast night sky, full of stars that seemed like snowflakes, brittle and crystalline. The edges of my frosty pane were whorled with fantasy-like patterns of ice, and beyond it the light was brilliant, surreal, unearthly. It kindled strange imaginings to me. In my fantasy I saw beyond the pane the Snow Queen, ready to bear me away to her kingdom at the North Pole, and this vision was further enhanced by my own reflection in the blue glass, distorted like the goblin's mirror which had hardened the heart of little Kay, and which made all the world look ugly and unhappy.

Lights turned the windowpane a glazed orange, and I saw a car coming along the far side of the road. It slowed, then pulled into Lady's drive. She had returned. The Colonel got out and trudged around to hand her out from the other side. They went in together, and the door closed. I felt the pangs of jealousy; Colonel Blatchley was now my rival.

I kept watch at the window until finally he left, Lady showing him to the door. She lingered for a moment, looking over at the snowmen, then the carriage lamps went off and the door closed. All was dark, except for a light behind the living-room shade, then the outside lamps were turned on again. Leaving the door swung wide, Lady came out. I raised my window softly, and heard the strains of music floating through her open doorway as, holding her evening coat closed, she came down the walk, crossed the street, and walked onto the Green.

Her arms were crossed in front of her, the palms of her hands resting on her shoulders, her head slightly tilted as she looked at the snowmen, Mister and Missus and the children. Closer she came, the ends of her light scarf trailing, to walk among them, stopping to inspect each as she passed it, like a woman undecided about merchandise in a department store. When she got to the last figure—it was Mister—she gazed at him for a longer time than she had at the rest, finally changing the angle of his hat.

From over the way the music sounded through the open door; I couldn't tell if it was the radio or the phonograph. I remember it was a waltz, and one part of it sounded like "Sweet Rosie O'Grady." (Later I learned it was *Swan Lake*.) Lady uncrossed her arms and held them slowly and gracefully out to her sides, her body dipping slightly as she moved. She turned and turned again, swaying, looking up at the sky. She danced lightly in time to the music, now moving her arms in the conventional form of a waltz partner, as if one hand were held by a man, the other gathering up her gown and coat together. The coat shone in the light, and her veil-like scarf, and her twinkling shoe tips—everything shone, her long white gloves, her white face, the diamonds sparkling on her ears.

Then she moved into the circle of snow figures around the tree, and while the music continued she halted her steps. Again she looked up at the sky and I fancied her imagining all the things I had imagined, that in her silvery coat and gauzy scarf and smooth-gloved arms she was the Snow Queen.

Ah, she was my Snow Queen, and I her willing prisoner, and did she live in a frozen palace on the Mirror of Reason, I would take the pieces and spell the word "Eternity" and she would give me the whole world—*and* a pair of skates, good as the ones Rabbit had received. Unable to resist, I took the flashlight from the table and shined it at the pane. She saw the light, and again her feet twinkled as she swept across the snow.

"How was Ignatz?" I whispered down between cupped hands.

"Ignatz who? Oh—Paderewski? Mag*ni*fishent! *Won*dafil! What are you *doing* up there, l'il Ignatz?" She giggled like a fellow-conspirator.

"I'se waitin' fer Krazy Kat. Plotz plotz."

"You little dickens, you plotz yourself to bed before you catch more cold."

"Will you come up and tuck me in?"

"I will not. But I'll come tomorrow. Good night, l'il Ignatz." She started away, then turned back briefly and waved the end of her scarf to me. "Good night, friend of my youth." The words came in a whisper on the cold air and I didn't know what she meant, really, but it sounded like such a lovely thing for her to say, tender, affectionate, and personal, and I loved her for it. She floated away, stumbling slightly, and I thought that while the Colonel had had a nightcap my Snow Queen must have had one or two herself.

The snowmen melted, leaving only soggy clothes to be picked up and dried on the line, the canes and hats returned to the attic, and the first of Lady's planned larks was the promised musical evening, at the end of the week I returned to school. This was early in April; though the snow lay in gray mushy patches around the Green, Mrs. Sparrow's forsythia was already in bloom. It was Sunday, and Jesse and Elthea had departed at their accustomed hour to go upstreet for dinner and the movies. Shortly thereafter, Ma brought us over the Green where we gathered in Lady's front room with our instruments: Lew his banjo, Harry his cornet, Ag and Nonnie their violins, me my French horn, and Ma at the piano. Some of the dining-room chairs were pulled into a semicircle in the bow of the piano, while Lady sat embroidering in one of the roomy wing chairs beside the lighted fire.

"Well, come, children," Ma said, slipping off her rings and settling her music on the piano rest, "play for Lady."

"No, you first," we said, and so Ma began, as she usually did, with "Keep the Home Fires Burning," which was always for our father, and then "The Parade of the Wooden Soldiers," which she used to play for us as babies, and then the "Going Home" movement from the *New World Symphony*, which one by one we all joined in.

"Now, now, I think we'd better start that again," Ma said, laughing, with a rueful look to Lady, "Agnes, dear, you'd better tune, you're flat." Ag blushed and tuned her violin to Ma's A, and when we began again it went better. We all felt a little foolish at first, never having performed for company before, but it remained for Lady to cause us to shrug off our inhibitions and play our best. Exchanging looks with Ma, she sat plying her embroidery needle with a rhythmical stitch, listening quietly, her smile saying that this was the best sort of evening, that this was what friends were for.

The time for Jack Benny's "Jell-O again" came and went and no one even noticed. After dinner, Lady expressed her concern about the septic tank in her back yard. Her plumber had told her the tank must be dug up and emptied, a nasty job, but a necessary one. Ma's eye fell on Lew, Harry, and myself, and we knew what was coming.

"Why, the boys can do that for you," Ma said with Her Look, "can't you boys?"

"I wouldn't think of it," Lady replied, shaking her head. "Perhaps I can get someone from the Town Farm." The Town Farm was the poorhouse, where Pequot's indigents were housed, but Ma said not an inmate there would be up to such a task. No, the boys would be happy to do it, "*Won't* you, boys?"

Around eight-thirty Colonel Blatchley stopped in for a visit, taking the wing chair opposite Lady and lighting up one of the expensive cigars she kept him provided with. The Colonel, a retired banker, handled Lady's money and holdings for her, and advised her carefully on all financial matters. I never learned why he was called "Colonel," though it was generally assumed it had something to do with the British regiment he had served in during the war. Only half American, he spoke with traces of an English accent, and he "sported" rather than wore his clothes: tattersall vests, baggy knickers, shoes with fringed tongues, sometimes even spats. He was well past fifty, bluff, genial, and portly, a good old duffer; wifeless for years, he loved playing the ever-youthful courtier to Lady. But, serving him his "twenty drops," which was what he called his ample bourbons-and-water, Lady would say, "What does the landed gentry want with baggage from the wrong end of Knobb Street?"

The Colonel had come at the instigation of Mrs. Porter de Sales-Sprague, who had maneuvered herself into the position of planning and writing a pageant to be mounted that summer in celebration of the town's tercentenary. With the Colonel as intermediary, Mrs. Sprague was requesting that Lady open the Josiah Webster House, Built 1702, to the Daughters of the Pilgrims Club and their guests during the festivities. Lady laughed, saying she couldn't imagine who would want to pay good money to see her parlor.

"My dear," said the Colonel gently, "yours is one of the most historical houses in our town—surely . . ." The truth of the Colonel's statement was well known. George Washington had visited in this very room at the time of the Yorktown Conference, though he had bedded down over on Main Street, where he and General Rochambeau had made the final plans for the Battle of Yorktown, which ended the American Revolution. Still, historical site or not, Lady did not seem inclined to favor Mrs. Sprague's suggestion. She crinkled her eyebrows with amusement and asked, "Will she want my tea service as well? Must Jesse get out the silver polish? And will there be *only* tea? No cocktails?"

The Colonel gave us all a broad wink. "Yes, I should think cocktails—surely the 5:10-ers will be invited."

"Ah, yes, the 5:10-ers could hardly get through a party without cocktails, even if Eamon Harmon doesn't have to mix his own gin anymore. Well," Lady continued dubiously, "if it's a case of the 5:10-ers . . ."

The 5:10-ers were members of the Pequot Landing establishment, so-called because of the active politicking that took place at the back of the 5:10 trolley car from Hartford, a local version of the "smoke-filled room" of convention fame. During these half-hour rides from the city, the 5:10-ers discussed events as they pertained to Pequot, and made certain determinations, picking various candidates for office, and seeing to it that certain appointments were filled. There was nothing underhanded or nefarious in this; it was simply a way of doing things.

These same personages formed the "Academy Parliament,"

known thusly because, often unable to transact all of their political dealings on the trolley, the 5:10-ers would meet outside the old Academy Hall before or after court sessions, or following Town Meeting, and make further dispositions regarding civic welfare. Most of the men were business executives in the city, others had local enterprises, and all were white, of English descent, and went to First Church. They were the town's Old Guard, sons of the original settlers, and were comfortably secure husbands and fathers. They played golf at the country club on Saturday afternoon, returned to dance and get drunk on Saturday night, and went to church bleary-eyed on Sunday morning.

Among the 5:10-ers were Eamon Harmon, whose family were seed growers; Sam Merriam, in insurance; Walt Bricker, president of the bank; Jack and Phil Harrelson's father, a lawyer; and Porter Sprague, retired and under sentence to his wife.

"You may as well say yes to Mrs. Sprague, Lady," Ma said lightly, "you know she won't stop until she has your house." The Colonel was quick to agree, but still Lady demurred. While the discussion went on, I found my eye straying to the gate-leg table between the back windows, and the shrine Mrs. Sparrow was forever talking about: little faded flags; a medal in a box lined with blue velvet; a framed speech; an array of photographs, most prominent among them the one that had been taken when Edward Harleigh was welcomed home from France, five months before his death.

"It's going to be a beautiful spring," Lady whispered as we left with our instruments. She kissed the Colonel's cheek warmly, but I noticed how adroitly she had avoided giving him an answer; Mrs. Porter de Sales-Sprague wasn't going to have *everything* her own way.

At Easter vacation we tackled the job of digging up the septic tank behind Lady's house, under the supervision of Jesse Griffin, who was a little of a plumber and a little of a carpenter and a little of just about anything else you could think of. But Lady didn't want him doing the digging, and so it fell to us to open up the lateral pipes which had gotten clogged and consequently caused the tank to back up. It was hard, dirty work, and it took most of our vacation to complete the job.

Lady meanwhile had spoken with some of the 5:10-ers, who agreed that what the town needed was a proper sewage system, and

Eamon Harmon and the others agreed to put the matter before the Town Meeting. There were two people who could be counted on to oppose any proposal that smacked of progress: Porter Sprague, who was still Keeping Cool with Coolidge, and No-Relations Welles, who opposed everything on general principles. Once he held Town Meeting in session way into the night because he was against the town having to pay for the laundering of gymnasium towels at the high school.

But while the problem of sewage was discussed at the Academy Hall, we dug in and dunked out, and emptied Lady's septic tank. She paid us handsomely for our labors, and we were always in and out of her house. Having keenly felt its emptiness, she tenanted it with us—a population explosion that never seemed to mar its serenity or elegance. We were, as she often said, her family, and though she got us ready-to-hand, with all our faults intact, she interested herself in every detail of our various small existences. Her instinctive consideration and understanding, the quiet delving into our individual personalities, the precise knowledge she had of each of us stemmed, I think, more from her powers of intuition than anything else. She quickened our interest, sharpened our perceptions, encouraged our temperaments, fertilized our imaginations, and added zest to all our lives.

She exemplified all the German virtues of housewifeliness and industry—it was the way her mother had brought her up. Hard work, thrift, and cook with potatoes. She loved cooking and baking and canning—it was always such a pleasure to see her in the kitchen—and she kept a good housewife's garden behind the carriage house, priding herself on the size of her summer squash, and the healthy issue of her pole beans. In her less active moods she was forever doing needlework of some kind: embroidery, crewel, petit point; to this day I have a unicorn she stitched up for me, seemingly overnight. She enjoyed and respected art—painting, music, sculpture—and she valued good, careful writing.

Though it would have been easy for her to cause her influence to be felt in the town, she most often withheld it. She believed that you could get a lot more flies with honey than with vinegar; flies she got, and friends galore. But while she had the respect and admiration of the community, she held herself aloof from its common currents of daily life, only bringing her power to bear when it seemed most needful.

As the weather became warmer, the carpets were taken up and put in mothballs, and the bare floors echoed with our footsteps, the walls with our shouts and cries. The living room became a place where Things Happened. Imagine sitting there and hearing Rosa Ponselle, our first Carmen, and having Lady tell how she rolled cigarettes and switched her hips and was stabbed by Don José. Or putting a Rachmaninoff roll on the player piano. Or looking at Renoir's glowing women in a picture book. We got paint sets and began painting. We went to the Athenaeum in Hartford to see the statues, Greek, unclothed, fig-leafed.

There were larks galore: an Easter-egg hunt in Hubbard's meadow; an outing to Pope Park to see some daredevil pilots; birthdays celebrated with trips to the movies—Grace Moore in *One Night of Love,* and Rudy Vallee in person. She took us all in the Minerva to see Rudy at a vaudeville-movie house; Jesse drove us, and saw the show, too. Lady loved it when Rudy sang "Good Night, Sweetheart," albeit through his nose, and I thought of Edward's carolers singing "Good Night, Lady," on the night they'd become engaged. I watched as her hand slid inside her pocketbook on her lap, and then dabbed at her eyes with a handkerchief.

Once, I remember, we piled in the Minerva and drove to Holiday Lake, an amusement park some distance away, where we rode the roller coaster and the merry-go-round, and saw the midway. Later, we were in the funhouse, prancing around in front of the crazy mirrors, making our heads disappear and our sides widen. I thought the mirrors were like the goblin's mirror in the Snow Queen. Lady was hanging back with Jesse, who'd come in with us, and I tried to get her to stand in front of one. She was politely reluctant while I, taking advantage of my new position of prominence, got smart and was overly persistent. She flung my hand away and stamped her foot angrily. "No! I don't want to see. They're horrid!" Jesse didn't say anything, but he gave me a look. I felt hot with shame, that I should have made Lady lose her temper. I never tried a trick like that again.

But still, there were the Dreams of a Welsh Rarebit Fiend to be concerned with, and we got into the habit of watching Jesse Griffin's face, as a sort of bellwether which we could read to tell how the atmosphere really was around the house across the Green. Sometimes I would see him at the window, and if he was frowning or otherwise looking dour, I wouldn't go in, knowing that Lady had been seeing Edward's ghost again, or that she'd been having bad dreams. Elthea, too, would touch her finger to her lips for quiet, saying Missus wasn't feeling well, and we'd tiptoe away and try to find something else to do. We soon learned that if you wanted to get on with Lady Harleigh you got on with Jesse and Elthea first.

6

Porter Sprague made a remark to Mr. Pellegrino, the barber, and somehow it got back to Lady. Mr. Sprague said, watching Lady go by in the Minerva, with Jesse driving, that she was too familiar with her inferiors, and that servants should be kept in their place or there'd be a Communist revolution in the country.

But Lady didn't care. She only laughed and said that Porter Sprague was the sort of man who drops his cigar ash on your rugs and says it's good for moths.

"Besides, everybody has their inferiors. A parlormaid has the upstairs maid; even the lowest person on the scale has the whole race of apes, so he's still more superior than someone else. What Mr. Sprague is afraid of is that the Griffins are superior to *him*. Which, let me add, darling, they are. Fa' goodnitz sakes (she was doing Krazy Kat), Porter Sprague wears lisle ankle socks with clocks on them!"

I knew what she meant, though. When you got to know Jesse and Elthea, you realized that in their way they had few peers. They were, in fact, a most special couple.

There was something in their looks and manner, their carriage and walk, that called up a mixture of the best of the races, African and Caribbean, black and white. To me the sound of their voices had the whisper of ginger and honey; imprecise but lilting cadences which spoke of palms and beaches and ever-sunny skies. They had their own way of expressing things that was unique. Before running the vacuum Elthea would say, "I'm going to make a noise in your ears, now." Or when a kitchen philodendron fell off the windowsill she said, "He must have dropped itself." Or again, if the soda pop was in diminished supply she'd say, "Ginger ale's singing the Doxology," which meant Lady was practically out. Any irritation or complexity Jesse deemed to be "stupidy," and I lived in fear of his judging me so. In their soft accents our commonplace words

changed and sounded more beautiful—"man" become "mon," or
"family" "fahmly"—and altogether they made me want to run away
and join the Navy, to see those sparkling islands they had left, where
women carried baskets of fruit on their heads, and nobody ever wore
galoshes.

"He's an odd number," Colonel Blatchley sometimes pronounced
about Jesse, but for all his forbidding frowns he seemed all right to
me, as he did to all of us. Still, I don't think he ever got used to having children around the house.

Elthea did, though. Except when Lady wasn't well, she never
seemed to mind having us underfoot or trooping in and out of her
kitchen, her special domain. We decided it was because, like their
mistress, she and Jesse had no children of their own. Elthea Griffin
may have been only a cooker of roasts and washer of pots and
duster of cobwebs, but, thinking back on her now, I remember her
as a person who asked for nothing more than what life had already
bestowed on her. All day long we'd hear her softly humming or singing as she went about the house, leaving a trail of melody behind.
She may have seemed lackadaisical and carefree, but she was a bar-
relhouse of energy all right.

I remembered the first time I'd seen her, at the seashore, at the
Manor House Inn, and how strange I'd found it—I was shocked,
really—watching her and Jesse in their swimming suits, discovering
that they must be brown all over. Until then I'd thought of Negroes
that just their hands and faces were colored, the rest of their bodies
white.

Like Jesse, Elthea was tall and thin, with a long neck, and such a
graceful way of walking. I decided this was because she'd been
allowed to go barefoot year-round as a child. She had a smooth,
glossy look, as if she'd just gotten out of a bathtub, and when she
was enthusiastic her eyes rolled around like great white marbles.
And she had the biggest, widest smile—how different she was from
the grave and dour Jesse. But, as Ruthie Sparrow said, opposites attract; we supposed she was right. Elthea's high humor kept her well
in Lady's graces, Lady enjoying people's fun as she did; they were
good friends, Lady and Elthea.

She devoured the newspaper, morning and evening, sitting with
Lady over coffee and cigarettes at the kitchen table, exclaiming in
delicious horror at the latest lurid ax-murder trial or giggling about a
raid on a Manhattan love nest. All she wanted to do, she said, was

go down to New York City and go dancing at the Aloha Room at a big New York hotel.

Once I asked her why she didn't wear saucers in her lips like we'd seen Negroes wearing in the circus.

"Oh, hon," she exclaimed straight-faced, "they're African folks, I reckon. We're islanders and fisher folks, we just wear geegaws and such."

"What's geegaws?"

"Bangles and rings, you know, like these here." Out shot her arm loaded with bracelets that clattered and rang: Elthea loved all sorts of flashy jewelry, which she wore if it was her day off or not.

"How long have you and Jesse been married?"

"Oh, long time. Just the longest. He's a fine mon, my Jesse."

"Does he like me?"

"Jesse? You? Sure, hon, he likes you just fine." She laughed at the thought of Jesse not liking *any*body; that was just his way, she said. "Only thing Jesse doesn't like is my laundering."

"Why?"

"I like to do a shirt nice and soft, so's it's comfortable-wearing. But that Jesse, all he wants is for me to do him a shirt with enough starch to stiff a corpse. That's what he says: 'Elthea, stiff me a corpse with that shirt.' Lord, he likes a shirt board-hard."

"Do you miss the island?"

"Sure, hon, folks always misses home. But I like it fine wherever I am. Like it fine right here. This is my home now, me and Jesse, looking after Missus. I must confess it, I like being with rich folks. Back home's nothing but poor folks mostly."

"We're poor."

She shrieked and whacked, first her thigh, then my shoulder, then her bosom; I thought she must have hurt herself. "No, you're not, honey, not by a sight. You're rich. You don't know it, but you're rich. Mon, you don't know what poor *is*. Take Daddy—that'd be Jesse's daddy—he lost his work and he was poor, I mean dirt poor. Till Missus helps him out."

"Lady?"

"Yes, hon. She sends money all the time to Jesse's daddy, and Jesse's daddy's family."

Sometimes I'd tried to get Jesse to talk about his island, and what it was like to have grown up in a place so exotic and different from our town, but he'd just hunch his shoulders and say, "Oh, that was a long time ago, I forget." But little by little, from conversations such

as these with Elthea, who was always willing to talk if she could
work at the same time, I gleaned certain facts and put them together. His people had been fishermen, and earned their living from
the sea. Jesse's father was a sort of island patriarch and had had
many children. Somehow he'd had an accident and couldn't sail anymore, and Lady, learning of this, had been generous with funds, and
for this she'd earned the Griffins' undying devotion.

But still I wondered about Jesse; he could have such a frowning,
disapproving air about him, particularly when people came around
who he felt oughtn't to come around. Such was the case one afternoon when Mrs. de Sales-Sprague called on Lady. Since the renova-
tion of the septic tank, Lady had made elaborate plans for changes
in her gardens, which were now to include the summerhouse, already being built by Mr. Seifert, the carpenter, and a path of herring-
bone brick to a particular spot where she was going to have a larger
birdbath, which would stand in a circle of brickwork and greenery.
We were out back, watching the work, Mr. Seifert on the summerhouse, Jesse laying the bricks, when Elthea came across the lawn and
announced that Mrs. Sprague was at the front door. Jesse grumbled
as he rose, dusted his knees, and went to put on his black coat.

"It's all right, Jesse," Lady said. "Elthea can show Mrs. Sprague
out here." Presently Mrs. de Sales-Sprague appeared, large-beaked
like a bird—though hardly a *rara avis;* she was common enough—
and looking as if it hurt her to smile. Evidently she didn't like gain-
ing Lady's presence by way of the kitchen door.

She had come, she said, to verify for herself Lady's decision not
to open her house and gardens for the Daughters of the Pilgrims
Club after the Tercentenary Pageant. Excusing herself to us, Lady
drew her guest across the lawn by the bird feeder, and while I pretended to be interested in Mr. Seifert's carpentering, I indulged in
my habitual pastime of eavesdropping.

Mrs. de Sales-Sprague was married to Porter J. Sprague, the
richest man in town (Lady was generally conceded to be richer)
and they referred to themselves as P.J. and Spouse. She was his second wife, and in a prenuptial arrangement he had been forced to
agree that she would not surrender her family name, she being a de
Sales of Talcottville (which meant merely that they had been in
onions when onions were practically legal tender in town), and as
she had joined Porter Sprague in body, so she had appended herself
to him in name as well. Large, granite-faced, and hyphenated, Mrs.
de Sales-Sprague could cast aspersions as seed is broadcast: wide

and by the handful. She was never so kind as to howdeedo a child unless an adult was within earshot; like her husband, she abhorred the young, but when there were grownups around she practiced her blandishments inordinately.

After their marriage they had bought the old Harleigh house, which had been Edward's father's and grandfather's, where they resided in aloof affluence, but maintaining a niggardly standard of living that would put Knobb Street folk to shame. They were frequently on view at the A. & P. or the Pilgrim Market where they would for a quarter of an hour pick over the roasts and chops, settling at last on a half-pound of ground meat which did them both for dinner. Spouse thought nothing of marching down to the parish-house kitchen after a church supper and filling up her basket with the leftovers.

I had good reason to dislike her. Because our family were newcomers to Pequot Landing, none of us had been invited to participate in Mrs. de Sales-Sprague's pageant. Ma temporized, saying it was merely an oversight, but while other children were being fitted for Pilgrim costumes, and were given lines to learn, we were decidedly ignored. I felt the snub keenly, and could hardly look at her as she marched back from the bird feeder with a satisfied smirk.

"What a lovely frock," she cooed to Ag. I glanced at Lady, whose expression hinted at a mysterious bargain struck in the matter of her premises and the garden party, a thought reinforced when Mrs. de Sales-Sprague announced that all of us were to be given parts in the pageant. I thought I detected Lady's fine Italian hand in the business as she casually drifted over for a word with Mr. Seifert, disclaiming any immediate interest in the matter.

Shortly after rehearsals commenced, however, another accident befell me which promised to keep me from performing my part.

One day Lew, Harry, and I got the idea of emulating the daring of some barnstorming aerialists Lady had taken us to see at Pope Park. We brought the skate sail out and put it together, proposing to use it to fly off the roof of the chicken house where we all were gathered. It was a simple matter for Lew to climb up and, holding the sail over his head, to make the easy leap into the mulch bed. Then Harry tried it, and, at last, myself. It wasn't much of a jump and certainly no test of Man in Flight.

Lew said what was needed was a higher roof, and the one most readily suggesting itself was that of Lady Harleigh's carriage house. Carrying the sail, Lew led the way across the Green while we followed. Blue Ferguson, who was pulling a Pilgrim Market basket from the back of his truck in the drive next door, came through the Piersons' hedge to see what we were up to.

"We're going to fly," I told him.

"Sure thing? That's pretty high, isn't it?" He sighted up to the roof and gauged the distance to the ground. I could tell that it had become a question of who was to bell the cat, for I saw that both Lew and Harry were having doubts. Seizing my chance to show off in front of Blue, I took the sail and climbed up into the loft above the space where the sleigh was stored, and from there by ladder to the roof, close to the gilded weathercock.

"Don't!" cried Ag, who had run up to join us, and though I hoped Blue would try to dissuade me, he merely watched with interest as I battled the sail and tried to maintain my precarious position.

"Go ahead," Lew said, daring me. I grabbed the sail more tightly and leaped out into space. For a few seconds I felt the wind catch and lift me, but when the air slid from under the canvas I plummeted straight down. There was a terrific crash, the sound of splintering glass; as I struck the ground, I felt a sharp pain in my left leg. I had fallen into Jesse's cucumber frame.

Dizzily, I tried to assess the extent of my injury. I had felt something snap, and the amount of blood spurting from my leg sent the others dashing in panic for help, while I lay bleeding in the shattered frame, with the sky spinning overhead. Suddenly I knew what heaven must be like, for it seemed a vision appeared before me, an angel with a sweet smiling face, and I was enfolded in a pair of smooth, gentle arms.

"Oh, my dear," said Lady, cool as one of the cucumbers I was sprawled in, "you've really done it this time, haven't you? Didn't anyone tell you you're not Icarus? No, don't move. You've cut yourself rather badly. Here's Jesse, to get you fixed up."

Wiping away my tears, she helped Jesse lift me out of the cucumber frame and lay me on the lawn, ignoring the grass cuttings staining her afternoon dress, holding me while he made a careful examination. "Stupidy thing," he said in succinct West Indian tones, fashioning a tourniquet with strips torn from an undergarment hastily snatched from the clothesline, then improvising splints from a garden stake. The pain was nothing to the new importance I now felt, being the center of concern: poor Ag's white face, Blue Ferguson, Lew and Harry looking sheepish, and Lady bending over and calling me Ignatz, and saying I was just as Krazy as Kat.

Again I was brought home in Jesse's arms and popped into bed, where Lady watched beside me until Ma returned from the Sunbeam. Dr. Brainard, who had by then arrived, agreed he couldn't have done a better job himself, and said Jesse ought to be a physician, and Harry said it sure was lucky Elthea's bloomers happened to be hanging on the line for bandages.

While I hobbled around in a cast, the Pequot Landing Pageant continued its rehearsals. It was to be a weekend-long anniversary celebration of the founding of the town. The pageant itself would take place on the Green and would depict various periods of the town's history. Lew and Harry and I were to be Pilgrim children, while Aggie was to be a fawn in a Dance Interlude. All the ladies of the town were busy sewing costumes and we boys had already been fitted for our gray serge suits with white collars and tall hats with buckles on them. Aggie got a spotted jumper with little ears.

During rehearsals, Lew, Harry, and I had been giving our all, preparing for the moment when we would dash across the Green toward the stockade, hollering bloody murder as the Indian warriors descended for the Pequot Massacre. Blue Ferguson and a number of other husky athletes were the Indians, and if they came tearing after us with loud savage whoops as they brandished their tomahawks and threatened us with the loss of our scalps, our cries of horror as we sought to evade capture were equally fierce.

It was Blue himself, and another, who were to carry off two Pilgrim girls (historically, their last name had been Rose) and kidnap them. I got what I thought was a brilliant idea: fleeing with the others, I would pretend to stumble and fall and almost get caught by one of the Indians—a moment of great suspense—but at the last moment leap up and race for the stockade. I broached the idea to Blue Ferguson, my hero, one morning after rehearsal.

"How about that, Blue?"

"Sounds okay to me."

"Hot dog! You want to be the one who catches me?"

Blue rumpled my hair and shook his head. "Listen, kiddo, I've got my hands full carrying Mabel Talcott—she's *fat*. Better get someone else." He gave me a friendly punch and ran off to his delivery truck, and next I sought out Mrs. de Sales-Sprague herself.

I waited until she had finished directing the Dance of the Vegetables—we were great seed growers in Pequot Landing—then told her my idea. To my surprise, she thought this a clever theatrical stroke and wrote it into her script, and I considered myself a big shot because it was my own invention.

I needn't have felt so smug. The first morning after my accident, when I limped out on the Green to join the others for rehearsal, Mrs. Sprague sailed up and informed me that owing to my injury the part of the fallen Pilgrim boy had been given to Gerald Morrisey, and furthermore I would not be permitted to participate at all; my costume should not be wasted. Too sorry, cooed Mrs. Sprague, and sailed off to direct the burning of the witch. My anger was boundless. In the first place, Gerald Morrisey: a sneak, a cheat, and a liar —all the things I myself was. But he was one thing more: teacher's pet. Awful Miss Grimes took particular pride in making Gerald an example to us all, and while I was kept in for recess, Gerald Morrisey got to clap the erasers, a prized chore. How I hated pantywaist Gerald Morrisey!

I spoke my woe to Lady.

"Is that a fact?" she blithely queried, then, spying Mrs. de Sales-Sprague directing the maypole dances, she swept out to her while I limped after.

"Dear Mrs. Sprague," Lady said in a sugary voice, "it seems we must give this matter second thoughts."

"Whatever in the world do you *mean*, Mrs. *Har*leigh?" asked the other in her own sugary voice.

"I *mean*, dear Mrs. Sprague," Lady said in a sugarier voice, "exactly what I said. We must give this matter second thoughts." Butter wouldn't have melted in that smiling mouth as she produced me from behind her skirts. "This boy wants to be a Pilgrim."

Spouse's smile was equal to Lady's. "I'm afraid that is impossible, *dear* Mrs. Harleigh. As you can see, he has a bad leg."

"But, *dear* Mrs. Sprague"—in her sugariest voice—"so did the Pilgrims from time to time, I should imagine. Have a bad leg, I mean. Can't we just pretend *this* Pilgrim boy has received an injury trying to warn the town against marauding Indians?"

"But, *dear* Madam," said Mrs. de Sales-Sprague in *her* sugariest voice, favoring Lady with a condescending smile, "if he hobbles so, I shouldn't think he could get *any*where in time to warn *any*one about *any*thing."

"Very well. Then he must have a horse to ride." Lady's smile was so bright as to be astonishing. She did not fling the gauntlet, but dropped it, carelessly, as she might a glove.

"A horse?" snorted Mrs. Sprague. "There are no horses in my script."

"Then may I suggest you write one in?"

"Lady Harleigh, are you presuming to tell me what I may or may not have in my pageant?" Mrs. Sprague gathered herself up, trying to tower over Lady, which was difficult because Lady was quite tall.

"I presume nothing, Edith Sprague. . . ."

"Very well, then. No horses and no boys with game legs. I cannot have the lad gimping around and holding up cues, now, can I?"

"Certainly not. I quite agree. No horses and no gimps. Come," she said to me, taking my hand and starting to pull me along after her. Having won the day, Spouse turned back to have a word with the witch whose agonized screams were not quite as loud as the directress might have wished.

"One other thing, however," Lady recollected over her shoulder as we went, "no more can I oblige you by opening my house for the Pilgrim Club." She tossed her head and I wondered how she could make her way across the turf, so grandly oblivious was she.

When Mrs. Sprague sailed toward us again, it was on another tack. "One moment, one moment—please, let us not be hasty about this matter," she called breathlessly.

Lady halted in her tracks but did not turn. "Then you agree," she said as the other hove to, "we must give it second thoughts."

The directress peered at me through her pince-nez. "Do you ride, boy?" she demanded.

"Of course he rides, don't you, darling?" Lady quickly put in (I had a photograph of me taken on a Shetland pony in the schoolyard), "and if he does *not* ride perhaps Mrs. Sparrow will open *her* house for tea."

Mrs. Sprague was, of course, forced to capitulate. "You can catch a lot more flies with honey than you ever can with vinegar," Lady whispered gleefully as she led me away.

"But you told her I could ride a horse!" I urgently returned.

"Can't you?"

"No."

"Always say you can, even if you can't, darling. It's how to get on in the world."

Whether I would get on or not remained to be seen, at least in the matter of my heroics in Mrs. de Sales-Sprague's pageant.

To begin the celebration, there was a flurry of dedications. Plaques and inscribed boulders were unveiled at various historical sites around town, an address was made by the Governor, and then a parade. The following day, a fine, fair June day, was the pageant, and the bleachers around the Green filled rapidly. Since the Great Elm was to all of us a sturdy and venerable symbol of the town, it was fitting that the pageant should take place more or less under its spreading branches, and that the title be "Beneath the Boughs." Each scene was introduced by a narrator, The Spirit of the Elm, and it may be imagined who this narrator was. Mrs. de Sales-Sprague's purple prose was amplified through loudspeakers the length of the Green, she being cleverly concealed at the base of the tree trunk behind some fast-wilting shrubbery. Exits and entrances were made from beside the Piersons' garage, next door to Lady, where, obscured behind the heavy screen of firs hiding the house from the street, the actors gathered before their entrances. And it was from this place that on cue I was to ride full tilt across the Green, shouting the line I'd been given, "The Indians are coming!" to warn the Pilgrim settlers of the approaching Pequot war party. Painted and feathered, Blue Ferguson held the reins as I clambered into the saddle astride the sorry nag who usually pulled No-Relation Welles's horseradish cart.

"'And lo, the seeds that had been planted sprang up, and this was good,'" came Mrs. Sprague's voice, "'and the Founding Fathers knew that the Wongunk braves had been right—Quonehtacut was a good place. But then one day, as they tilled their plenteous crops, they heard the sound of madly flying hooves and a valiant voice cried out—'"

Fiercely gripping the reins, I dug my one good heel into the spavined horse's flanks the way Blue had showed me, and old Dobbin took a step or two in the drive, then stopped. I looked wildly at Blue, almost unrecognizable under his feathered bonnet.

"'. . . the sound of madly flying hooves . . .'" came Mrs. Sprague's cue, "'and a valiant voice cried out—'"

Again I kicked the nag, again she moved a step or two. I could hear the "Indians" snickering behind me. I kicked and yanked and urged, to no avail. The horse wouldn't go. I looked at Blue again, who seemed to be paying no attention to my dilemma. He was over at the bushes beside the garage.

The cue came again. "'. . . the *sound* of *mad*ly *fly*ing hooves! And—'"

And a valiant voice cried out. Mine. Suddenly the horse whinnied, dodged from one side of the drive to the other, then took off, with

me holding on for dear life, across the lawn, into the roadway between the bleachers, and onto the Green. Turf flew in all directions
as I blindly headed for the group of farmers and their families. All
eyes were on me as I shouted, "They're coming! They're coming!"
though it could have been the British for all I managed of my line
about the Indians. But Indians quickly made themselves apparent
when Blue and his wildly shouting tribe dashed onto the Green.
There was a moment of confusion as my mount continued wildly
gyrating and threatening my fellow-actors with injury. While the
horse wheeled and the Pilgrims headed for the stockade, I saw a
rush of feathers and a painted grimace. I was yanked from my saddle, and a tomahawk swished past my head. Before the horse could
spring away, the savage reached and pulled something from under
its tail and the animal immediately receded into docility again.

Flat on the ground, I watched Blue dash toward the stockade, run
nimbly up a ladder, and give out with a loud Tarzan cry. The crowd
was spellbound as he disappeared for an instant, then reappeared
with ferociously protesting Mabel Talcott slung over his shoulder.

When the smoke of musketry had dissolved, the appointed people went about to carry off the fallen, but no one had been assigned
to me. As Mrs. Sprague paused in her narrative, I groaned awfully,
rolled over, got to my feet, alternately clutching my head and my
chest, and staggered to the palisade where Mr. Pretty, the vegetable
man, helped me from view behind the palings.

"You were extraordinary!" Lady exclaimed later. "Jesse—some ice
cream for the young man. He was born to the sock and buskin."
After hugs and kisses and ice cream, I got my Kodak Brownie from
Ag, who had photographed all the parts of the pageant I was in, and
then I went around snapping people in their costumes, making sure
I got one of Blue Ferguson in his feathers and war paint. He
obliged me by re-enacting the abduction of the "Rose" girl with the
hefty Mabel Talcott. A small crowd had gathered around, and
watched admiringly, saying that Blue Ferguson was the greatest guy.
And he was. If ever he could have been called "True Blue," he was
that day.

"Some ride, eh, kiddo?" he whispered, taking me aside and giving
me a friendly jab. "I'll bet you never thought that glue-bait could
shag like that." Then he made his confession: he'd gotten some burrs
from the bushes and stuck them on the horse's bum, hence my thun-
derbolt entrance.

"You're pretty good, kiddo. You really saved the day." He said it loudly, so everyone overheard it; praise from Blue Ferguson was praise indeed.

And though the events of that weekend ended happily enough, there was an aftermath which, though inadvertently brought about by me, could scarcely be considered my fault. But it upset Lady to the degree that she withdrew from all our activities—"retired," as Ruthie Sparrow so often put it—and it came about in this way. When the rolls of film Ag and I had taken were developed, we decided to show them on the magic lantern in the garage. We invited the neighborhood to come and see the pictures of the pageant, which would be projected onto a sheet hung on the back wall. The audience was seated on benches and chairs, the doors were closed, and I showed my collection of postcard views; then everyone gave their undivided attention when I offered the main attraction.

As photographers, Ag and I seemed without peer, for the shots projected clear and large on the sheet, give or take a wrinkle or two in the fabric. There was old Mr. Lyman, our local Civil War relic, waving in the parade. There, on horseback, was Eamon Harmon, in tricorne and wig, playing the treacherous Stamp Agent for the Crown, Jared Ingersoll, who'd been stopped by the angry revolutionaries and forced to resign. There was the Pequot Massacre, with me riding full tilt onto the Green. There were all the guests at the tea in Lady's gardens; there we were on the terrace wall watching the boat flotilla down in the Cove; there was Blue Ferguson, repeating his role in his war bonnet, hoisting Mabel Talcott over his shoulder as I'd snapped the picture, and the crowd laughed. . . .

I had my head down, trying to adjust the focus slightly, when I heard the sound of a chair overturning. Lady had sprung to her feet, her hand to her mouth, staring at the picture on the sheet. Then, shaking her head, she hurried out the side door. The garage darkened again, and while everyone made astonished talk I stared down the beam of light to the picture on the sheet, seeing what I had failed to notice before, and which, enlarged, became immediately apparent. There, at the front of the group around Blue and Mabel Talcott, a little to one side, observing with thin amusement, the tight mouth twisted askew, was the blurred but clearly recognizable image of the red-haired man.

PART TWO

New Songs

PART TWO

New Scrip

I

So it was that Lady "retired" and we lost her for some time to come.
For endless weeks no one saw her, and all you needed was to hear
Ruthie Sparrow over the fence to know that the bedroom blinds
were down. Everyone was at a loss to understand what had
frightened her, and I for once withheld what little I knew, revealing nothing of the existence of the red-haired man. Secretly, I
studied the snapshot under my magnifying glass, perusing the fuzzy
features and wondering what his sinister power was over our friend,
and how he came by it.

But, as we were to learn, even without Lady life continued however it might, and while she retreated into some unfathomable fear
and hid behind drawn shades, and as July came on, we were now
left to our own devices.

Those acquainted with the tedium of summertime in a small town
are those who have lived through it, year after year. School vacation
may have its charms, that infinite and airless vacuum of unvarying
temperature looming up before the boy who in May anticipates the
end of classes and who in September laggardly returns with some
small sense of regret for time lost, but who by mid-July wonders if
the days will ever pass, pondering on how to fill those monotonous
hours of what-to-do-now.

Such times become a test of both ingenuity and will; the attempts
to discover something new and diverting prove more taxing in that
steamy season when those who can afford it have gone to camp,
others to their lake or seashore cottages. These are the days of list-
less inaction and infernal boredom when the green leaves are already shriveled, the lawns burnt off in sorry patches, the flower beds
too soon tired and gone to stalks. The businessmen come off the
5:10 in shirt sleeves, carrying their coats, with ties yanked, while at
high noon people look for their reflection, children for mirages, in
the baking tar of the streets.

One Saturday in canning season, Ma sent me over to Elthea to borrow some rubber jar rings. Elthea was ironing in the kitchen, shirts and a stack of Jesse's collars, dazzling white, one for each day in the week, and with enough starch in them to stiff a corpse. But no, she said, they were out of jar rings.

I asked for a cruller from the breadbox, but she said crullers were singing the Doxology. I knew Lady hadn't been baking. Elthea cut me a piece of her own banana spice cake, and gave me a glass of ginger ale, which I drank in morose silence.

"What's the matter, hon?" Elthea looked at me as her iron zipped around the buttons on a shirt.

"Nothing."

"Come on now, you look dark as thunder. Is it Missus? Don't you fret. Missus is all right, I just gave her a fine lunch and she ate it all. That's always a good sign." While I finished my cake, she told me about the show she and Jesse had seen Thursday night. Elthea loved going to the movies, or to the State Theatre where they had vaudeville and she could hear Cab Calloway sing "Minnie the Moocher."

Just then a truck pulled in the drive and backfired as it came past the window.

"Hol-*ee*, that'll wake the dead, or Missus, if she's napping. Blue Ferguson, whyn't you get yourself a new truck, sound like guns going off out there."

Blue came through the doorway with a market basket which he put on the table. Elthea pulled her cord plug and began taking the things out. "Here now, you call this veal?" she asked, slipping me a wink as she inspected a parcel.

"Elthea, that veal came off the fatted calf, believe it." Blue knew she was joshing him; Elthea loved to joke with all the delivery people and, like everyone else, she appreciated Blue. She sat him down and gave him a piece of cake, too.

"Say, that's good cake, Elthea," Blue said around a mouthful. "If you didn't have a husband, I'd marry you myself."

Elthea stifled her laughter and gave him a playful swat. "You better not let Jesse hear you talk that way, Blue Ferguson." Still, I could tell she was flattered.

"How do you get around on those high heels, Elthea?" She gave him a sassy look and did a little sashay as she replugged her iron.

"Same way you get around on those flat ones. And if Missus doesn't eat her dinner tonight because the veal's tough, I'm coming after you all the way to Main Street. With this." She shook a rolling pin at him.

"Lord, that one," she said, giggling, when he'd gone, "he's True Blue, all right." When I asked where Jesse was, she said he'd taken his pole to the Cove and was probably fishing. I ran to the back of Lady's yard and looked down to the river: there was Jesse in his little skiff, edging along among the willows near the bank as he trolled.

I went down and stood waving until I attracted his attention. "How's about a ride?"

He nodded, I kicked off my sneakers, waded out, and clambered over the stern of the skiff. "How's fishing?"

"Fishing's fishing. Few perch, is all."

"You like fishing, huh?"

"I like it."

That was Jesse; you could hardly get more than a sentence out of him at one time. Being the sort who seldom talked, he gave you the feeling he didn't enjoy talking, but was full of all sorts of thoughts, and that if you could only discover them you'd be better off. He was a wise old bird; that is to say, he was wiser than some, which made him wiser than most.

I have called him a wise "old" bird. Maybe he was old, maybe he wasn't. He never seemed to age much, and Mrs. Sparrow said that in earlier days he was as hale a fellow as one could hope to see. He must have made quite an impression; there were not many Negroes living in Pequot Landing, just Andy Cleves, who ran the Noble Patriot tavern, some families at the end of Knobb Street, and a scattering of housemaids around town.

Jesse rowed a little, fished a little, was silent. I said, "How's Lady —Mrs. Harleigh?"

"Fine."

Silence.

"Jesse?"

"Um?"

"Don'tcha think Colonel Blatchley'd make a good husband for her?"

"Um."

"He likes her a lot."

"Missus tell you she wants to get married again?"

"Nope."

"Colonel Blatchley?"

"Nope."

"Then what?"

"Just seemed like a good idea."

"Maybe, maybe not."

For all his uncommunicativeness, Jesse Griffin was hardly a man to be taken for granted. During the time we had become friends with Lady and been given the key to the house, so to speak, he was to us as much a fixture of the place as the walls or the roof, and if it was Elthea who fed us and looked after us, Jesse's quiet presence was nonetheless affirmed in a hundred small things. And as we grew older and he came more to trust us, in some strange, unspoken way he took the place of the father we had lost.

To me he had the look of a corsair, a strong, hawklike face, with prominent nose and cheekbones, the lips chiseled, almost etched, with an outline around them. When he smiled, which was rarely, his evenly set teeth flashed white, though there was little of this color in his eyes whose dark centers were surrounded with whites that were more often than not reddish, or even yellow. His short-cropped hair (Elthea used hand clippers on it on the back porch; Mr. Pellegrino at the barbershop would never cut a black person's hair) was like a woolly cap, and we wondered what it was like to touch it.

His hands were long and beautifully articulated, all the tendons and veins showing beneath the dark skin, with lighter palms, as if he'd scrubbed them too hard, and fingernails of a perfect shape, blunt at the ends, plum-colored, with paler, perfect moons, and always well looked after, like a doctor's.

He never did care much for our New England winters. He was always bundled up in sweaters and scarves and caps, but in the warm seasons his blood seemed to thin out and rise like sap in a tree. He was the hardest worker.

The pride he took in that house, the zeal with which he looked after it! We used to say he was Doctor, Lawyer, Indian Chief, he did so many things—gardening, plumbing, building, repairing. You'd see him sitting on a windowsill in one of his striped shirts (he wore violet suspenders to keep his pants up), a red bandanna wafting from his back pocket, as he Bon-Amied the panes, and always finding time when everything else had been seen to to lay out on the kitchen table and polish all Lady's good Georgian silver that was part of the Harleigh inheritance. How often I would find him down on his knees at the sideboard with his flannel rag and can of polish, and when he had waxed and buffed he ran his fingers over the worked surface of the wood as if the pale whorls of his fingertips by some tactile sense informed him of the "doneness," the same way Lady's careful poking with a broom straw into a cake layer told her when it was baked.

He was large and lean and strong, but for all his size you never heard him coming and going: as soon as he got home after driving Lady somewhere, he would remove his good shoes and put on his old ones, with X's cut in to ease his corns, or a worn pair of carpet slippers. He could tell the weather by those corns. In later years he began wearing glasses to read the newspaper or the books he was so fond of, though neither he nor Lady would ever admit to his failing eyesight.

Like Blue Ferguson, Jesse was my hero, if for different reasons. It was the simple fact of the quiet presence that bespoke an authority urging both respect and obedience. As he became more familiar to me, I saw him not simply as Lady Harleigh's Negro houseman, but as a human being, as individual and particular as any white person, even though, as we knew, it was the whites who'd inherited the earth.

And so, in those years in the house on the Green, it was the man Jesse, rather than the women Lady and Elthea, who made us all feel the most safe and self-assured, for what did women know of hunting and fishing, of the intricacies of a motor, or how to lay a brick properly? We were afforded ample opportunity to observe his dignified if somber ways, his never subservient but almost courtly demeanor, his flashes of wry humor, his intelligence, the bright look that said we had done well, the darker one that said we hadn't, or the disapproving guttural sounds he made in his throat when we were out of line.

It was just such noises as these that I encountered as I tried to make further conversation: "Jesse?"

"Grmm—hmp?"

"What happens to her?"

He gave me a look and positively growled. "What happens to her when?"

"When she's—you know, funny. Like—now."

He thought a moment, giving the matter consideration, as if how best to explain the matter to my young mind. At last he puffed out his lips and said, "Missus, she gets feeling breakedy sometimes. Her brains get breakedy, she has to give them a rest."

I had been thinking of Mr. Ott, and how he figured in matters, and was looking for a way of discovering if Jesse might know anything about him.

During the ensuing silence, Jesse gave me a keen, studied look. He said, "Missus, she's a fine person, and when she gets feeling trapsetty, best thing is just to let her get through it. She'll come downstairs again."

"When?"

"One of these days. It's never good to dig into God's business too much."

I nodded, deciding that maybe Mr. Ott was part of God's business, and that I'd better leave it to Him. There was a *plop!* in the water near the bank, and I looked, thinking perhaps to see a frog, but instead it was a rabbit—Rabbit Hornaday, under the willows, shooting stones with a slingshot.

"Don't you think Rabbit's a jerk?" I asked Jesse.

"Doesn't matter what I think. Point is, do you?"

"Sort of."

"He's no humbug, that Hornaday fellow. You boys all go nugging round just with each other, but you ought to let him come and nug with you. He spends too much time by himself—not fitting, not proper, doing a person that way. He's a handy fellow."

"No kidding?"

"No kidding."

"How?"

"That's what you ought to find out. He might have a trick or two up his sleeve you don't know about. You listen to what Jesse tells you."

"Yes, sir."

"Agreed?"

"Agreed."

"Then shake, son."

"Shake, Jesse."

We shook, initiating a formula that was to become ritual between us. Later, when he tied up his skiff, we walked back up the hill, where Elthea had his lunch waiting for him. Mine was waiting for me, as well, and Ma was hot under the collar because of my not having brought back her rubber jar rings. When lunch was over, she dispatched us to buy some, and some more Mason jars as well.

"Just *go* to the store, *buy* the jars, and come right *back;* don't go *any*where else," she admonished us, giving Lew money for the pur-

chases. "Okay," we said, and soon as she was back at the piccalilli
on the stove, we sneaked around the fence into Gert Flagler's pasture
and had a ride on her cow. Poor Bossy, with us seizing every opportunity to ride her, had never learned to buck us off—our most
ardent desire—but only loped about the enclosure in dull frustration.
Hearing her frantic moos, Gert came thundering off the back porch
with blood in her eye, flailing the air with her great pocketbook,
while we tumbled off the cow and fled from her wrath.

We got to the Center later if not sooner, where we bought the
Mason jars and divvied them up for carrying. We came out of the
hardware store just as Porter Sprague was leaving the barbershop.

By his own admission, Mr. Sprague was important, but not to us.
He was, in fact, our archenemy. Even with all Gert Flagler's blustering threats to "get us kids" or to "tell our mother on us," it was difficult to think of her as other than an object of ridicule. Porter
Sprague was another case entirely. He was a cheapskate and a
grouse, and we sensed the general air of disapproval for him among
the older generation, which heightened our own dislike. Mean, ar-
rogant, and given to airs, he was a boy-hater through and through.
You never went crosslots through his back yard or he'd set the dogs
on you.

He looked like a shorter, fatter Ned Sparks, the movie comic. He
always had a cigar butt jammed in the corner of his mouth, and his
expression was eternally sour, his clothes were rumpled, his tone one
of grating contentiousness. (It always made me think of Shredded
Wheat without the milk and bananas.) His dogs, a line of beautiful
Irish setters, had long, silky coats of a rare cordovan shade, and those
great dark eyes full of love and intelligence, the sort of dogs you
yearned to pet—but of course you didn't, not Porter Sprague's dogs.

Here he came, freshly barbered, strutting out like a bantam
rooster, all puffed up in that important way of his, and almost col-
liding with Harry. "Careful, there!" he snapped out. Then, more
jovially, so as to be heard by Mr. Marachek, taking his empty morning mailbag into the post office, "Say, boys, heard the one about the
three holes in the ground?" We hadn't. "Well, well, well." He was a
card, that Porter Sprague. We snickered politely and watched him
strut off to his house, speaking sharply to one of his dogs which was
barking on the side lawn.

Next, we headed for Miss Jocelyn-Marie's Gift and Novelty
Shoppe where we nosed around the counters, the proprietress, as
usual, keeping strict watch and ward over her merchandise. Plump

and sly, she wore a flowered smock, and her hair was like a hat of blue sculptured waves, hard as steel, her round baby face blank as a dish—her mind about as deep—but she was always ready to cry "Thief!" at any one of us whom she caught stealing. Because of our small depredations, her inventory never balanced at the end of the month, and as customers we were given short shrift, but if you wanted to hear what was going on around the Center, all you had to do was lend an ear to Miss Jocelyn-Marie. As eager a gossip as Ruthie Sparrow, she seldom missed a trick.

Her attention diverted by a loud commotion over at the Spragues', I snitched a wax pipes-of-Pan, while Lew and Harry each lifted a peashooter and some Fleer's Double Bubble Gum, and when we sneaked past Miss Jocelyn-Marie, and out onto the street again, we saw that the noise at the Spragues' centered around the barking dog.

That winter one of Mr. Sprague's bitches had whelped a large litter. The best of them was his particular pride, and he had derived a good deal of amusement by announcing to the boys at the Noble Patriot that he had named the dog Lady, for reasons too obvious to bear mention. The dog, however, proved one of that overly bred strain that, from either nervousness or some other complaint, continually barked. Sitting in church, you could hear it setting up a howl, and at night its cries continued until the whole neighborhood was aroused. And if the townspeople were angry, Mr. Sprague was angrier.

So here he was, out in his side yard, the dog chained to a tree and barking for all it was worth, and Mr. Sprague shouting "Quiet!" for all *he* was worth, while on either side of the street passers-by and loungers were attracted by the racket.

Then, to everyone's horror, Mr. Sprague smacked down his Panama hat on the grass, kicked it into an iris bed, and marched around the corner of the house, reappearing in a flash with the garden hose spraying full blast. He turned the jet on the dog, while the poor animal tried to escape, running this way and that, finally circling the tree until it was hopelessly twisted up in the chain. The water hardly quieted it; she cowered on the ground, shivering and making yipping sounds that were even more painful to the ear. Now Mr. Sprague's notable temper really got the best of him. Angrily throwing away the hose, which snaked and writhed about in the iris bed, and wetting his Panama, he undid his buckle, snicked his belt out, and began belaboring the dog about its rear quarters.

It was a pitiful sight. People were so shocked that no one had even made a move to stop him, until a voice rang out from the steps of the Academy Hall.

"Porter Sprague—govern your temper!" It was Miss Berry, our neighbor, coming out of the library. With some books in her arm, and wearing a straw hat with a little red bird perched on the front, she marched across the lawn and seized Mr. Sprague's upraised arm before it could descend on the dog again. "For shame," she said, stepping back and inviting him with her look to strike another blow. Astonished, Mr. Sprague began a series of furious gestures, loudly proclaiming that Miss Berry was trespassing on private property, and ordering her to remove herself or he would call the constable. Meanwhile, a window flew up and Spouse's head popped out and immediately disappeared. Mr. Sprague's choleric tirade continuing, Miss Berry stepped to the irises, retrieved the hose, and turned it on Mr. Sprague, dousing him from head to foot. At that moment Spouse shot out the door and came flying from the porch.

"How dare you!" she cried, bristling, as she advanced on Miss Berry, who was now calmly watering the portulacas. "Porter Sprague is a Selectman, if you don't know it. That is my hose—give it to me instantly."

"Very well," Miss Berry was heard to murmur mildly, obliging Mrs. Sprague by handing her the hose—full in the face. Quite dry and in utter tranquillity, she stepped to the curb as Gert Flagler's Chevy swooped out from the post office. Miss Berry got in, and off they went together, in a trail of exhaust.

"Damn morphadite!" Mr. Sprague did everything but shake his fist after them, then turned as his wife spoke.

"Mind your tongue," she said shortly, trying to kink the hose and stop the flow of water. Mr. Sprague, soaked to the skin, started up the front steps.

"Porter Sprague!" snapped Spouse, also drenched, "not in my front hall you don't! Use the back door!"

He did, obediently, like a little boy being punished, but he managed to give the screen door a good whack which everyone heard out on the street.

Things quieted down after that, and nothing more was thought about the dog until some weeks later, when the sequel to the story took place, a sequel which involved Lady Harleigh herself. She treated Porter Sprague as little more than a joke, and we knew she had small regard for him and his pretensions—and not without reason. Porter Sprague had once asked Lady to marry him, and people still laughed about it. We'd all heard the story, not from Lady but from Ruthie Sparrow, over the fence to Nonnie while they were hanging out the wash. After the first Mrs. Sprague had died, P.J. cast his greedy eye on Lady Harleigh as a likely marital successor. Having decided that joining his large fortune with her larger one would be a clever financial ploy, and always having coveted the house she lived in, he pressed his suit. Later he declared that Lady had been leading him on, but of course she hadn't, was only being polite. Mr. Sprague came to call several times, and hinted that, considering the fact he was now a widower and she a widow, matrimony might be of mutual benefit. Lady turned him down cold, and, his suit rejected, he found solace among the de Saleses of Talcottville, and brought his horse-like bride back to Pequot, but since that time he harbored a grudge against the snippety upstart from Knobb Street who'd spurned him.

But to get back to the matter of the dog, Lady's namesake. We'd heard through Jesse and Elthea that her ire had been aroused at hearing of Mr. Sprague's maltreatment of the poor animal; she could never bear to see any living thing hurt or injured. I hadn't been across the Green for some days, but I had an idea that things were about to return to normal as far as Lady was concerned, because with the windows up and the doors open behind the screens, you could hear the vacuum running, could hear Elthea laughing, and, finally, could hear Lady calling. Sometimes it sounded almost as if they were having a party over there, such was the merriment within doors, though these genial scenes were being played offstage, as it were, since we still hadn't actually seen Lady.

One morning Jesse rolled out the Minerva, and I thought we'd get to see her then, but no, he was just taking the car over to Orcutt's Garage to have it serviced. He gave us a ride to the Center, and asked us to buy a pack of playing cards at Miss Jocelyn-Marie's and take them back to Elthea. She and Missus were going to play pinochle that afternoon. We thought pinochle was a step in the right direction, and when we'd bought the cards, we saw Porter Sprague hanging around in the barbershop doorway, regaling Mr. Pellegrino with a story. At his side was Lady, the Irish setter. It was a curious thing about the dog. Mr. Sprague's terrible notions of training must have been effective, because the word had since gone around that the animal had ceased its yowling, had, in fact, not uttered a sound. She still shivered whenever her master came near her, and he kept her close to heel on a tight leash when he paraded her on the walk, taking palpable pride in having so mastered the poor beast.

We said hello to Colonel Blatchley as he came out of the drugstore and went in the barbershop, passing between Mr. Pellegrino and Mr. Sprague, who followed the barber and his customer, still chortling over whatever joke or tale it was he was telling.

When we brought the cards back to Lady's, Elthea came to the door and took them. Lady was baking—always a good sign—and the smell of fresh crullers hung in the air. But the usual invitation to treats and ginger ale was not forthcoming, though I could hear Lady's voice from the kitchen, calling a thank-you. She sounded perfectly fine, but not a glimpse did we have of her, until later, and then her disposition was quite another matter.

We were out on the Green, having a game of one-o'cat, when, running back for one of Lew's fly balls, I saw Colonel Blatchley hurrying down the walk from the Center. He didn't answer when I yelled, nor did he stop at his house, but went directly to Lady's door, where Elthea admitted him. Moments later, Lady appeared in her apron, her hands still floury, and clutching the shotgun we knew had belonged to Edward Harleigh.

At first we thought it was a joke; she looked like something out of the pageant, a Colonial wife taking out after marauding Indians. But angry was not the word for Lady Harleigh at that moment; she was on fire. Lew struck Harry out and we let the ball roll while we followed close behind her, with Colonel Blatchley also coming along, protesting feebly.

Ruthie Sparrow, who hardly ever left her bay window, came hurrying down her steps to catch up with him, her Seiss-Altags clutched in her hand. Near the Center several others joined them. They clustered around the Colonel, wondering what Lady was doing in her apron with a gun. We retarded our steps enough to hear the Colonel's response: Lady was going to kill Porter Sprague. Was going to call him out and shoot him dead on his own doorstoop. For what Mr. Sprague had told the barber and what the barber had told the Colonel and what the Colonel had told Lady Harleigh was that the dog no longer barked because Mr. Sprague had surgically severed its vocal cords.

"Jeez," Lew muttered under his breath as we started off after Lady again, she marching on in magnificent fury, her head held high, apron strings flying. As luck—ill, in this case—would have it, who should be coming out of the A. & P. bearing their quotidian allotment of chopped beef, but P. J. Sprague and Spouse, with the maimed dog on its leash.

Without an instant's pause Lady halted where she stood, hiked the stock of the shotgun to her shoulder, and, feet spread, called out in a voice terrible to hear: *"Porter Sprague."*

P.J. and Spouse turned at the same time and saw the gun raised against them, Spouse crying out, then wilting to the sidewalk in a faint, P.J. dropping the butcher's parcel of chopped meat and the dog's leash and putting out a fumbling hand as though to stave off the shell marked for him. His other hand joined the outstretched one and he clasped it in a dumb show of entreaty, and in this reverent attitude (he who never went to church) he sank to the sidewalk in abject terror. He removed his stained fedora and clutched it to his bosom while his wrinkled mouth tried wordlessly to articulate an appeal, yet no words came.

But: "Stand up, you *puny* man," ordered Lady Harleigh, the sights of her shotgun still trained on him. No printed page could possibly transmit the contempt in that word "puny." Mr. Sprague arose, cringed, wheedled, again became speechless. By this time a considerable crowd had gathered to witness his ignominy, and just then Constable Keep's tin lizzy was seen chugging up to the curb. He got out, calling sharply to Lady. When she looked at him, Mr. Sprague turned tail and ran, abandoning Spouse, prostrate on the sidewalk.

The gun went off. A single sharp report thundered, and before it died away Mr. Sprague cried out. He gave a little leap in the air, faltered, but did not drop. Another shot. Another cry, another leap, slightly higher, and this time he clasped his crushed fedora over his rear as he tottered on, stumbling up the walk to his house and disappearing inside.

"Holy God, Lady Harleigh, what the hell're you doing?" demanded Constable Keep.

Lady, who had lowered her gun, turned to him and swooped her eyebrows in that elegant way of hers. "Good day, Constable Keep. I am out shooting varmints, if that be the phrase. Perhaps you and some of these gentlemen would like to see Mrs. Sprague home. She seems to have fallen to the pavement." With that she shouldered the shotgun like a militiaman, took the setter's leash in her hand—the crowd parting as she passed the astonished Colonel Blatchley and his group—then swept gloriously down the walk, the dog trotting docilely at her side.

The end of the story was Porter Sprague's end—a sore one too, for it turned out the gun was loaded, not with buckshot, but with rock salt, and he had to sleep on his stomach for a week. As for the setter, Mr. Sprague never got her back. Lady kept her, renamed her Honey, and at last she had a dog again, to replace the little one that Miss Berry had given her years before. Lady and Honey were affectionate companions for many years. Colonel Blatchley's admiration of Mrs. Harleigh increased. Porter Sprague failed to press charges. Lady never mentioned the incident again.

2

"What d'you suppose has got Nonnie so happy these days?" Harry wondered.

Lew said, "I think she knows something we don't know."

"Like what?" I asked.

"That's what we don't know." Lew had brought the matter to its furthest possible conclusion, logical if unenlightening; then, it not being polite to discuss family matters in front of others, we changed the subject.

There were six of us: Lew (with Patsy, his dog), Harry, and I; the Harrelson brothers, Jack and Philip; and Rabbit Hornaday; and we were on a camping trip. It was further proof of Nonnie's new amiability that I was permitted to go along on the outing, Ma having objected to my being away from home overnight. But Nonnie had stood firm in my defense, and so I found myself with the others on Hermitage Island. The island, situated some four miles below the town, was a low-lying shoal, covered with scrub and alders, and poplar and basswood trees. Nobody ever went there much, except an occasional hunter or fisherman, but in our hot month of July the Hermitage was like a small secret pocket of the world, and at night you could lie with your arms under your head, looking up at the sky (the "starry feermameent," as our teacher Miss Bessie called it), and you felt the island was almost rocking, like a boat, and that it was taking you somewhere, anywhere; a little piece of safe space belonging to you and no other.

We had rowed there in the leaky scow Lew had traded a stack of bubble-gum cards for, and we had built huts and made camp. Each morning two members of the expedition would row back to town to do the day's food shopping, the menu consisting mainly of hot dogs and things from cans, with bakery doughnuts or jelly rolls for dessert. The first afternoon, we found the huts too stifling to use and, abandoning our labors, we flung ourselves into the river. Rabbit Hornaday cut himself a pole, to which he hitched a line and a hook, and went off fishing. Though we had invited him along, we regarded his presence among us as something of a curiosity; he was such a strange fellow, with his constantly perplexed look behind his thick glasses, as if he couldn't really see what was going on in the world and, what was worse, couldn't understand it. But, having harkened to Lady, who'd hinted that Rabbit "might be smarter than we knew," and to Jesse, who'd said he would be a handy fellow to have around, and that "he was on to some tricks we weren't," we now were offered instances of his handiness. Everyone said he'd never get any fish with that old pole, but an hour later back he came with four catfish on a stick. When the sun started sinking, we built a fire, and he took his jackknife and without a word went about gutting the fish.

"You gonna eat 'em?" Phil Harrelson was astonished. "I wouldn't eat a catfish ever." Patsy trotted over for a sniff; she didn't like catfish, either. She had canned liver for supper, and Phil ate what we ate, a couple of tins of beef stew warmed in a pot, and yams roasted in the fire. But Rabbit savored his catfish, saying we didn't know what we were missing.

Next day, instead of fishing, he went hunting. That is, he hunted without even stirring from where he sat, whittling on a stick at the riverbank. His eye had been more or less riveted on the branch of a tree, and at a certain point he grabbed up Lew's BB gun and popped off a shot. *Bang!* and something fell; he ran to retrieve his quarry, a squirrel, picked off neat as you please. You wouldn't have thought Rabbit could see that well, with his sweaty glasses. But in no time he had the body skinned and eviscerated; we would have squirrel for supper, he announced. Phil turned green. "No, sir. I wouldn't eat squirrel ever." Rabbit paid him scant attention, taking the skinned carcass to the river where he tied it in a bag to keep it cold.

We didn't do much for the rest of the morning, just swam and lay around in the sun, talking. Inevitably the conversation veered toward Lady. Rabbit said, "Huh, Porter Sprague sure got what he was asking for." Though we'd hoped that the explosive event would bring Lady back into our midst again, we had shortly discovered that this was not to be. The playing cards were in use a lot, and once, sneaking up for a peek in her dining-room window late one evening, I could see through a crack in the drawn shade, and there were the three, Jesse, Elthea, and Lady, playing pinochle at the cleared table. Lady was flicking out the cards like a movie gambler, and they seemed to be having a high old time, just like anybody might do in their house after supper. During the day you could hear the radio, and we supposed she was back at her calisthenics, and Elthea would bring fresh crullers out to us on the Green on baking days, and the house seemed to be enveloped in its own shared life, but to our sorrow it was a life unshared with us.

Everyone was at a loss to explain her mysterious behavior at the magic-lantern show, and while Mrs. Sparrow mourned "Poor Lady" from her piazza, we on our island mourned, too; we weren't even halfway through July. Lew took to throwing a stick for Patsy to fetch from the river, and she'd come back dripping and shaking out her wiry coat all over us. Later, when Lew chased Patsy up to the end of the shoal, I nudged Harry, and out of earshot of the others I finally confided my secret about the red-haired man's face appearing on the sheet, and that his name was Mr. Ott, that he'd come to the door the previous winter, had frightened Lady, and that I'd found her crying. That was all I had to tell, and though we mulled it over between us, there seemed no adequate solution to the circumstances.

Along about noontime, we heard a whistling off behind some alders and Blue Ferguson appeared with his gun. He'd docked his boat at the tip of the island and was out to see what he could shoot. He admired our huts, and then the squirrel Rabbit had gotten, and spent part of the afternoon swimming with us, treating us not like kids but as if we were his friends.

I have said that Blue Ferguson was our hero, but I think he was more than that, a kind of demi-deity. I used to try to imitate him in his various particulars, his walk or laugh or the way he had of cocking his head at you—"Hey, kiddo"—practicing these effects in the mirror of the boy's room at school or in our bathroom at home, later using on people what I considered the "Blue" look, but succeeding only in making myself ridiculous. The girls, including the waitresses at the River House, were crazy about him, and he knew this, too, but I could see that he mostly had more serious things on his mind, and wasn't interested in capitalizing on his glamour.

He took us into the woods and showed us how he used his rifle, a beauty of a Winchester, and though he said he ought to be getting

back to town he seemed to want to linger on into the evening, and
we persuaded him to stay and eat with us.

We got the fire going and Rabbit and Blue quartered up the squirrels they'd shot, and soon had them cooking in the pot, while Jack
Harrelson and Harry prepared the rest of our meal, salami sandwiches and potato salad. We were sick of salami sandwiches, and
the salad, having been put with the squirrels to cool in the river, was
swamped and watery, more like greasy potato soup. We all tried
some of the squirrel, eating it from the bone like chicken and saying
it was okay, but it wasn't much of a meal for the lot of us, so our ap-
petites were hardly appeased.

Later, almost without our noticing it, it grew dark; the entire sky
had filled with stars, and the moon had risen. Our talk continued
meandering and desultory when suddenly we sat up, hearing the
soft slip of oars in the darkness. We hushed and listened. Far off
on the water came the unmistakable sound of dipping oars, and then
we recognized the low sibilances of Jesse Griffin's voice, and next
the light sound of laughter that could be only one person's—Lady
Harleigh's!

We all jumped up and halloed, and I ran and got my flashlight
and shined it out on the water. Soon we could make out the prow
of the skiff, and Jesse's white-shirted back as he bent over the oars,
and then Lady herself, a bright scarf tied around her hair, and
Honey, the setter dog, beside her in the stern.

"How are all the Huckleberry Finns doing?" she called gaily as,
with a final lunge on the oars, Jesse beached the craft. I waded
out and helped her from the bow onto the shore. Shipping his oars,
Jesse carried onto the shoal an enormous wicker hamper, holding
it aloft on the top of his head like a safari porter. Honey sprang out
and began making joyful circles with Patsy.

"And there are some blankets, Lew," Lady called, seating herself
on the log near the fire. "Who's that—Blue? It's nice to see you. Jesse,
here's Blue Ferguson."

Blue showed his teeth in the firelight as he took Lady's hand.
"Good evening, Mrs. Harleigh."

"Are there mosquitoes? No? Thank heavens—I never saw the Connecticut River without mosquitoes, what can have happened to
them? But fireflies—look, so many. What have you had for dinner,
more hot dogs?"

Squirrel, we said.

"Ooph—squirrel. Jesse, open the hamper."

And he did, to a feast of Belshazzarian proportions. Passing plates around, Jesse chuckled and said in his husky voice, "Missus and Elthea been cooking. The day long."

Lady was wearing navy-blue slacks, a white blouse, and white beads and earrings, which she'd borrowed from Elthea. She looked —wonderful!

"We would have been here sooner," she explained, "but Minnie broke down coming back from the store. I must think about getting a new car."

"No!" we chorused; to trade the Minerva in on a Cadillac was unthinkable. Lady laughed, saying she liked the new Packards; she wanted whitewalled tires and a radio, and we'd just have to see. She was in her element, playing hostess there on the riverbank as she so often did at home, and while we filled our stomachs with Elthea's good West Indian cooking we listened as Blue and Lady kept the major portion of the conversation going.

"How are your mother and sister, Blue?"

"They're both fine, Mrs. Harleigh. Estelle's working for the WPA now. And Mother's doing pretty well."

"Wouldn't you like another piece of chicken? That squirrel can't have been much of a meal."

He grinned and patted his stomach. "Thanks, Mrs. Harleigh."

"Perhaps you might like to call me 'Lady.' All the boys do."

"I think—well, if it's all the same I'd rather just say 'Mrs. Harleigh.'"

"Of course, Blue. Is that your nickname or a real one?"

"It's my real one, Ma'am. Not like the color, you know. It's really Ballew—a family name on my mother's side, but people think it's just plain Blue."

"I think 'just plain Blue' is fine. How are things up at the high school?"

"I'll be a senior next year."

"And then college?"

"*If* I get my scholarship. I've got to earn more money somehow, though." His voice flattened out slightly. "It's tough, making a dollar these days."

When the lid of the hamper finally creaked closed, everyone sat contentedly digesting the meal, nobody saying much, and all of us caught in the spell of the summer night. Lady leaned back on her elbows on the car blanket, looking up at the star-strewn sky. The placid plane of the river gleamed and glinted in the moonlight; somewhere a whippoorwill sounded. Still the silence held, as though all of us were afraid to break anything so grand and fragile. A pale light glimmered behind the treetops, floating up from the horizon like the cold blue-green glow of phosphorous. But try as I might to let my imagination make of it some minor aurora polaris, I knew that the source of the glow was no more than the prosaic city lights upriver.

Harry, who liked to show off for Lady, began picking out the more recognizable constellations, the Big and Little Dippers, the North Star, Orion's Belt. Then Jesse spoke, showing us some stars we didn't know about. There at its zenith, was a diamond-bright Vega, and over there, Arcturus. It was this very star, he told us, whose beam of light, begun over forty years before, had turned on all the lights at the Century of Progress Exposition in Chicago. That gave us something to think about, and Harry prosaically marveled at how it took a star beam forty years to travel through space to light up Sally Rand's bubble dance. Again we lapsed into silence until, moon and water and the night casting their spell, Lady was prompted to say, "Isn't it sad, not having the riverboats anymore? All of them gone."

"Did you ever ride one?" Jack Harrelson asked her.

"Yes . . . I did." She replied vaguely, looking out across the river, and in the firelight I saw the little furrow deepen between her brows. "I took an excursion trip once, from Hartford to New York. With Edward." She looked down and brushed some sand from her foot.

"What was the boat?" Harry asked.

"It was called the *City of Springfield*."

The *City of Springfield!* We'd seen it ourselves, we said, and Lew, Patsy haunched between his bare knees, told the story. The spring we'd moved to Pequot Landing, our father had taken us to the river. It was the first time we'd seen it. How wide it seemed then, swiftly flowing and reaching away from us in three directions, up, down, and across. Pa said "Look!" and there it came: the *City of Springfield*, her tin stack puffing black smoke against the sky, the white prow gracefully cleaving the water as she drove toward us. Coming abreast, the great round paddle wheel was seen, churning up the water and spewing it behind. Up on the deck passengers leaning against the rail waved to us, and higher up, in the pilot house, the captain saluted, then pulled the whistle handle, making sharp toots for us. We ran along the bank, prancing and cutting up, until the boat vanished around the bend. Voices floated after, and there was one final toot as the great craft disappeared from sight.

Until only a few years before that night at Hermitage Island, the boats continued plying the river, and we saw them frequently. It was the sons and grandsons of the old ship captains who piloted them, but then, one by one, they'd disappeared, and now there were none left.

"You went all the way to New York on one?" Harry asked Lady, and she smiled and shook her head.

"No, darling, not all the way. Only half, I should say."

"How come?" Harry persisted.

"We—just never got there, that's all." She dismissed the subject with a small wafting gesture, then tied her scarf and let the ends flutter in the breeze. "And now the boats are all gone."

"Progress," muttered Jesse, picking one last chicken bone clean.

"I'm afraid so. People want speed today. Trains and planes, but I miss those steamers."

"But the future's in aviation," Blue said. Like the rest of us, Blue was a bug on flying, and though it was sometimes said that lighter-than-air craft like the new *Hindenburg* zeppelin the Germans had built would be the great thing, our own *Akron* had crashed, and Blue said it would be wings that would win the air.

"Look at Lindbergh, look at Wiley Post—he took the *Winnie Mae* around the world in seven days. Seven *days!* And that *GeeBee* the Granville brothers designed, that's the most dangerous racing plane ever flown, but she beat every record at the Cleveland Air Race. Planes like that can outfly any gasbag built. And those new flying boats—what I wouldn't give to fly a China Clipper! That baby's going to make history, see if it doesn't. With planes like that, America could win any war that comes."

There always seemed to be talk of war these days. The Germans had twice repudiated the Versailles Treaty, once by the reintroduction of conscription and the beginnings of a new army, and again by the occupation of the Saar. Everyone laughed at the League of Nations, because they had turned their backs on what was happening with the Japanese in Manchuria, and the threats Mussolini was making against Ethiopia. Along with our Indian and baseball bubble-gum cards, there was now a new series depicting The Horrors of War. Still—a real war? We'd had one all too recently. We had our father's helmet and pistol to prove it.

Blue stretched out his long legs and crossed his arms over his stomach. "If there is a war, America'll be in it, one way or another. And I'm going to fight, you bet."

"I'm going to join the Navy," I loudly boasted.

"That so?" Jesse darted an appraising look at me. "A good life, a sailor's."

"Jesse's father is a sailor," Lady said, but Jesse shook his head.

"No more a sailor, Missus." He looked around at us. "Daddy's near ninety—he doesn't do much of anything now. But once upon a time he sailed practically the world wide. He's been to Los Angeles."

"Yeah? Where else?" Jack Harrelson asked.

"Hong Kong. Russia. Montevideo. He sailed in the four-masted ships, before there was steam or engines. Had to quit, though."

"How come?"

"He got him an addled pate, went stupidy. Derrick caught him in the head and they put a steel plate in. But his balance was gone —can't sail without balance." He gave me another look. "You ever read Bowditch's?"

"No, sir."

"You'll never be a sailor worth his salt without Bowditch's. That's the sailor's bible. Tells you everything about sailing, tying knots, rigging, navigation."

We all knew Jesse to be a reader. He had an amazing book collection: one by one they'd appear around the kitchen, a shoelace or a gum wrapper marking his place. He seemed to read everything, history, biography, mythology, philosophy, religion, even medical books from time to time. If the truth were known, he was probably one of the best-educated men in Pequot Landing, and we often speculated on why he'd settled for being a butler.

"We've got the finest ocean in the world," Jesse went on, "our Caribbean Ocean, no finer sailing or fishing anywhere." He loved the softness of the air, he said, the bright sun and the sunsets, the birds flying, fish that leaped for yards across the water or took your line for miles. And he spoke of the life of island fisher folk, where everyone sat down to table together and sang and then got up and danced, drank, and sat down and ate some more.

I thought Jesse must be a lot like his father. Though Jesse had lived in Pequot Landing longer than any of us could remember, still he was never native to it, never really got used to it and I always had the feeling that not only did he view our New England extremes of temperature with dissatisfaction, but viewed with equal dissatisfaction our small-town puritan ethics and folkways, as if our often narrow viewpoints were distasteful to him.

"Lordy," he said, with a woeful shake of his head, "hereabouts folks burned witches, isn't that so, Missus?"

"Indeed, yes, Jesse. Think of poor Mercy Higham." Mercy Higham was our local witch who'd been denounced as a demon-fancier because she could stick a needle in her finger without drawing blood. "But," Lady continued, "it's the part of the New England ethic which, even after centuries, still hangs on. Look at poor Elsie Thatcher—you boys are too young to remember her—she worked at River House, and was drummed out of town."

"Why?" Phil Harrelson asked.

"She was requested by some of the town ladies and gentlemen to depart elsewhere. The committee serving notice on Elsie was headed by P.J. and Spouse—the Spragues."

What had Elsie Thatcher done? we wanted to know.

Elsie, to her sorrow, had borne a child out of wedlock. Elsie was a sinner. Elsie could no longer draw lager at River House. Elsie could no longer live in Pequot Landing.

"She ought to have gone to Holiday Lake," I said.

"What ever do you mean?" Lady asked in surprise.

"You know—the roller coaster? Lily Marini?" I thought everybody knew. One of the Knobb Street Marinis hung out with the boys on the depot platform at night, and when she was going to have a baby she went to Holiday Lake and rode the roller coaster backward and she didn't have the baby. "But it took five rides," I added.

"Oh, Ignatz, you're making that up." Lady laughed and laughed. "But we're very Old Testament in our thinking," she continued. "From Abraham to Selectman Standish, we are guilt-ridden and fearful of impropriety. Narrow lives make for narrow minds. Or perhaps it's the other way around? But one day it may change."

"Change how?" Harry wanted to know.

"Well, today our population is around five thousand in the town. But it will grow, what with the new highway, and the factories being built. There will be more houses—little houses, you may be sure, but the people living in them won't necessarily be of English stock, or Protestant, or even white. They may have other ideas than the 5:10-ers have. Did you know there's only one Jewish family in town? The Rosens?"

We didn't know much about the Rosens, except that their son George was a good student, and his sister Anne was one of the prettiest girls around. But we did know that because they were Jewish, and went to temple in Hartford, like Catholics they were somehow "different."

"And," Lady continued, "one day, when the farms are gone, and the streets are laid out, and the little houses are built, these new people will be the ones Mr. Welles will want to sell his horseradish to. One day we may even have a mayor and a town council, and one of the Marinis could be on it."

A mayor and a town council! That was unthinkable; Pequot Landing had always been, and always would be, run by the public voting at Town Meeting. As for the Marinis, it was hard to think of any of them ever attaining a position of importance in the town.

The Marini farm was down at the end of the Green, almost across from Colonel Blatchley's house. Papa and Mama Marini were Tuscany peasants who'd come to America with little more than their clothes, steerage all the way from Genoa, and not speaking the language. Now Mr. Marini had a prosperous farm and owned land, and a large family—there were Marinis all over the place, it seemed. His brothers had immigrated as well, one to the grape country near San Francisco, and another lived with his family up on Knobb Street —they were considered poor relations, and two of the girls were often out back of the schoolyard, trading looks with the fellows. But our Marinis, the ones on the Green, were industrious, friendly people. Johnny, the oldest boy, worked hard for his father, and Teresa —scrawny and shy, like Ag, only darker—was always in the kitchen helping her mother. You couldn't walk by the house without getting a whiff of something good cooking. In addition to truck farming, Mr. Marini sold greenhouse plants, and his front yard was crowded with a display of stone birdbaths, brownies sitting on mushrooms, little animals, benches, and other garden ornaments.

But enterprising as they were, good, upstanding people, still the Marinis were only farmers, and Italians, and Catholics—they wouldn't go far in Pequot Landing.

Continuing the conversation, Lady said, "Blue wants to fly, Woody wants to sail, how about the others?" Jack Harrelson said he wanted to go to Harvard and study law, as his father had. His brother Phil wanted to be an architect, and design buildings like they had in Radio City, or like the Empire State Building, or even bigger ones. Lew said he might like to be a basketball coach—he didn't care at what school, as long as it was not in Pequot Landing. Harry wanted to go to MIT and study mechanical engineering. Well, Lady said, maybe he could team up with Phil. That left Rabbit, who'd played dumb most of the evening.

"How about you, Harold," Lady asked, "what do you want to be?" He blinked behind his glasses in his usual perplexity, scratched himself, and finally came up with the astounding information that he wanted to be a veterinarian. I suppressed a laugh, thinking it funny that he wanted to take care of animals, after how he'd treated Colonel Blatchley's prize hares. And, what was funnier, he wanted to set up business right here in Pequot.

"The way I figure it, this is about as nice a town as you could hope to find. It ain't city, but it's close enough. And Mrs. Harleigh's right —it's going to grow, and people are going to do things. And they'll have families, and families ought to have dogs and cats and things, and I'd like to take care of them. You can always find a doctor if you have to, but when a dog gets runned over, who's around to put it back together?"

He said it so soberly and so earnestly, you couldn't doubt him, but of all of us who spoke that night, I think he was the only one who was content to stay in Pequot when he could as easily go elsewhere.

Then Lady, in her gently inquiring way, asked questions about Rabbit's mother and how she was getting on at Middlehaven. I could tell that he didn't like talking about it, but it didn't look as if she was ever going to get out of the reformatory. She couldn't keep her temper, and the matrons had a lot of difficulty with her. As for Dora, part of her trouble had something to do with her ear canals, and that was why she wasn't right in the head.

Lady seemed to be paying particular attention to the recital of these woes, and when she reached and tousled Rabbit's hair I felt the Green-Eyed Monster rising in me again. That dumb-silent Rabbit Hornaday, he knew how to get the attention all right. All you needed was a dippy sister, a mother in the hoosegow, and dreams of living on Knobb Street and having a pet shop.

But it was as this subject of getting away ended that we learned why Nonnie was singing again. Lady told us. In September our sister was going away to college, to the Norwich Normal School. I glanced at Lew and Harry, wondering where Ma had managed to come up with Nonnie's tuition, but however it was to be arranged, I was happy that Nonnie was finally going to realize her dream of becoming a teacher.

Lady sat up and hugged Honey to her, pointing her moist muzzle at the sky. "Look, Honey—see how bright the moon is!" Honey cocked her head, seeming to agree with her mistress. It was a spectacular sight all right. Having risen high over the trees, the moon was making a path across the water, big silvery pieces floating in the black, and adding to the magical spirit of the night. "It looks like one of the gazing-globes Mr. Marini sells. Wouldn't one look pretty in the garden?"

"Mrs. Pierson has one," Harry pointed out.

"So she has," Lady agreed. "Well, I can't have Lilah Pierson thinking I'm keeping up with the Joneses. Papa Marini will have to find us something else. Jesse, Elthea's going to be wondering where we are if we don't start back." She smiled around the circle, then rose. "It's been a gorgeous night, boys. Thank you for letting us share it with you. Can someone put the hamper in the boat?"

While Lew took the hamper, I helped her into the skiff where she sat in the stern with Honey. Jesse put the oars in the locks, then struck out with a forceful stroke. The skiff seemed to hang in the darkness, with only the white of his shirt and of Lady's blouse and face briefly visible. Then they too became shadows, became only voices as they spoke.

"Thanks for the food," we shouted, and her merry laugh floated back to us as she said she had enjoyed it more than we.

Later, Blue left, the fire dwindled, we talked some more, then went to the huts and bedded down. Lying in my sleeping roll, I looked up at the moon at its zenith. It seemed there had never been so many stars in the sky as on that night, and they looked warm and close and comforting. I thought about Blue, wondering if he would ever really do what he wanted to do, if there would be a war and he would go to fight, or if he'd end up stuck in Pequot Landing, driving the Pilgrim Market truck, and stopping to swap jokes with the boys at the Noble Patriot. A hundred-horsepowered boy in a one-horsepowered town, trying to make an honest dollar in a day when, as Blue had pointed out, a dollar wasn't easy to come by.

Not that we were really aware of the Depression, and the fact that people elsewhere were suffering through hard times. At home there was always food enough on our table, and even if it was shepherd's pie or goulash or slumgullion, it was both filling and tasty, and to stretch the budget even further Ma could make the best cheese soufflé. If we had roasts only on Sundays, with the leftovers curried on Mondays, no one complained. We knew of something called the NRA—there were Blue Eagle stickers everywhere, in the barbershop, the drugstore, on people's windows, even at our front door, an emblem of the period—and if the banks had closed in '32 they opened again soon enough, not that we had money in any of them. Since like almost everybody else in the whole town, we were Republicans, nobody in our house ever bothered to tune in to Mr.

Roosevelt's fireside chats, but had we cared to, we could have listened to the radio blasting from next door at Gert Flagler's. She was a rabid Democrat. If we didn't have a surfeit of wardrobe, we had enough, though Aggie and I suffered from hand-me-downs.

We had no car, but there were others who didn't either, and they didn't have Lady Harleigh across the Green with her Minerva, and anyway the trolley ran right past. We received an allowance, which we earned by doing chores, but of soup kitchens and bread lines and alphabetized relief programs we were ignorant, except what we heard on the radio or read in the papers or saw in the movies. We all knew what we wanted to be when we grew up, which was to be better than our antecedents, to build taller and wider, to fly higher and faster, to make more money and be more famous, and at all costs to get out of Pequot Landing.

Lying there, looking up at the stars, I wondered if any of us would ever get to do what we thought we wanted to, and I was conscious of yearnings I couldn't define, vague yet distressing, and the realization of how hard it was to grow up, and what an unnatural process it seemed. I couldn't wait for it to happen, and I wished for a way to make it happen more quickly, to be grown and away, away from Ma and Nonnie and Ag, away from our house with its tan papered walls and katty-cornered furniture, away from Pequot Landing. What I didn't realize then, and perhaps never thought about until much later, until Blue Ferguson was dead, and my brother Lew, when all the war casualties were counted and we really were grown, was that we were living in a time of peace, and that that was a most valuable thing.

3

Then, after Hermitage Island, August came and went, September was here, summer had gone, and it was back to school again. I was in the sixth grade that fall, and Miss Grimes, the principal, was my teacher. Next year I would go on to junior high, and I would not be sorry to see the last of the Chester Welles Grammar School, a Gothic pile of dirty red brick, slate-roofed, with floors so heavily varnished you could skate on them; a hall of lower learning, with the constant clatter of shoes, the smell of damp woolens in the cloakrooms, the heavy cardboard reading charts, where knowledge came at the end of a pointer and punishment at the end of a razor strop.

Nor would I be sorry to leave Miss Grimes, the terror of any schoolboy. How often had I been sent to her office in disciplinary matters to be importantly adjudicated and then summarily dealt with. Oh, the rulers struck on the hand, my small one fiercely gripped by her large one, she grimly frowning as she whacked my palm with a worn, heavy ruler inscribed with an advertisement for the local hardware store. Oh, the wicked leather shaving strop she wielded with such mastery, for Miss Grimes knew full well that "This was what such a boy needed," and what Miss Grimes knew to be true was readily conveyed by the handiest and most thorough means.

Though her tenure at the Chester Welles Grammar School continued for many years after I left, and though I would occasionally see her about town, I do not recall ever seeing her smile, and if she saw me, it was with a dubious expression, as if to say, "There's *that* boy, thorn of my flesh." I have not missed Miss Grimes.

That fall, the Italians invaded Ethiopia, and I was given an assignment in Current Events dealing with this subject. At the library, I got from Miss Shedd (Lady had kept her promise, and we all saw the librarian often these days) everything she could find that pertained, and history-laden I made my way home one afternoon where I found Nancy in the kitchen.

That September, after Nonnie had gone away to normal school, Nancy came to us. Nancy was a Negro who had been at Meadowland, the institution where Rabbit Hornaday's mother was. Though we knew Nancy had been in some kind of trouble, we quickly accepted her as the person she came to be, a friend and helper. No one ever questioned the private facts of her previous difficulties, but it had been arranged for her to come to us so that Ma could continue at the Sunbeam Laundry, where she had been made a superintendent and did not have to work on the mangle anymore.

There were a number of these so-called "wayward" girls placed in homes around town. Having fallen foul of various petty charges of immorality or delinquency, they had been sent to Meadowland for rehabilitation, and were "paroled" to whatever kitchens required their services and could afford their nominal upkeep. They were all good-hearted girls, not overly bright, perhaps, but willing and honest. They lived in cramped, unattractive attic quarters, froze in the winter, roasted in the summer, shared the bathroom, and worked twelve hours or more a day. But if you gave a little love or affection to them they returned it in the fullest measure. Nancy did all the things Nonnie had done, and more, and faster, if more noisily, but within a week she had established proprietary rights over all our family and was a familiar sight around the Green.

"Woody, you boys haven't got such big feets, why you make so much noise with 'em?" she demanded as I came in the kitchen door with my library research.

"It's my boots—they clump."

"Then unclump 'em."

"Okay."

"You take your Iradol-A? No, you didn't. You take your Iradol-A."

Nancy was a nonbeliever in castor oil, our most common winter household remedy, and had convinced Ma that Iradol-A, a thick, molasses-like syrup with a terrible taste, was a better tonic for us, and as we had quickly discovered, what Nancy said usually went. I took my Iradol-A, then made my usual peanut-butter and Marshmallow Fluff sandwich, and carried it with a glass of milk into the living room to get my French horn, since I was due at Mr. Auerbach's at four. Nancy followed—she never missed an opportunity to talk with someone—and as I ate my sandwich, sorting through my music for the *Poet and Peasant Overture*, she interrupted herself to peer out the window.

"Men's diggin'," she observed, watching the WPA men at their labors. Shortly after school had begun, an interesting form of activity had developed around the Green, as workers came with trucks and equipment to dig a trench for the new sewer line. Lady had made her influence felt at Town Meetings, and, the Spragues and No-Relation Welles notwithstanding, the town fathers had voted to replace the irksome septic tanks, thus defeating P.J. and Spouse, who had been, most people thought, properly squelched; and it was generally felt that poor old sleepy Pequot Landing was showing a little progressive spirit, at least in the matter of public sewage.

"Who's that one over there?" Nancy was still peering out the window, and I went to look.

"That's Dumb Dora. She's—" I tapped my head with a peanut-buttered finger. Dora Hornaday was lollygagging around in the Piersons' driveway, looking vacantly upward as if expecting to see a zeppelin go over.

"That's the one's mother's at Meadowland? She's a holy terror that one. Rambunctious. I seen her take after one of the girls with a butcher knife. That's her crazy kid, huh? And she's got another one —stomped rabbits, I heard." Nancy went to see what mischief Kerney was into; I took my music and horn, and left by the front door. I heard a motor starting up, and as I came down the walk the Pilgrim Market truck pulled out from the Piersons' driveway. Blue waved, then turned his wheel quickly, and was only missed by the narrowest gauge as Gert Flagler's Chevy careened around the roadway and she slewed into her drive. In another moment there was a shattering crash. I raced to peek through a hole in the fence, to see the front end of the car sticking out the back end of the garage.

"God damn it—that was the *gas* pedal!" Gert's exasperated voice boomed from inside. "I thought it was the brake." Miss Berry came to a window, then, commiserating, coaxed Gert into the house.

I crossed the Green, and next door to Lady's, Mrs. Pierson came out on her porch with a parrot cage and hung it on a hook to air. Mrs. Pierson was nice, but a little strange. Her husband traveled on business a good deal of the time, but she never went anywhere or did anything. Her face was forever pale under the heavy make-up she always painted on, and her hair, a variety of reddish hues, looked, Mrs. Sparrow declared, like an Italian sunset. She lounged around all day in a Japanese kimono, and Mr. Pierson complained that she was always forgetting her lighted cigarettes, which would sometimes roll onto a tabletop, scorching it, or making burns in the rug beside the davenport.

As I passed, Mrs. Pierson came out again with a pan of water which she slid into the parrot cage. I heard her call, not to me, but to Dora, who was lurking under the heavy screen of firs that almost engulfed the house. Dora ducked around back; Mrs. Pierson made the parrot talk, then went back inside.

When I got to the Center, I saw Elthea Griffin coming out of Miss Jocelyn-Marie's Gift and Novelty Shoppe. Wearing her muskrat coat, she was decked out with beads and bracelets, and she sashayed through the doorway on her spike heels, clutching an enormous box of candy. Seeing me, she struck a pose, throwing her arms wide, snapping the fingers of her free hand, and singing, "Ah'm gonna *sit* right *down* and *write* mah*self* a *let*-ter—and make believe it came from *yoo-o-o-ou!*" She gave out with her marvelous laugh, and lifted the lid of the candy box and let me poke around for a nougat. I took a couple and she gave me a swift kiss, plunked the lid back on, and went into the drugstore.

"God in heaven, don't that boy know that woman's black?" Porter

Sprague was, as usual, bending Mr. Pellegrino's ear. I tried to get past, but Mr. Sprague buttonholed me. "Listen, son, you got the wrong idea—that gal's a nigger, don'tcha know that?"

I stepped by, saying nothing as I headed for the corner of Church Street.

"Folks'll be calling you a nigger-lover, if you don't watch it," Mr. Sprague tossed after me. I ducked my head and started to run.

I hated his saying that word. Nobody used it much, except talking about some of the Knobb Street gang. Everyone liked Andy Cleves and his wife, who ran the Noble Patriot, and I knew that while the word was used a lot down South, in Pequot it didn't sound right, particularly when talking about my friend Elthea. I couldn't imagine anyone using it about her, or about Jesse.

On Church Street I saw Dora up ahead of me, and by the time I'd gotten to the freight depot she was already on the platform, swinging her legs and throwing rocks into the rail bed as the train whistle sounded down the track.

The striped wigwag arm began moving, and the red light blinked. The train came around the curve, her stack puffing clumps of black smoke. I fished out a penny and laid it on the track, while the engineer tooted for all he was worth to get me out of the way, which I did only at the last possible moment. Forced to slow down, he glared at me as he went over the crossing, but he should have been used to it: there wasn't a boy in town who wouldn't try to slow the freights if he had his wits about him.

"Hey!" Dora Hornaday piped at me, tossing rocks from the freight platform across the street. She wagged her head and beckoned. Steadying my horn under my arm and balancing myself on a rail, I footed my way in her direction, but not coming too close: Dora had a good aim and was often indiscriminate in its employ.

"Hello, Dora," I ventured, "what's happening?"

"About what?" She swung her legs and chuckled as if she'd gotten off a good one.

"Okay, Dora." I reversed my path on the tracks and started in the other direction.

"Hey—c'mere." I edged toward her again. "Which one're you?"

"I'm Woody."

"Woody-poody." Lank, straw-colored hair hung down in her eyes, and she brushed it away absently as she studied me. Several years older than I, she was a big girl with thin arms and legs and large hands and feet. "This is Lala." She stood a curly-haired doll on her knee and made it bow.

"Shirley Temple," I said.

"Lala—where's Agnes?"

"She's at the library."

"She's WPA."

She said it as if there were something wrong with Ag's earning money by re-binding library books. I started off again.

"I know somethin' you don't know," she chanted. I stopped. She sucked a finger and winked, her smile revealing long, irregular teeth.

"So?" I sneered, daring her. "What do you know?"

She brushed a trickle of saliva from her mouth with the doll's head and leaned her face on top of it. "I'm not going to tell."

"Okay, Dora, so long."

"Wait—I'll tell. I'll tell just you." She glanced over her shoulder to see if the stationman was within earshot. "Hand me that stone," she ordered. I picked up the stone and put it in her hand. She licked it and held it out into the light. "Sparkly," she said as the wetness evaporated.

"There's mica in it," I explained. "What did you want to tell me?"

"About the parrot lady—you know—" She put one hand on her hip, the other behind her head, and wiggled like Mae West.

"Mrs. Pierson?"

"Know what she does?"

"Nope."

"Want to know?"

"Sure."

"I'm not going to tell." She licked the stone again.

"Okay, Dora."

This time I really went. Who cared what she knew. I had gotten a short distance away when the stone struck my back.

"Dora!"

A woman appeared on the porch of a little house set back from the depot. This was Rabbit's aunt, and she was a shouter. "How many times do I have to tell you not to throw rocks! Your ribbon's all undone. You come in here!"

Dora paid no attention. Leaving her doll, she jumped down between the tracks and came after me. "This is what the parrot lady does." I knew well enough that she was speaking of Mrs. Pierson, whom she'd obviously been spying on, but I stared uncomprehend-

ingly as she made a rapid pantomime of inserting an index finger in
the closed O of her other hand. "This is what she does, see, like this.
She does it with—"

But before I could learn who Mrs. Pierson did it with, the aunt
came rushing onto the tracks. She fetched Dora a smack and yanked
her off toward the house. Wondering about the obscene pantomime
all the way up to Valley Hill Road, I was ten minutes late for my
lesson, and Mr. Auerbach told me my heart wasn't in the French
horn. Mr. Auerbach was right.

4

Though all the Pequot Landing weather prophets were predicting
record snows for winter, and Jesse's corns were substantial corroboration, autumn showed no signs of proving them right; the weather
continued mild for the most part, and the leaves turned slowly. We
decided that Ma must have been really striking it rich at the Sunbeam Laundry, because now, in addition to our music lessons, and
Nonnie's tuition, she announced that we were to be enrolled in Miss
Lee's dancing class. Ag received the news with a terrified look and
quickly retreated to her room, and we saw little of her for the next
few days. Though we heard strange clumpings and bangings around
in there, nobody investigated; Ag's room, which she'd taken over
from Nonnie, was sacrosanct, and you didn't intrude without a
proper invitation. What the noises were, nobody knew, but then,
suddenly, the door would be flung open, and Ag would go dashing
across the Green to Lady's house, where she'd stay for an hour or
two. Then she'd return, calmed and docile, retire to her room again,
and cut out pictures of Joan Crawford, whom she'd just seen being
soignée in *No More Ladies*. Not so soignée herself, Ag resumed her
bumpings and bangings behind the closed bedroom door. Still, I had
an idea I knew what all the racket was about.

Lew, Harry, and I felt that Aggie, with her shyness and blushes,
was going to be the class wallflower, and that we would have to bribe
someone to ask her to dance. And though we tried, we failed, and it
was Ag herself who brought it off, beautifully. Our dancing teacher,
Miss Lee (beautiful Miss Lee!), drove down each Friday night from
Hartford, with a piano player named Gus, to the Masonic Hall

where she set up shop, Gus at the piano on the stage, Miss Lee in a long evening dress (practically a different one each week), and the boys on one side, girls on the other. I was that year wearing a salt-and-pepper tweed knicker suit of Lew's, six years old and itchy, but it was the best that could be managed for these Friday-night sessions. Miss Lee had promised that by Christmas we would be doing the rumba the way they did it at the Rainbow Room in Radio City, but before any rumbas there was the inevitable grand march around the room to the strains of "When the Saints Go Marching In," then the rush to choose a partner, then the painful process of learning the basic one-two steps, and fumbling our way into the simple rhythms Gus had devised for us. I always made a beeline for Cookie Bunder, who was big and jolly, and was willing to take me off to a corner and give me private instruction.

Meanwhile, there was the problem of Ag. As soon as the time approached when boys got to choose girls, we looked around, trying to decide who would take on our sister. Our choice lit on that paragon, Gerald Morrisey, who we figured would be just the ticket to push Ag around the hall in return for a consideration. But when the time came, the plan backfired. Gerald took the bribe all right, and pocketed it, but, having gotten it, he now retired to the washroom where he proceeded to splat his pimples on the mirror and wouldn't come out. As with Krazy Kat, feckless was the word for Gerald Morrisey. And there was poor Ag, sitting at the end of the row under an arrangement of artificial gladioli, twisting her gloves into rags, the plastic pocketbook I'd given her for her birthday clasped in her lap, and her brown school shoes scuffed like mule saddle.

She turned scarlet when Miss Lee brought Gerald, the only remaining unpaired male, from the washroom, and waited until he had proposed his invitation. Ag rose; Miss Lee walked to the center of the hall; Gerald simpered; Ag sat again; the music began. Round and round went the class, while Ag, still blushing, ducked her head, refusing to look at perfidious Gerald, who was fidgeting as if he needed to go to the bathroom he'd only just quitted.

Then a group appeared in the doorway of the vestibule: Lady and Colonel Blatchley, and Jesse, liveried and standing in the background. I went dancing by with Cookie Bunder, and we both smiled as we passed; but Lady's glance was not on us but on Ag. Lady had a quick word with the Colonel, then slipped off her fur coat, which Jesse stepped up and took, and together she and the Colonel walked to the end of the hall, where Lady whisked Gerald onto the floor

with the other dancers while Colonel Blatchley, with a debonair
bow, persuasively took Ag's hand and led her out. Her face was still
red and she hung her head so her hair hid it, but he raised her chin,
making a joke that caused her to laugh in spite of herself, and as she
laughed he took her in his arms and began dancing with her. I
stopped pushing Cookie around, riveted by the sight because,
wonder of wonders, old Ag could actually dance! And thereby lay
the explanation of the strange noises from her bedroom: she had
been practicing the fox-trot with a chair, until frustration drove her
over to Lady, who would show her the correct way to do it.

After class we usually spread out in the drugstore for a soda, because, it being Friday night, Mr. Keller kept open till eleven, and
when he closed, Constable Keep patrolled the street in his tin lizzy
until the last of us had gone to our houses.

One night when we went to the drugstore, I escorted Cookie
Bunder, Lew was with Jack and Phil Harrelson's older sister, Marge,
while Harry sat in a booth in the corner with a bunch of stags.
Cookie ordered a lemon phosphate, and I had my usual root-beer
float, and we all said hello to Blue Ferguson as he came in and went
to the back of the store. Mr. Keller provided him with purchases
unseen, the cash register rang, Blue gave us his "Blue look," and
went out. Seconds later the door opened again, letting in another
blast of cold air. I stared at the customer who'd come in. Even with
his back to me, I knew immediately who it was. I darted a signal to
Lew, who leaned across the table and I whispered the name in his
ear.

"Ott."

Lew tossed a sugar cube into the corner booth to attract Harry's
attention, and we all three cautiously observed the man. Above the
babble of soda drinkers and sundae eaters, it was impossible to hear
what he was saying to Mr. Keller, but the druggist came around
the counter to the rack where chewing gum and life savers were
displayed. Mr. Ott bought cough drops. Opening the flap of the box,
he put a lozenge into his mouth. Harry had extricated himself from
the corner and was standing behind Lew, and I held my breath when
the man came in a straight line toward us as if he intended speaking. In one hand he carried the battered briefcase I had seen before.
His expression was bland, and he made sucking motions with his
mouth, his cheeks pulled in, his white lips pursed into an ugly little
pocket.

At the last minute, he changed his direction and went out. Lew jumped to his feet and ran to the door, peering through the glass. Harry went behind him, and I behind Harry, all of us looking. Cookie broke off her conversation with Marge Harrelson and demanded to know what was going on anyway?

Out on the street Mr. Ott put another cough drop into his mouth and slipped the box into his coat pocket. He hefted the briefcase once or twice, and stood looking up at the church clock. I was sure he would go off toward the Green, and planned on following him to Lady's house, but when he moved it was in the opposite direction, to the trolley stop in front of the Masonic Hall. He stood under the street lamp, lit a cigarette, waited. When the trolley came along from Talcottville, it stopped and he got on, swinging the briefcase aboard ahead of him. The door shut, the car started up. We stepped out to watch as it gathered speed, rocking as it grew smaller along the track, and the tip of the discarded cigarette glowed as it spun through the lighted window into the darkness.

Again the old questions arose. Why had he come? What did he want here? What was in the briefcase he hugged so importantly? Why was he frightening Lady? How I hated him, that red-haired man. Hated the thought of him, hated his existence, hated the pale freckled face, the red rabbity eyebrows. We pondered the mystery all week, discussing it only in fragmented conversations, and never mentioning it to anyone else. At night I lay awake imagining a confrontation, what I would say to him, and what I would do. And I secretly resolved that I was finally going to bring Mr. Ott's case before Jesse.

This came about one day when Jesse had taken us out hunting in Hubbard's woods. Rabbit Hornaday was along, and Lew and Harry with their air rifles. While they prowled on ahead, the ping of their BB guns occasionally sounding through the woods, and while Rabbit drifted off somewhere with the slingshot he was taking pot shots at the squirrels with, I tried to lengthen my stride to keep up with Jesse. He moved, as might be expected, with a slinky sort of Indian walk, making hardly a sound, his head erect and turning periodically from right to left and back again. Once I heard his low-throated chuckle, and ran to ask what he was laughing at. He stopped in the footpath and pointed across the ravine.

It was Mrs. Pierson, Lady's next-door neighbor, having a fall walk in the woods, but in such a way: done up in a fur coat, a turban, with gloves and thin shoes, as if she were going upstreet shopping, her fingers toying with a cigarette, and laughing, who knew at what?

She disappeared immediately, and Jesse, still amused, sat down on a sawed-off tree trunk.

"Lordy, white folks." He removed his plaid hunter's cap and ran his hand over his shiny brow. "Sure do funny things."

"White folks?"

"Yes, sir."

I nodded. "Yes, sir."

He laughed again, and gave my shoulder a little punch, and our looks connected. His humor held for a moment, then by degrees disappeared, his expression becoming Jesse-still and sober.

"Jesse," I said.

"Yes, sir," he said, the "sir" a kind of imitation of mine to him.

"Are we friends?"

"I guess if we thought it over, we are."

He bent to tighten one bootlace and I looked at the top of his woolly head for a moment, then said: "Jesse?"

"Mm-hm?" He was still fiddling with the lace.

"Is Lady—Mrs. Harleigh—in trouble with someone?"

"Not that I know of." Head still down, he hunched his shoulders once or twice. "You think she might be?"

"There's a man. He comes around sometimes. Lady—Mrs. Harleigh, she's scared of him."

He raised his head and his eyes looked into mine again. "What man?"

"We don't know who he is. He comes around and—he's been to her house. He's got a briefcase and—"

"Lawyer?" I could tell from his look that inside that dark head he was doing heavy calculating.

"I don't know. She wouldn't say. I don't think he's her lawyer."

"What's his name?"

"Ott. Mr. Ott—O-T-T. He's got red hair. . . ."

Jesse's arms had shot out and his fingers curled around my elbows, pulling me to him. I could smell the bay rum and the life-saver scent on his breath.

"Red hair, you say?"

"Yes, sir. He's been twice, and this time makes the third."

"Which time?" His eyes narrowed so only the dark parts showed.

"Last Friday night." I related the incident at the drugstore after dancing school. Jesse held me firmly for several moments, thinking, then released me, staring at his mushroom-colored palms. He made a little sound in his throat, as if to clear it, shot me an appraising look, and dropped his glance again.

I looked at him, then down at his shirt buttons, not knowing what to say. His fingers moved to my shoulder and he tapped it ruminatively, as if he, too, didn't know what to say, either about Mr. Ott or about my knowing about him.

"Who else knows?"

I wanted to say no one did, that the secret was between us, only it wasn't. We all knew, Lew and Harry, and Ag, whom we'd thought it right to tell. "But they won't say anything, honest. They'd go to their graves before they'd—"

"If he comes back again"—Jesse's voice was soft and low, but with the cut of steel—"if you ever see him around here again, I want you to come and find me. Find me wherever I am, and tell me—can you do that?"

"Sure, we can do that."

"If he comes and then tries to go away, you've got to make up some story to keep him around till I get there, you understand?"

"Yes, sir."

"And you don't say anything to Missus or Elthea. You don't tell them you told me, understand?"

"Yes, sir."

"Good boy. Let's go along."

"But who is he? Why's he frightening her? What's he want?"

"Did you ask Missus?" he replied evasively.

"I asked her, and she—she didn't say anything, she wouldn't tell."

"Reckon she wouldn't."

"He's bad, isn't he?"

"Bad? Who can say what's bad, son?" His voice was husky but gentle as he rose from the stump, seeming taller than ever as he hung the shotgun in the crook of his arm. "Still, I guess a fellow who comes around and bothers the lady of the house, yes, you could say he's bad."

He went off down the path, and I followed. A little way along I heard a familiar whistle: it was Blue Ferguson with his rifle. He'd been out hunting, too, but when we all got home none of us had shot anything, except Rabbit, who had knocked off two squirrels with his slingshot. Leave it to Rabbit.

Before bedtime I got Lew and Harry alone and informed them of what Jesse had told me that afternoon, that if Mr. Ott showed up again we were to detain him until we'd gotten word to Jesse. This required further examination, and Harry brought Ag in and we put our heads together, evolving various stratagems to work under a variety of circumstances during which we would attack, tie up, and otherwise impede the intruder if and when he came.

We didn't have long to wait, for he returned on the following Thursday, which was Halloween night and, as it happened, Jesse and Elthea's day off. We'd been down in Lady's cellar helping Jesse paint the storm windows. For whatever reason, Lady had been especially nervous and jumpy during the past few days, and it occurred to me that she might have known about Mr. Ott's earlier visit, or that in her sensitive way she was somehow anticipating it. In any case, Elthea had cautioned us to move quietly downstairs and not make unnecessary disturbances. These admonitions I had momentarily forgotten as, continuing the painting work, I began singing. There was a rhyme we sometimes sang, and it went:

> *There was an old, old, old, old lady,*
> *And a boy that was half-past three;*
> *And the way that they played together*
> *Was beautiful to see.*

We'd put a tune to it, and it caught on among all of us, but today I saw Jesse giving me one of his dark looks.

"Don't sing that—Missus might hear."

I clammed up immediately. Still, I thought, why would such lines bother Lady, and while the words "old, old, old, old lady" kept going through my mind, I thought I had made the connection. She never liked the thought of growing old; it seemed to preoccupy her unnaturally.

We'd gotten almost to the bottom of the can of green enamel when Jesse discovered there wasn't enough to finish the job, so we decided to go to the hardware store. As we were turpentining our hands, a window banged open and a strange, grimy face appeared. "Say, ain't you got your own coal chute down here? Boss says you do."

It was a coal man, come to deliver; his boss was right. Typically, Lady had her own chute, which swung down on iron hooks from the ceiling beams. Jesse went to undo the latch and lower it in place under the window while we all trotted up the hatchway stairs and around front to watch the work.

The truck, emblazoned with dual legends of "Pequot Landing Blue Coal" and "Copper's Coke" on the sides, stood in the road, while the two coal men, with rubber capes fastened over their shoulders, heaved the burlap sacks off the truck and carried them to the open cellar window. There they were emptied into the chute, and the shiny chunks slid down into the bin below, amid choking clouds of dust. In a moment Nancy's Don't-care-who-hears-me stridencies were ringing from across the way.

"LewisHarryWoody, get yourselves out from under those old coal folks, hear me?" The workers digging the sewer line stopped to chuckle at Nancy's continuing salvos, while Gert Flagler came out on her stoop with some of the dogs and watched with a menacing look on her face, as if to say those coal men sure better not raise so much dust when it came her turn for Copper's Coke. And, inevitably, Ruthie Sparrow had her Seiss-Altags trained on the proceedings from her bay window. So much interest and concern did the ordinary delivery of a winter's worth of coal occasion around the Green in Pequot Landing.

After Jesse and Elthea went off on the trolley car, for their usual Thursday evening, Lew and Harry went home to hear the radio, and Lady called to me, asking if I would take a walk around the Green with her—to look at the leaves, she said, finally turning in that late, coldish October. She had, she confessed, been feeling melancholy all day—I suddenly recalled that it was the anniversary of Edward's death, and this perhaps accounted for her edgy behavior. Her mood seemed colored by the close of autumn, by the heightened sense of change, and the dying year. So it was not the red-haired man at all, I decided.

We had often walked like this, Honey close at her side, we hand in hand, and I thought what a tragedy it was that she had lost not only her husband, but, in another sense, herself; lost to what seemed an irrevocable widowhood. I thought, too, of Colonel Blatchley by his own solitary fire, and I wished they might be together, as seemed fitting and proper, with that kindly old fellow to look after her and to keep her from feeling lonely. The street lamps blinked suddenly on, and in the oncoming twilight and the mist which was not quite rain there formed incandescent circles of blue and gold, like little glowing halos around each lamp bulb. With the waning of the mournful day Elthea had lighted the candle of a jack-o'-lantern carved by Jesse and me only yesterday, setting the jagged orange pumpkin grinning in the front window for the time when the younger fry would come ringing doorbells for candy and giveaways. The air was layered with visible striations of haze from leaves raked in piles along the roadway, ablaze earlier but now only dully smoking. The men digging the sewer line had long since left, and their kerosene torches, like sooty black cannonballs, flickered in the gloom. Wetly shining branches dripped onto the half-raked Green, a carpet of deep musty red, and our feet crushed the fallen leaves as we strolled along. Lights came on one by one in the houses, though none but Lady had thought to show a jack-o'-lantern.

"Lovely trees," she said of the elms, in her low voice, its timbre strangely muted. "Next spring they'll be young and green again. They never change, do they?"

"But they're *old*. . . ."

"Ha! A clever observation." Her laugh was short, staccato, and too brief to make me believe at that moment in its sincerity. "Old is old, any way you look at it. And here we are, my young man, your old lady—"

"*You're* not old—"

"But I verge, darling. On the ancient. And here we are, in our old town. We did her proud this year, didn't we? She must be feeling very happy after her three-hundredth birthday. Still, it's not very old, is it? Not like 'Paris France' or 'Venice It'ly.'" Here she gave a nod toward the Sparrows' bay window where the mistress of the house had her binoculars trained on us. "Paris France" and "Venice It'ly" were Ruthie's dreams of romance, and neither city could be spoken of without its country.

"I wish I could leave," I said, throwing Honey's rubber ball for her.

"Of course you do, darling, that's what towns are for, to be left. But they're there to come back to again. Promise that when you're all grown up and gone away, you'll come back and visit the poor gray-haired antique across the Green who once made crullers for you."

"I promise." Honey came panting back with the ball. "Why don't you ever leave?"

"I can't." She said it with an air of utter finality as she took the ball from Honey and tossed it again. "That is to say—" She ran to the dog, retrieved the ball, and came back breathless. When she spoke again, she lightened her tone, a trick I had come to recognize.

"What I mean is, I'm a homebody. I have everything I need right here. Mama always said that little girls should play in their own back yards, and I've taken her advice." Turning to me, she shivered a little despite her warm furs, then gave me an affectionate hug which seemed to say to Mrs. Sparrow, This is why I will not go away, because I love this boy and I will stay with him.

"I like it here," she continued, urging a little gaiety between us. "New England may not be Paris France in age, but it's not like the American West, either, where if some Panamint thundermug is sixty years old it's considered an antique. Still, Paris France *is* older. The trouble with New England is that it falls between two stools. I don't think Boston should put on such airs, do you? Hartford doesn't. But then maybe Hartford would if it could manage them. But as for myself, I would like to sit in my warm kitchen with my family, and smell bread baking and listen to the rain on the roof. Ah, my family? Why, that is Jesse and Elthea and all of you, and dear Nonnie, who'll be coming tomorrow night. You are all my family. Families are not necessarily relatives, do you think?"

I guessed not, scarcely daring to notice how, rather than being singled out, I had been generally lumped with my brothers and sisters.

"I think the important thing is caring about someone. It's being by themselves that does people in, makes them old and bitter." Her voice slid into a musing tone, and though she spoke to me I could tell that her thoughts were elsewhere. "Everybody's so busy looking for happiness, but I think real happiness only comes when we are joined to another human being. Otherwise we are lonely, and we suffer for it."

"You like to be alone sometimes. . . ." This I ventured tentatively, and she quickly seized upon it.

"You will learn, my Ignatz, that there is a vast difference between loneliness and solitude. Solitude is a kind of food, we eat of it and it sustains us, but loneliness is a starvation diet—no one ever got healthy being lonely. To be alone and unloved must be the most terrible thing in the world."

I nodded, knowing she was referring to her having been without Edward for so many years. "Then you're really not lonely?"

"Why . . ." She paused, carefully choosing her response, and looking up at her I could see the rich luster of her eyes, and in them a half-thoughtful, half-dreaming expression. "We are all lonely," she continued after a few more steps. "It's why people keep pets or use the telephone or listen to the radio. It's why they go into bars or write letters, join clubs, have meaningless affairs. . . ."

I said I did not understand this word and she laughed. "Romances, darling. What people are always hankering after—romances. You'll find out one day. But, to suffer loneliness—" She gave a little shrug, then patted Honey, who kept ever close to her side. "Man is made to suffer, they say."

"Why?"

"I've no idea. It's the way of the world, I guess." She considered this with some gravity, then laughed lightly. "I really don't know. I really don't. But just imagine—think of the people who go through life and never suffer. Who never feel a thing. There *are* those who do. Be glad you can suffer, be glad you can feel. It's not such a bad thing, do you think, to be made to feel?"

"I'd rather feel good."

"But that's the whole idea. How can you tell if you're feeling good unless you've felt bad, so you have something to compare it to?"

"I'll bet Eskimos know it's cold even if they've never lived in Africa."

"I'll bet they do, too, but I imagine they can get pretty hot, wearing those furs and eating whale blubber—whale blubber causes body heat, doesn't it?"

I guessed so; that was Lady, always making sense out of my nonsense.

"And," she added, by way of summing up her remarks, "every day, every single day we live, we should live to the fullest, for who knows what tomorrow holds? And we may be sorry that tomorrow came."

"Will you be sorry if tomorrow comes?"

"I hope I shall be very glad if it comes. And when it does, I'll try to live it like today, or yesterday, or—" Again she broke off, in the gently abstract way of hers, as if suddenly, for her, I had disappeared from sight and presence and she were alone. Then, abruptly, she came back. "Well, let's just say that not every day is to be lived like every other day."

This seemed to conclude the conversation, and for some moments we walked along in silence, Honey running to sniff in the leaves and then quickly returning to her mistress's side. I was whistling a few bars of Miss Lee's dancing-school march, then broke off, the attraction I felt for Miss Lee making me feel unaccountably guilty or disloyal to Lady.

Then, a thought coming to mind, I asked, "When the saints go marching in—does that mean that sinners don't get in?"

"So we are led to believe."

"*None* of them, not even a *good* one?"

"A good sinner—what, I wonder, is that?"

"Well, someone who—maybe someone who sins but doesn't really mean to?"

"The Bible tells us that God forgives. Maybe there are some things He will forgive, but not all. There are things people do that not even God may forgive."

Again the silence fell between us as, lost in our individual consciousnesses, we walked back along Lady's side of the Green. My thoughts were suddenly diverted as we came abreast of the grinning orange face in the window, when a troop of Halloween kids appeared among the dripping trees, giggling and growling behind their masks in disguised voices. There was a boy in black sacking painted with white bones, too fat by far to be a skeleton; one something like a witch; a tramp; and two or three other unidentifiable characters in an assortment of attic odds and ends. Lady applauded them enthusiastically and showed them to her doorway, where she turned on the carriage lights and sent me to fetch the trays of candy from the dining room and the bowl of shiny pennies, fresh from the bank that morning.

Then, kneeling before each child in turn, Lady removed the papier-mâché faces one by one and exclaimed over each marvelous disguise. The smallest girl—she must have come from up Main Street somewhere, for I didn't recognize her—kept behind her redly grinning mask the saddest expression imaginable, and nothing Lady might do could coax the slightest mirth from her until she was again safely hidden behind her paper face; then there came a peal of baby laughter as she filled her paper sack with candy, took a penny, then another, and ran away in glee with the others into the darkness.

"Yes," Lady reflected, watching the grinning faces dash up the Piersons' walk, "extraordinary what a mask may do for one." And, "Extraordinary," she mused as she rose and softly closed the door. She drew me to her, and gave me a great hug, and Honey ran about us in circles, thumping her tail against the radiator.

"I love children," Lady said exuberantly. "I love them."

"Why?"

"Because, dear l'il Ignatz, children are grend and magnifishent creatures—even when they break my windows. Anyone can make them—except me, of course; I couldn't—that requires little enough. But children should be taken as the gift they are. To be happy and rejoice in them, to appreciate them—that's something grownups often forget to do. To watch them grow, and become, to find the person they really are, that's a wonderful thing." She called me her "boom compenion" then, and with another hug prepared to send me on my way.

"But you'll be left alone," I said as she opened the door.

She fell on her knees and threw her arms more tightly around me. "Darling, don't think such a thing!" She raised my chin and I could see her eyes sparkling in the light from the carriage lamps. "Don't ever feel sorry for me. I have had all that life has to offer. I have lived it as I have wished to, and for me it has been the perfect thing!" She said it so ardently, and with such passion, I could not doubt the truth of it. Still, by lingering and by my own oft-tried brand of implacable wheedling, I got her to agree that we might come over after supper and keep her company until Jesse and Elthea returned.

5

The old trolley cars are gone now, those splendid, ancient, well-beloved vehicles of yellow-painted wood, whose shape and line were so familiar, whose sight and sound and very odor we knew so well, the clang of the motorman's gong, the buzzer to make the car stop, the worn raffia seats, the leather straps, the rows of cards above the windows advertising "Ipana for the Smile of Beauty" and "Sal Hepatica for the Smile of Health," and Carter's Little Liver Pills. When the day finally came that the trolleys were replaced by buses, and the tracks dug up and removed, we felt a loss, as if part of our lives were gone, that it was one more change among so many changes, and that we were somehow threatened.

It was just such a trolley, with clanging bell and rumble of iron wheels along the track, that marked the arrival of the red-haired man on that Halloween night. I remember it was around nine, for I glanced at the clock just after the trolley went past, stopping to let someone off and then continuing to the end of the line. During supper Ma had been in a particularly gay mood because Nonnie was coming home next day, and afterward we carried our stamp albums over to Lady's, to spend as much of the evening as would be allowed.

She was at that time doing some needlepoint which proved to be a pair of slippers, red and black, with handsome gold designs on the toes, and though she had begun them only that week, with her nimble fingers the work was progressing fast. The slippers were to be a Christmas present for Jesse; she couldn't stand his old carpet slippers any longer, or the shoes with the cut X's for his corns. And the corns, as we knew, were prognosticating a winter of heavy weather. I deftly turned the moment to remind Lady of her promise that if there was enough snow we would have a sleigh ride, earning only the usual response, "We'll see."

It was then that I heard the trolley car stop, and a few moments later the doorbell rang. Lady put aside her work, patted Honey's head, and went into the hallway. Presently the sound of low voices rose from beyond the door. We all exchanged glances, then the front door closed, and Lady came back.

She ran her hand along her forehead and then onto her hair, saying, "Well, children, I'm a bit tired, and we have a big day tomorrow with Nonnie's party, so perhaps we'll say good night now. It's all right, Lew, I'll set the fire screen. You all just go along. Don't forget your stamps." Well, I thought, she sure was in a hurry to have us out of there.

Lew put down the poker with which he had begun pushing the logs apart, reset the screen, and we closed our albums and put on our things, each stepping up to kiss Lady's cheek. She led us into the hall and opened the front door for us. When Lady bent to me, her hand brushing my cheek, I glanced over her shoulder into the dining room and saw the dark figure of the man, half hidden behind the doorjamb. The front door closed and, suppressing a gasp, I hurried down the walk after the others as the trolley went by again, heading upstreet.

I waited until we had gotten to the Great Elm, then stopped everyone and looked back. The carriage lights had been turned off and the shades already pulled; I stood with one hand on Lew's arm, breathing hard.

"What's the matter?" he demanded.

"He's in there. He's come back."

"Who?" Ag said, "who's come back?"

"Mr. Ott!"

We all started whispering at once, deciding what to do. I was for returning and listening under the windows, but Ag said Ma wouldn't like it. I, who still didn't hold myself above the practice of eavesdropping, thought the circumstances called for it. "Damn it," Harry said, "why'd he have to come on Thursday? If Jesse was only here . . ." Then we remembered what Jesse had said in the woods: if Ott returned we were to tell him, keep the man here. . . .

Quickly we made a plan. Lew would go to the movie house and find Jesse. Harry and I would remain, and if Ott came out, we would somehow detain him. The trolley having already gone, Lew would have to hoof it up to Packard Lane and try to catch another streetcar there to take him to the city. He went off at a run and we leaned against the tree, puffing with excitement and exploring the situation in whispers.

At this point Nancy came to our door to answer the last of the Halloween callers, and seeing us she began hollering to come in before we catched our death, so we left the tree and followed her in, trying to act as if nothing had happened. When Ma wanted to know where Lew was, we lied and said he'd gone over to Jack Harrelson's for something—hoping that she didn't plan on waiting up for him. She went to bed, Nancy bumped up to her room in the attic, and we sat huddled and hushed in the darkened sleeping porch where we could see every move that was made across the Green.

We had only a half-hour to wait for further developments, for when the next trolley came by, Elthea and Jesse got off—without Lew. We didn't know what had happened, but plainly Lew hadn't connected. I raced down the stairs to tell Jesse the news, but before I got out our door he and Elthea had already gone in theirs. I went back up to the window again, where Harry and Aggie were whispering in the dark. Having heard the door open and close, Ma called, "That you, Lew?" I poked Harry, who, deepening his voice like Lew's, gave her an "Uh-huh."

"Come and kiss your mother good night, then."

Oh, cripes, I thought; then Harry called back in his own voice, "He's in the bathroom." Ag quick as a wink ran to turn on the water and flush the toilet. There was no further response from Ma. A few minutes later a car stopped on the far side of the Green and Lew got out. The car drove off toward Talcottville; Lew glanced over at Lady's house, and hurried up our walk. I signaled with my flashlight in the window to let him know where we were, then the front door opened and closed downstairs.

"Now who's *that?*" Ma called from her bedroom.

"It's me, Lew," he replied up the stairs.

"I thought you were in the bathroom—"

"Me? No. I was at the drugstore."

I dashed to the banister and gestured frantically that he'd been at Jack's. Ma was confused. "The drugstore? What time is it? Isn't the drugstore closed?"

I hurriedly whispered to Lew, who called heartily, "That was before, Ma. Then I went over to Jack's for a *National Geographic.*"

"Then you *did* go to Jack's. Come and kiss your mother good night."

"Just a sec, I've got to go to the bathroom."

"I thought you just went to the bathroom."

She sounded exhausted, trying to keep up with it all. When we got back to the sleeping porch again, Aggie reported no further moves from across the Green. The four of us knelt, leaning on the sills and watching with all our might and main, while Lew recounted what had happened upstreet. He'd gotten to the movie house and told the manager there'd been an accident and he had to find Jesse, and he went poking along the rows, whispering "Jesse? Jesse?" in the dark. With Jesse's color, this wasn't easy, and he never located him at all. (As it turned out, they hadn't even gone to the movies, but had dinner in the Franklin Street Diner, then gone for a walk, after which they'd come straight home.)

The church bell rang ten o'clock, and another trolley came down the tracks and went to the end of the line. It was just after it had passed that the gun went off. We recognized immediately the blast of the shotgun, as we had heard it the day Lady shot at Mr. Sprague. It was only one barrel, but enough to wake the neighborhood.

"What's happened? What was that gun?" Ma called while we knelt frozen at the window. A light went on in Ruthie Sparrow's bedroom, then we headed for the stairs. Ma appeared in her nightgown at her door, and Nancy's footsteps came thundering down from the attic.

"Why ain't you kids in your pajamas?" she demanded, ignoring the drama of the moment, as we raced pell-mell down the stairs and out in front. Ruthie Sparrow was already on her porch with her Seiss-Altags, and on the other side Gert Flagler appeared wearing a flannel Indian bathrobe and galoshes, and clutching a broom, prepared for alarums and excursions.

"What the hell's going on? Who fired that gun?" These questions were demanded of the Green at large, but, seeing us, Gert came clumping off her steps, wanting to know if we'd been playing with firearms.

Then, over at Lady's, the lights went on, the door opened, and Elthea came out, laughing to beat the band. We hurried to her, meeting halfway across the Green, where she explained that Jesse had thought maybe he'd seen a prowler out behind the carriage house and had fired at it, but it turned out to be only a bush.

This explanation accepted, all retired to their respective houses, and the Green fell silent again. We went upstairs and, under Nancy's loud supervision, got into our pajamas. When she'd gone up to the attic and Lew had finally kissed Ma good night, Ag sneaked back into our room; we yanked off the covers and threw ourselves at the windows for further observation.

Shortly thereafter the trolley car was heard returning from Talcottville, and when it appeared down the tracks a brief glimmer of light showed at Lady's front door as it quickly opened and closed, and someone hurried down the walk. There was just time for the figure to catch the trolley, using both hands to climb aboard, and as the car passed we got a closer glimpse: the figure wore an overcoat with the collar turned up, and a wide-brimmed hat.

So much for the visit of the red-haired man.

Except for one thing: when I'd seen Mr. Ott in the dining room, he had been carrying a pair of gloves in his left hand and the briefcase in his right. But when he had gotten on the trolley his hands were empty.

Why, I wondered, would Mr. Ott leave his briefcase behind?

6

According to weather statistics, the nation never saw such violent extremes of temperatures as were recorded during those mid-thirties years. The country was beset with droughts and dust storms, the summers were dazzling in their heat, and the winters bitterly cold. The winter of 1935–36, as the local prophets had foreseen, was a humdinger. The first snow flew before Thanksgiving, always a robust sign, and it snowed off and on through the early part of December. But with all the snow there came no sleigh ride as promised, for Lady Harleigh did not appear. She had gone into

"retirement" again. Jesse or Elthea came out with Honey and
walked her around the Green, but of her mistress, not a sign. I supposed she had forgotten her promise to let us polish up the runners
and bring the sleigh from the carriage house, and get No-Relation's
horse. Each time the snow fell anew, I hoped that at last she would
come out, but still there was no sign. When queried, Elthea and
Jesse volunteered no more information as to Lady's state of health
other than that she was "doing well."

School let out for Christmas and we went sledding or toboggan-
ing on the second nine at the golf course, and bought or made presents and wrapped them. Remembering Ruthie Sparrow's story of
Edward Harleigh courting Lady, I came up with an idea I thought
foolproof in effecting her reappearance, and on Christmas Eve we
carried our box of presents across the Green to her front door and
rang. Elthea came to answer, and accepted the box, setting the gifts
one by one on the table and ohing with Jesse over the wrappings,
but throwing anxious glances up the stairway. When she got to the
bottom of the box she presented us with the holiday basket that
Lady had taken to sending over to our house. It was heavy, which
meant lots of homemade jellies and relishes. Elthea kissed us (from
the Missus, she whispered) and Jesse solemnly shook hands all
around, and we went out with the basket, the door closing gently
but firmly behind us.

Then we gathered on the stoop, I raised my hand, and together
we began singing "Good Night, Ladies," but changing the word to fit
Lady, just as the carolers had when Edward had asked Lady to
marry him:

> "Good night, Lady, Good night, Lady,
> Good night, Lady, we're going
> To leave you now . . ."

But I knew it was not we who were leaving her, but she who had
left us, and though the carriage lamps stayed on, there were no holiday candles at the windows, no colored lights on the trees, and if the
wind sang old songs I did not hear them, for Lady would not come
out.

It was a sad Christmas that year.

In January there was a thaw, the river started rising, and people
were talking about the dikes not holding if there were a flood. But
before there was further talk of flood, there was much talk of snow-

storms, for when the temperature dropped and it snowed again it did not take long for everyone to realize that this was no ordinary snowfall. It continued day after day, and those old enough to remember were comparing it to the blizzard of '66 or the one of '08.

It seemed impossible that it could snow so much, as if the sky had been storing it up to dump on us all at once. By the end of the first afternoon we were brought indoors for good, and spent hours watching from the windows of the sleeping porch, unable to see even the Great Elm, so dense was the snowfall. The wind rampaged through the town, eddying and whirling, driving man, beast, and vehicle from sight. Soon the telephone service was interrupted because of downed lines, and the radio told us to use as little water and electricity as possible; this was an Emergency.

But not to us. With the schools closed, it became another lark, and seldom had we found ourselves all in the house at the same time. It was impossible to get to the woodpile, and after we had burned the load that had been brought into the cellar at Christmas we were forced to rely solely on the coal supply, carefully rationing each shovelful, with all of us wearing sweaters and our heaviest clothing indoors, and sleeping under extra blankets at night.

Lying there on the sleeping porch under the slippery comforter that Ma had tucked over me and I had untucked, I thought of Lady, and the mystery surrounding her. I went back in my mind, recalling each circumstance that veered at all from the norm, hoping to discover some answer, some clue. I went over what I had come to call "the difficult times," adding up again the total of her furtive looks, her snatches of talking to herself, all those curious manifestations of erratic behavior; but the result was only the same old total—zero. I tried to imagine what it was like for her, living over there, alone except for two servants, and seeing ghosts—or, more precisely, one ghost—Edward's.

At the end of the fourth day the snow stopped. We awoke to the strangest sight we had ever beheld. From our windows in all directions, we saw the earth lying buried under a giant cloak of whiteness, thick, deep, astonishing. Familiar roofs of farm buildings were not even to be seen, small trees whose heights we knew well were girdled higher than we were tall. In places the wind had drifted the snow up to the eaves of houses, lending them an unfamiliar, muffled look, while all the chimneys had tall white caps on them. The only way we could guess where the roads were was from the telephone and light poles.

By the time the town had dug out and school reopened, things had returned more or less to their humdrum pace. Still the weather continued bitter, not only because of the lashing wind that got down your collar and up your coat, and the snow that grew stale and boring, but bitter mostly because of never seeing Lady through all those long months. In February we spent hours making valentines for her, going to Miss Jocelyn-Marie's for packets of winged-cherub stickers and cutting the edges of doilies to decorate hearts scissored from red construction paper, and when these were properly fashioned and bore suitable sentiments, I collected them from Lew and Harry and Aggie, and adding my own, I brought them around the Green to Lady's house.

I dropped the envelopes in the box, rang the bell, ran down the walk, and hid behind a snowdrift. Jesse appeared in a wool sweater and picked out the cards. He wiped his feet on the mat, and I saw that he was wearing the red-and-black slippers with the gold designs on the toes that Lady had needlepointed him for Christmas.

I lay back against the drift, and, glancing over at the Piersons' house, I felt a sharply rising thrill: smoke was pouring out from behind one of the living-room storm windows. The house was on fire!

I dashed back up Lady's walk, grabbed at the doorknob, and the door swung wide, my momentum carrying me into the hall. I ran to the telephone table, shouting for Jesse and Elthea at the same time. When Elthea came through the kitchen door, I handed her the phone, told her to call the fire department, and ran out again.

The smoke was billowing out more heavily around the storm window, and there were no signs of life at the house. Not bothering with the walks, I plunged over a high drift, laboriously pushing my way across the stretch of snow between the two houses. When I got to the Piersons' front walk, I rushed up onto the porch. I rang the doorbell, pounding with my fist on the glass at the same time. I turned the handle, flung the door open, and ran in. The hall was filled with smoke, which was creeping through the heavy oak doors that met on a track, closing off the living room. "Mrs. Pierson, Mrs. Pierson!" I called, looking wildly in all directions. Then, through the haze, I saw her come to the banister above, clutching her kimono across her chest.

"Oh, my God, the damn house is on fire!" I blinked as Blue Ferguson appeared. "Jesus Christ," I heard him say; then he leaped behind Mrs. Pierson, but not before I saw that he was stark naked.

A moment later Jesse came through the front door followed by

Elthea. I ran and slid the living-room doors partly open, then slammed them again as I became engulfed in smoke, through which I glimpsed a sullen orange glow and heard the crackling of flames. Jesse was moving Elthea out onto the front stoop and in the distance I could hear the whistle blowing at the firehouse. Without thinking, I started up the stairs two at a time, grabbing Mrs. Pierson's arm as she continued leaning over the banister in silent horror; Blue Ferguson was nowhere to be seen. I pulled Mrs. Pierson around the newel post and down the stairs. Seeing Elthea just outside the door, she drew back and tried to free her arm, but I clung fast and got her through the doorway where Elthea took her down the steps.

Running to the kitchen to look for a pail, I found one on the back steps, an empty Pilgrim Market basket beside it. Filling the pail at the sink, I heard a sliding sound from above; chunks of snow were dislodged from the eaves, and something dark flashed by the window. I stood on tiptoe and saw Blue floundering in the deep drift by the drainpipe, trying to make it to the driveway where his truck was parked.

I was reasonably certain no one had noticed the truck slip out of the driveway, for the fire engine was coming in the opposite direction, and there was a great deal of commotion as hoses were screwed to hydrants and run into the house. There was no need now for my pail of water, so I set it down, and when no one was looking I returned to the back steps. I took the market basket out behind the garage and buried it in the deepest drift I could find. When I got back to the front again a fireman was carrying out the parrot's cage, with the asphyxiated bird at the bottom, while two other men came with the smoldering davenport, and dumped it into the snow. The heat it still contained made a large melting ring around it, which gradually turned black.

7

Fire, and then—a judgment from on high?—flood, though I doubted that there were any so foolish as to call the devastation which lay in store for us that spring a mark from heaven. March had come in like the proverbial lion and as proverbially bade fair to go out like a lamb, but between these two extremes there befell our town a dis-

aster whose effects were as far-reaching as they were famous: the
Great Flood of 1936.

But before this major event occurred, all of us children had been
afforded ample time to dwell on that last appearance of the red-
haired man. We had given ourselves over to endless hours of speculation regarding his mysterious visit at Halloween, to the point
that by degrees it had become a dead horse which even I was no
longer inclined to flog. Yet I held my own reservations about the
matter, and these I had steadfastly confided in no one. Despite our
having seen a man get onto the trolley, the thought had entered my
head, and it stayed there, buzzing around my brain like a bee. I
was sure that murder had been committed; that, in fact, Lady Harleigh had shot Mr. Ott, and that Jesse had disposed of the *corpus
delicti* somewhere on the premises, though what happens to *corpus
delicti*'s in a state of decomposition hardly came to my mind. There
was one particular circumstance which only served to bolster my
feelings in this regard.

Before the river froze, we had brought up Lew's scow which we
used to row to Hermitage Island, and it had been down in our cellar for months, waiting to be caulked and repainted. With spring in
the offing, Lew decided it was time we got down to brass tacks and
started refurbishing the craft; confronted with the battered hull, we
saw that the first thing to be done was to strip off the old paint. I
remembered that among Jesse's tools was a blowtorch, and accordingly one afternoon I went over to borrow it.

Lady's bedroom shades were drawn, not at all unusual that winter,
and I felt that little tug of pain and sadness, like a kind of home-
sickness, recalling the endless weeks that had passed without our
having beheld the Lady of old—indeed, without having beheld her
at all. I trudged down the drive to the back kitchen door, where
Elthea let me in. She seemed happy to see me; Jesse as well, though
you never could tell with Jesse. He was at the table in one of his
pink-striped shirts, the violet suspenders crossed over his back, his
lap protected by his gray apron as he polished the candelabra
from the dining-room sideboard. When I explained about the blowtorch, he thought for a second, rose, directing a look to Elthea
at the sink, and went to the cellar door, motioning me to follow him
down the stairway.

The wooden furniture from Lady's summerhouse was arranged
on newspapers near the furnace, where Jesse had been painting
them for the spring. Beyond them was the coal pile, with the shovel

leaning against the wood siding of the bin. The supply had dwindled considerably since the day we painted the storm windows and the coal had been delivered, and there were long scrape marks across the cement floor where the shovel had been slid at the coal before carrying it to the furnace.

Jesse was filling the blowtorch with kerosene, pouring from a gallon can through a little tin funnel, and I caught his eye as he glanced up from this work, looking first at me, then at the coal pile. His lower lip jutted out in a pitcher-like curl—the way it did when he was thinking hard or he disapproved of something—and he began depressing the torch primer in a rapid series of strokes. I noticed how the coal was being used up, not from the front of the pile, as would ordinarily happen, but along the right side almost to the rear of the bin, leaving an unnatural-looking heap on the left side. I found this a curious way of shoveling coal, but it was not until later that the truth of what I was thinking just then struck me. Still, there was enough import in the moment to cause me to start slightly when Jesse put his hand on my shoulder, as if directing my attention away from the bin. He wiped the blowtorch off with a flannel square and handed it to me.

"You know how to work it?"

"Yes, sir."

"Take the kerosene can and funnel in case you run out."

Back in our own cellar, Harry and I scraped with putty knives while Lew used the blowtorch, I turning over in my mind the small pea of doubt that had become lodged there. It was then that I discovered what I had been thinking all the time: the *corpus delicti* was hidden in the back of the bin in Lady Harleigh's cellar, where the coal had been piled so irregularly.

Of this fact I grew more and more certain through the early weeks of March while the snow melted all around the town, and sometimes I would sneak along the side of Lady's house where, crouched down, I could see through the grimy pane of the cellar window over the coal bin, watching the pile recede as the furnace was stoked, wondering what would happen when the coal supply was at last exhausted.

My carefully evolved theory was put to the test several weeks later at the height of the flood. For weeks now, with the sun growing warmer, the snow first turned to slush, then melted altogether, running in roiling channels along the roadside, the eaves and gutters of the houses dripping, the drainspouts rattling tinnily from the overflow. The ice in the river had begun breaking up, and the current carried it south in a steady and speedy flow, and the river day by day rose alarmingly. The boys from the nearest CCC group began working around the clock, sandbagging the dike northeast of the town near the airfield—at night we could look from Nancy's attic window and see the blue glimmer of their lanterns—but these labors proved fruitless as the water level continued to increase, threatening the lower town.

For days excitement ran high around the Green with rumors of evacuation, and there was only a skeleton crew at the firehouse, the firemen having joined the CCC boys at the dike. Late one afternoon they drove back to the Center in Joe Paulus's car and emerged wet and tired and disheartened. The dike, they said, would not hold through the night. We raced up to the north end of Main Street and climbed the tall tree in the back of the Town Farm. From this vantage point we watched the last of the CCC trucks pulling away, and behind them the river already spilling down the steep slope of the high-banked earthwork, cutting gullies and channels as the water ate away at the sides.

Next morning the National Guard was called out, and we awoke to find our back yard knee-deep in water. The dike had gone. The radio told us that the schools were closed and we looked forward to a watery holiday of undetermined duration. By the following afternoon the Green was a proper lake, and water was coming into our cellar. The trolleys had stopped running, and Ma stayed home from the Sunbeam, but neither her remonstrances nor Nancy's could keep us indoors. After putting on our rubber boots, we sloshed our way up to the Center, then down toward the River Road, where—astonishing sight—River House was flooded to the first story, and only the second-floor gallery was visible. People were going by in rowboats, women and children and dogs and possessions being taken to dry land. The current was rapid, swirling with mud as it sluiced along its swollen course, carrying with it anything that would float, tree branches, crates and boxes, here a barrel, there a porch chair. It was when we saw the residents of the Town Farm being loaded into a bus that the real drama of the situation struck us. People were being driven from their homes, and if it was bad today on the River Road, what might it be tomorrow on the Green?

We raced to the hardware store, full of customers buying lanterns and fuel, coils of rope, candles, and—what Lew had said we must get at once—siphon pumps. We bought the last one. Ma, naturally, was worried when we got home, and we reassured her and Nancy, who was wailing in the kitchen, and then went down cellar to investigate. There was over a foot of water, and the sawhorses on which we had set the scow were already being inundated. We got the boat up through the hatchway and moored it to the trunk of the crabapple tree in the back yard. We spent the early hours of the night fashioning a drain out of some old pipes our father had left stuck up along the ceiling beams, which we fitted together section by section, joining the last to the siphon pump. Then we took turns plunging the handle up and down, the suction created emptying the water from the cellar floor and carrying it away through the improvised drainpipe.

It was no use. By next day water surrounded the house, and if the river continued to come up, we would be as homeless as those along the River Road, would in fact be flooded out before nightfall. Lew said we must pack, and get Ma, Ag, Kerney, and Nancy out as quickly as possible. When we came upstairs again, Nancy was sitting at the kitchen table squeezing her knuckles and biting her lower lip. Ma came in bearing an armload of clothing, with Aggie carrying more behind her, and Kerney looking frightened.

The National Guard, Ma explained, was coming to evacuate us, but this might take some time, since the Guard had its hands and boats full elsewhere. At these words Nancy flung her clasped hands toward the ceiling and cried, "Mercy Jesus!" The telephone had gone dead and there was no electricity. All the food from the Frigidaire was in boxes in the back porch, ready to be transported with us. I didn't think the National Guard would be interested in rowing cold pig's hocks and sauerkraut around town, and then realized that if we were being driven out, the Sparrows and Miss Berry and Gert Flagler would most likely also be in peril. Lew and Harry and I ducked out on the back porch and had a hurried conference. Lew, being the tallest, went out the door and down one step, where he was almost up to his boot tops in water, and slogged his way to the tied-up scow. We had brought the oars up as well, and he maneuvered the boat to the steps where we got in, calling inside that we would be back.

We rowed first over to Ruthie Sparrow's—strange and wonderful to be boating across our own lawn—and found her sitting in her bay window, her Seiss-Altags sweeping the watery vista. She saw us, and was already in her hat and coat and galoshes when Mr. Sparrow opened the front door, both of them only too happy to be rescued.

Not so Gert Flagler, to whose house we next rowed. Miss Berry was shivering on the stoop, the dogs clustered around her feet and quiet for once. While we transferred Miss Berry and the dogs to the boat, Gert Flagler appeared in high wading boots. No damn National Guard was going to get *her* out, she said, sloshing her way down the drive to rescue her cow.

Manning the oars, Lew and Harry rowed us down the Green toward the Center. There was no sign of life over at Lady's, and I wondered if they had all left, though there seemed to be no reason to; her house was on higher ground and relatively safe from the rising water.

Our passengers were taken from us at the Masonic Hall, which had been turned into a refugee center, and I spelled first Lew and then Harry at the oars on the return trip. Ag and Kerney were on the porch, Ag with a small suitcase with books and other belongings; Kerney clutching the silver candlesticks Pa had bought for Ma when they were first married, and our crystal set and earphones.

But what about the food on the back porch, Ma asked; heaven knew what there would be to eat where we were going. When they were on dry land, Lew said, we would come back and bring whatever we could manage. Ma followed Ag into the boat, we loaded Nancy and Kerney in, then Patsy, and pulled away from our house. Gert was on her stoop, while the cow stood knee-high in water on the lawn.

"You tell old Keep not to send any soldiers around in a boat, I'm not leaving unless Bossy goes!" she stormed, as if it were our own personal flood. Her face screwed up in a pugnacious grimace, she watched our boat slide away from our door. I sat at the stern in order to bail, for the scow, though seaworthy, was leaking water along the keel where the caulking had split. Lew and Harry had us headed on a course for the Great Elm, where the current seemed easier going, but still it was hard work.

Then I saw the front door open across the way, and Lady appeared, bundled up in Jesse's old sweater and running down the walk toward us.

"Where are you going?" she called, and we answered, to the Masonic Hall.

"Nonsense," she returned in a tone I remembered. "Lew—Harry, come this way—this way, boys. Hurry before your poor mother gets all wet. Hello, Agnes, hello, Kerney. Nice weather for ducks, isn't it? Don't be afraid, Nancy, the boys will have you safe in a jiffy."

There she stood at the end of her brick walk with Honey beside her, the laughter in her voice, suggesting that this was all some marvelous adventure and sure to prove diverting. She called back to the house for Elthea and Jesse, saying guests were coming and to make ready; then she grabbed the painter as I tossed it to her from the bow, relinquishing it to Jesse, who came behind her in his butler's coat, as if expecting company. Meanwhile Patsy sprang to dry land and went frolicking with Honey. Elthea and Lady helped Ma, then Ag and Nancy onto dry ground while Jesse waded out in rubber boots and carried Kerney to safety. We pushed off, to row back across the Green for the things from the Frigidaire; and half an hour later, grouped around the fire Jesse had built, with hot coffee and tea or cocoa, Lady's laughter floating about us as she talked of the house party we were going to have—"Larks, my dears, we'll have such larks"—I openly rejoiced, knowing then that she had come back to us again.

8

Had, in fact, never left us; or so it seemed. She was the Lady of old, brimming with fun and plans, and unable to do enough for us, our whole family scattered helter-skelter about her house. It was large enough, certainly, and sleeping arrangements were easily made, and the extra leaves put in the dining-room table to accommodate us at mealtimes, and plenty of food to put on it from Elthea's pantry. We stayed five days, and they were among the best I can recall. We seldom were alone, and there was no chance to probe Lady's latest and longest retirement. Nor was the last visit of the red-haired man spoken of. It was as if she had blocked out all the unpleasant things that had happened since that Halloween night.

But this was the end of March, and at the final phase of an historic flood; for almost from our transference to the house across the Green the river began receding. Isolated from the world, we were hungry for news, which we got on the crystal set, and were thankful that we had not had to go with the hundreds of others who had been evacuated throughout the valley, including the redoubtable Gert

Flagler. Who that was there doesn't remember with a smile the
sight of Gert being carried, under protest, into a waiting boat by two
husky National Guardsmen? Her furious bellows could be heard
even over on our side of the Green, and she swatted her husky
saviors with her pocketbook as they rowed away, cradling her latest Spencer corset catalogue in her lap.

"My cow—my cow—"

"Lady, we'll get your cow."

"Tell it to Sweeney!"

They did. Two men came poling a makeshift raft, got poor Bossy
on it, and, mooing loudly, she was taken to dry land.

Lew, Harry, and I were meanwhile spending a good deal of time
in Lady's cellar, using another siphon pump, for it had been discovered that the ground, which had soaked up so much moisture,
was depositing it through the stonework of the foundations, and
this, too, was taking on a foot of water. We pumped it into buckets
and carried them up the hatchway stairs and emptied them off behind the carriage house, and I watched with fascination as the level
gradually dropped, revealing the bottom of the coal pile, the lower
twelve inches of which had gotten soaked.

Harry and Lew began moving the dry coal to the other side of the
bin, and I stared in horror as their shovels worked at the place where
I had made up my mind that the *corpus delicti* had been hidden.
Then, to my surprise, they were down to the watery floor, with not
enough coal left to hide a midget.

The matter remained a mystery as the flood tide continued to
recede and the water ebbed back from the Green, leaving an ugly
stretch of mud and debris. But, the water line dropping, I knew
that each inch brought us nearer to the day when we must leave
and go home. Traffic was once again negotiating the roadway along
Broad Street, people were seen coming and going on various
errands, while a work crew began the job of cleaning up. It was at
this point that Lady announced that she was going to give a party—
an end-of-the-flood party, combined with her birthday celebration,
where, like Noah, everybody could get as drunk as they wished.
The house now being accessible, she would invite all the neighbors,
and we would have a high old time. Since it was also to be our fare-
well to her house, she intended to make it a memorable celebration.
So on went the apron, down came the recipe books, out came the
baking pans, and she began preparing enormous quantities of food
for a buffet supper. Ma, Ag, Nancy, and Elthea helped her, while

we boys worked under Jesse's supervision, cleaning, waxing, and polishing in all the downstairs rooms.

Meanwhile there began a parade of deliveries from the Center, where things had gotten back to normal: wine from the liquor store, meat from the market, and ice from Mr. Pretty, the vegetable man. Mr. Pretty's industriousness was the talk of Pequot Landing. At one time he had made a comfortable living selling ice, but with G.E.s and Kelvinators on everyone's back porches he changed to peddling vegetables door-to-door in the summer to support his family (large jolly wife, nine kids, all fat) while during the winter he sold firewood and kindling, and trees at Christmas time. In the spring he odd-jobbed, in the fall guided businessmen on hunting trips in Maine. Evenings he took a correspondence course in dentistry, when he wasn't meeting with the Boy Scouts, the Masons, or the church deacons. He was so busy that people said they didn't see where he found time to oblige Mrs. Pretty with so many offspring.

He brought Lady a hundred-pound block of ice, and departed, and behind him came Colonel Blatchley, supervising the laying in of the various liquors, and after he had scouted a suitable spot at which to set up the bar, and a place to set out the champagne, he and Jesse put the wine bottles in a snowdrift to cool until the party.

We had attacked the sideboard in the dining room, and I was making faces in the watery mirror when Lady came in. Remembering the episode with the mirrors in the funhouse at Holiday Lake, I broke off, and she asked us to go up to the attic to find the pads for the table before she laid the cloth. There was a large platter up there which she wanted as well, and she sent Ag along to carry it down.

Warmed by the bricks of the giant chimney at one end, the attic was a cozy spot. We discovered a number of trunks of a size to hide any number of very large men in, and I wondered if the remains of the red-haired man had not found its way into one of these instead of the coal bin. Harry already had one of them open, but no mortal bones did it contain, only clothes from earlier periods.

With a delighted sigh Ag drew out a long robe and tried it on, a sort of dressing gown covered with a feathery pattern of turquoise peacock tails, with gold dots in the eyes, and it made soft swishing sounds as she knotted the sash and moved in it. Lew, meanwhile, discovered an old army tunic, and when he had put it on we went to look in the mirror in the bedroom under the sloping roof at the other end of the attic. This room we knew to be Jesse's and Elthea's, sparely furnished and, not surprisingly, neat as a pin, for Elthea was unfailingly a good housekeeper. There was a large bed which took up nearly all the floor space, with a great carved headboard and a smaller footboard, and a mattress under the counterpane that sagged toward the middle.

Lew and Aggie were posing side by side before the mirror on the wall, and none of us heard the footsteps on the stairway until Lady's voice was heard to say, "Where are my table pads—" She broke off as she appeared in the doorway, staring at the figures, her face gone white as if she had seen a ghost. Which, I suddenly realized, was precisely the case—a pair of ghosts. Lew had struck a smart attitude of salute, while Aggie's languid-model pose dripped peacock from sleeve to hem.

Lady's half-moan froze them like figures in a tableau. Her brows drew together in an angry line, and her voice was a harsh whisper. "Get out, all of you, get out of here! Take those things off. Do you hear? Take them *off!*" We stood, speechless, then Lew plunged past her through the door. Tears came into Aggie's eyes as she looked at Lady, then turned to follow Lew. Lady's hand came out, seizing one of the sleeves, and the delicate fabric tore at the shoulder seam. Then, giving me an impatient shake, she hurried me through the door after the others.

Lew was unbuttoning the tunic, while Ag was trying to unknot the sash of the torn gown. Lady had closed the bedroom door and was stopped at the stairway railing, one hand supporting herself, the fingers of the other pressing at her mouth, and she continued to stare as Aggie's movements grew more agitated in trying to undo the knot. It was Aggie's tears that brought Lady back to herself. Visibly controlling the emotions that had shaken her, she came around the railing, hurried to Ag, and drew her into her arms.

"No, no—mustn't cry—mustn't . . ." She made comforting sounds and smoothed Ag's hair down, then helped her untie the bow. When the clothes had been replaced in the trunk and the lid closed, Lady sank down on it, still gripping Ag's hand.

"G-Gosh," Lew stammered, "we didn't mean to—"

"Oh. Ohh," Lady said, her tone one of relief. She was half laughing and trying to make a joke of it, but we all could see how badly upset she was. "I'm sorry—I'm sorry—darling Agnes, Lew, I'm sorry —I can't imagine what made me—"

She looked from one face to another, then opened her arms and we all crowded around her, and she was still laughing and crying, clutching Ag's hand and patting it. She found her handkerchief and blew her nose, and shook her head aghast at the fierceness of her earlier reaction.

"I'm sorry," she murmured again. "I wondered what had happened to you, and here you were playing ragpicker in the attic."

"I didn't mean to tear the dress," Ag said.

"Darling, *you* didn't, *I* did. It doesn't matter. It was just an old thing—it doesn't matter. . . ."

When we found the platter and table pads, and came down from the attic, Ma was at the foot of the stairs. Lady excused herself, saying she wanted to rest before the party, she would set the table later, and when she had gone Ma turned her eye on us.

"All right, what was going on up there?"

We tried to explain what had happened, but Ma would hear none of it. "You've upset Lady, all of you. Now I want you boys to bring in some wood, then go to your rooms and get your schoolwork. Agnes, give me the platter, and bring the pads. Elthea can use some more help in the kitchen. The very idea, going through trunks that don't belong to you." Cautioning us not to make noise, she hurried us downstairs. The party preparations were well underway in the kitchen; Jesse had been polishing the silver, and the good crystal and china had been washed, and there were wonderful smells coming from the oven.

When we went out to the woodpile in the carriage house we found Jesse, in an old sweater, his hunting cap, and rubber boots, carrying a long stick over to the summerhouse. He explained that the heavy weather had ruined the brick walk he'd set down the previous year. He laid the stick across the brickwork, which had heaved in places, sunk in others; then he broke the stick into pieces, drove these stakes along the sides of the walk, and began tying string to them. The walk, he grumbled, would have to be pulled up and reset.

We brought the wood in; then Lew went down cellar with Elthea to fetch relishes and pickles from the cold cellar, and Ma told me to go ask Lady for the tablecloth. I found her on the wicker chaise in her bedroom, having a cup of tea. She said the tablecloth was in the linen closet at the end of the hall but I would need her footstool to stand on to reach it.

In the linen closet, hidden behind the square tin cakebox Lady kept her sewing things in, I made an exciting discovery: Mr. Ott's briefcase! There it was, pushed all the way to the back of the shelf, and, realizing I had been right all the time, I pulled it toward me. I was trying to undo the straps when I heard footsteps on the stairs. It was Elthea coming up. She went into Lady's room, and I quickly replaced the briefcase, grabbed the tablecloth, and ducked out, shutting the door. As I came along the hall, I heard Lady's voice.

"I don't see why, dear."

"He thinks it'd be a bit more tactful," Elthea replied. "With so many people coming."

"But those things have always been there. Why should I rearrange a room—*my* room—to please others?"

"It's just really pleasing him."

Colonel Blatchley, I decided, had suggested the removal of her shrine for the party, a request Lady took exception to.

She paused, and I heard her moving the things around on her vanity table. "All right. If you think so."

"Thank you. Have a nice nap."

"Thank you, dear. I'll try."

I pretended to be just approaching the door as Elthea came out. She took the tablecloth, but wanted the napkins as well. She went to get them, and I brought the stool back into Lady's room.

Sitting at the dressing table, her hair hidden with a hand towel, she was using a wide camel's-hair brush to paint her face with egg white, a beauty treatment, she explained, that she'd found in the *Delineator*. I leaned against the fourposter bed with its crocheted counterpane, and as she painted I saw how she examined her face microscopically in the large mirror, looking for flaws.

While the egg dried, she removed the towel, let down her hair, and, moving to the chaise, began brushing it with long, powerful strokes. She handed me her pins and I put them in the little pewter dish on the linen runner, with its curly, curvy A.H. monogram. The lid of the dish had a fake pearl for a handle, and held not only Lady's hairpins but sewing pins, as well as the small iron key to Edward's chifforobe. She made no mention of the incident in the attic but, glancing out the window, asked what Jesse was doing in the yard. When I repeated what he'd said about the brickwork, she rapped her ring on the pane and motioned for him to come in. "It's too cold out there, doesn't he know that?"

I can still see her as she was that afternoon, her gold wedding band flashing on her finger as she used the ivory-and-silver brush on her hair (she continued doing it up behind in a knot, the way Edward had liked it), and next she used the suède buffer on her nails. Again she paused to rap on the windowpane, and Jesse, who had paid no attention before, now shrugged his shoulders inside his sweater and, leaving his work, headed for the kitchen.

"All that snow and wet," Lady said dismally, "it will have rotted my bulbs."

"There sure was a lot of snow—but we never got our sleigh ride. . . ."

"Sleigh ride? Was there to be a sleigh ride?"

She'd forgotten again. I was willing to let it go, but she put down her nail buffer and drew me to her. "Ah, my dear," she murmured, "you mustn't pay any attention to Lady. She doesn't mean to hurt you. She wasn't well this winter. She wasn't herself." No, I thought; and knew the reason. It lay behind the cakebox in the linen closet. She took in a shuddery little breath, and held it. She reached for a tissue and blew her nose, then felt the dried egg white. "Why do I let you see me like this—I must look awful."

"You look funny."

"I'm sure I do. A very funny-looking, foolish lady." Her expression grew grave. "If—if you should ever find Lady acting that way again, you just give her a little shake to wake her up, and tell her to remember that we're boom compenions, will you do that, Ignatz? And be a little forgiving of her? Just a little forgiving?"

"I'd forgive you anything!" I vowed fervently, and as I nestled closer and put my arms around her waist, I truly believed my words.

9

When I think of her now, I see her, most often, as she was that night: never lovelier, never more elegant or exquisite, never more shining or alive. I remember her, seated in her favorite wing chair by the fire, auburn-haired Honey at her side, the black velvet skirt of her dress spread around, her diamonds, one clipped to each ear, sparkling in the firelight. Her hair was dressed simply, the curve of her white throat, catching glints of red and orange, was beautiful. She wore a necklace of garnets that had belonged to an aunt, and had been given to her by her father before his death.

And from the chair she greeted her guests and was hostess for her party, while we rubbed elbows with the 5:10-ers, the members of the Old Guard she had wanted to join us. The Harrelsons were there, and Eamon and Eva Harmon, of the seed family, and the undertaking Foleys, the banking Brickers, and Mr. and Mrs. Merriam—Mrs. Merriam played the organ at church. No one could believe the buffet that had been laid out on the dining-room table—the chairs moved elsewhere so everything was easily accessible—the hors d'oeuvres, the hot dishes, the desserts, cheeses of all description, wines of both colors, beer, and, with dessert, champagne.

It was perfectly in order, and the first time I ever tasted champagne—on Lady's birthday. She was fifty that night, but I heard Eva Harmon saying she looked more forty than fifty, and Eva, who had both wit and style, never said much that she didn't truly think. I agreed. Beyond accepting congratulations, Lady wanted no fuss made. Except for us, she had told no one because she didn't want presents, but wished only to give her friends and "family" a party. There wasn't even a cake; Elthea had had her orders.

I had never known a party like that before, and have known few since. It was lit by a kind of conviviality that comes only from an infusion of spirit into those gathered, and this radiated from Lady herself. Hers were not "hostess ways," but real, honest charm, and profound feelings of warmth and solicitude. It was as if she were thanking these people of the town for having let her live among them. Never was Colonel Blatchley so funny, never was Ma so gay, never were the 5:10-ers so ossified—to use Mrs. de Sales-Sprague's word—never had the brick house exuded so much good-heartedness or bonhomie. Even Jesse, in his best black coat, passing trays and fetching drinks, couldn't keep a smile off his face, while Elthea, bangled and braceleted at every visible appendage, laughed as loudly as any of the guests as back and forth she went from the kitchen.

When people had heaped their plates at the buffet, and were seated around the living room, Jesse filled the wineglasses with champagne, and Colonel Blatchley led the birthday toasts. Lady acknowledged them, and proposed one of her own.

"To present company," she offered, moving her glass in a semicircle and taking in the gathering, "and absent friends. . . ." Her glance went to the gate-leg table where the champagne cooled in a large porcelain bucket filled with ice, beside a bouquet of hothouse flowers, these things replacing the familiar shrine to Edward Harleigh, the photographs, the war medal, and other mementos. Earlier I had realized this must have been what Lady and Elthea were discussing in the bedroom. Jesse, popping another cork, inclined his head and refilled the Colonel's glass.

The toasts honored, Lady sat again, the rugs came up, and there was dancing to the radio in the living room, card games in the back parlor, and the stairway was dotted with sitters and watchers, eaters and drinkers. Lady maintained her chair through most of the evening, and I kept close to her side, with Honey. Outside it was cold, but inside—I could feel the warmth not only of the burning logs but of the whole room closing in around and enveloping me. Seeing how Lady was loved, I loved her more.

It was a time of friendliness and goodness and cheer, and I said, leaning to her while eating a small boiled potato stuffed with caviar and sour cream, "Can't we do this *every* year?"

She leaned down to me and wiped my mouth with her napkin. "But I won't be fifty every year."

"Then do it when you're fifty-one!" I had drunk wine and was rejoicing in its effects. Please, I cried, it would be like an anniversary, like weddings and birthdays and such things should be, and yes, she said, a party every year until she was white-haired like Barbara Fritchie and we would all be grown up and married, and would bring our children to see the old lady across the Green, and who touched a hair of yon gray head—

" 'Dies like a dog—' "

" 'March on, he said.' And march, sir, please bring me some coffee." With sugar, the way she wanted it. Jesse was nowhere to be found, so I prepared the cup myself, and when I came back, I sat again beside her and Honey, as though to be in close proximity gave me status with my elders—which seemingly it did.

"Well, sir, and who's this young fellow?" Eamon Harmon asked, knowing full well.

"This," said Lady Harleigh, "is the friend of my youth. He is my boom compenion."

It was the accolade, and I toasted myself with more champagne. But what about next year, I asked again; would she promise?

"We'll see," came the reply. And then, too soon, it was over. In spite of floods risen and abated, and we Ark-like in Lady's living room, there were banks to open and seeds to be sold, and funeral arrangements to be seen to, and group by group the guests departed, while I sat hugging Honey by the fire, praying Ma would not round us up, too.

But no, not a word was said about bedtime, and while Elthea saw to the cleaning up, our group, Lady's "family," drew together by the fireside, the rugs still rolled against the wall, and Ma played piano. Lew, Harry, and I rounded up every lighted candle we could find, ringing them around Lady in her chair, and we sang "Happy Birthday." Then there was "Home on the Range," and "Yes, We Have No Bananas," which always amused Lady, and "Don't Bring Lulu." Then Ma played "When I Grow Too Old to Dream," one of her favorites, and I knew from her misty eyes that she was thinking of Pa when she played it.

When Ma finished and took more champagne, we shouted for Lady, who replaced her at the piano bench. "What shall I play?" she asked around the room. "Anything, anything," we chorused, and then she provided the best part of the evening, a coda of her own devising to what had preceded. Fingers resting lightly on the keyboard, she thought for a moment as her gaze went to the cove molding at the ceiling where paintings hung on cords of gold tasseled silk. Reflecting, she used the fingers of her right hand to twist the ring on her left, a trace of a smile playing about her lips; then she redirected her gaze in front of her—the music on the rack was something entirely different—and began. Several bars, and then without pause she returned to the beginning, and with one or two introductory passages began again, her fingers spreading across the black and white keys to form the chords, a soft, economical accompaniment underlining rather than stating the music.

It was a sad song, I could tell, not only from the title she had given, but from her facial expression and the register of her voice. She did not try to make it sound sad; it was simply so, a sad song. The German words, all unintelligible to me, sounded husky in her throat. (Mother had said once, "I don't care for German, it sounds so harsh"; but from Lady's mouth it didn't—sounded soft and fluid, romantic, and spoke of the lost-in-love.)

As the lines continued, it was almost as if we were not there at all and she were singing them for herself, or for someone who was not there in the room. Edward, perhaps? There was a play of emotion on her features, something sweet and at the same time painful, that which is sentimentally called "bittersweet," I suppose, and I, too, became lost in the German words whose meaning I did not understand.

It ended. She paused, her fingers still on the keys.

"What's it called?" Ag asked.

"In German, it is *'Das Lied ist aus,'* which means 'The song is over'—'*Frag' nicht warum ich gehe*,' 'Don't ask me why I'm going.'"

"It's pretty."

Lady nodded, more to herself than to Ma's remark. "*Ja, das ist schön.* That is a good thing, the music is the German soul."

She turned her head away and used her handkerchief, asking over her shoulder for Jesse to bring more coffee in. He came, with his tray and cups, and I could feel the cold on his coat as he bent to serve Lady. I wondered what he'd been doing outdoors, and decided he must have been to the woodpile, for he was wearing overshoes, hastily wiped on the kitchen mat.

Then it was really and absolutely time to go to bed, and Ma began her usual refrain about upstairs, Now, children. And up we went. Lady, still in her jewelry and gown, came and kissed each of us good night. Before she went out, I said again what a wonderful party it had been.

"I'm glad you liked it, l'il Ignatz."

"Boy, if you'd invited P.J. and Spouse—would they have been surprised."

"Not half so much as I, darling. I did invite them. They turned me down cold."

10

The next night found us returned to our own house: damp, musty, and all too common in its familiarity. It bred contempt within me; I longed to be back at Lady's again. But, as Ma said, "All good times must end," and morosely I conceded the truth of it. The flood was over, our stay at Lady's likewise, and what lay ahead except more school, with the dullest of prospects at every turn? March went out baaing, sure enough, though April resembled February in its cold and blustery particulars, and the remaining snow froze fast again.

It was then that I suddenly remembered the Pilgrim Market basket I had buried in the drift behind the Piersons' garage on that fateful day. I took a hatchet, sneaked across the Green, and found the basket, upended in the half-melted drift. I freed it, chopped it up for kindling, and no one was the wiser as it fed our late Sunday-afternoon fire, and I sat on the living-room davenport, watching Blue Ferguson's shame go up the flue in smoke and ashes. It made a cheerful light.

To me, it had been an awesome fall from grace, Blue Ferguson's. Many things had become clear to me—low, deceitful things. I knew now why the Pilgrim Market truck had so often been parked at the Piersons' kitchen door, hidden behind the screen of fir trees from Mrs. Sparrow's prying eyes. I knew now why Mrs. Pierson had been in the woods the day we'd gone hunting with Jesse, and had found Blue there also. I knew now the precise reason for his trips to the back of Mr. Keller's drugstore. He was no different from anybody else, just one more of the common mold, a god with feet of clay. True gods must be at pains to disguise their frailties; True Blue had revealed his, naked to the eye, in Mrs. Pierson's upper hallway, and what hope did he have of disguise? For if I had thought that the secret lay buried with the market basket I was mistaken. In some way the news had leaked out, and the next thing we heard was that Blue had left town. But who, besides myself, had known? I thought immediately of Dora Hornaday, and the scene at the railroad tracks, when she had done her pantomime about the parrot lady. I was right—she'd been spying. The talk that subsequently went around was that Mrs. Pierson, in a fit of remorse, had confessed her sins to Mr. Pierson, and had sought his forgiveness, which had been withheld until the culprit had been dealt with. Mr. Pierson made all sorts of threats against Blue, even to declaring he'd sue the Pilgrim Market, though on what grounds no one could imagine. Then we learned that Blue had run off, nobody knew where, and his mother was sick with worry.

In no time the story was all over town. People talked of nothing else. True Blue Ferguson—the fair-haired boy, pride of the Academy Parliament, dealer in wit and sound intelligence—profane and sullied, and skulking out of town, tail between his legs. He was to have been graduated from high school in June, and had his scholarship arranged for in the fall, considerations which seemed slight in the face of his ignominious departure.

People had said Blue Ferguson would go far, and they were right. Far had he gone; but where?

Then the Piersons also left. Nobody saw them go, and no one even knew they were gone until a FOR SALE sign went up in the front yard.

Though Blue's exact whereabouts remained a mystery, Mrs. Ferguson had received a postcard from somewhere in New York City, telling her not to worry, but this was small solace for her. The embarrassment of Blue's illicit connection with Lilah Pierson was as cold as yesterday's mashed potatoes, but still people picked over the leavings, and when I thought of Blue, as occasionally I did—not without meanness, for I felt some sort of personal, if undefined betrayal—it seemed incomprehensible to me that he would have just sneaked off, and not met the situation head-on and taken the consequences, as I thought someone like Blue ought to have done. But now Mr. Pierson was gone, Mrs. Pierson, too, and reflecting on it, it seemed to me a business both shabby and ridiculous.

The more I dwelt on it the deeper the funk I got into, and as the last of the snow melted away and the weather warmed, what I considered to be my old world seemed to melt too; I would gladly have had winter come again, narrowing my horizon and imprisoning me with its familiar white boundaries. Spring was lurking, and I became fearful of it.

Then a dreadful scene occurred. It happened on a Friday after school when, suffering from I knew not what vague longings, I walked across the still-soggy Green to a favorite spot of mine, on Lady's side terrace. As I would sometimes do, I took along the little bedroom radio Ma had bought us after the flood. At home Nancy always had *The Romance of Helen Trent* or *Lorenzo Jones* or *Backstage Wife* on during that part of the afternoon, and I liked sitting on the terrace, the radio plugged in the outside jack, leaning back against the brick, listening to some music, and feeling the pleasant warmth of the absorbed sun through my windbreaker.

Lady needn't have worried about the wetness affecting her bulbs; there were tulips and jonquils and white narcissus everywhere, and hyacinths all along the terrace wall. The forsythia had almost gone by, but the rhododendron and dogwood were in bloom, the lilac was ready to burst, and the lawn was a deep, velvety green that looked unreal. In later years, after a dreary New York winter, with everything bleak and gray to dullness, when I yearned for flowers—a hunger for spring color that was like an unsatisfied craving for sweets—I used to think of Lady's springtime flower beds, particularly that year after the flood.

Jesse was finishing up his project of re-laying the brick walkway from the summerhouse to the birdbath, but instead of setting the bricks in sand, he'd used cement to make sure the work would hold firm. The birdbath had been placed in the center of the little circle, likewise brick and also cemented, with a border of upended bricks around it, in which ivy and flowers had been planted.

I must have been dozing, for, the sun making colors behind my closed lids, I only distantly heard the sound of voices. The window over my head was partly open, airing out the living room, and the words, traveling through from the kitchen, rose in conflict. Lulled by the sun and the music, I was not aware of their precise content, but one voice was unmistakably Jesse's. Opening my eyes, I saw that he had left his work on the bricks, and had gone indoors. Then I heard Elthea speak, and I realized some sort of argument was in progress, Jesse protesting with unheard-of vehemence, while Elthea seemed to be trying to calm him down. Next I heard the familiar sound of Lady's heels on the kitchen flooring, and her tone matched Jesse's in firmness and intensity. I opened the side door and crept into the living room, halting by the wing chair and listening. Still I could not make out all the elements of the conversation, only its tenor, and that in fragments.

". . . don't think that way," I heard Jesse saying.

"I may think any way I choose, may I not?" Lady retorted airily. "After all, it's my house."

"True enough."

Then Elthea: "Now, hon, don't you go fretting yourself into a stew."

"Don't she go fretting herself back to bed, you mean," Jesse interjected.

"I'll fret myself where and when I choose," Lady replied.

"You must suit yourself, then," Jesse replied. "As in all things."

"But I got *rid* of it!"

"Then be happy. . . ."

"*How* shall I be happy? Aren't I a little too old for that—now? 'Rapunzel, Rapunzel, let down your hair, let your lover climb up'? Shall I let down my hair? My *long* hair? That Edward *loved*? Shall I? Tell me, Jesse—shall I? It's easy to put photographs and medals away, but I can't put him away, I can't!"

I listened, astonished. I had never heard Lady speak that way, with such calculated sarcasm. Still, I couldn't tell what precisely the argument was about. Something, obviously, to do with the shrine on the gate-leg table. Jesse spoke again.

"You can't because you won't let yourself. And you won't let anyone else—"

"Missus. Or *ma'am*. Don't you say *ma'am* to me? Call me ma'am, Jesse." Again her voice rode on an unsuppressed wave of sarcasm as if she were mocking him for his subservient position.

"Yes. Ma'am," Jesse replied in a dull tone.

"Thank you, Jesse. That was very nice. Very well, Elthea. Your Jesse thinks it best, and we must oblige him. Leave the things where they are."

A moment later Jesse came down the hall. I ducked behind the wing chair as he went out and closed the front door behind him. Meanwhile Lady had begun singing, not in her usual lovely voice, but in a raggedy, oddly kiltered range. I instantly recognized the rhyme Jesse had warned me against letting her hear: "There was an old, old, old, old lady," she sang, and a few more bars; then there was laughter, not a pleasant sound, but ironic and mocking.

Then she broke off and cried out, "Oh, I am being driven mad in this house. Old old old old and *mad!*" These words were followed by indistinguishable ones in Elthea's flowing murmur of protest, then more from Lady, ending with "old old old old" in a tone of anguish. I heard her rapid footsteps down the hall, and the sound of her sobs, and Elthea coming after her.

"Where are you going?"

"I am going," Lady returned with another cry, "to cut off my hair."

"No!"

The word escaped my lips before I realized it, and I rushed through the living room. Elthea was holding on to the newel post, looking up the staircase as I plunged past her and ran to Lady's room.

She sat at the dresser, her eyes wet, her features contorted, a pair of large silver scissors from her sewing box clutched in her hands. Her hairpins lay scattered about and her hair hung around her face. Coming through the doorway, I saw the shears close on a large hank, slicing it clean. I stared in horror as, like a demented thing, she hacked and cut in a fury of resolve, scarcely noticing me as she went about her awful work.

Clump after terrible clump fell while she chopped around her neck. When the furious energy had expended itself, her hands dropped to her sides and she stared dumbly at the unfamiliar image in the mirror and the havoc she had wreaked upon her person. The scissors slipped from her fingers. She burst into a torrent of remorseful tears. She snatched up a hairbrush and began pulling it through the unevenly chopped hair, moans alternating with cries of rage and anger.

"What have I done, what have I done?" She stared at her image in the mirror, and suddenly her hand lashed out, the back of the silver brush striking the glass and shattering it. Broken pieces fell onto the top of the vanity, and I could see blood along her knuckles. Unmindful of the cuts, she abruptly stopped crying, as if spent, and said in an empty voice, "Well. That's that. Goblin—goblin— Ugly people doing ugly things."

Drops of blood were falling on the linen runner. Her face was an awful white, drained of color, and she clutched her abdomen as if such an expenditure of fury had made her sick. There were red smears on her white blouse, and the pewter dish was overturned, scattering pins and the chifforobe key. I stepped quickly forward to take the brush from her, then laid the palm of my free hand against the back of her head and looked at her fractured image in the mirror.

"I think you'll look good with short hair." With a whimper she buried her head against my arm and sighed exhaustedly. I put the things back in the pewter dish and righted it. When she lifted her face again, tears streamed down her cheeks.

"Please don't see me like this."

"You've hurt yourself."

"I'll fix it. Please go—now?" A little-girl's voice, in a childlike appeal. Obediently I laid the brush down and left the room.

I went back to the side terrace for my radio and, replugging it in our sleeping porch, I saw her, with a scarf tied peasant-fashion around her head, as on foot she turned up the street, heading for the Center. Several hours later, she came back still wearing the scarf. I decided another retirement was in the offing.

I mourned the cut hair. Even though it might grow back, I thought it would never be the same. Something had been taken from me, the structure of my world had in some way been altered, and Lady's tantrum—for I considered it such—had in some indecipherable way threatened me. Now, no matter what, it would be a new Lady, a different Lady, and this was painful to contemplate.

I did not see her for some time after that, and though the bedroom shades were not drawn in daytime, still I felt sure the spring boded her absence from the Green. But somehow I didn't care. I considered her cutting her hair for spite as childish, and I was bored with the idea of a grown woman letting her emotions run away with her like that. If her presence had been made available to me, I would have let her know my attitude by acting cool, or shunning her altogether, to teach her a lesson. However, I did not see her, and the opportunity for such ridiculous melodrama did not arise. But I sulked plenty around our house, feeling disagreeable, out of sorts, disgusted with my fellow-man—and woman. I loved no one in this world, no one I knew or could imagine, for I was sure no one loved me. I was a solitary boy. What had Lady said—one feeds on solitude? I fed, but was hungry.

Perhaps it was nothing more than spring fever, and if Nancy had been more aware she would have double-dosed me with Iradol-A and given me a good shaking. But my desperate mood—I was by that time considering running away, as Blue had—was altered by a chance but memorable encounter, in which existed the opportunity of a greater understanding of myself, and of others, and a realization of what we so often forgot or did not want to realize, the fact that my bones were lengthening, my teeth settling, my cheeks drawing in, and, confirming the measuring marks on the kitchen door-jamb, that I was that most average of creatures, a boy growing up.

This meeting came in that time of kindest April when, the flood having devastated and then receded, the whole Connecticut River Valley was drenched with a picture-book sort of spring. It was on a Saturday after lunch, with a sky bright but scudding with clouds, and when they passed across the face of the sun they cast giant flying shadows over the pastures like the shadows of giant flying birds. Alone, I walked down toward Talcottville by the back road, the collar of my windbreaker turned up, the zipper pulled to my chin, and the inner thighs of my corduroy knickers rubbing with manly, audible friction.

I climbed to the top of Talcott Hill, which rose between the end of Pequot Landing and the nearer side of Talcottville. No-Relation Welles lived in the large house topping the crest, and I could see his horseless cart in the drive. I cut diagonally down and across the pasture to the pond behind the Paulus farm. Mr. Paulus was a kindly man who never seemed to mind our swimming in his pond, and sometimes Mrs. Paulus, a big, blond Scandinavian woman, would bake an apple pie and leave it on the kitchen sill, pre-slicing it for us to help ourselves. I could see Mr. Paulus going down the lane to fetch his cows at the far end of the pasture, where they were already chewing down the young grass. Birds sang, their dark forms spaced out like bits of Morse code along the telephone wires, while others perched in the branches of trees that everywhere already bore the faintest touch of lettuce-colored green, testimony to the greener foliage to come.

When I got to the pond, I followed the course of the stream it made into the woods, where little pockets of clean snow still lay sloped against some of the tree bases, and the thinnest lace of ice trembled against the undersides of the stream banks. I had worn my freshly oiled jackboots, laced with rawhide thongs to the knees, and I could easily wade along the bed of the stream, higher than usual from the flood, feeling the throbbing current against my shins and the crunch of the clean turned stones under my thick soles. I saw a lot of different birds, blue jays and nuthatches eagerly feasting after the thin winter pickings, others only recently arrived from warmer climates, cowbirds, robins, some red-winged blackbirds. I flopped down in a sunny dry spot, taking in all the spring sounds and sights around me. The sky was clear, clouds gusted on the wind, the soft clank of cowbells drifted across the pasture, and at every turning the stream gurgled coaxingly.

"Am I interrupting you?" asked a voice I knew. I opened my eyes and looked up at Lady Harleigh. She was dressed for walking, with heavy shoes and her old flannel skating skirt, and the wool cardigan sweater that hung in the back porch and that Jesse sometimes put on, a scarf around her neck, and her knitted skating cap pulled over her head. "I thought perhaps you were asleep. Just thinking? May I join you?"

She took a place beside me, leaning back against the tree trunk, her eyes sparkling as she explained that she, like me, was out for a walk on this day of days, and had been following me as I came into the woods from the pond. Not having seen her since the awful day she cut her hair, I stared at her, trying to imagine what it must look like now. She sensed, rather than saw, my curiosity, which I tried to disguise, and she slipped the cap off, dropping her head a bit as she ran her fingers lightly around behind, then lifted her face. "You said I'd look good with short hair. Do I?"

She looked wonderful. In place of the familiar twist or knot at the back, there was now a short roll, with soft waves at the sides, and lightly sweeping down at the temples, leaving the brow clean. It was a striking change. Then I noticed something that had escaped my eye before: here and there were strands of gray. Ruthie Sparrow had sworn for years that Lady touched up the color, but we knew what dyed hair looked like, Mrs. Pierson being witness to that, and Lady's seemed of quite another sort. But here she was, turning gray. It hardly seemed possible, and I remembered that pitiful cry, "Old, old, old, old." But she wasn't old, of course, only the littlest bit gray, and on this day she was young both in face and in spirit, the complete and final rejuvenation of the Lady of the winter past.

After we had talked for a while in the manner of people becoming reacquainted after a separation—the weather, friends, the price of eggs in Denmark—we resumed our walk together. From her talk and her manner I could tell that she was feeling the magic of the day, glorious as if all the things that had gone before, all the bad things, might be forgotten, and that hope, as the poet said, truly did spring eternal.

Still, within me I felt that surge of things not understood, of wishing—what? Wanting—what? Needing—whom—? I turned away, staring down at the stream where it rushed fast over some rocks, and a pair of catfish nibbled at the waving grass near the bank. Presently I felt her light hand on my collar, and the finger touching my ear was warm.

"What is it?" she asked gently. I shook my head, trying to press my ear next to her finger. She cupped my chin and turned my head, looking at me with those dark, sparkling eyes. "You can tell me if you want to."

"Blue Ferguson's never coming back."

"How do you know?" Her voice was gentler still.

"I just do." I became suddenly angry at the thought of Blue's having put everything behind him, of having struck out on his own, of having gotten out of Pequot, of having left me there, abandoned, frittering away my time. "Blue Ferguson can go to hell," I added hotly.

"Let's hope he's not gone quite that far. But wherever he's gone, you'd like to go, too, wouldn't you?"

"Sort of." I thought my grudging reply would put her off, would be enough of an excuse, but she continued her gentle probing.

"There's more, isn't there? More about Blue? About Blue and Lilah Pierson?" The words came out so unexpectedly and with such frankness that I pulled away. She came a little around to face me. I felt a flooding of embarrassment, that she of all people should have brought up the subject.

"I saw it all, you know." I stared in surprise, and she nodded. "From my hall window. You were getting a pail on the back steps. Blue's market basket was there. He came out of a snowdrift, and drove away. You took the basket out behind the garage." I silently concurred in her recollection of the events. "Where had Blue come from?" she asked.

"He jumped out the upstairs window."

She put her hand over her breast and laughed in dismay at such a ridiculous picture.

"Did you tell?" I demanded.

"Heavens, no, not I. His secret was safe enough with me." She laughed harder at the thought, then grew suddenly grave, as she often did. "Whom do you feel badly for? Blue? Mrs. Pierson? How do you feel about Blue's being in the house that day?"

"It wasn't just that day! It was lots of days. Lots and lots. When Mr. Pierson was away. Upstairs with her, in the back room. Everybody knows—at the barbershop, the firehouse. They're laughing at him. It must have been Dora Hornaday who told—everyone's laughing and—and—"

"And it's dirty."

I blinked at her in shock. Surely she wasn't going to—I felt more embarrassed, more ashamed, and growing angrier I wrenched myself away from her.

"Is it?" she insisted, reaching for my hand. "Is it dirty?"

"Sure it's dirty. Like Lily Marini in the bushes—like the girls at River House."

"Why?"

"Everybody knows what *they* do."

"And you're disappointed in Blue, that he could do dirty things."

"Yes."

"And you can't forgive him."

"I hope he never comes back, I hope I never see him—"

"Oh, my dear, you mustn't use that word."

"Why not?"

"Because never is a long, long time. Longer than we may know. Come, let's sit a minute."

Taking my hand, she brought me to a pile of timber and we sat side by side on the sawed logs, our fingers entwined together in her lap. I could not possibly reconstruct the words she used in this troubled moment, but whatever hurts I had suffered—the disappointment in Blue, and the contempt I felt for his having been caught doing dirty things with Mrs. Pierson—were salved, and the thoughts that were causing me turmoil lay where they could be examined and, possibly, understood.

She talked about the incalculable differences between men and women, not only the physical, but those others that are harder to analyze. She talked of love between them, and of how there was a vast difference between what Blue had been doing in the back room with Mrs. Pierson, and the love a man may have for the woman he sets his heart on, and she for him. It was not at all like that—firehouse smut and beer-hall jokes. And the River House girls—she knew a thing or two about that. It was not necessary to mate as animals, but as human beings, one to the other. Never did she employ such pat tritenesses as "One day, when you are old enough . . . you will understand." I was old enough on that day, at that hour and minute, and if I chose, she told me, I could understand it at that precise moment, not waiting until I "grew up" or "came of age." And though she spoke of serious matters, of things I had never talked or scarcely thought about before, she did so with such a light touch, with such color and emphasis, yet with such warmth and humor, that I realized that the circumstances of the Ferguson-Pierson intrigue were no more than the joining of two forms for immediate release and profit.

Lady looked down at my hand lying in her palm, enclosed it with her other one, and pressed it warmly. "This you must believe," she said, holding my gaze with an intent and profound expression, her eyes searching mine, "this you must absolutely believe if you will ever believe anything I shall ever tell you. It is not the coming together or the parting of two people that counts, or where or when, but those two people themselves, and in what manner they are joined. And if it is not with hate but with love, not with impatience but with understanding, and never with boredom but with interest, then nothing can be wrong with their being together, no matter how wrong it may seem to others. But those others, they do not count, they must not be permitted to count, for it is only between the two persons themselves that it must have meaning. It is not so difficult for people to arrange their lives sensibly if they behave sensibly, but to arrange their lives happily, that is a far, far different thing. Can you understand this?"

It was a lot to understand, but I tried, and she saw that I tried, that I knew somehow it was in that moment most important that I should understand.

"You cannot hope to do it all at once." She lifted her top hand again and traced the lines in my palm with her fingernail. "It can only come with time. But if you will try to start believing this now, when you are just so old, it will be easier and more profitable to you when you are ready."

"What will I be ready for?"

"You will be ready to love someone in the way that you can hope to love someone, with all of yourself."

She plucked a leaf from my sleeve, and absently ran her fingertips up and down. "You see, life is hardly ever one thing or another, and things don't ever stay the same. Perhaps that's one of life's tragedies. But who knows, perhaps it's one of life's blessings as well. And blessings, as we know, always come mixed. But meanwhile— isn't it a beautiful world? Look at that sky, doesn't it make you feel *good?* It's not such a bad place, is it?"

"What isn't?"

"The world. It's not our enemy, you know, but we treat it so badly. And the same with people. And you will have your share of mixed blessings, l'il Ignatz."

Later, we walked back up Talcott Hill together, and standing at the crest we looked back upon the scene, the pond and pasture, the Paulus farm, others more faintly distant, the woods where we had walked, where winter had become spring, where the whole sense of change was apparent to the eye. And I sensed, even if I was not completely aware, that in the farmhouse and the barn, in the field and the meadow, there were pain and joy and hurt and love, all the good things and the bad, too, all those mixed blessings of life; but that where the sky could look so blue, the grass so freshly green, there lay hope as well, that the human heart was lifted and that God was inclined toward it.

"It could all be so beautiful," she said as we turned to go, "if people were just kind." I said I thought she was very wise. She laughed and tugged my ear. "Ah," she said, taking my hand again, "what is more wise than to be kind? And what is more kind than to under- stand?"

PART THREE

Sad Songs

I

It seemed a new beginning, but perhaps it was only an old ending, the end of innocence merely, not a beginning at all. I had thought I had learned something, had advanced a stride or two in the painful process of maturing, had responded in measure to Lady's summons to my awareness of that greater and more enigmatic life at work around me, but in this I was to be proved wrong. Understanding does not necessarily come with the accumulation of years, but with a willingness to understand, and when my chance came I was unwilling, and thus incapable; and through this stubborn unwillingness a breach opened between us that was to alter our relationship forever.

But, for the moment, her reappearance in our lives was a sort of epiphany, for like the spring itself, she in her full-flowering way had shone forth again, once more to establish herself as the center of our lives, and for a time all proceeded in what appeared to be our normal fashion. Yet there were signs indicating that though things might seem the same, in truth they were not. Changes in people, external changes, do not immediately make themselves apparent to children, yet children, with those sensitized antennae they develop for their own protection, are often aware of things no one gives them credit for. They perceive things unnoticed, they are privy to small, unspoken bits of knowledge which they hoard like misers, fitting one bit to another and forming a picture which suits, or sometimes fails to suit, their needs. And so, though I was not even into my teens, I saw, or thought I did, changes in Lady which troubled me. She had often seemed vague, preoccupied, even melancholy, but now, although she was much in evidence around the house, around the Green and the town, the symptoms appeared aggravated by who knew what causes. Whenever I went over after the day of our spring walk, as I had come to think of it, I noticed that she was particularly nice to Jesse, as if in apology for her harsh words and bad behavior;

was especially nice to everyone. But there were other things. She developed a habit of unconsciously rubbing one palm against the other in a light, circular motion, then spreading both palms in her lap and idly staring at them. Her hands were always one of her greatest beauties, and Aggie said that a woman's age often shows itself first in the extremities. Perhaps it was only that; but I didn't think so.

One day, in the summerhouse, she lifted her hand, inspecting its back closely, and I thought she was distressed by the liverish-colored spots that had begun appearing there. Then I saw it was a small insect that had captured her attention.

"Ladybug, ladybug, fly away home," she softly recited, "your house is on fire, your children will burn. . . ." She flicked the insect with her nail; it parted its spotted carapace as it sailed upward, spreading little transparent wings which bore it away into the blue of the sky. When it had disappeared, she turned her hands over and studied her palms.

"Are you reading your future?" I kidded.

"Read the future?" She looked at me blankly, then folded her hands and brightened her tone. "Palmistry is an inexact science, darling. Better you should look there and play gypsy." She pointed to the gazing-globe, which stood in the center of the brick circle at the opposite end of the walk from where we were sitting. The gazing-globe had appeared shortly after the hair-cutting episode, and seemed to have some special, if undisclosed, significance for Lady. Bought from Mr. Marini, it was a handsome ornament: the large silver ball crowned a curved stone pedestal cast in the ornate Italian fashion, and gleamed brightly amid the green foliage and white flowers behind it. Lady's immense fondness for the globe was manifested by the extended periods she would spend looking at its curved reflection, and, as now, her glance was often directed to it while we sat in the summerhouse and conversed quietly and the dusk came on and the bats flittered in the pine boughs and the fire-flies started.

Still, she appeared so jumpy and nervous that people other than myself or Jesse and Elthea began noticing it. Ruthie Sparrow took it upon herself to bestow a few ill-chosen words, and for her pains got what she might have expected: the back of Lady's hand—figuratively speaking. Capturing her briefly while Lady was out with Honey for a stroll, Mrs. Sparrow had advised her "sensibly," as she later put it to Ma, that what Lady wanted was a change, that she ought to go away ("for her health, poor dear") and take a nice trip. (Paris France or Venice It'ly immediately suggested themselves.) These humble profferings Lady had accepted with her usual grace and good humor, but then Mrs. Sparrow went a step too far, saying that in her opinion Lady was dwelling too much on the long-ago past; what she really ought to do was lock up all of Edward's pictures and the war medal, and his clothing in the chifforobe should be got rid of, and she should accept one of Colonel Blatchley's oft-repeated proposals and make a December-December marriage.

Lady was not inclined. She did not fancy being referred to as a winter bride, nor was she receptive to the remarks about Edward's things.

"The chifforobe will remain as it is," she had declared coldly, her face turning white, her eyes tossing sparks. As on the occasion with Mr. Sprague and the dog, her anger could be awe-inspiring, and so it proved this day. Stay the chifforobe did, contents and all, though the shrine on the gate-leg table, having been put away, did not re-appear, and in its place Lady set out framed pictures of each of us, "her family."

The actual reason for what may have been troubling Lady during these weeks seemed to me, possessed of private knowledge, quite clear. Since the flood, the Green had dried up again, and all had resumed its natural appearance, except for one curious instance which occurred early that summer. Water began continually seeping up through the turf close to the roadway just opposite her front door. This soggy phenomenon became the cause of conjecture, and when the WPA engineers arrived to survey the situation it was thought that something was amiss with the new sewer line. They decided to dig up the spot and discover the trouble, and as the re-excavation commenced, and we stopped over to observe its progress, we could see Lady in her window, watching with concern.

It was the *corpus delicti,* of course, that was causing her alarm. I felt more certain than ever that Mr. Ott had not left the house on that fatal night, but that Jesse had somehow managed to sequester the body in the open sewer excavation, and had shoveled in enough earth to bury it before the job had been completed. But by the end of the week, when fifteen feet of the line had been dug up, nothing untoward was found, other than that the pipes had been laid on an upgrade, a fact Porter Sprague and his clique of Roosevelt-haters made capital of: the WPA couldn't even lay a sewer properly. The mistake rectified, the excavation was refilled, the turf tamped down in squares, and the workmen retired from the scene. Lady evinced visible relief at this, while I, ever the detective, racked my brain. If the *corpus delicti* was not in the coal bin, not in an attic trunk, and to all appearances not in the sewer line, what had become of it?

Some weeks later, Ruthie Sparrow was pleased to discover that her helpful hints had not been totally wasted, for Lady announced that she was going away. An elderly German couple named Hoffman, friends of her father's, who lived in Garden City, Long Island, were traveling to Europe, and Lady was driving down to New York to see them off on the *Queen Mary*. She would also visit her old friend Mrs. Hooper, the woman who had given us Patsy, and afterward she planned to go on to Virginia Beach for a short stay. Elthea and Jesse would accompany her. On a Friday afternoon the house was closed, the keys and Honey given into our safekeeping, and off they went in the new Packard Lady had bought that spring.

Alas for the Minerva landaulet; it seemed to us the end of an era.

Before leaving, Lady had loaned Ag her newly purchased copy of *Gone With the Wind,* and our romantic sister holed up in her room with the book, playing Tchaikovsky on the record player. We hardly saw her for the better part of four days. I, for one, couldn't understand all the fuss about this "O'Hara" person and someone called "Red" Butler, but when Ag turned the last page she emerged in delirium, declaring tearfully that Scarlett just had to get Rhett back. Next day she went out and fell in love with the third-oldest son of the vegetable man.

Unhappily, the romance did not proceed well. It was first stormy, then flaccid, then it petered away to nothing. The vegetable man's son did not want our sister, so poor Ag, drippy, dreamy, and all forlorn, shut herself up again and reread *Gone With the Wind* for another four days while the house echoed with the *Pathétique*.

Soon after, we made an excursion with Nancy, one that was to have far-reaching consequences. A small fair was to be held at Meadowland, and Ma gave Nancy the Saturday off so she might visit her friends at the correctional school in Middlehaven. Between them they coaxed Ag to go along, and though I didn't want to, I ended up on the trip as well. Since both Lew and Harry had been invited to watch the National Guard drill team practice at the armory, and I was unable to tag along, Nancy included me in her junket, a prospect which did little to cheer me.

Miss Beale, the social worker who made trimonthly visits to the houses around town where the various hired girls were employed,

came in a jitney with a driver to pick up the girls, and Ag and I
were loaded aboard. I was feeling plain mean, my mood aggravated
by my being the only male, but there was so much joking and
laughter among the riders that my cloud of discontent gradually
dispersed, and Ag, in spite of herself, was soon laughing along with
the rest.

It wasn't much of a fair, the merest of makeshift booths set up on
the grounds, displaying handicrafts and hobby trifles made by the
women. Though I looked for bars at the windows of the various
buildings, I saw none. Meadowland was nothing like my idea of a
reformatory, but more like a college campus, with its white-trimmed
brick dormitories, its broad lawns and neat landscaping where visitors casually strolled among the flowered borders.

Nancy led us from booth to booth, renewing old acquaintances
with girls she had known when she'd stayed there, and telling them
how things were in Pequot, pridefully producing us from behind her
skirts as specimens of her new status. Ag, shy as always, was not
very talkative, and presently she drifted off and sat under a tree by
herself; but I, having shaken off my earlier sullenness, found myself the center of considerable attention, and boldly engaged the girls
in talk, dragging out my repertory of schoolboy jokes, accepting a
piece of bubble gum from one, a taffy apple from another, popcorn
from a third.

I saw a car pull up the drive, and Mrs. Sheffield, the supervisor,
and Miss Beale went to meet it. Mrs. Sheffield was an imposing
woman whose geniality belied the importance of her position. She
was all smiles as she greeted the new arrivals: Porter and Mrs. de
Sales-Sprague. We had heard that, as one of Pequot's selectmen, Mr.
Sprague was representing the town at the proceedings. He fell
quickly to striding about in his cocky way, inspecting the girls as if
they were army privates and he a general on parade, while Mrs.
Sprague scanned the scene and plied Mrs. Sheffield with questions
regarding the "welfare of the inmates." Terminating her interview,
she mingled with the girls, and put on her dreadful smile as she
fingered braided place mats and poked at crocheted doilies with
fanatical interest.

Nancy said we'd be eating soon, and not to go far. I sat down on
some steps, where the American flag hung limply on a flagpole,
watching Ag, who was still under the tree, poring over a book of
poems Lady had given her. I felt sorry for her, she was so unhappy.
There she sat in her freshly ironed dress, a dreamy schoolgirl moon-

ing over the vegetable man's son, but I thought how pretty she was, how she was losing that gangly, all-legs-and-arms look. She'd put some curl in her hair and tied it back with a pale blue ribbon, and it shone from the nightly brushings she'd been giving it under Lady's instruction. Her chest was getting bumps, her complexion had cleared up, and her cheeks, which had always been red, were a new, peachy kind of color. She was like a summer flower about to bloom.

Then, in the background, Rabbit and Dora Hornaday appeared. Nancy had said they'd be there to visit with their mother, but just now they were alone, and each stayed separate from the other as if they were embarrassed by one another's company, Rabbit staring up at some birds on a wire, while Dora looked both blank and disconsolate, and tugged at the end of the bow her aunt had stuck in her hair.

A bell sounded, and Mrs. Sheffield came along with the Spragues, calling for everyone to go to the dining hall for lunch. Spying Dora, Spouse tittered to her hostess and hurried across the grass, arms outstretched.

"Why, here's little Dora Hornaday. Now, now, now, Dora, mustn't pull our pretty bow." She made an elaborate to-do of retying the ribbon, while P.J. stopped with Mrs. Sheffield on the walk. I could tell it was all for her benefit, one of Spouse's I-love-kiddies acts. "Isn't it a lovely fair, Dora? What have we been doing today?" Dora's thumb swooped into her mouth, sparing her the necessity of talk, but Mrs. Sprague was having none of that. Unsticking the thumb, she reiterated her question. "Dora, tell Mrs. Sprague what you've been doing today. At the fair?" Bending, she made a large lap, and drew the protesting Dora onto it. I hoped that maybe Dora had a rock handy, but she submitted with her usual scowl, ignoring the fuss being made over her.

Mrs. Sprague dug in her pocketbook and produced a Reed's paloop and wafted it under Dora's nose. When Dora grabbed at it, she held it beyond arm's reach. "No, dear, you may have the lollipop when you have spoken nicely to Mrs. Sprague. Now what have we done today?"

Dora scrunched her eyes, and then blurted out one expanding stream of words, retailing every last item of possible interest since she had left home for Meadowland, speaking so fast that Mrs. Sprague's brows shot up above her glasses as she took it in. Then Dora was set back on her feet, and Mrs. Sprague rose and marched off with her husband, promising that Dora might have the Reed's

paloop after lunch. Mrs. Sheffield called to Dora and Rabbit Hornaday, and they went off toward the dining hall. When Nancy found
me and Ag, I asked where Mrs. Hornaday was.

"Her name's not Hornaday, honey. Her name's Zelinski. Kids
took that aunt's name. *She's* a Hornaday."

"Why'd they do that?"

"Maybe she don't want folks to know they're Polacks."

We went to the dining hall, where Ag and I got in line with the
girls. There was meat loaf, mashed potatoes, and eggplant and
coleslaw. I ate the meat loaf and potatoes and coleslaw readily
enough, but we'd never had eggplant at home, and I found it very
foreign. Seeing my untouched portion, Ag gave me a look, and while
no one was looking she switched plates with me.

Our table was served by one of the women, who had already
eaten, and when we had finished, she began clearing the things onto
a tray, which she carried toward a service door. She held the tray
on the flat of one hand, and had reached with the other to push the
door, when it sprang open in her face. She stepped back quickly,
the tray slipped to the floor, and silver clattered and glass and china
crashed. Through the door backed a chef in a tall white hat and an
apron, while behind him came a kitchen worker. She seemed the
most woebegone creature imaginable; her green uniform was
wrinkled and stained, the white collar limp. Her face was blotched
red from her labors in the kitchen, and in her hand she held a saucepan, which she wielded threateningly at the chef.

It was a chaotic scene: the girl who'd dropped the tray cried in
dismay as she bent to pick up the scattered things, the chef and
the other woman loudly confronted one another at the open door,
and the other kitchen helpers crowded around to watch.

"You think you're God Almighty in there, don't you!" the young
woman railed, while the chef turned with outspread hands to face
the hall in frustrated appeal. "Whatsa to be done with her—she's a
cra-zee!" His further remonstrance was silenced as Mrs. Sheffield,
who had risen from her place at the staff table, marched down the
aisle, clapping her hands for silence.

"Go back to the kitchen," she ordered the chef, then turned to the
woman. "Helen, go to your room."

The poor thing started to protest angrily; then her face flushed
even more and she looked about uncertainly.

"At once, Helen." Mrs. Sheffield's voice rang through the hall with
formal authority. With a despairing gesture, the chef retreated into

the kitchen, while Helen fled to the corner, barricading herself behind a chair, saucepan at the ready.

"Helen, give me the pan." Mrs. Sheffield's voice was firm but calm. I felt sorry for the woman; her face was pinched with emotion and she needed to blow her nose. She looked both pathetic and vulnerable, yet her expression was defiant as she cowered behind the chair in fear and embarrassment. Still she would not surrender the saucepan.

"Very well, Helen." Mrs. Sheffield turned with a resigned air to Miss Beale, who rang a small bell at the table. The doors at the far end of the hall bulged inward, revealing a large female officer in a gray uniform and badge.

"Mama!"

Dora Hornaday's voice cried out as she stood. I realized that the woman with the saucepan must be her mother, Mrs. Zelinski. Rabbit scraped his chair back and stood beside her, watching the matron advance. Her grim expression read trouble as she came with a menacing scowl toward Helen's corner. Rabbit's napkin was tied around his neck, and he blinked behind his glasses, his mouth opening and closing several times, but no words came. Then I realized he was wetting his pants: a dark stain spread down the front of his shorts and a puddle grew on the floor beside his chair. He seemed unaware of what he was doing as the matron continued purposefully down the aisle.

"All right, dearie, no nonsense, now." About to step around our table, the matron found her way blocked by a chair. Ag darted forward, with a glance to Mrs. Sheffield, then hurried to Helen, who lofted the pan as she approached. The matron halted at Mrs. Sheffield's signal, and Ag began speaking to Helen.

"Mrs. Zelinski, my name is Agnes Woodhouse. That's my brother, Woody, and that's Nancy—she works for us. We're all friends of Rab—Harold's. And Dora's, too. Last summer Harold went camping with my brothers. And Dora comes around to play sometimes. And Harold and Dora came today to see you. They've been waiting for you to get off work."

Helen Zelinski had lowered the saucepan and was listening with bewildered interest. There was not a murmur in the room. Neither the matron nor Mrs. Sheffield had made a move since Ag started talking.

"Maybe," she continued, "—well, if you put down the pan, maybe you could get to see them. I know they'd like that. I'm sure they've been looking forward . . ."

I couldn't believe it. There Ag stood, before the whole hall, talking in that sweet, quiet voice of hers, as if she were in Sunday school, the focus of everyone's eyes, and she wasn't even blushing. Boy, Ag, I thought, do I love *you!*

"He's awfully clever, you know," she was saying to Helen. "He knows all sorts of things—about animals and cars, and I'll bet he doesn't tell you about his report card. He just gets the best marks at school, and—you should really be very proud of him and—my goodness, why don't you let me take the—the—?"

Mrs. Zelinski's look flashed surprise as Ag reached and drew the pan from her unclenched fingers, handing it in back of her to the astonished matron. Then, taking Mrs. Zelinski's hand, she moved the chair aside, and brought her from the corner. She glanced at Mrs. Sheffield, who nodded, and led Mrs. Zelinski back up the aisle toward the far doors, guiding her with one hand cupped on her elbow, the other making comforting patting motions at her back.

"Very well, girls," Mrs. Sheffield called when they had gone out, "let us continue our lunch." The matron barged out through the kitchen door with the saucepan, and the hall quickly broke into a thunderclap of talk.

After lunch, during the sack and potato races, I heard a constant flow of comment about what a dreadful person Helen Zelinski was, with several people wondering who the little girl was that had calmed her down. Didn't she know Helen was dangerous? Apparently not, for Ag had spent the period of the races engaged in a conversation with Mrs. Sheffield on the steps of the administration building, and later I saw her run into one of the dormitories. Nancy had gotten Rabbit cleaned up and dried off, and he and Dora now sat idling on the swings beside the softball field. A few moments later Ag came out with Mrs. Zelinski, and they went to join them.

Later, when the races were over, the visitors began their leave-taking. I looked around for Nancy, then walked over to the swings, where Ag was pushing Dora, while Rabbit spoke with his mother. They talked back and forth for some time, she nervously running her hands along the chains and scuffing the toes of her shoes in the dirt. Then she took something from her pocket, and Rabbit ran off toward the ring of booths, which were being closed up and dismantled.

The matron was marching about the grounds with a megaphone, announcing that it was "quarters hour" in five minutes, and Nancy

came to round us up; Miss Beale was ready to drive us back to
Pequot. I went over to find Mrs. Zelinski with Dora on her lap,
earnestly talking to Ag. As I approached, Dora yanked away from
her mother, retreating to the farthest swing, where she put her
thumb in her mouth and eyed me silently. When Ag said I was her
brother, Mrs. Zelinski caught me by both arms, pulling me to
her and looking at me with tearful eyes.

"Geez—thanks. Just—thanks."

I had no idea what she was thanking me for, and my glance
traveled to Ag, who said nothing, only went over to push Dora's
swing.

"You know my boy, Harold," Mrs. Zelinski said. "Harold was telling me about you and your family. He says he wishes he looked like
you."

"He must mean my brother, Lew. I'm Woody."

"That's who. He says he wishes he looked like Woody." I didn't
know what to make of that. I thought Rabbit could have chosen a
more likely model; still, I was pleased.

"Be friends with him, please? It'd mean a lot to me, knowin' he's
got friends like you kids."

I marveled at the change in her. She'd put on a clean uniform,
and her hair was brushed and held back with a celluloid barrette.
Her outburst in the hall aside, I thought her mild-mannered, meek
almost. There was something particularly engaging in the way she
caught my glance and gave me a good look, trying to establish some
bridge of communication, and then dropped her eyes, as if unused
to such contact with another person.

"It makes it a lot easier, being in a place like this, to know your
kids are doing okay. You in the same grade as Harold?"

"He's a year ahead."

Just then Rabbit came running up, holding something in his hand.
He darted a look at me as he gave it to his mother. It was a cheap
Woolworth's compact, decorated with designs applied in nail polish,
and some sequins glued on.

"I guess you don't use rouge yet, Aggie," Helen said, calling her
over and giving her the compact, "but one of these days you will,
and when all those boys start comin' round, you want to look your
best. . . ."

Rabbit took his mother's hand and put a duplicate compact in it.
"What's that for?"

"For you." Rabbit stuck his fists into his pockets and blinked.

"Harold—you shouldn't ought to spend your money on me. Geez." She shook her head, then drew the children to her and kissed them both. "You gotta spend it on yourself, money's hard to come by these days."

"Don'tcha like it?"

Her chin quivered, and her eyes teared up again as she looked at the cheap compact. "Sure," she said gruffly, then she buried her head against Rabbit's shoulder. Ag grabbed my hand and we walked away from the swings to where Nancy and Miss Beale were waiting with the others for the ride home.

2

Lady Harleigh came back with Jesse and Elthea ten days later. She looked refreshed and healthy, and though she didn't talk much about their trip, she seemed to have enjoyed her stay away. Elthea had a crepe-paper lei for each of us, having realized her dream of going to the Aloha Room at that hotel in New York. Lady had seen her friends the Hoffmans off for Southampton on the *Queen Mary,* whence they were to go on to Germany, where they had relatives. Jesse, however, was not feeling well after his return, and though he insisted upon cleaning and sprucing the house up, he soon took to his bed for several days.

Lady was most interested to hear of our visit to Meadowland, which Ag related in all its details one evening in the summerhouse, and the next day together they drove down in the Packard to Middlehaven, where Lady had an interview with Mrs. Sheffield, and another with Helen Zelinski. Upon her return, she conferred with Dr. Brainard, and Dora Hornaday was put into the hands of doctors at a Hartford clinic who were to investigate her ear trouble. I also noted that Rabbit was soon wearing new glasses.

It was August when we learned of Blue Ferguson's whereabouts. We knew that his mother had received some letters, postmarked New York, but with no return address. Now the Hartford *Times* had a story that he was listed as leaving for Spain with members of the Lincoln Brigade, who had volunteered to fight with the Loyalists. Porter Sprague took up his post in front of the barbershop, insisting that the Lincoln Brigade was nothing but a pack of Communists, and that Joe Stalin was sending planes to the Loyalists they were fighting with.

I was happy for Blue. In my mind the tarnish of previous events had worn off, and I no longer regarded him as that sullied delivery boy whose market basket I had buried in the drift to spare him shame. Somehow I knew that Blue was going to redeem himself, and that he'd come back to town a hero.

Ma had managed to scrape up the money to send Ag—still mooning over the vegetable man's son—to camp for two weeks, and while she was gone, an unhappy incident befell our house. Lady had left Honey with us while on her trip, and the dog had become used to being around our kitchen. She and our Patsy got on well enough, until one day in the hottest weather Patsy must have been feeling the heat, because she went for Honey at feeding time, and there was a wild scramble on the kitchen linoleum. Lew safely dragged Honey off by the collar, but when Kerney tried to catch Patsy, she bit him. It was only Kerney's toe, and he had a sneaker on, but there were teeth marks. Lew took Patsy out to the back yard while Harry and I diddled Kerney until he calmed down—he was more frightened than anything else. When Ma came home, she patiently heard the story; then, without saying anything more, she put down her purse, took off her hat, and went out back to talk to Lew.

We watched through the downstairs bathroom window. Lew was leaning against the crab-apple tree, with Patsy haunched between his knees while he stroked her, listening to Ma, who sat talking beside him on the grass. None of us could imagine why Patsy had done such a thing, except that she was already pretty old when she originally came to us. We figured she must be fourteen by now. Lew had always said she looked like Asta in the Thin Man pictures, and he really loved that dog; never went anywhere without her.

Ma stayed under the tree when Lew came in carrying Patsy in his arms. He was crying. It was an awful moment—Lew was the oldest and while we'd seen him mad often enough, neither Harry nor I had ever known him to cry. He went upstairs, washed his face and combed his hair, came down with a piece of rope which he tied to Patsy's collar, and led her away. Harry and I went out and sat on the porch and waited until he came back just before supper, without Patsy. He went up to his room and wouldn't eat. I felt terrible for him, remembering that evening we'd gotten Pat from Mrs. Hooper at the Manor House Inn and how I'd gone off behind the hotel crying, and wouldn't eat my dinner.

We knew what had happened to Pat. Ma had told Lew that she must be put away. She'd offered to arrange the matter herself, but Lew had said that Patsy was his dog and if anybody was going to take her to be gassed, it would be him. After that, he always kept her empty collar hung over the post on his bunk, until he went off and was killed in the war.

One evening Miss Berry called over the fence from her kitchen steps, and I went to see what she wanted. It was cereal boxes, about six months' worth, stacked on her back porch.

"Gee, Miss Berry, we don't send box tops anymore."

She peered at me through her spectacles with a dubious expression. "Aren't they any good?"

"Oh, sure, but that's for kids."

"Goodness, no more Tim McCoy? Well, I guess you're growing up—pretty soon you'll be tall enough to see over the top of my fence without peeking through the knothole, eh? And I s'pose Kerney's too young for box tops." She sighed, plugged in an outdoor cord, and came down the steps with some electrical paraphernalia. "Now I'm all tangled up, aren't I?"

"Yes, Ma'am." I followed her out to her front lawn, untangling a maze of wires for her as we went. Selecting a spot on the grass, she drove two metal shafts into the ground, explaining that they were electrified, and then sat on her stoop awaiting the bounty of night crawlers which soon came winding up through the lawn, numb from the storm of current buzzing below ground.

"Sorry to hear about your dog, little Patsy. Will you be having another?"

I shrugged; Ma hadn't said anything about another dog. Miss Berry patted my hand, and arranged herself more comfortably on the step. I liked Miss Berry; everyone did. I suppose people more or less took her for granted, like Miss Shedd at the library. She was just around, like a fact of life. She was prudent and wise and respected, but no one really knew her, unless it was her friend Gert Flagler. Though she kept to her own sun parlor and doorstoop, seldom mingling with the townsfolk, she had for years been part and parcel of the community. Hers was the blood of her Puritan ancestors, and the sturdy fiber of the New Englander, hewed and strengthened since the days of the Pequots. Fortitude is not an assumed guise; it is formed in the marrow, bred in the bones through generations. Miss Berry had the virtues of the Yankee, without his vices. She was no bigot, no horse-with-blinders, and if she had her prejudices she kept them well to herself. To me, she smacked of other, older days, of collecting maple sap on frosty mornings, of sun-dried apples, stone walls, spade-bearded farmers, unspoiled woods and fields; days gone by.

The Berrys had been among the earliest settlers in Pequot, boasting a number of sea captains back in the trading days when the town had been a river port. One of her forebears had sailed as mate on the first American ship to circumnavigate the globe, three hundred years after Magellan. Others in her family had piloted the riverboats I so treasured the memory of. Miss Berry could recall much of the town's history and was full of stories about things she'd heard as a girl from her grandfather, about what life had been like around the Green a hundred years ago. In her great-grandfather's time, cattle and sheep had grazed right there near the Great Elm, fenced in against the wolves that would come and carry them off. Over there, at Colonel Blatchley's house, there'd been an inn, for the first Boston Post Road had gone right past our doors before George Washington's time. Over there, where the Piersons had lived, a spinster miss had devised a way to harvest the local marsh grass and weave it into ladies' bonnets that were every whit as good as the Italian leghorn ones. Where Mr. Paulus's barn stood was the original site of the first corn mill in Pequot, while the old Academy Hall had originally been a seminary for young ladies. Miss Berry herself had once attended the "little red schoolhouse," a one-room antique which still stood at the corner of Valley Hill Road and Welles Street.

It was presently used as a police station, and was close to the house that Lady's mother had lived in when she moved from Knobb Street. I mentioned the fact, and asked what she had been like.

"Old Mrs. Strasser?" Miss Berry gathered and smoothed her ample skirts and folded them onto her lap. "She had a mind of her own, I expect." I suspected Miss Berry was being tactful; most people who'd known her didn't care for Lady's mother. I'd seen pictures of her: a short, squat, stolid-looking woman, with a grim-featured peasant face that made me think of a large potato. She had never lost her thick German accent, and was generally considered to be well below Mr. Strasser's station. Mr. Strasser had been an intellectual, a college professor, and from him Lady had inherited both her looks and her passion for conversation and the arts. I always thought that perhaps her Katzenjammer voice was poking fun at her mother, a mild reproach to beyond the grave.

"She sewed well enough," Miss Berry added. "But she didn't make Adelaide's life any the easier, I can tell you."

"Why?"

"I suppose because she ruled the roost. Ruled her husband, ruled her daughter, and had it all her own way. Such folks usually do. She sent Lady out to bring home the bacon for her, so to speak. Lady has always been too generous a soul. A dear one, if ever there was."

She fell to reminiscing of that long-ago time, even before Lady had married Edward Harleigh and moved to the Green, when she had lived on Knobb Street and kept house for her mother and father. Another Lady, not much older than I, in pinafores and braids, carrying a lunch pail to school, a Bible to church, Lady in button boots and a fur muff, a Lady of maiden innocence and propriety, a girl when McKinley was President, when there were oil lamps on Main Street, and the horsecars went by. I basked in the warmth of Miss Berry's words, she spoke so admiringly of Lady, and when she had done I bragged that Lady's name for me was Ignatz, that we were boom compenions, and that she called me the friend of her youth.

"Then you are most fortunate," Miss Berry replied, "to have someone to remember always. She will stay with you. But as you are the friend of her youth, so you must be the friend of her age, too. She has needed friends."

"She's got lots of friends."

"I venture to say she has. And deservedly so."

"But if you're friends," I said, "how come you never—" I bumped my head toward Lady's house. Miss Berry smiled.

"She lives on her side of the Green, and I live on mine. It is not always necessary to exchange visits to be a party to another person's life. We are both private people, she and I, and I respect her privacy as she does mine. I am here if I can help her; she knows that." She began gathering the stunned worms which had wriggled up, and putting them in a coffee can.

"What do you do with them?" I asked.

"Feed them to the birdies—or save them for Jesse—he uses them fishing." She wiped her hands on the grass and resumed her seat on the stoop. "You walk with Lady often, there, around our Green, don't you? I see you from my sun porch. Adelaide has sometimes been sad, and not without reason, but with you she has been gay, and that's nice to see. It was always good to hear her laugh." She gave me a quizzical glance. "I heard you, Christmas Eve, singing to her."

"'Good Night, Lady.'"

"'Good Night, Lady,' yes."

"What was Mr. Harleigh like? Her husband?"

"Edward?" She considered for a moment, looking over to the Green where Elthea and Jesse had appeared in the roadway, with Honey on her leash. "Edward was like any man who has too much of one thing and not enough of another. He expended himself very quickly. He was a prodigal, Edward Harleigh. Jesse must be some better, eh? Heard he'd been feeling poorly."

True; it was the first time I'd seen Jesse outdoors since he'd taken to bed after his return. Elthea, her arm through his, was leaning to his ear and confiding something in a private way, and he laughed, then unsnapped the leash, and Honey ran in circles around the Great Elm.

"I never thought to see Adelaide Harleigh with another dog," Miss Berry observed thoughtfully.

"Why?"

"Oh—" She became suddenly aware, and gave a half-hearted shrug. "I just didn't. That poor, voiceless animal—I suppose Adelaide was determined to give it a home. They're the best couple, Elthea and Jesse," she continued, "though I'm not sure he ought to be frolicking so." Jesse had gone chasing after Honey, and Elthea called for him to come back.

"How come they never got to New York?"

"Eh? How's that?" Miss Berry was always a little hard of hearing.

"Edward. He took her on the *City of Springfield*, to New York. But they only got halfway there."

"Ayuh." She nodded in recollection, as if discussing something that had taken place only yesterday. "Got off at Saybrook, come back t'other way."

"How come?"

"Bless you, you're full of questions this evening. I expect you'd better ask the person most nearly concerned about that. As I recall, it was a part of their romance. Lady was ever a romantic, and Edward was the apple—"

"What apple?"

"Of her *eye*, dear. But she was German as well, stubborn as her mother, if it came to that, and I suppose she got balky somewhere down about Essex. They got as far as Saybrook and come back. Lover's spat, nothing more."

"Why does she see his ghost?"

"Pshaw, ghosts are just the workings of a vivid imagination. What she ought to do is clear all those things out and put them away; such reminders aren't healthy for a person."

"That's what Mrs. Sparrow says—"

"Good for Ruthie Sparrow."

"And she did. I guess Colonel Blatchley got her to put the photographs away for the party—and the medal, all of it."

"Why, good for Colonel Blatchley, then. Lady's mind is elaborate, I can say that. Like most thinking folks. Trouble is, hers won't let her rest. Won't let Edward rest, neither."

"But why is she so sad sometimes?"

"We all have hurts. Some are harder t'heal, some never do. A dog licks its wounds in the thicket. Adelaide Harleigh was never one to show her sorrow. We will be her friends and let her come to us if she chooses, or chooses not, however. But what we must do, most simply, is to remember that she is there, and that we are the friends of her youth. Let me include myself, for I am always her friend. And another thing"—here she peered at me most gravely from behind her spectacles— "it is not good to expect too much from people. They give what they can. Sometimes it is all they can give. Ayuh." She confirmed her words with a precise nod, patted my shoulder, and rose. "We all ask too much of one another anyway, I think. But," she concluded before going to collect the last of the worms, "it's good when one feels the affections of the past. They are among the lasting things—they will never leave us."

3

We had noticed that though Jesse was a devout Catholic, he had not recently been attending Mass. Had not, in fact, since the previous autumn around Halloween time, when Mr. Ott had last appeared. But Elthea was a regular churchgoer, and on a Sunday morning I saw her coming down the front walk in her last-Easter's hat and spike heels, but wearing only a modicum of her usual array of jewelry. I was dressed for our own services, and when to my surprise she suggested that I might want to go along with her instead, I quickly agreed; I had never been to the Catholic church, and I looked on it as a sort of adventure, having often wondered what "they" did there.

I still recall the peculiar sensation I had as we went in, as though I were venturing into sinister terrain. I remember that I saw a host of Marinis, taking up the better part of two pews, and a look of surprise on Teresa Marini's face as I followed Elthea in. I watched with awe as she dipped her fingers in the holy water and made the sign of the Cross. I wanted to do likewise, but thought perhaps Protestants weren't allowed to use the Catholics' water. Why didn't we have our own, at our church? I stared at the gilded plaster figures placed in niches along the walls, and the little altar-like affair near the door, with rows of flickering candles in red glass cups. I waited while Elthea dropped a coin in a box, took a taper and lighted a candle, then extinguished the taper in a trough of sand, and knelt to pray. People were always saying that the Catholics were money-minded; I wondered at buying candles, and if I might do the same. I had some change in my pocket.

Then the priest, Father Huegenay, walked in with Gerald Morrisey on one side and another boy on the other, all wearing ankle-length black robes with shorter white garments over them. I had never seen a surplice and I marveled at the elaborateness of their design. Leave it to Gerald Morrisey to be wearing a satin tie like Little Lord Fauntleroy. I stifled a giggle, and the congregation rose while the priest moved up some steps to the altar and the Mass began. It was a strange experience, the hollow-voiced Father chanting in Latin, the congregation repeatedly sitting, kneeling, standing, sitting, then kneeling again—a tedious procedure, I thought—and all by some signal I could not recognize, the ringing of little bells, the smoking censers, the costume and ritual, the small panoply and pomp. I did not trust it. It seemed to me exotic, foreign, even barbaric. I was too young to realize that what "they" were doing was little different from what we in our own church did; different only in the way the service was performed, the worship of God. I became bored and restless by turns, then even irked, thinking that if I must go to church I'd have done better at my own. Didn't they have flowers? Hymnals? Elthea was fully preoccupied with the service, making the ritual response in her soft voice, her head almost continually bowed, her eyes reverently closed, a rosary clutched in her dark fingers.

No wonder Lady had switched to First Church, I thought, scarcely able to imagine her in these pagan surroundings. Again I let my eyes wander, following in the footsteps of my mind. Father Huegenay was a fairly young man—there must have been another priest when Lady used to come here, probably the one who had visited with her after Edward's death; Father O'Brien, Mrs. Sparrow had said his name was. Father Huegenay was in the pulpit—Catholic sermons, I now learned, were every bit as long and boring as Protestant ones—while Gerald Morrisey and the other boy sat on a bench to one side. Gerald had another pimple—he should have splatted it before getting all dressed up in that silly-looking outfit. I felt Elthea's glance as I suppressed a small mirthful noise inside.

I lowered my eyes dutifully until the prayer was concluded; then when Communion began, I watched with interest as people rose and began going to the railing, where the priest offered the Host and Gerald Morrisey followed him along the row of communicants, holding a little gold salver under the wafer as it was given. When a place fell vacant at the railing, Elthea rose and took it.

"*Domine, non sum dignus*," droned Father Huegenay, while Gerald Morrisey showed off in his Sunday costume and Sunday calling, with that same condescending look he always had while clapping the erasers at school.

When church let out, Elthea and I shook hands with the priest, then went to say hello to Papa and Mama Marini, while Teresa stood in the background, watching me with her great dark eyes but saying nothing. I had the feeling she regarded me as an intruder in her church, and then I thought that if she'd come to ours, I would have wondered what she was doing there. Congregationalists, I decided, ought to go to their church, and Catholics to theirs.

On the way home I asked Elthea why Jesse didn't go to church anymore. Though her replies came easily enough, I had the feeling that she was in some way disguising his defection, and passing it off as a mere trifle.

"Jesse doesn't like coming to Mass lest he takes Communion," she explained.

"Why doesn't he take Communion?"

"Well, hon, we can't take Communion, lest we go to confession."

"Do you go to confession?"

She threw her head back and laughed. "Oh, *yes*, every Saturday afternoon. I expected Father Huegenay's got cramps, stuck in that box, listening to me tell my sins."

"What kind of sins?" I couldn't imagine Elthea having any sort of sins to confess to anybody.

"Oh, sins aplenty, hon. Not mortal sins, mind you. It's what they call venial sins—like—"

"Like what?"

"Oh, like lying, fibbing, things like that. You look into your heart, there's plenty enough there to confess, without too much looking."

"Has Jesse sinned?"

She clutched her purse and held it to her bosom, and her eyes rolled white. "Lord, no, Jesse hasn't sinned. He *hasn't*."

She said it with such fervor that it had an opposite effect on me. He had sinned, I was sure of it, and I knew how. And because he'd sinned he wouldn't go to church, wouldn't make confession, couldn't take Communion. For his sins he was denied churchgoing, and not the sins of lying, either. His was a mortal sin.

But whatever I thought about Jesse and sinning was soon forgotten, because when we arrived home we learned that Jesse, who had been taking down the awnings during our absence, had fallen from the ladder. Lady had found him among the rhododendrons, and had gotten him to bed. She was waiting for Dr. Brainard. Just before Sunday dinner, the doctor's car pulled up and he got out with his black valise. That afternoon we heard that Jesse had had a stroke and was confined to bed again.

Though no one would admit it, least of all Elthea or Lady, it was a serious matter. Jesse's heart had been weak for a long time, and the doctor had cautioned him against overdoing. But Jesse had never liked sitting around, dawdling, as he called it; there were too many things to do about the house, and though it was Lady's house he took it as his responsibility. Everything always had to be just right for Missus.

Two days later Jesse was taken to the hospital for tests. Released again, he was put to bed in the back spare room and told to stay there. He grumbled and carried on, but even he would now admit that his condition warranted a little care and looking after.

That year, 1936, was an election year, and nearly everybody in town that autumn was boasting a sunflower button enjoining "Vote for Landon"; if it had been up to Pequot Landing, the Kansan Alf would surely have been in the White House by January. Gert Flagler, however, swore that 1937 would see Roosevelt in for his second term, and wouldn't she have whooped if she could have forseen that he would be elected to four terms! Mr. Roosevelt was out stumping the New England states and though he was damned in practically every house in town, we were given time off from school to line up along the Hooker Highway and see him drive by in a motorcade.

Republican or Democrat, I thought he looked as a President should, and I felt proud that I was an American.

After the motorcade, I came straight home from school, since I had an appointment with Lady. Dr. Brainard was just leaving, Jesse was resting, and Elthea was too busy to talk to me. Lady had wished to visit Edward's grave, and would I go with her? We would have a nice fall walk.

Elthea said Lady was upstairs changing, and I went to round up the needed tools in the carriage house. There was a long-handled cultivator she particularly favored when gardening, and I found it up in the loft. Glancing out the dormer window, across the lawn, I could see into her bedroom. Far from dressing, she was sitting on the chaise longue, her chin resting on her hand as she stared down at the gazing-globe in the garden with a thoughtful expression. Because of the angle of the light, the room and all its contents were plain to my eye; it was almost as if I were in the room with her; I could in fact recognize the *Ladies' Home Journal* which lay on her lap, and the gold wedding band gleaming on her finger.

But what of our gardening? Had she forgotten? I rapped on the dormer pane, but she didn't hear. As she changed her position slightly, the magazine slid unnoticed from her lap. When Elthea went and got her, she was all apologies. Yes, she admitted, she'd forgotten our plan, and hurried to change.

At the grave we set in the bright autumn flowers we'd bought at the Marini farm; they would last until a frost, Lady said.

"How old is Jesse?" I asked as I troweled and she cultivated.

"Do you know, I've never really been quite sure."

"What does the doctor say?"

"Oh, pooh, Jesse will be fine. Certainly he will." She said it with such conviction it only brought home to me again how dependent she was on her two faithful friends, Jesse and Elthea, for all that people considered them only servants. In my mind's eye I could see them, Elthea in her starched cap and apron, and he coming into the room in the late afternoon in his slippers, asking, "Will that be all, Mrs. Harleigh?" Knowing he would in a moment bring in the martinis he'd already prepared; and later we would hear his slippers on the stairs as he followed Elthea up.

We washed off the flowerpots which Lady always saved for sprouting seedlings at home, and though the work was done, still she seemed inclined to linger at the grave, fussing and making further small adjustments to the plantings. Finally she said the last

"There," which meant she was satisfied; then she spent some minutes in the church, and we left for home.

We arrived almost at sunset. I put the tools back, and when I came out I found Lady sitting in the summerhouse. It had grown chilly and she had put on the old sweater from the back porch. She seemed tired. In addition to the cemetery gardening, she had been working around the house all day, helping Elthea, whose many duties had increased since Jesse's collapse. When I joined her in the summerhouse, Lady gave me a fleeting smile and said she was having a moment by herself. I started to leave, but she asked me to sit with her. I remembered what she had told me once about "solitary feeding," and was willing to respect her silence. But this afternoon she seemed communicative, saying that Mr. Marachek, the postman, had brought a letter that morning from the Hoffmans, who were in Berlin, where Lady had been born.

"What is Berlin like?" I asked.

"Heavens, it was so long ago. Very beery, I should think."

"Don't you remember anything about it?"

"Well, there was a little garden at the back of our house with a fruit orchard, and in the spring all the trees would be in bloom. Like the ones your father planted."

"Is that all?" I was disappointed, imagining she'd have all sorts of stories and recollections.

"I suppose there are other things. I remember Christmas was always wonderful there."

"Better than our Christmases?" For some years now, all of our family had been coming to Lady's for Christmas Eve and Christmas dinner, while she, Jesse, and Elthea, would come over and help us trim our tree. It had become a tradition.

"No, not better. Just . . . different. . . . Childhood Christmases are always different, somehow. I remember the ornament that went at the top of the tree. Papa would hold me up and let me set it on. It was a Saint Nicholas—not a Santa Claus, but an old man with a long white beard and a white robe."

"Like God?"

"Yes, I suppose so—if that's how you picture God. But Germany isn't a good place to live in anymore." She took the letter from her sweater pocket and read parts of it to me. It was filled with news and items of interest, but it sounded as if the Hoffmans were not enjoying the trip to their homeland. Mrs. Hoffman, who'd written the letter, related several witnessed incidents of brutalities in the public streets. I wondered why Germans were being attacked by their own countrymen.

Lady explained that the people beaten were Jewish, but I couldn't understand this. What did their being Jewish have to do with anything? Were they as different as all that? Was it because they had all the money, as I had overheard Mr. Sprague saying? Because they'd put the X in Christmas, making it Xmas, so the Jewish merchants could sell more on the Christian holiday? Miss Berry's mother had been a Rose, descendant of the same Rose family whose daughters had been kidnapped by the Pequots. George and Anne Rosen were the only Jewish kids in town. Rose—Rosen. Was the difference an "n"?

Hitler was a dictator, and we all knew about dictators. Mussolini, Franco, Stalin—there were plenty of those. Totalitarianism was becoming an everyday word in our lexicon. Here in America there were people who said Roosevelt wanted to be a dictator. And there was an entire echelon of minor demagogues, each of whom bore the earmarks of incipient dictatorship: Huey Long (assassinated the year before), Father Coughlin, Senator Rankin—even Mr. Bilbo from Mississippi, who wore gravy-stained shirts in the Senate. Father Coughlin, once an ardent Roosevelt supporter, now damned him from the pulpit, even calling him a Jew, and saying his name was actually Rosenfeld. (This, it appeared, was worse than being a Rosen.) If people knew about these men, I asked Lady, why did they listen?

"Because they want to believe in them," she answered. "But people are seldom really who they appear to be. They are only what they are. Sometimes it takes a lot of work and many years to discover what a person really is." She leaned her chin on her hand and absently ran the edge of her sleeve under her nose—that old back-porch sweater, whose frayed tips fell over her fingers. Her voice was quietly reflective as she continued, "We all wear other faces, it's true. The good are not nearly so good, and, as for the bad, I'm sure they're much worse than people think. But there are bullies the world over. And very shortly the world won't be a very pleasant place to live in anymore—not anywhere. Trouble has a long finger—it can touch so many places."

"There's lots of bad people in the world, aren't there?" I suggested, as if just having counted them.

"I'm sure there are probably more good ones than bad, or else we couldn't have progressed this far. At least it's something to believe in, all the good ones. We must find something to believe in, totally, with all our hearts."

"What should people believe in?"

"My dear, who can tell? That's up to the individual. Perhaps God is as good as the next thing. Until you find a person, someone living . . ."

"Have you believed in someone?"

"Yes, I have. I have believed so much sometimes I thought it would be the death of me . . . the very death. But never be incredulous of people—they will always manage to surprise you."

"How?"

"In all ways. People are people wherever you go—they run to type, they fit categories. At least in my experience they do. But look out for the exception to the rule—they're the ones you have to watch."

Falling silent, she let her glance drift to the gazing-globe, and made a few indistinguishable murmurs, lost in some private reverie. I pictured the grave in the churchyard we had left earlier, and it occurred to me that it was Edward she had been speaking of, that it was his memory she had believed in, and that had sustained her for all these years.

Presently she said, "We must remember to bring the globe in before it gets colder. I'd hate to have it crack in a quick frost."

"Could it?"

"Couldn't it? The glass is very fragile. It's lovely there, isn't it?" she went on musingly. "The perfect spot. Come and look."

She led me down the walkway to the circle of brick, and the globe centered in the middle on its stone pedestal, with a stone bench close by. I glanced at Lady, then picked the globe up between my fingers, and held it.

"Careful, darling, that's a mirror, you know—seven years' bad luck." Unconsciously she touched her hair, and I supposed she was remembering the day she'd smashed her vanity mirror. I replaced the globe, carefully fitting the small glass projection on its underside into the hole in the pedestal, which held the globe in place.

She took my hand and we walked around it, watching ourselves as we moved, first with the shrubbery behind us, then the large elm tree, then the back windows, the drive, the carriage house, another elm, the slope of the lawn, and the bushes again. But we two, we remained the same, and it was like seeing ourselves caught in a little silver world of its own.

"You see what that's like?" she asked.

"Sort of . . ." I voiced my thought about the little silver world.

"But exactly—that's how it is, just that way. If you walked and walked around it for a long, long time, the leaves behind us would turn and then drop and become new leaves again, and the trees would grow taller and older and you would, too, but everything would go on, it would all continue, and you wouldn't even notice the changes." She touched the silver sphere with her finger, whose tip, reflected, enlarged as she made a little circle on the top. Then she drew me down on the stone bench.

"You see how things look whole? Not only your little piece, or someone else's little piece, but all the pieces, all unbroken, all flowing together. It seems to me that when I look in there I can really see what God meant the world to be like. The earth is round, and so is this globe. All is visible, you can see everything in its place, and each thing is in relation to each other thing. Everything is in balance with everything else. That's the way the world should be."

I could see it. I could understand what she was saying. I knew it was exactly that way. We were side by side, seeing ourselves, and our surroundings. It was a way of looking at things, at images, at life, the whole world. Everything seemed to proceed in one unbroken line; everything continued, in time, in space, in existence, all held in that silver globe, and reflected by it.

Still seated on the bench, we fell silent. Around us could be heard the sounds of leaves falling—light, papery sounds. A squirrel rummaged in the chrysanthemums behind us. There was the tang of smoke in the air, and a crisp chill. A bird popped out of the hole in one of Jesse's birdhouses, darting its head about as if wondering where summer had gotten to. Kerney's banged-up tricycle lay where he'd left it, overturned amid the dying hydrangeas. Everywhere the plants had been cut back, tied up, some covered for winter. The luminous dusk came on, the sky dimming in the east, while beyond the Cove long fingers of clouds drew down over the hills of Avalon. Mauve, rose, gray, the colors of the pearl on Lady's little pewter pin box, these were the colors I saw in the sky.

I looked at Lady. Her lips were curved into a smile that I can only describe as bittersweet. She was looking into the gazing-globe, and I turned to see what she might be seeing now. As we watched, behind us, toward the west, the sun, a small autumn ball of cold fire, was held in the curved silver surface, reflected as if from deep within, as light shows the fiery heart of a jewel. Then it dropped, slowly, slowly, seeming to slide down the lower part of the globe as if into another hemisphere. And was gone, and there were only shadows and the light from the sunset sky, and the wind blew cold. Lady pulled her sweater across her front, hugged a shiver out of her, and we went in for tea.

4

By Thanksgiving, Jesse was up and around again, but it became clear that however old we may have imagined him to be, he was yet older, and since the stroke his years were beginning to show. He shuffled, rather than walked, as if by some inner instinct he were purposely shortening his stride to lengthen his life. The skin on the backs of his hands was like dusty dark paper; his face had gradually lost its healthy sheen. His black woolly hair, rather than going gray or white, seemed to have turned rusty, and he fidgeted when Elthea gave it its customary shearing every month or so. He seldom spoke unless spoken to, but was constantly making the growling sounds in his throat, as though in protest against some unseen hand. And if the hand were unseen, still we knew whose hand it was he feared: the hand of death. He appeared grateful for any little attention, or the slightest display of affection. He seemed to draw nearer to Elthea than he had in the past, spending hours in the kitchen in a chair, clasping and unclasping his long fingers, and silently moving his lips or grinding his jaws; when I was there, too, I would catch him looking at her in a way that said he desired to establish some secret communication with her. He kept his chair as near to the stove as he could without getting in Elthea's way, and sought other places to provide himself the warmth his body seemed now to need: by the living-room fire, in a sunny window, even the cellar, where he would position himself close to the furnace or, if the fire was banked, put his back against the asbestos insulation as though to melt the marrow in his old bones.

One day I found him down there, and sensing that he was grateful for the intrusion, I pulled up a box and sat with him to keep him company, whittling on a stick and aimlessly whistling through my teeth. Once he caught my eye and the corners of his mouth twitched in a reluctant smile.

"You've grown some, son."

"I'll be thirteen."

"Twelve's old enough." He nodded, more to himself than to me, I thought, as if remembering what it was like to be twelve. "I think twelve's just fine. You goin' some, mon?"

"I'm sorry—"

"You going 'way from this place or you goin' stay 'round, like some folks do?"

"Well, I'd like to go away, yes."

"She's big."

"Who?"

"The world. Big place, the world. Never seen it, but Daddy did say. Don't you get cotched."

My inability to follow his words made me feel "stupidy," but the finely honed edge of his speech had become blunted; he seemed to have lapsed into some early, recollected speech pattern, the patois of the islands. It was as if he were seeking the safety of his earliest memories, a familiar place he had been too long away from.

"You get cotched by the world, son," he continued reflectively, "you gets your se'f in trouble." "Cotched," I translated as catched. "Well, you go 'way," he went on, "you come back sometimes. You'll have to look after Missus. Someone got to look after Missus after ol' Jesse done turned in his receipts. She a fine lady—*fine* lady. Reckon how long it's ben. Mean, reckon how long I ben hyere. I ben hyere eighteen year come Easter. Long time to live in a house that ain't your own. Well, I guess old Jesse c'n just do some settin' and a-rockin' now. Never will see next Easter."

"Sure you will—"

"No, mon. Never see no mo' Easter. Reckon they'll put me in the ground 'fore then."

He made a bowl with his palms in his lap and stared at them, like a seer divining the future in the creases and wrinkles, but the small repetitive shake of the head seemed to see no future there.

"Not so bad, though. We done better'n collards and chitlins and cabin-cookin'. Elthea cook a good dinner, Missus set a fine table. My, my, all that crystal glassware and silver spoons. Reckon how many silver spoons I polished in my day . . . silver spoons and forks and knives and trays and pitchers, and that one sugar bowl, who could say how many times? My, my, think of a island nigger in such a fine house. Wrote Daddy all about this house, he say, 'Boy, you doin' just fine.' Daddy say, 'You ain't a wasted man.' No, sir, no wasted man with no wasted life. Elthea, now, she's a good girl, don'tcha think so, son? Gives a lot, that Elthea. She a giver, all right. And Missus—Lord, if she don't take the cake and the muffins, too, that Missus woman. Folks set a store by Missus, which is right an' fittin'. Right *an'* fittin'. . . ."

He crossed one leg over his knee, tugging his slipper over his woolen sock, gazing soberly but vacantly into space. After a while, taking notice of his slipper toe, he said, "Reckon how many stitches in such a slipper? Missus does fine needlework, agreed? Sewin' such a pair of slippers for Jesse."

He made a few ruminative sounds, as if assaying for his own satisfaction such a pair of slippers, and the rightness and fitness of the town's esteem for Lady Harleigh. Closing his palms together, he pulled at the finger joints so they cracked in the musty silence, and he leaned his head back so his Adam's apple protruded to fuller prominence. He drew in a breath, then expelled it wearily, as if the next would be more tiredly drawn.

Without looking at me, he asked, "Son, whatcha gonna do with yourself? Still going to be a sailor? Read your Bowditch's, you want to be a sailor. But you got to get your schoolin', that's the thing."

"Why didn't you get to be a doctor?" I asked.

He scratched, rubbed his back against the chair slats like a luxuriating animal, and gave a tentative tug to his suspenders. I wondered why old sober-sided Jesse favored such colorful gear: the violet suspenders, one of his favorite pink and white striped shirts, a gold collar button winking in the hole, but no collar since he'd gotten ill—it was as if he'd removed a badge of office. "Why-y," he drawled at last, "things . . . intervened, reckon. Sometimes there's things more important than just being something."

"Like what?"

"Like? Oh, like folks. Other folks can be more important. Anybody can be a doctor if they want to bad enough. Trouble with me . . ."

"Yes?"

". . . was a woman. There's a thing; a woman surely can be the downfall of a man, surely can. Upfall—no such word, of course—but sometimes she could be the upfall. The making of a man. Certain women make a man more a man than he'd otherwise attain to. But that's a rare creature indeed. A woman can be a good deal of trouble. There's sinning, and then there's *sinning*. Lord *God*, there's sinning!"

And then he was down on his knees, his hands clasped and lifted to the steam pipes above, while tears rolled down his cheeks and he mumbled an anguished prayer, "Lord God, help this poor sinner, help me, Lord," and his plea was fervent and I saw that he suffered. Then, still on his knees, without looking, he groped for my hand. I gave it to him and he clasped it hard, still mumbling to God, squeezing my fingers together, and I relished the pain of it.

"Where'll they bury me, Lord God, where'll they put me? Where'll they put old Jesse for his sins? Got to find me a spot, God—got to find me some little place, God."

His tears made two silvery lines down the deep creases beside his nose, and the Adam's apple rose and dropped in the thin column of his neck. He looked at me with the same frantic expression he had offered to God.

"Son, listen—God's going to turn his back on me. He's going to look away from me, won't take me, won't ever take me, but when I'm gone, you got to look after Missus . . . got to look after her. You do that for old Jesse, will you?"

"Yes, sir."

"You don't have to 'sir' me. You just make me that promise and Jesse'll die happy. Shake, son?"

"Shake, Jesse."

We made our ritual handshake. Then, drawing his neck into his shoulders, Jesse sagged, and before he could topple I caught him in my arms. The bony point of his chin notched against my shoulder, and he settled against me as if in gratitude. Flesh and bone seemed to have lost their weight, to have relinquished their ability to displace volume. He had no heft, he was like a log whose cortex has dried to pulp.

Holding him, I thought, Who is he, this sleepy dark man? Heavy-lidded, fuzzy-headed, red-eyed, what did I know about him? He had been a part of all our lives, we had at times slept under the same roof, had worked and eaten together, but he was a stranger in our midst. And what did we know of him, really, any of us? He was a person who in some indefinable way I could say I loved. If he died, I would be sad. I would miss him. But who was he, really? When he had gone what would I remember about him? With every tick of the clock he was nearer his end, but what would I have of him when he was dead? A boat ride on the river, a hunting trek in Hubbard's woods, a trip in the Minerva landaulet to hear Rudy Vallee, some Christmases and Thanksgivings, and he in his apron and slippers. Perhaps that was all I would remember of him, a pair of slippers padding in the halls, on the stairs, through the kitchen.

And when the time came, when he was gone, dead and buried, I remembered all of these things, but I came to discover that it is not always the larger things that we recall in someone, but the smaller. So it was that in afteryears I often recollected how he cracked and ate his morning egg, using his spoon just so, neat and dexterously, economically, with no wasted motions, a little daily breakfast surgery, and never with his pinkie finger sticking out.

5

Winter came on, if not apace, then by degrees, and if not with the harshness of the previous blizzard year, then with enough snow to give the semblance of winter. But what fell soon melted and by the time school let out for vacation all signs pointed toward no white Christmas.

Jesse had good days and bad, spent more time upstairs than he did down, but when down was affable and cheerful, as if in leaving this life he wanted to present as good a face as might be managed. One afternoon I heard him make a remark that I found odd, he who had never cared for cold weather.

"Wish it would snow," he said hopefully as I came in through the kitchen with an armload of evergreen boughs for Lady's mantel. All of us had been over through the afternoon helping with the usual pre-holiday procedures: setting the electric candles in the windows, swagging the doorway with its accustomed garlands, hanging the evergreens with Noma lights, rerouting most of the interior lamp wiring with clumps of three-way plugs, and seeking out the carol songbooks, which somehow were never in the piano bench where Lady always insisted they would be. We went over to Mr. Marini's to pick out the Christmas trees, one for our house and the larger one for Lady's, and these lay beside the respective driveways in readiness for Christmas Eve decorating. The titillating smell of baking hung in the kitchen as I stopped, hearing Jesse's remark, and Elthea, who was peeling rutabagas at the sink, tossed a look over her shoulder.

"Why, Jesse?" I asked.

"Why? Christmas comes, ought to be snow, oughtn't there? It's fittin' and proper." He was bundled into his old sweater, and wore his needlepoint slippers, and, as if in a way of maintaining his status in the household, was making a pretense of polishing the silver sugar bowl with a felt cloth. But as he replied his dark eyes had a twinkle

in them, a light that I had not thought to see again, and I knew him
well enough to realize there must be something behind his comment
that I should be able to decipher. Just then Lew and Harry came
in with more branches, and when they had passed through to the
hallway I saw Elthea steal another look, first at me, then at Jesse.

"Jesse, honey, Indians have rainmakers for when it won't rain—
maybe what we need is a snowmaker."

He polished and growled and then said, "Got my heart set on one
more Christmas with snow."

"That's what you say every year. You'll be saying the same thing
in this same kitchen to that same boy next year, except he'll have
grown a foot."

Jesse winked at me in secret complicity, though of what nature
I had no idea, and I went through the door still wondering what
he wanted with snow.

As always, he had his reasons, whose source was revealed when
in fact snow did fall two days before Christmas Eve. This seemed
to offer him satisfaction, and though he chose to remain upstairs that
afternoon, Elthea said he was sitting by the window watching it
come down. We all wondered what would happen if it continued;
the plows would not be out on Christmas Eve. Later, and more mys-
teriously, Lady telephoned to say she would not be over for our
traditional tree-trimming—nor did she mention seeing us for hers,
another odd thing—but, immersed in the holiday activities at our
own house, what with Nonnie's arrival home and the usual cheerful
bustle her visits always provided, we forgot about both the snow
and Lady until I heard a sound out in front, one unmistakable to my
ear. Before anyone else could get to it I had rushed and flung open
the front door.

"Anyone for a sleigh ride?" Lady called, bundled up beside Colonel Blatchley, whose chestnut mare was hitched between the shafts,
the sleigh twinkling in the streetlight gleam. "Put on your things,
come along while there's still snow!"

And so I finally got my sleigh ride, and having come so unlooked-
for, it was the more memorable. The sleigh could take only four at
a time, and I let the rest go first, one load, then another, while doors
opened around the Green and the neighbors waved, and Gert Flagler tromped out on her stoop to see what the racket was about. At
the end of each trip the sleigh deposited the passengers at Lady's
doorway, then drove around to ours for the next load, and when it
came my turn Lady arrived in the sleigh alone. The Colonel, she

said, had gone in to mix the punch, and did I mind if just we two went?

I didn't mind.

She wore her fur coat and little fur hat, and when she had us bundled under a warm car blanket, she snapped the reins, the horse stepped smartly out, and off we went. Along Broad Street and then up to Main Street, past the church and the silent graveyard, down Main to the end, then off onto a country road whose path was unmarked by any former tracks.

If a sleigh ride in July is merely being taken for a ride, a hoax of sorts, my sleigh ride that December eve was none. With Lady Harleigh? It became one of my most memorable recollections. The darkened sky above, the snow falling lightly around us, the air tingling, pristine, the cold making my nostrils pinch, the jingle of the brass bells, the muffled beat of the horse's hoofs, the breath pouring from its nostrils like dragon's smoke, the feel of Lady's fur against my cheek, and in the cold the slight trace of her flower perfume; and if no fox came to view out in the whitened fields, nothing else was lacking. She was my Snow Queen, and I her willing prisoner.

We returned the way we had come, talking now and then, but mostly feeling the spell of the moment. I thought what a handsome town we had, how elegant the fronts of the houses along Main Street, with what care they were presented for the passers-by, their lighted doorways and windows and the colored lights over the trees and along the fences, green wreaths over the knockers fluttering red bows.

"Where would anyone live but here, if they could?" Lady said enthusiastically. If her feelings toward the owners of these houses was soon to alter, and theirs toward her, tonight all was as it should be, tonight it was as though the street itself were bidding us a happy Christmas.

We rounded the flagpole in front of the church, brightly lighted for Christmas Eve services, with the organ playing and the choir singing, and when we got to the cemetery drive, Lady turned the horse from the road and we glided in.

How still it was, how quiet. The tombstones rose darkly in rows and clusters, their tops catching the increasing fall of snow. Lady drew gently on the reins, slowed, then stopped the horse, and, handing the leads to me, she lifted the corner of the car robe and got out.

"Just for a moment," she said lightly, and I felt the cold air slide in under the blanket as she walked across the white space toward the stone marking Edward's resting place. In the flurrying snow and the pale light, I could just make out the dark shape of her figure as she stood motionless, looking down at the snow-blanketed grave. Behind her was the small rise of the ancient burying ground, with its markers like great, four-legged tables, where the earliest settlers lay buried.

"I must bring some winter cherries," she murmured when I helped her back into the sleigh and we continued along the snowy aisle between the graves, at last passing out onto the street again. "They're the only things that give color in this weather." I recalled the bowl of orange papery blooms like Japanese lanterns that had been on the table on the night of the "little veal-cutlet supper," the night of the first visit of the red-haired man.

As we circled the flagpole again, church was just letting out; the steps were thronged with worshipers being greeted by the minister and his wife.

"Merry Christmas!" we called, and they returned the greeting, all heads craning to see the charming sight of the sleigh and its driver, who waved her gloved hand and nodded as we went along. Lady grew serious as we passed from earshot of the jocund gathering, and again her hand sought mine and she squeezed my mittened fingers in hers. We came at last back to the Green, stretching away from us into a hazy infinity, but the snowfall was not heavy enough to obscure the height and breadth of the Great Elm, and again I felt the surge of pride and pleasure that this was our elm, the largest in the country, here in our little town. The wind had stolen away the final leaf, and its stripped but telling form rose grave and somnolent, venerable as ever.

"Trees are God's noblest race." Lady's face looked pallid in the shine of the streetlights, and though the cold should have put color in her cheeks, they were pale, her eyes smoky and encircled with a purplish cast. "Still, trees last, don't they? While we die quickly. Each of us."

"Look at all the Christmas lights," I said, trying to bring her out of her melancholy. But it was no use; her thoughts that night, for whatever reason, were on death.

"Jesse looks better this week, don't you think?" she asked in the child's tone she sometimes fell into. Yes, I said, he definitely looked better. "He's dying." No, I said. "He will not last the year." But I said Jesse was a tough nut, hard to crack. "Dying," she persisted; "and he's so patient about it."

We continued along the Green, and when we pulled into her drive, she started to get out, then drew me back against the seat and took my hand. "It's true that you'll be going away. Sooner than I could hope for, and one day there is something I should like you to know."

"About you?"

"Don't be a great booby, of course about me."

Aha—the, as I thought, defunct Mr. Ott. "Is it a deep terrible secret?"

"All secrets are dark and terrible. It's the way of the world. They are like 'The Dream of a Welsh Rarebit Fiend.'"

"I think," I said, "I know something."

"Ah," she returned, with that mischievous look, "a little knowledge is a dangerous thing." She laid my hand against her cheek and I could feel the cold through my mitten. "But it can wait. Come, we must make a merry Christmas. I'll send Lew and Harry out to help you unharness Colonel Blatchley's horse." She donned a mask of lightness, forcibly putting aside her earlier morbid thoughts, and went in, all gaiety, disappearing through the brightly lighted doorway when Elthea answered her ring, stamping her little boots on the mat, the sound of her laughter rising as she went to greet her guests.

The door closed behind her. The snow still came down. The horse clopped her hoofs in the drive, snorted, shivered. I did not know it then, but it was the end of all the Christmases of my childhood, for the closing of that door really marked the end of Lady Harleigh as I had known her. Later, when the party was the merriest, when all went with Christmas good cheer, when the presents had been opened and the fire was dying, we sneaked out through the kitchen, reappearing at the garlanded front door to sing "Good Night, Lady," and this time she did come out to hear, with tears and smiles, and was touched; but after that it was never the same, never could have been, for within months I had made my terrible discovery. And as Lady had told me, never is a long, long time.

6

Easter came and Jesse was still alive, was indeed a tough nut to crack. During that spring vacation, Lady engaged us to give the summerhouse a fresh coat of paint and we worked diligently in the warming April sun, with ladder, bucket, and brush. Dora Hornaday hung about as she so often did, spying on us from beside the gazing-globe, or sometimes from the loft of the carriage house where she liked to idle, staring out and hatching whatever hidden thoughts went on in that ill-shapen brain of hers. The weather was fair, the spring flowers were already up in the gardens, and Elthea would bring a plate of sandwiches and cups of soup out to us at lunchtime. Jesse, seated on the wicker chaise, watched from Lady's window as the work progressed, his gray face imprisoned behind the pane like an ancient tribal sage. Often, Dr. Brainard would stop by when he came home from the hospital, coming out back to see how the work went, then going in to see, in effect, how Jesse's heart went. "Old fellow's strong as an ox," he would say when he came down again, shaking his head in amazement, though I noted he always managed to say it in front of Elthea, as if to allay her fears at the threat of losing her husband. And he would call a hello to Dora, whose presence now was more or less regular, as she stationed herself in the carriage-house loft.

Once, when I came over with my Kodak to take pictures of the newly painted summerhouse, I saw Dora appear from the side door of the carriage house, having descended from her solitary aerie. I watched her circle the lawn warily until she stood by the gazing-globe, staring at her curved reflection.

"What's happening, Dora?"

She seemed not to hear, and I saw that her ears were plugged with large wads of cotton, part of the treatment that was being administered at the clinic Lady was sending her to. The doctors had determined that it was Dora's ear trouble that kept her in her continually half-realized, dreamy state. I clicked my shutter at her, and "Don't!" she said. When I lowered my camera, she leveled her look at me and said nothing more, and presently she disappeared.

Then, suddenly and from nowhere, the blows fell, one more calamitous than the last. Jesse had been taken to the hospital for more tests, and though Dr. Brainard's report was positive, when Jesse came home again both Elthea and Lady were more worried than ever. Dora stopped coming around altogether, and except for Lady's taking the Packard out on her various errands, there were few comings and goings across the Green. It was as if the house were holding its breath, waiting.

It was several weeks later. Heavy rains had set in, and it proved a wet spring. The water in the Cove was high, though never so high as the flood. I sloshed my way home from school in rain gear, ate a sandwich in the kitchen with Nancy, then went across the Green. I was working on a large model of the *Hindenburg* zeppelin, pinning the intricate maze of struts and crosspieces to a board for gluing. Having used every pin available from Ma's sewing box, I went to borrow some from Lady.

The carriage-house doors were open, the car gone; Lady and Elthea must have gone shopping. Jesse, I supposed, was resting. As usual, the kitchen door was unlatched, and I kicked off my rubber boots and padded in on my stocking feet. Lady had been baking; there were cake layers cooling on racks on the sideboard, and a bowl of frosting sat on the table. I had a lick, then went upstairs to find the tin box she kept her sewing things in. I found it beside her bedroom chaise. I began picking out what pins I could find, then put back the cover and dropped the pins into a paper cup I had brought along.

Outside, the rain had stopped, and the afternoon sun was gleaming palely through a rift in the cloudcast over Avalon across the river. The broad plane of the Cove shone brightly, and boats already launched for the summer bobbed in clusters at their buoys. In the distance, through the just-greening treetops, I could see clumps of smoke blossoming as the freight train came down from Hartford. I watched closely, wondering if someone would try to slow it. These days there was a new engineer, whose ire was easily aroused, and I could hear his whistle making querulous toots as the engine neared the crossing at the Rose Rock soda-pop works.

I left the sewing box on the floor and started out, glancing at Lady's dressing table. I remembered she kept an assortment of pins in the little pewter dish, and decided I might as well have those, too. I spilled the dish out on the runner, picked out the straight pins from the safety and hair pins, put them in the paper cup, and replaced the rest. Among them was the little steel key for Edward Harleigh's chifforobe, which I returned with the pins, put the cover on, then again started out.

They were there on the floor, just a part of them. I nearly missed them, except that my head was angled slightly down as I came around the bedpost. I stopped, stared. Something occurred; a thought, the merest. I dismissed it, or tried to, but then I felt a sort of panic, an enlarging sensation that expanded my stomach and made my knees buckle. I think I said something aloud. It was the numb, stricken feeling one gets, the slow-rising flood of realization, of fear, that sets the intestinal juices flowing, the adrenal glands secreting. My hand had closed on the paper cup of pins: without thinking, I crushed it; their points stung, pricked me. I dropped the cup, the pins spilled on the carpet. I stooped, not to pick them up, but to examine more closely my discovery.

Still I had not realized all of the truth. It was proof, but not enough. I wanted, desired more. I rushed to the dressing table, tipped over the pewter dish, spilled out the pins, and took the key. I unlocked the chifforobe. I felt the blood charging my neck, my cheeks, all of my head, as shame, fear, disgust, engulfed me. I wanted to vomit.

It couldn't be.

Yet it was.

I would not believe it.

Yet I had to.

Stopping my breath because I could not stop the sight of what I was looking at, I yanked out the drawers one by one from the bottom to the top, each only further illustrating the truth to me. As if needing more proof, I flung open the closet door and began pulling things on hangers from the pole, threw them out on the floor, dragged out hats and shoes and furs.

"What on earth—"

Panting, I wheeled at the sound of the voice. Lady Harleigh stood in the doorway. I hated the sight of her.

She looked about at the confusion of strewn things, the ransacked chifforobe. "Oh, my dear." A faint smile appeared at the corners of her mouth, a sad smile, the smile of things remembered—or perhaps of things best forgotten.

"My dear," she said again, reaching out her hand to me. The bracelets slid on her wrist, and I stepped back against the bed, away from her, but still staring at her.

She came into the room and began closing the drawers one by one, and she locked the door with the little key, which she held in her hand. She eyed the things on the floor with a faint glance of distaste, then moved beside me at the bed. I stepped quickly away, but she only bent to pick up the slippers. She held them in her hands and, outraged, I saw with what affection her fingers stroked the needlepointed toes. Jesse Griffin's slippers, which I had seen sticking out from under the dust ruffle of the bed.

I stared, not at her but at the closed chifforobe, its inventoried contents vividly colorful: the stacks of starched shirts, striped in pink and white, the seven white collars, the violet suspenders, the undershirts and drawers, the little compartment of gold collar studs —not Edward Harleigh's, but Jesse Griffin's things. I started to feel sick again.

"Pick up those pins, please." She moved to the chaise and sat looking out the window, the slippers on her lap. I could hear Elthea humming downstairs in the kitchen. I knelt and picked up the pins. My hand hurt where they had stuck me, but the pain seemed nothing to the pain in my chest.

"Will you come and sit?" I rose and she nodded toward the vanity bench. I moved to her but did not sit. Two steps away was close enough.

She began speaking. "Do you remember—last spring? When we walked? By Paulus's pond? I told you then that you were old enough to understand some things, old enough at that moment. And so you were. As you are older now, you must understand more. Will you try?"

I refused to answer. I would never speak another word to her as long as I lived. I dug my fingers into the openwork of the crocheted spread that covered the bed where she slept with Jesse Griffin.

"It would be easy for me to say that Jesse's things were only moved in here since his illness. I will not say that, because it isn't true. His things have always been in this room, for almost twenty years, ever since he came. This is our room together. That is the truth of it. I would like to tell you why."

Still I refused to speak; didn't want to hear; hated the sound of her lightly modulated voice, as if she were preparing to recount the events of a summer vacation. She leaned back against the pillows, slightly averting her eyes as though better to search out her thoughts.

"Will you try to understand?"

I said nothing. The train whistle sounded distantly down the track. It sounded like a small, drawn-out cry. The room was utterly still.

"Will you try to understand?" she said again.

"*No!*" I craned my neck at her, jutting my jaw and letting the word rip out at her. I wanted to hurt her, as the wounded lover wants to hurt, to retaliate, to reject her thought of ever understanding, a renunciation of her entire person.

"You're not a child any longer, a little boy. I told you there were things you must understand about life and about people if you are ever to be happy. Things that are a part of life, and of people."

"Why?" I was the sassy boy, mocking her with the question; as if I or anyone could ever understand such a gross thing.

"Because if we love people we try to understand. Even when it's difficult. We try to feel what they may be feeling, and think what they may be thinking. We try to know their pain." She was holding the slippers, her fingers absently stroking the toes. She was not aware that she was doing it; still it was a loathsome sight. She paused, then talked some more. "It's easy to pretend to an understanding, to run about giving sympathy, but unless it's really, truly felt, it's wasted energy. I beg you—"

She did not entreat with her eyes, but gazed at the slippers in her hands with such caring, such devotion, such—love. . . .

My fingers clenched at the bedspread, my arm shot out, pulling it away from the blanket, and I swept it to the floor.

"He's a dirty nigger!"

I shouted the words and though their sound died in the room their echo continued inside my head as I flung myself toward the door. "Nothing but a dirty nigger," I repeated. *"And you're nothing but a nigger-lover!"*

Jesse was standing in the doorway, blocking my passage. A little light glimmered in his dark eyes as he put his hands out to slow my onrush past him. I butted at him, trying to get by, but he kept me caged inside the room. I began flailing and kicking and batting at him. His arms came around my chest and he held me, lifting me from the floor. I saw Lady sitting on the chaise, saw Jesse's ransacked clothing yanked from the closet onto the floor, saw above me his dark chin with its dusting of talc, heard the growl in his throat.

"Easy, son, easy."

"Elthea's your wife!" I shouted, trying to free myself. I could feel his heart beating under my back.

"Let him go," Lady said, not rising from where she sat.

"Your wife!" I spat the words at him.

"Let him go!" Lady sprang from the chaise and crossed the room with one-two-three quick strides. Then, using the flat of the slipper, she slapped me once across the face. "You make me ashamed of you." She pushed her way past and went out.

"Your wife," I repeated dumbly as Jesse lowered me to the floor and made me stand by myself.

"No, son," he said as he bent to pick up the things from the floor, "Elthea's not my wife. She's my sister."

7

His sister—not his wife, his sister!

And there it was, the truth revealed. And I lived with the dreadful knowledge, all my fears centered around that one dark secret, but I quickly saw that this was the core of the fruit, and that the flesh around it was rotten as well. There was much more to be discovered, and it came, one thing leading to another until I realized how incredible it all was. I ate of the tapioca and the scales fell from my eyes; I saw all.

It was just that taste, a dish of tapioca Ma served one night, that took me back to that time at the seashore, at the Manor House Inn, when the lady came in the great Minerva automobile with her friend and her maid and chauffeur, and I watched her walking by moonlight in the rose garden. She had been discovered then. She and Jesse: somehow Mr. Stevenson had come across them in a compromising situation, had asked her to leave, and she, laughing, had gone. The roses might have shriveled, died for shame.

Seeing this, I saw more: the rides about town, Jesse in front, she in back, the speaking tube connecting them—laughing. The drawn shades, they behind them—laughing.

Jesse following Elthea up, but not as far as the attic where she slept, but only to the bedroom where *she* slept—laughing.

"You make me ashamed of you. . . ."

Those were Lady's last words to me for a long time, and still they rang in my head, echoing and re-echoing. But how ashamed was *I* for *her!* Lady Harleigh, Jesse Griffin—linked; coupled. How could she, how could *they?* No wonder she pleaded for understanding. No wonder that on the threshold of the hereafter he trembled in fear of judgment. God would judge them, but until He got his chance, I would do. I judged them, damned them, hated them, plotted against them. He who had touched, had defiled her, would live in eternal hell of my own imagining. Die, I thought, die quick, and let her live alone in the greatest of loneliness. Let her live with the ghost of Edward Harleigh, whose honorable name she had dragged down, whose memory she had betrayed. How clever she was, how cunning her duplicity, the pose of devoted widow, mourner. Nothing could ever be so base as for years to have continued the deception. Here on the Green where she had lived among decent people, let them discover her ignominy, let her be damned from the pulpit, let her wear sackcloth and ashes, let her be driven from her home, from the town, as Elsie Thatcher had been. Let her be stoned on the steps of First Church, let her fall, regenerate but unforgiven. Let him be sent back to his island, to the fisher folk, black men, black, different, nigger. No wonder she wore that old back-porch sweater of his so often. She'd loved it; it had his smell in it.

Nigger.

Wretched, I sat in undiminished anger at the worktable in the sleeping porch, staring across the Green and praying for a bolt of lightning to strike the house, to see the finger of God point, and destroy all three. I resolved I would tell, that I would run into church on Sunday and announce it to the congregation: she has sinned, she has fornicated, with a *nigger!* When Lew or Harry or someone else came in, jarring me into reality again, I would retreat to the cellar, or to Hubbard's woods—anywhere to get away from the mortifying knowledge I had gained. "Original sin?" This, in the brick house across the way, was more original than any, and I would expose it in all its shamefulness.

But before I could, it was accomplished otherwise, and though I was blamed, and would have been equal to the blame, it was not of my doing. And it was the greatest injury to my friend—for though I didn't know it, or care, Lady was still my friend—that she thought me responsible.

School let out, and in one of her confidential sessions Ma told me that the following September I would be allowed to go away to school, an event I regarded with mixed emotions, but since she was to manage the tuition out of her own pocketbook I went willingly enough to make the obligatory visit and meet the faculty and teachers. Blankenschip School was up on the north New England coast and it was a long bus ride to and from the school.

When I returned, it was just before the storm of scandal broke over Lady's head. If I had looked for a change across the Green, some reading of the emotional barometer forecasting weather to come, there was none. Jesse was up and around again, and I would see him as he came out to take in the mail, stopping for a word with Mr. Marachek. And it was our Czechoslovakian postman-friend who, unwittingly, now performed the service which revealed to everyone the secret I alone had known. Gossip in small towns often starts over the wash lines, wipes its feet at the back door, and soon is welcomed in the parlor, and so it often was in our small town.

But in this instance the gossip came by way of the front door, in the mailbox. For from door to door went Mr. Marachek, to all the important houses, with letters "from a friend," disclosing the information that Adelaide Harleigh née Strasser, widow of Edward, was living in sin with her houseman, with—as I had so often reiterated to myself—a nigger.

One letter came to our house; I saw it; even recognized the stationery, a cheap variety that could be found on the counter of the Gift and Novelty Shoppe, and I secretly rejoiced that Miss Jocelyn-Marie's untidy typing was disseminating such gossip to all quarters and strata of local society.

First the letters, then the talk, then a full-blown scandal. Notorious was the word! People took to walking on the Green, stopping in groups to peer over at the brick house, or to driving by. It was a topic of prime importance on the 5:10 trolley car, and following court sessions and Town Meeting. The convenings of the congregations after church were no different at the Protestant bastion from those of the Episcopal or the Catholic. There was as much talk at the drugstore as at the A. & P.; and Spouse's expression at the meat counter was as vindictive as P.J.'s was at the soda fountain. The gang at the firehouse explored the situation in all its shabby details, as did the boys on the platform of the seed store, while Mr. Phelps at the freight depot went across to talk it over with the cappers at Rose Rock.

There were nasty doings. As testimony of what Northern gentlemen thought of ladies who had truck with gentlemen of color, who as everyone knew were eaters of watermelon, a dozen of these were smashed on Lady's lawn, their juicy guts and seeds strewn as far as the doorstep. The mess cleaned up, a sign appeared, its whitewashed scrawl the same words I had used—"NIGGER-LOVER." Then someone remembered about Blue Ferguson and Lilah Pierson, and comparisons, odious but inevitable, were drawn. But Blue Ferguson was a saint next to Jesse Griffin, Mrs. Pierson no more than a misguided creature, while Lady Harleigh . . .

I thought the sinners justly punished. It was as Jesse would have vowed, right and fitting. Let them skulk out of town, hiding their faces, like thieves in the night. For, as the whole town knew, the mistress of the brick house on the Green was no better than the girls at River House, or the Knobb Street Marinis, who did it on the platform of the freight station at night and who took roller-coaster rides at Holiday Lake backward to get rid of the baby. I gloated; how I gloated! Miss Jocelyn-Marie's poison-typewriter letters had accomplished what I could not.

But if any of the participants in the affair were shamed, none showed it. During the following weeks, their faces were everywhere in evidence as Jesse drove Lady about: at the post office, the A. & P., the Rose Rock soda-pop works for her monthly case of pale dry ginger ale, and at the freight station to send off a package. Never did she create embarrassment by starting a conversation, but in each instance stated her wishes clearly and with candor, saw them carried out, and departed, head held high. Jesse, tough nut to crack, seemed to have rallied, and on his own part showed as much effrontery—or bravado, call it what you will—as did his mistress. Between the country-clubbers and the boys at the Noble Patriot, no opportunity was missed to plumb the humorous possibilities inherent in this hitherto harmless term. "What's the difference between a mister and a mistress?" "A mattress," and so on.

Then, horror of horrors, it was the sanctum sanctorum itself that was invaded, the house of Porter J. Sprague and Spouse. The Daughters of the Pilgrims were granted unscheduled admission to the premises, the house having been cleaned, dusted, and aired the week before. Inasmuch as Spouse had already provided the ladies their once-annual entrance at Washington's Birthday, clearly this connoted emergency measures of the sternest order. Ostensibly a meeting to vote on funds for the Town Farm, everyone knew it was called to blackball the name of The Person who had brought shame upon the organization, she who in any case never appeared at such functions. Except in this case she did, and even I, reveling in her disgrace, admired her courage in facing that doughty gathering. The ladies had been requested to bring foodstuffs for the indigents at the Farm, and the meeting had already been called to order when up drove the Packard to deposit at the curb Lady Harleigh, carrying several cakeboxes. The boys rushed to the doors of the firehouse, the loiterers at the Noble Patriot pushed out onto the walk, and the barbershop emptied as up the walk she went, wearing a new hat, not waiting for Mrs. de Sales-Sprague's door to be answered, but ringing and then entering.

What happened next was food for thought at every supper table in town. The Person deposited her boxes with the rest of the provender inside the door, and assumed an empty seat at the rear of Mrs. de Sales-Sprague's parlor. Whereupon the hostess interrupted her speech—whose contents had been carefully rehearsed, and dealt with the taint of immorality upon the children of the village—announcing that The Person who had just sat down was unwelcome, and the meeting would stand adjourned until The Person departed the premises; would someone second the motion? Someone did, and all was silence, heads turned, eyes staring, until The Person slipped on her gloves, which she had removed, directed her attention to the hostess, saying that she would consider it a kindness if her name might be struck from the rolls of the Pilgrim Club of Pequot Landing, founded 1898, and, as requested, vacated the premises.

Far from my original fervent prayer that just such disgrace should be visited upon her, I now was of two minds, still gleeful that she was getting her comeuppance at last, but proud that she wasn't hiding and afraid to show her face. Around the Green, war had broken out between the two factions: those for and those against. Colonel Blatchley, who might have been a staunch supporter, had left for London that spring to see the coronation of George VI. Ruthie Sparrow led the "against"s, and was full of I-knew-it-all-the-times and I-always-thought-there-was-something-funny-going-on-over-theres. Oddly, it was Gert Flagler who led the "for"s, stating in her loudest tones that what people chose to do was their own damn business and she wished other people would mind theirs. It was not known what Miss Berry thought, for she kept her own counsel.

Thus the *vox populi* of Pequot Landing.

8

During the following year, the scandal more or less ran its course—by then Porter Sprague was stirring up the America Firsters—and while people still talked about it, everything that was to be said had been said, every opinion ventured, every good (read evil) gained. In the end Lady was considered no more than a rich person with eccentric proclivities. And so matters remained for some time. For my own part, I was mortified for her, and for Jesse as well. The slow realization grew in me that though I had kept the secret and felt betrayed, it was nothing to my own betrayal of the years of kindness I had received across the Green.

Then, who reappeared on the scene but Rabbit and Dora's mother, Helen Zelinski. She got off the streetcar one day, as nice as you please, spoke a few words with me from the roadway, and then went across the Green to Lady's house. We had heard that she had been released from Meadowland, and was working as a waitress at a place called the Red Fox Café—up on the outskirts of Hartford—which you passed on the trolley line. If my thoughts had been kind toward Helen Zelinski when she went in, they were of a different nature when she came out. For she reappeared with Rabbit and Dora, a nice little family group, stopping to chat with Lady on her stoop while Jesse brought the car out, and in they got and off they went. I hated Rabbit all over again, hated Dora, and most of all hated Helen Zelinski. There they were, all three, in those precincts where I had once held center stage, and where I could no longer go. I could picture them sitting around the kitchen table, having cake and ice cream, and laughing, and talking—about me, undoubtedly. I could hear them—"Poor boy, he couldn't understand. He doesn't know what he's missing. But he'll find out. I'll bet he just feels terrible." I did, and I knew, too, what I was missing. The visits became more frequent, and on Saturdays I'd see Rabbit over there doing the chores that Jesse had been forbidden. Mrs. Zelinski, too, in bandana and apron, helping Elthea around the house and yard. One day they would be out fertilizing the gardens, the next time shining the windows, the next doing a full spring cleaning. Now there were six of them over there, and over here, two: me and the Green-Eyed Monster, and I couldn't tell whom I hated more, them or myself.

I knew that Ma knew that something was amiss, for how could she help it? Being Ma, she said nothing, but I could tell she was watching for a sign, waiting for me to spill everything. But I wouldn't, couldn't. How could I tell anyone the words I'd said about Jesse, and what Lady had said to me? Ma aside, it was Aggie who realized first what had made me silent and mean for so long, that somehow I had known. She kept at me until I admitted that I had called Jesse a name—I would not say which name—and she pleaded with me to make it right, but I could not. Nothing could send me up the walk to that front door, or even to the back one. I would hang around the Elm, drawing day by day nearer to the far pavement, thinking that in their comings and goings I would receive some kind of recognition that would be the signal for a rapprochement, but though they came and went and though I lingered, there was no sign that I existed or was even visible to any of their eyes. No one wanted any part of me over there.

One day I saw Elthea in the A. & P. She was buying dog food for Honey. She caught my look, and I ducked around the cereal counter, hiding myself behind a pyramid of Quaker Oats boxes. I waited, wondering how I could get out without her seeing me again. Then, from the other side, I felt a hand on my shoulder. Taken by surprise, I whirled, and looked up into Elthea's face. My sudden movement caused the pyramid of boxes to come tumbling, and I knelt to retrieve them as they rolled around in the aisle. Elthea stooped and helped me.

"You ought to come back," she whispered, bringing her face close to mine. "Ought to talk to Jesse. Ought not to go treating him that way."

I dropped the Quaker Oats boxes and stood. She reached for my hand. I pulled away.

"You ought to. Otherwise, it may be too late, and you'll be sorry."

I ran from the store. When I looked back, Elthea was just standing there, watching me go.

The ultimate tragedy came late in the summer, just before school began. One afternoon, Lew, Harry, and I went to dig clay for a cliff-dwellers' model we intended building, the clay to be mixed with shredded paper and dry asbestos, a makeshift adobe which we would bake until hard.

Clay of the sort we needed could be found around the culvert in the bank below the railroad crossing, and there we went, with a garbage can, a shovel, and a wagon. Dora Hornaday was in her accustomed spot at the freight depot, throwing rocks in the cinder bed. Dora's treatments at the clinic had been proceeding, the stoppage in her auditory canals alleviated to a large degree by the drops which were administered daily, and she still had wads of cotton plugged in her ears; thus, if formerly she had pretended to be hard of hearing, now she gave evidence of hearing nothing at all.

At the crossing we saw Lady Harleigh's Packard pulling in at the Rose Rock soda-pop works. She announced to one of the cappers, standing on the steps, her intention of purchasing a case of ginger ale. While Jesse got out of the driver's seat and opened the car trunk, she took a parcel from the back and carried it toward the station, intersecting our path just as we got to the tracks.

"Hello" was all she said, giving me not the smallest glance as she crossed the road to the freight station and walked up the loading ramp. But a great hello to Dumb Dora, sitting on the platform play-ing with something. Her ears wadded with cotton, she made no acknowledgment of the greeting. "What's that you have there," Lady continued, "a hoptoad?" I saw something dark leap in Dora's hands before she imprisoned it again. "I have another package, Mr. Phelps," Lady told the stationmaster as she went inside. Dora re-leased the toad and let it hop along the platform, while she crouched behind it and intently watched its every move.

I trundled the wagon after Lew and Harry, who crossed the tracks and descended the bank to the culvert. At the bottom Lew waded in with the shovel and began digging out the clay, while I knotted the end of the rope on the bail of the garbage pail to pull it up to the wagon above. Where we were certain we could discover plenty of clay there was little, and Lew found it necessary to make his way farther along the stream, Harry following after with the bucket, while I played out the length of rope, tying the end around my waist, preparatory to pulling the pail up. When Lew signaled, I began hauling away, the bucket sloshing water onto the dirt bank as it moved at an angle toward me. When I had it in my grasp, I dumped the clay into the wagon. Digging my boots into the slippery mud, I tossed the bucket back down to Harry, who tossed it to Lew, who began refilling it. The train whistle sounded from up the tracks. I hoped the new engineer didn't think I was planning on slowing the freights that day. Just then Lew called to haul away, and I began arm-over-arming the bucket up the embankment. I glimpsed Jesse on the Rose Rock steps, with a man carrying the case of ginger ale and stowing it in the car trunk. Jesse backed out, and just before the striped wigwag arm began signaling, he started the car across the track.

What followed took only seconds. The train whistle blew three sharp blasts in rapid succession. I thought they were warnings for Jesse, who inexplicably had jerked the car to an abrupt stop just short of clearing the crossing, had thrown open the door, jumped out, and was hurrying along the railroad ties. Then I saw what was happening: Dora, crouched over the hoptoad, was directly in the path of the oncoming train. Behind her, I saw the front of the engine as it bore down on her, the whistle shrieking fiercely. People were running from all directions, Jesse from the crossing, Lady from the freight office, Mrs. Hornaday from her porch, while Dora—her ears plugged with cotton and oblivious to her peril—remained intent on her toad.

"Dora! Dora!" Lady cried.

A shower of sparks flew up from the train wheels as the engineer at last applied the brakes. Jesse was straining as he raced along the ties. I heard Lady call out to stop him, then my foot slipped and I slid part way down the muddy bank. The train thundered past above me. As I got the rope untied and clambered back up the bank, the cowcatcher struck the Packard with a grinding concussion. Gradually the train slowed to a stop. I leaped over the coupling of two freight cars in time to see Jesse safe beside the tracks as he handed Dora over to her aunt.

He pushed his hat back and wiped his brow with relief, then drew his shirt front from his chest and blew inside it to cool himself. As the trainmen came hollering from both directions, he seemed to be fumbling for a handkerchief. He took an awkward step forward, and a second. Then his arms went rigid, his head snapped back, and his hat fell off. Lady cried out, and as she reached him he toppled forward, the weight of his fall too great for her to stop, and he collapsed next to the tracks as the engineer and the other trainmen came running up. Dora stood silently by until her aunt pulled her away. I ran to Lady.

She knelt in a patch of cinders, which must have bruised her knees painfully. Oblivious, she cradled the body of the black man in her arms. She gave me a quick frantic look as I knelt beside her and looked down at Jesse. His breath came in a raspy sound from deep in his chest, which his hand spasmodically clutched, released, then clutched again. Lady held herself practically motionless, trying to quell the results of her exertions, as if of itself her panting might cause Jesse to expire. His gaze rested on me for a moment, but whatever expression was there remained for me unfathomable. He called for God, once, then twice. Lady looked up at the circle that had gathered around and asked that someone call a doctor and a priest. Mr. Phelps said it was being attended to. Jesse's eyes closed and I thought he had died. The others did, too, for I could hear the whisper of breath that went among them.

Lady tried to change her position slightly, and Jesse's head fell back against her breast. In a moment he opened his eyes again; the darks seemed to roll downward from under his lids, focused on me.

"Stupidy," he whispered with a little smile. I did not know why he said it, or what he meant, nor do I know now. But I have often thought of his lying in the train tracks with that pale, gray smile, and it seems to me it perhaps was his comment on the indignity of his dying—the foolish, unhearing child, the train bearing down, his running despite the doctor's orders. Or perhaps it was the fact of the breach between us, that after all it had mattered little, that things that came between people, that made them unhappy or drove them apart, that caused grief and pain, that scarcely matter—all of these were "stupidy." Or perhaps he meant all of life.

"Shake, son?"

The sight of his face blurred with my tears as I put my white hand into his black one and I felt the smallest pressure.

"Shake, sir," I whispered back, clamping my other hand between my knees until it hurt. Still he looked at me, and his expression seemed to say, We are different, but what does it matter now; it all comes to the same thing.

He lifted his chin slightly; then his face was obscured as Lady's head bent toward him and her hair fell across. I heard a mumbled sound, several, then a pause. When Lady raised her head, calling again for a priest, Jesse was dead.

I felt someone's hand on my shoulder, and Mr. Phelps helped me up, while the Rose Rock man moved about the circle of faces repeating, "Give 'im air." One of the trainmen knelt to Lady and tried to extricate her from her position. Mute, she shook her head, folding her arms around Jesse's shoulders and holding him fiercely against her. We backed off, silently watching until Dora, eluding her aunt, approached and looked uncomprehendingly down.

"Dead?" she asked in her thick voice. Lady looked up at her and nodded. A siren wailed out on the street and in a moment a policeman's motorcycle slowed up, scattering the watchers. Lady meanwhile was struggling to get her arms out of the sweater she was wearing over her blouse. She moved herself from under Jesse's head, then pillowed it on the bunched-up sweater. I watched with horror as Dora bent and set her hoptoad on Jesse's motionless breast. Lady drew back in one quick recoiling movement as the toad sprang from the dead man's chest onto his thigh, then into the cinders, where it crouched, blinking and not knowing where to move next.

"Dead," Dora murmured again before her aunt came and led her away. "My hoptoad. My hoptoad."

I looked at Harry, at Lew, and stepped around Jesse's body to crouch by Lady, offering her my hand. She stared at it, then at me, then at Jesse, then spurned my help, getting to her feet unaided. Someone came from a car that had pulled up and helped her to-

ward it. The train engineer stepped up for a closer look, then shook
his head.

"Listen," he said, "someone get this coon's car off my tracks, can't
they? I got a late train here."

9

Jesse's body stayed by the railroad tracks for two hours more, while
it was decided what must be done with it. Mr. Foley, the local undertaker, was called, but when he arrived and discovered whose
body it was, he found that his schedule did not permit him to do the
undertaking. Finally a firm in the city agreed to make the funeral
preparations and Jesse was taken away.

Interment became another problem. Three freed slaves were
buried in a corner of the village cemetery, and Jesse might have
joined them, except that since Edward's remains already rested
within the grounds, and Lady herself would one day join him, the
cemetery was deemed unsuitable. The Catholic church had no
burial ground of its own, and so, after services, the body was held to
be returned to Barbados, whence it had originally come. Lady and
Elthea were to take it home.

Helen Zelinski, Rabbit, and Dora were there to see them off, also
Colonel Blatchley, and members of my family. I did not go over,
but sat on our porch steps, working hard to put my roller skates on.
I watched across the Green. A taxi arrived, the bags went into the
front seat beside the driver, Lady got in, and Elthea. The door
closed. Everyone waved. The taxi pulled out of the drive. I skated
down our front walk, and turned up the main walk. I kept my head
down, fists jammed in my pockets. Then I heard the taxi stop. The
door was flung open, and Elthea came hurrying across the Green on
her high heels, the bracelets on her wrists jangling. I stopped skating, watching her come, and when she reached me she threw her
arms around me and pulled me to her. I could smell the Midnight in
Paris perfume I'd given her last Christmas.

"I'm sorry," I said, "I'm sorry. . . ."

"I know. I *know*."

She hugged me again, then let me go, and I skated away up the
walk. I heard the taxi door slam again, and the driver stepped on the

gas. I skated as fast as I could, trying to catch the taxi, but it disappeared up Broad Street. I stopped, breathless, and leaned against a tree. Crying, I punched the tree trunk until my knuckles bled.

The coffin had been brought to Lamentation Station, where Elthea and Lady boarded the train with it—Jesse in the freight car, the two women in a passenger car—seeing it first to New York, then by ship to the Caribbean.

With the nigger, the coon, the whatyamacallit dead and gone, removed from sight and a little from memory, people, not discounting myself, found they could afford to milk the dry teat of whatever human kindness could be managed. Notes of condolence were delivered daily by Mr. Marachek—whose mailbag had been the original source of the misery—lines in longhand on monogrammed stationery offering regrets that Mrs. Harleigh's houseman had departed this vale of tears and hoping that when Mrs. Harleigh was more herself the undersigned would be permitted to call.

No one was. It was the death of Edward Harleigh, twenty years before, repeated. When Lady returned, without Elthea, she closed herself up in her house again. It was to be her final retirement. Aggie brought the unopened notes home and answered each one "in the name of Mrs. Edward H. Harleigh," with thanks to the sender.

Summer ended, and I prepared to go away to school, as had been promised by Ma. Lew and Harry and Aggie had already returned to their respective classes, and because Blankenship opened later I was left practically alone, packing my belongings in two laundry cases which would convey my things and would also serve as containers to send home my shirts and underwear in for Ma to take to the Sunbeam and then ship back to me.

Daytimes, there were only Kerney and Nancy around, and she, usually so talkative, was stunned, almost mute, seeing to her household duties soberly if not grimly. The scandal had been as great a blow to her as to anyone else, or so I believed, though she had never discussed her feelings, but as we went about our various activities I could feel her dark eyes on me, as if with Jesse's passing I, a white boy, had become a kind of enemy, though she never slackened in her work, or in her efforts to please me. But when at my accustomed time I came into the kitchen for my sandwich and milk she always found an excuse to be elsewhere, and never did I hear the old refrain to take my Iradol-A, or to zip up my windbreaker when it got cold.

Meanwhile there was Ag, whom I had come to regard as my

Lady

nemesis, whose blue accusing eye seemed to follow me wherever I went, scornfully blaming me, and waiting for me to make a move toward Lady, and ask for her forgiveness, and for Jesse's.

"But we shook hands," I told her fiercely. "He forgave me—I know he did."

"It's easy for the dead to forgive," she replied, equally fierce, "but it's the living you've got to ask it of!" I stared at the scuffed toes of my shoes, not telling her how Lady had ignored my hand, had in fact shown exactly what her sentiments were regarding me. And the more Ag argued, the more I found it impossible.

I tried. Time and again I tried to force myself to march up that front walk, an oft-rehearsed apology in my brain if not on my lips. I could not do it. I could not face Lady Harleigh. I hurt for her, was sorry for her, sorrier for myself, but nothing could make me go to her. In my peevishness I had thought only of how I had been tricked, in my jealousy I realized that I was scarcely the figure of importance I imagined myself to have been, and in my despair I was unable to make the necessary amends.

I reasoned that I had been made a goat of, victimized in the first instance, excluded in the second. It was a shabby business, those three over there, and I their dupe. What I failed to realize was that it was none of my affair. I was a child among adults who were involved in the very real business of living their lives, while I had scarcely begun mine. I could not see that the relationship served to illustrate the endless variety of human congress, and that kindred spirits sought each other out in many guises. Nor did it occur to me that far from being the lonely widow we had thought her to be, Lady Harleigh had until Jesse's death been living a full, domestic existence, for all that it took a less conventional form, and that what she seemed to be most of the time she truly was: that rarest of creatures, a happy woman.

It did not matter that she had been open and honest with me, had in fact already declared her intention, had prepared the ground for my eventual understanding of the matter, or that she had treated me as a rational person, capable of understanding; that is to say, mature. Nor could I then see that in her intelligent way she trusted me to understand, was in fact counting on it, and that in this regard I did mean something to her, and in the same regard I was letting her down.

But in my selfishness I did not consider Lady herself, or how she was suffering. I would not think of the sudden, intolerable loss of

both her closest companions, that she had returned to live in the
house across the Green with the ghost of the dead Edward. I refused
to picture her bearing her grief, not in solitude, but in loneliness,
which she had always feared: mornings at the kitchen table with
the newspaper, cigarette, and coffee cup, but alone; evenings stitching in the wing chair, but alone; nights in the fourposter, but alone.
What did I care for her real agony when, to me, mine was realer?
Or her tears or pain? *Someday*, I thought, she would come out and
smile and wave, and *then* I would run across, and *then* I would say
I was sorry, and *then* everything would be all right; but not now.
Now I was a coward.

And yet, staring from my window past the Great Elm, I thought
of the house that had once been our Ark, keeping us safe and dry
while the floods rose around us. I thought of the living room where
we had found consideration and grace and good will, where we
had eaten bounty, where we had been together in a chain of love
that Lady herself had forged, that room of my youth, with the friend
of my youth, for hadn't we been boom compenions when we had
drunk to "present company and absent friends," where she, in her
velvet gown and diamond clips, had played and sung a German
love song to me—to me—in a time of friendliness and warmth and
cheer; and, Yes, we had said, we will do this every year, an anniversary to be remembered, even as weddings and birthdays, till she
herself was white-haired and we had children and they would be
brought to see and hear, with Jesse silent in his slippers to and from
the room.

No more; never anymore.

I thought of that mostly, that it was somehow Nevermore. But
the future lay ahead; who cared for bygones? I cleaned out my
childhood, putting into cartons to be consigned to the attic all the
things I felt reminded me of the past, for I was a grown boy now,
and the past would never be again. Secretly I planned on tacking
up banners and school insignia and rah-rah pictures of track and
crew teams as I packed away the Roxy Radio Junior magic lantern,
the postcards of Paris France and Venice Italy, the books from my
shelves, *Robin Hood* and *King Arthur* and *Treasure Island*, illus-
trated, to make room for *The Way of a Transgressor* and *Knight
Without Armor*.

It was while I was carrying up just such a box of books that we
learned about Blue Ferguson. His mother had received word that
he had been killed in Spain, and was to be buried there. It was a

bitter blow to her—she was frantic, wanting him to be brought home
to our own churchyard—a bitter blow for all of us who had been his
friends. No one now remembered about Mrs. Pierson or the reason
for his leaving; we thought only of the Blue Ferguson we had
known, Blue of Hermitage Island. As we had lost Jesse, so we had
lost Blue, though I suppose there was none to draw the parallel.
Both I had loved, both I had felt betrayed by, both were dead. I put
my *Hindenburg* model on the table, set a match to it, and watched
it blaze, smoke, crumble, become ashes, and long after Lew and
Harry were asleep, I stared across the Green where until late, and
later, a solitary lamp burned behind the drawn downstairs shade.

And so the days wound down, until shortly before I was to leave,
and still I had not gone across the Green. And still Ag watched
and waited, and was disappointed in me, and I hated her for it, but
could do nothing. And then the storm came, and it did for me what
nothing else could do: it drove me back where I should have gone
of my own accord.

There'd been a wind brewing for days, with small-craft warnings
posted along the Sound. As the wind continued, the rain came in
squalls; the frequent radio bulletins kept us informed of the progress
of the storm, calling it a hurricane as it thrashed its way up from
the Caribbean to Florida, then into the Carolinas. It approached the
town in a gradually consuming fury, as if by coming slowly upon us
it could rob us the quicker and to greater profit.

As usual, Ma had gone to the laundry, and the schools, as usual,
were open, and as usual Nancy was ironing under the cellar stairs.
She emerged in time to make lunch, then, frightened by the storm,
retreated to her ironing board and radio programs; she didn't want
to see or hear none of that nonsense.

Back at my worktable, with the broad panorama of the Green
below, I watched Miss Berry make her way from her door, crossing
the Green and heading for Lady's house. This was a strange thing,
for to my knowledge she had never paid a visit across the Green in
all the time we'd lived there.

Her umbrella unfurled, defying the storm to turn it inside out,
clutching the collar of an old black coat, and trying to keep the red
bird from flying off with her hat, she made her way up the walk. I
thought the wind would blow her away, but she got to the door and
was admitted.

Later, I persuaded Nancy to come up and watch the storm with
me, which she did only with reluctance, wringing her hands, her

dark lips taking on an ashen hue as she offered admonishment to the phenomenon.

"Oh, Lord, you's bad, you's a bad thing, lookit what you's doin' to Missus Sparrow's snowball bushes"—Mrs. Sparrow's snowball bushes were scudding across the lawn like tumbleweed. "Here, now, you ain't got no call to blow like that, Lord, that streetcar's goan' pop offa that track"—and so it appeared, the trolley having come up the track listing like a foundered ship, until debris blocked its path and the motorman fled to a nearby house for safety. "Done broke that glass!"—the butt end of a branch drove through a passenger window. "Lord help us, this whole house is gone to shakin'" —it had; we could feel the timbers quake in the walls and flooring.

"Lord God bless us, what's she doing out in that?" Nancy exclaimed as Miss Berry closed Lady's door behind her and marched back across the Green.

"She's coming here"; I had a feeling of dread as I got up and went down to open the door. Rage and contempt were on Miss Berry's windblown face as she confronted me, thrusting her black-gloved finger at my chest. *"You told!"*

"Told?" What was she talking about? The wind tore at the red bird, making it bob ridiculously. I tried to take her hand and bring her in, but she pulled away as if I were contemptible.

"You told about Lady and Jesse."

I felt amazement and then outrage. "No, I didn't. I never said a word."

"You did *not* tell?" She put her face close to mine, peering through her spectacles. *"No one?"*

"No . . ." My voice rose in a disconsolate wail on the wind.

Miss Berry darted me another look, then pulled the door to, leaving me behind it, trembling in anger. How could Lady have said it? Why was I blamed? I had never mentioned a word, not to anyone. Was she trying to get back at me? Would she put the blame on me for spite? It was the dirtiest trick I could think of, and instantly my feelings hardened toward her again.

When I got back upstairs, Miss Berry was heading up the Green, the wind buffeting her from behind, a frail craft abroad in rough waves; she looked hardly seaworthy. Colonel Blatchley, long since returned from his summer in England, came out and spoke to her, but Miss Berry shook her head and continued on. I watched her disappear, wondering what errand took her about in such weather. Leaves flurried across the grass in manic torrent, whirling, twisting, flying up in leaf-geysers, while water flowed in the streets as if the hydrants had been turned on. The radio said the hurricane was now ripping through New Bedford and heading for Boston. Again we had been declared a disaster area; the National Guard, the WPA, and other agencies had been called out. When Lew and Harry got home, Lew called Ma and asked her what she was doing: ironing shirts! In the middle of Connecticut's second-greatest disaster, our mother was back on the mangle! Lew told her not to try to come home. Where was Agnes, she fretted on the other end of the line. She agreed to remain at the laundry, but Ag must call when she got home safe.

We were all worried. The other schoolchildren had gone by, but no Ag, who always came home before going to the library to rebind books for Miss Shedd. Our worry increased as the storm did, and the real havoc began. The smaller, suppler trees were able to bend with the wind and still maintain themselves, but because of the wet spring the ground had been loosened, and one by one the larger trunks were literally uprooted before our eyes. A sixty-foot maple leaned, tottered, and crashed to the earth, taking with it a great cake of dirt and revealing its naked root system, which in no time was washed clean by the driving rain. Another tree went, then another, with great gaping holes appearing in the ground. "Look!" Harry exclaimed, and down went another; I watched it, then returned my eyes to the Great Elm, which I was sure would go at any time. Leaves flew like dark rain from the branches which tossed in thick green waves as the wind tore at them from every direction. Limbs broke off and were borne away, but still the thick trunk held.

By degrees the fury died, and though the rain continued all seemed eerie silence. The sky changed color, a sickly yellow, a Biblical signal of disaster or pestilence.

"Lord, I believe it's over," Nancy breathed gratefully, and I let her go down to the kitchen in her innocence, for I realized that we were now in the eye of the storm, that calm center around which the hurricane spiraled.

We waited, watched, talked among ourselves, worrying about Aggie, and as the rain slackened I looked across the Green to Lady's house. I wondered what she was doing. All was quiet; there were no signs of any activity. Like the others, her lawn was leaf-strewn, the blossoms of her plants had been torn off, leaving only the bare stalks, and the sheets of her afternoon paper were scattered over the grass.

Then into this calm chaos came Agnes, our sister, with Miss Berry. Her umbrella still intact, Miss Berry marched, rather than walked, straight down the Green, avoiding the carnage with careful steps until, arm in arm with Ag, she crossed the roadway in front of our house. Up the walk, up the steps, through the hall, upstairs, and into the room she came. Pulling out the long pin anchoring her hat, she threw the hat on the bed and sat down, looking straight at me.

I glanced at Ag, who'd come in behind her, then said, "Yes, Miss Berry?"

She composed herself by removing her gloves, then began. She had come, she said, directly from the parlor of Mrs. de Sales-Sprague, whom she, Miss Berry, had encouraged in no uncertain terms to surrender the truth concerning the poison-pen letters. It was indeed Mrs. de Sales-Sprague who had circulated them; the stationery had come from Miss Jocelyn-Marie's Gift and Novelty Shoppe, had been stamped and mailed in the post office, and had been delivered by Mr. Marachek. And how had Mrs. de Sales-Sprague come by this information?

Through Dumb Dora.

Spying from the carriage-house loft, Dora had observed certain things, which accounted for her frequent visits during the time we were painting the summerhouse a year ago last spring. From the loft she could see into Lady's bedroom window, where unnoticed she had witnessed demonstrations of affection between Lady and Jesse which even Dora's opaque mind could hardly construe otherwise. Had seen Lady kiss Jesse as she tucked a comforter around his knees. Had seen her sit on the chaise foot, holding his hand as she talked to him. Had seen her, while Jesse dozed in the sun, disrobe and change her clothes before going shopping.

So much for Dumb Dora. But how had Mrs. Sprague found out? By dint of one of her "What-have-we-been-doing-today-Dora-dear"s. Mrs. Sprague had coaxed, and Dora had obliged her by telling. Mrs. Sprague went to Miss Jocelyn-Marie's for the purchase of writing paper of the cheapest sort, and to the post office for stamps. The unwitting Mr. Marachek had done the rest.

Her recital finished, Miss Berry rose. "Lady said you were the one," she said, facing me with her direct look, "but I told her you weren't. Go, now—hurry."

Hurry? Where? There was a hurricane. I felt bewildered, not understanding what she wanted me to do.

"Go to her. She needs you. She still thinks it was you. Tell her you didn't."

I lowered my eyes, then sat down. "I can't."

"*You—can't?*" The words exploded with disbelief. "You shall! You must!"

I felt everyone's eyes on me, but I didn't care. I would not go. I thought Miss Berry was reaching for her hat as she flew across the room, but it was me she wanted. She seized my shoulders and pulled me to my feet with a strength I wouldn't have thought possible, and shook me until my teeth clacked. Then she sat me down, took up her hat, and left the room without another word.

I glanced around at the others, and went back to the window. No one said anything. Outside, the storm had begun again, the velocity of the wind, the intensity of the rain matching my own storm of feelings. I felt a hand on my back and was whirled around to face Ag, her young fury matching Miss Berry's elderly one. Who did I think I was? she demanded, her face redder than I had ever seen it, her eyes running with tears. I had never heard her talk so much or so fast or so angrily. Who had taken us in and opened her house to us when we were flooded, and we would have been sleeping at the American Legion for a week? Who had paid Harry's hospital bills when he was sick? Who had sent her, Ag, to camp? Who had given us Christmas and Thanksgiving and Lord knew what else year after year? Yes—and how did Nonnie get to go to normal school, except that Lady talked Ma into it, and paid her tuition. Paid for Nancy, too! And who did I think was helping to send me away to school! Who gave and nursed and took care of us, and not only us, but everyone—there wasn't a family in town practically who wasn't obliged to her—and who was now as miserable a woman as could be found?

"And if you want to know what I think of you," she ended, "I think you're—you're nothing but a stinker!"

Finished, she fled in tears. I looked at Harry and Lew, who turned and leaned on the windowsill. I looked the other way, into the mirror over the bureau, a true goblin's mirror where an ugly boy did ugly things—a mirror that . . .

Then, suddenly, I was running from the room, while Lew and Harry stared after me, and downstairs Nancy was pulling at me as

I tried to open the door, with rain and leaves gusting in around us. Unheedful, head ducked low, I ran past her into the storm.

It was an astonishing feeling to be out in it, both fearful and exhilarating. As I made for the far side of the Green, I was shocked to see that the Sparrows' house looked as if it had been suddenly repainted; the white clapboards were turned absolutely green from the leaves that the wind had plastered to it. Trees were going down all along the sidewalk, lifting the paving in serrated rows like half-extracted teeth. One of the elms in front of Lady's house had already fallen, and now the other went, toppling toward the street, branches sprawling over the driveway. Everywhere I looked I saw broken boughs and networks of projecting roots as I cut diagonally across the front lawn to the back.

The flower beds were in shreds, the plants crushed under fallen boughs. Even as I appeared, a huge tree near the carriage house started to go. I stopped in my path and watched as with an audible noise it tore the earth around its roots and tumbled, the left side of the top mass thundering down onto the roof of the summerhouse. There was a terrible sound of breaking wood and timber, the delicate lattice collapsed, and the summerhouse itself disappeared, engulfed in greenery. Beyond, the boats in the Cove bobbed furiously, some torn from their moorings and driven pell-mell toward the shore. The weathercock had fallen from the ridgepole of the carriage house and lay in the driveway, but it was not the rooster whose safety I feared for.

Miraculously, the gazing-globe sat unharmed on its pedestal. All around it lay debris and branches, any one of which might have struck it. Still it remained whole, and I could see myself in it as I dashed toward it. I seized it lightly but firmly in my fingers, drew it from the hole in the pedestal, and ran back across the lawn. Another branch broke off, tumbling in my path, and fearing I would never get the globe to safety in one piece, I changed course, heading for Lady's back door.

I pushed through, intending to leave the globe in the back entryway. I saw the inside door swinging to and fro on its hinges. I had a quick sensation something was wrong. I stepped into the kitchen, then called; there was no reply. I backed through the hall door, still holding the globe in my hands. Then I heard a sob. I ran down the hall.

In the living room, Lady was crouched on the Oriental rug, beside the wing chair. I hardly knew her, she looked so dreadful. Her hair was uncombed, her face swollen and red, her eyes stared wildly. I remembered her saying once that storms frightened her. Before I could move to her, she began dragging herself across the floor toward me, moaning like some wild mad thing. Then she stopped, came to her knees, and flung her hands up in supplication. Still clutching the globe in the crook of my arm, I dropped to the floor and threw myself into her arms, touching her hair and face, and telling her not to cry, that everything was all right now, that I was there.

She pulled herself together, sniffing and wiping her nose and eyes, and then she raised her tear-stained face and took my face between her hands and gave me a long, searching look. Then her look altered slightly, falling on the silver gazing-globe. Her laugh broke out amid her sniffles and she shook her head in disbelief.

"In this storm?"

"Yes."

"Oh, l'il Ignatz," she said, drawing me to her, "have you come to tell my fortune?"

PART FOUR

Last Songs

I

And so we became friends again. I came and went across the Green as I always had, and Ma and Ag were happy that we'd made it up. Each of us, Lady and I, renegotiated our relationship charily, not mistrusting each other, but aware of damage already done, and each wanting the wound to heal with the least amount of scar tissue. I, being younger, and more unthinking—but mature enough to recognize her value to me, for I loved her—entered into this new phase with more energy and zeal than she, but even I was aware that I must tread softly. I was also aware that in keeping my promise to Jesse I would have to "act grown-up," not "stupidy," and so it happened through the next half-decade that I became more and more the adult, and she the child.

But if I hoped she would provide an occasion for explanation, none came. Except for the culpability of Dora and the Spragues in loosing the scandal, she seemed disinclined to speak about anything of a personal nature, as if too much of her had been exposed, and though we often talked of Jesse, and of Elthea, who wrote frequently, and of things as they were before Jesse's death, neither of us mentioned the scene in the bedroom with the needlepoint slippers, and it was only over a period of years that I finally learned all the facts. Some of the story was to come from Lady, and some from Miss Berry, this second part being related to me after an interval of fifteen years. The truth is always made up of lots of smaller pieces of other truths, and so it was with Lady, but I was to discover how long a shadow truth casts, and over how much ground. The final truth was, to me, astonishing, as it would have been to anyone else, but no truth could hurt by then. Lady was gone, and Jesse, too; there were no others to know her secret and only two to keep it: Miss Berry and I.

That September of the hurricane had also been the time of "poor Czechoslovakia," and everyone said there would be a war that fall, surely by Christmas. But England's Prime Minister went to Munich, chatted with Hitler, surrendered Czechoslovakia, and came away saying there would be peace in our time. Next morning, making his mail rounds, our postman, Mr. Marachek, was crying over the fate of his country. It was a sad day, for him, for everyone.

Soon after, Mother came home with my bus ticket and I went away to Blankenschip. I would turn fifteen the following January. Though Lady wanted me to go to school, though she had helped provide funds to make it possible, and though I went, I did not like it. Blankenschip School was a preparatory academy near Portsmouth, New Hampshire, enabling its students to ready themselves for a naval career, and offered as part of its curriculum full sea voyages aboard a barkentine. It was, however, not a rich man's sons' school. Moreover, though it was nondenominational, to me it resembled nothing so much as a church afloat, for there were tedious chapel services twice—sometimes three times—daily.

It was, furthermore, part of the agreement made between the school and its applicants that each student must partially defray the costs of his education by work periods during the day, and it fell my lot to be assigned a dining-hall detail, where, under the flint-eyed scrutiny of the supervisor, I was required each morning and evening to put the chairs upon the tables, mop the giant floors, and when they dried, put the chairs down again. Betweentimes it was my job to polish the brass: brass kick plates on the doors, brass handles and brass hinges, or brass chandeliers with their scrolls and turnings, brass lamp bases, brass wastebasket rims, even the brass fittings of the tables themselves; brass, all brass, and all constantly in danger of turning green. It was my duty to see that they did not.

When I had finished, in time for morning chapel services, I washed the brass polish from my fingers and hurried to my pew for the pastor's harangue. After classes, and more chapel, I returned to continue my duties in the dining room, then to study, and then to bed. It made for a long and uninteresting day.

I returned home for the holidays, Thanksgiving, Christmas, Easter, then suddenly it was summer vacation again. To my surprise, I had completed my freshman year at Blankenschip almost without realizing it. That summer, Harry and I got jobs on the State Highway Department road gang; work that was hot and dirty, but built up muscle, paid well, and gave me time to think.

And though I had much that was new to consider, still my mind returned to the old, to Lady Harleigh, Jesse Griffin, and the house across the Green. For both Lady and myself there had evolved a tacit understanding that if things between us would never be the same—the old things—there would be new things. With Elthea gone she was alone now, and getting older. I was growing up, and had my promise to Jesse to keep, that I would in all things "look after Missus." But with Elthea gone it would not be an easy adjustment for Lady.

In a very special way she was spoiled and used to being waited on, to being looked after, taken care of. Now, as if driven by some perverse instinct, she refused to hire new help, and insisted upon doing all the household work herself. Many were the times I found her down on her hands and knees scrubbing the linoleum in the kitchen, or bending over the toilet bowl with a can of Old Dutch Cleanser. She ran the washing machine in the basement, hung out the sheets and pillowcases, swept, vacuumed, even hauled the trash barrels to the street on Wednesdays.

Still, such household labors seemed to take little toll of her. She had always been used to work, and even with servants to help she'd commonly managed a large part of it herself. She didn't look any older, at least to the cursory eye. Her hair got grayer, but it was becoming to her. She favored darker colors, a lot of black or navy blue or plum. She seemed to have given up wearing hats. Her shoes were not the dainty ones that I remembered, but of a more "sensible" sort. This was undoubtedly for her comfort, for her limp was more pronounced at times, and took on the responsibilities of Jesse's corns in matters of weather prophecy.

Colonel Blatchley, feeling that she was lonely, increased his visits, often stopping by several times in one day. Good old faithful Colonel Blatchley, he never gave up hoping. For the rest, Lady had only Honey, the dog, for company—Honey as faithful and loving as the Colonel. From visit to visit, as I returned over the years, I observed further changes, small, but all leading to the final result. She moved less quickly than I remembered, and since she was often drowsy she began taking regular naps in the afternoons. Her hands trembled increasingly, until she could not disguise the fact, and she had trouble holding her teacup on its saucer. She let her figure go. Not to say she became fat, but her body thickened, and she renounced the regime of calisthenics she had maintained for years, dutifully following a local radio gym instructor. But even with all that had happened to her, she accepted the challenge of that most commonplace of creatures, a woman bereft. It was as if she had been twice widowed, once by Edward Harleigh, once by Jesse Griffin. I suspect it was the second widowhood that was the truer one. She was then, in the year the war began in Europe, only fifty-three years old.

The light that was Lady Harleigh now burned with a mellow incandescence; she softened, and if her vitality diminished, her determination only increased. If in time she became querulous, argumentative, even unreasonable, as she called on the last of her resources and fought the specters around her—Edward's, and then Jesse's—these seemed the only means at her disposal to fend off the phantoms of guilt that plagued her.

That winter she had suffered a slight accident, slipped on some ice at her back doorstep and fractured her ankle. Dr. Brainard put her in a cast, which did not come off until early summer. And it was during that last summer of peace that she chose finally to explain matters to me, an interview which came about in a most natural way.

When the Highway Department truck dropped me off after work, Lady telephoned to ask if I would go with her in her new car for a "special little drive," it was such a lovely day. We went, at her suggestion, along the back country roads toward Lamentation Mountain, avoiding the new parkway that had been put through a few years before, and making our way slowly up the slope to a spot she seemed particularly to favor.

It was a sort of lookout where the road ended and there was turn-around space, affording a handsome view of the valley. To the west wound the railroad tracks, with the little country station people often favored over the larger and noisier one at Hartford for their trips to and from New York, and which was almost the only reason for going to Lamentation at all. East of us lay the river, and the steeple of First Church and the clustered roofs and chimneys of Pequot Landing. Nearer was Talcottville, which in the old days had been called Two Stone, and at the river Talcotts Ferry, where the oldest ferryboat in America still plied the water. Between the two lay the Paulus farm, and the meadow pond, where Chester Welles had built the first corn mill.

Legend had it that in searching for the site of the mill he had walked from Pequot Landing through the forest, until he became lost. He found a mountain, and climbed it to get his bearings. His friends, fearing for his safety during the night, had come in search, calling and sounding drums. Hearing this, Chester came down from his mountaintop, and the "lamentation" for his whereabouts ended, and to this day the place where we now sat was called Lamentation Mountain.

Lady took off her shoes and twiddled her toes while she scratched her left foot. She had been out of the plaster cast for some time still her ankle itched and she used a cane to walk with. Settling herself comfortably, she produced a pack of Pall Malls and gave me her lighter—an old habit; she always enjoyed having her cigarettes lit for her. She inhaled and blew the smoke out through her nostrils, a trick I had lately been mastering at school. "Will you have one?" she asked casually. I managed mine fairly decently, and for a time we smoked in silence.

Presently the distant train whistle sounded, and we could see the engine as it panted along the tracks through the leafy countryside. Simultaneously, down at the station, a long black hearse pulled in. The driver got out, then a female passenger. They were Mr. Foley, the undertaker, and Estelle Ferguson, Blue's sister. She stood shielding her eyes against the light and straining anxiously to see as the train came down the tracks.

It slowed, stopped, and amid gusts of smoke and steam a lone passenger descended: Mrs. Ferguson, peering uncertainly about as her daughter came to embrace her. She shook hands formally with Mr. Foley, who had come rolling a wheeled trolley from the back of the hearse. The door of the freight car was slid open, and with a pang I saw the end of Blue Ferguson's coffin. The stationmaster helped manuever the coffin onto the trolley and together they rolled it down the platform. Estelle had brought a flag and some flowers. The flag was draped over the coffin lid, with the flowers on top; Mrs. Ferguson followed each of these actions closely, her head moving this way and that, overseeing each detail in its minutest particulars.

I thought I knew where the money had come from to allow her to make the long trip into ravaged Spain, aided through various Red Cross agencies, to discover where Blue had been buried with the others who fell in the Abraham Lincoln Brigade.

The train pulled out, its whistle sounding a dirgelike wail, puffs swirling about the platform, partially obliterating the trolley and its burden. When it cleared, the small party had gone inside, and the solitary coffin was the only thing to look at. It stood out in all its starkness, while the breeze riffled the ends of the flag. It was a mournful sight. Lady said nothing. I tried to imagine Blue inside there but I couldn't. He was dead, that was all. He would have been twenty-one that summer.

The breeze continued tugging at the flag until it had dislodged it, dragging the flowers to the planking of the platform. No one came to fix it. Then the flag was blown into a sloppy bundle and became snagged against the wheels of the trolley. Mr. Foley came out with the Ferguson women, and he rolled the trolley toward the hearse while they fumbled up the flag and the flowers. The coffin was stowed, the rear door closed on it. Mrs. Ferguson stood back clutching the flag, smoothing her dress and patting her hair in several places as though trying to tidy herself for her son's homecoming.

"Why didn't anyone come besides Estelle?" I asked Lady, in a low voice, though there was no one to overhear. I distrusted the absence of pomp; Blue had died a hero and it was as if he were being sneaked into town by the back way.

"They didn't want it."

"Someone ought to have come for Blue."

"*We* did."

It had been planned, then, the little drive to this place. Her eyes were wet and her lips trembled as she gazed down on the empty platform. "He was a fine boy, Blue Ferguson. He'll be missed in our town." I thought again of Blue leaning over the banister without his pants, how he'd jumped into the snowdrift. Somehow it all seemed funny now, and long ago.

"You liked Blue, didn't you?" she asked.

"He was a good guy."

" 'True Blue.' Poor Mrs. Ferguson, she'll never get over Blue." Suddenly she changed her position, pulling me closer and pressing the flat of her hand about my head, gently, firmly. "Oh, be careful—do be careful. Promise me you will."

"Sure I will" was all I could think to say.

"It's going to be so—so—seeing you boys go."

"No, it won't. If there's a war, it won't last long. We won the last one."

"I'm not sure we did. If we had, Blue wouldn't have come home like this today."

"But that was different—that was just a war in Spain."

"No, my dear, it was not just a war in Spain. It was the beginning of it all. Europe will be a butcher shop. But you're right—maybe if America does fight it will end sooner, and better. And maybe there won't be any more wars after that."

I said I would be careful, and she found her handkerchief, sniffed in it, and dried her tears. I had sat up, and to spare her further emotion I looked off toward the place we had come from. I saw the hearse again, winding its way along the road toward the steeple of our church in whose cemetery Blue would be buried.

"You were a good friend," Lady said.

Wondering what had prompted the remark, I looked at her. "Why?"

"Because it's your nature, darling, that's why. You were a friend to Blue, and you are a friend to me. I have been twice blessed in this life."

"Twice?"

"Once with Jesse, once with you. Oh, I'd forgotten—I have a little present for you." She took from her pocketbook a small wrapped parcel and put it in my hand. I undid the string, and the carefully wrapped paper. It was a copy of *A Shropshire Lad*, the poems of A. E. Housman. I opened to the flyleaf, where she had written in her curly, curvy hand: "For Present Company from Absent Friend(s)," to which she had appended her initials, and the date. It was today, the day Blue Ferguson returned. I thumbed through the pages, stopping where I saw another bit of writing in the same hand, a marginal note indicating a particular poem.

"Read it," she said.

"No—you." I handed her the open book.

"Yes, better I to a young man, than you to an old woman—people might laugh." She took the book and read in her clear, crisp voice, without sentimentality:

> "Into my heart an air that kills
>   From yon far country blows:
> What are those blue remembered hills,
>   What spires, what farms are those?
>
> That is the land of lost content,
>   I see it shining plain,
> The happy highways where I went
>   And cannot come again."

And there it was; the perfect poem for the perfect time; "Right and fitting, as Jesse would have said," I observed.

"As Jesse would have said. Yes, he would have," she replied. Together we looked down along the valley, our eyes tracing the "happy highways" where each of us, of different generations, had grown up;

the valley which was the land, not of my lost content, for I was too young to know that then, but what seemed the land of my discontent, and I was more eager than ever to leave it, to be done with that church spire and those chimneys and roofs and all the people who lived there.

Once more I looked to the highway where the hearse had traveled; it had gone now, but still I thought of Blue, who had "come again." Well, there were ways and ways.

A plane flew overhead, low, one of the new commercial passenger planes, and we watched it become a speck, disappear. When its drone faded, Lady looked back at the river. Since the flood three years before, its course had settled in a new channel, and much of Hermitage Island had been eaten away. Where the river curved behind First Church, at River Road, had been the wharves and warehouses of the old trading ships, when the town was in its maritime glory. Now, beyond, there were two metal oil-storage tanks, and a dark, flat tanker was leaving its berth, chuffing up smoke. I knew from Lady's expression what she was thinking. I rotated my arms and made chooga-chooga sounds in imitation of one of the old paddle wheelers. She nodded.

"Yes, I much preferred them, the steamers. Well, they'll come again. . . ."

"When?"

"In another life, perhaps. Another lifetime."

"Reincarnation?"

"Oh, please. Cats, maybe, but not me. One life will have been sufficient, thank you." She plucked at a blade of grass and laughed, low, throaty, easily. When I inquired, she looked at me from under her brow, a particularly flirtatious way she had, and said, "I was just thinking of the *City of Springfield*, and that damn steamer ride Edward took me on."

"To Saybrook."

"Yes. Only the trouble began at—"

"Essex."

"Ye-es. How did you—"

"Miss Berry remembered."

"Did she indeed? I thought Mary Berry was as the tomb, both silent and final. What else did she tell you?"

"Nothing. Honest—nothing."

"Very well." Again she gave signs of private amusement. "Then shall I tell you? Now? Shall I tell you about Edward—and Jesse?"

The names slid out so easily, so unexpectedly, so out of nowhere, that it took me unawares, and it was there, on Lamentation Mountain, on a summer afternoon, that she told me the story of herself, and of Edward Harleigh, her husband, and of Jesse Griffin, who had been her lover.

But the story began with Edward.

2

"I did not want to marry Edward. I was in love with him, or thought I was, but I was afraid of him. That is to say, I wasn't sure I liked him—there's a difference between being in love with someone and liking him. I knew his reputation with the girls, his drinking and running around. The marriage was arranged by old Mr. Harleigh, who's been glowering down on our dinners for so long. He was old and ailing, and more than anything before he died he wanted to see Edward married and with children—an heir to the Harleigh name. I couldn't imagine why he picked me, except that he decided I was a realistic and sensible girl, and that if Edward found me attractive I could change him. And I thought I could, too. I thought that in his weakness I would be his strength. Mr. Harleigh felt that a bit of good German blood wouldn't hurt the family strain, either—he even checked up to find out what kind of housekeeper I was. Then Mama was at me and at me to accept Edward, who'd already indicated his intentions. He really gave me the rush. He'd come with Daddy Harleigh's sleigh—*your* sleigh, darling—and we'd ride all through the town, the rich part of town—remember we lived on Knobb Street—and he'd tell me what it would be like when we were married.

"Christmas came, and there was a big party at the Harleighs'; they always had open house on Christmas Eve—Mother Harleigh loved playing the *grande dame*. Everyone was there, Talcotts and Welleses and Standishes, and two Strassers from Knobb Street. Mother was impressed. Edward took me into the conservatory, and it was like something out of a play; there were palms in pots, and orchids; an orchestra—five pieces, imagine—had been brought down from a hotel in Hartford, they were playing in the bay, and Edward produced the Harleigh sapphire. He put it on my finger and it stayed there; then the carolers arrived and the musicians went to the kitchen while everyone came into the conservatory, and after they'd sung 'Silent Night, Holy Night,' Edward rapped on the pane, and they sang 'Good Night, Lady.' I cried, Edward kissed me, everyone applauded Daddy Harleigh's announcement, and we were engaged.

"I would have preferred a long engagement, but Mama was all haste for the wedding. Everyone seemed to be. Then I had no choice. Edward took me off on an excursion—on the *City of Springfield*. We'd only gotten to Essex when he was suggesting things I knew he oughtn't to be suggesting, and when we stopped at Saybrook for passengers he coaxed me off the boat. I never saw New York at all, and arriving home, I was a confused young woman. I agreed that we must marry quickly. I'd wanted to go to Europe for our honeymoon, but the Harleighs thought otherwise and so we went to Mexico instead. I was very surprised—"

"Why?"

"By the way things were arranged, and the way Edward behaved. It's not important, really. Anyway, it turned out I was going to have a baby, but—I didn't. We came quickly home again; it was hardly a honeymoon at all. Daddy Harleigh was very angry. But when we got back, there was the house—Mother Harleigh had picked it out, and had chosen the furnishings and the wallpapers, everything heavy, heavy, heavy. The only good things really were the dining-room Sheraton and Edward's chifforobe."

I couldn't meet her look as she said the word, remembering that awful day I had opened it. She went on.

"I became a good housewife. But it—just didn't work. Edward did some terrible things, went back to all of his old ways. He drank a lot. I was very unhappy. I thought if I could have a baby, it might change things. Certainly it would have made Daddy Harleigh happy. Then it turned out I *was* pregnant again and I was determined to keep the child this time. Miss Berry came over and looked after me, and I was glad to have her there." She gave an odd little laugh before continuing.

"At any rate, it looked as if there were going to be an heir at last, and Mother Harleigh was always having me over for tea, showing me off, and telling all her friends how wonderful it was going to be. Edward thought so also. Extraordinary how much he wanted that child, even though I knew he hated me.

"By this time I hated him, too—at least, I realized the mistake I'd made. There were terrible scenes. I offered to go away after the baby was born, and he said I could go, providing I left the child. I could never have done that. Daddy Harleigh tried to get Miss Berry to keep me locked up. But they didn't reckon on Miss Berry.

"There was a dreadful business about a dog she'd given me. After that I hated Edward more, and I never ever wanted to have another dog again. Edward had become terrifying by then. There was an awful row; Miss Berry tried to save the baby, but couldn't. It died. After that there wasn't any point in trying anymore. Edward said he'd go away and get himself killed in France, and I really believe he meant it. At least I don't think it was his intention to come back a hero.

"You know I limp a little. I'd had a—fall, and my foot had caught under me somehow, and broken, and Dr. Forbes set it badly. He was the worst doctor! The ankle never healed properly. He said I'd walk with a cane for the rest of my life, but I bet him I wouldn't. And I haven't—until now.

"After that it was all up with the Harleighs. They washed their hands of me. Daddy Harleigh was ill by that time, his final illness, but it wasn't until after he'd died that I found out that certain papers had been signed, first an agreement with my mother concerning financial arrangements, and another, entailing his entire estate in Edward's name, and stating that neither he nor I might inherit unless we lived in a 'suitably chosen property' in Pequot Landing for the remainder of our lives. That property, of course, was the house on the Green, which the old man had always coveted.

"But after my fall, things had gone badly with me. Something had happened inside my head. I'd get dizzy spells and have blackouts. I couldn't remember things, and I'd imagine I was seeing things that weren't there. I cried a lot—never could stop crying, for weeks. Then one day I woke up and couldn't speak. Literally. Not a word.

"Miss Berry took over again. She arranged for me to go South, to Memphis. Not Memphis, Tennessee, but Memphis, Virginia. I couldn't talk, but I could think, and I thought my life was over. But it was only the beginning. I met Jesse Griffin."

She pronounced the name with a firm downward inflection at the end, as if drawing her story to a conclusion, and for some moments I thought she wasn't going to continue, but I quickly saw that she was merely coming to the second part of her tale: Jesse, the sequel to Edward. I wanted to go back over what she had already told me. I felt there were so many missing parts, things I didn't understand, but I waited until she spoke again. And now the scene shifted from the small Northern town of Pequot Landing to the smaller Southern one of Memphis, to a place called Broadmoor, which was the only reason for the existence of the town. Broadmoor was an expensive rest home and sanitarium, catering to people with drinking problems, or mental trouble, or those who needed to recuperate from surgery. Upon arriving, Lady found the doctors curiously uninterested, and only conventionally attentive. She had made her mind up that she would never get well, that she was just another patient there, and that the best medical advice to be found had dismissed the case as hopeless. It was generally assumed that she would never speak again. But, unable to speak, and realizing her plight, she grew infuriated. She wanted to speak, wanted someone to give her the key, to help her release the words.

But the doctors had not reckoned with a West Indian black named Jesse Griffin. The son of a poor Barbadian fisherman, his father had recognized his potential, and the family was made to save and contribute to an educational fund for him. Jesse, knowing what a toll this took, wanted to become well educated, to get on in life, and help his family in return. He'd won the King's award for scholarship, and could have gone to England to study, but instead he chose America. But when he received his degree from Howard University, in Washington, he couldn't find the sort of employment he sought; hence he had taken a job as orderly at Broadmoor. And it was as he wheeled Lady's chair around the gardens that, little by little, he gained her confidence and, by patient instruction, got her to begin speaking again; first only sounds, then words, then sentences. It was a long, grueling task which the black man had set for himself, but by the very strength of his personality he gradually elicited the words from her.

Having been raised in the North, Lady was shocked at the treatment of Southern Negroes, that there were segregated bars, segregated stores, segregated parts of trains and busses. She was quick to realize that the man who was spending endless hours encouraging her to speak again was himself muffled, not by any fall, but by his fellow-man. Interest bred sympathy, sympathy bred love, and love bred an affair. They became lovers.

But there was a villain in the piece. He was called—and the way Lady said the name, it was with more ridicule than contempt, as we used to say Gert *Flag*ler haw haw—Eotis Thorne, pronouncing the E with a Y-sound—"Eee-yotis." And indeed she did laugh, though as she said the name and related the next part of the story, there seemed to me little reason for amusement. Eotis Thorne, also a Negro, worked in a different section at Broadmoor and, like Jesse, he too had graduated from Howard University. But, unlike Jesse, Eotis Thorne hated white people. "Hated them—hated me. He'd follow us wherever we went—I was out of my wheelchair by then—and he spied on us. And he used that dreadful word every chance he got."

"Which word . . . ?"

" 'Nigger.' " I thought her smile the most beautiful thing I have ever seen. There was forgiveness in it, and memory forestalled, and all the compassion a man might seek. It lighted her face, and I felt tears under my lids. "Not to worry, not to fret, darling. Eotis Thorne was a character out of Faulkner. Eventually he discovered that I was helping Jesse financially—I'd arranged through the bank to have some money transferred and it went to his daddy in Barbados. Eotis intercepted one of the bank letters. I was urging Jesse to go on with his education; he'd gotten almost through premedical studies when he graduated, but he felt he couldn't take the time to finish his full medical. He needed to send money to his family.

"I was better—well enough to go home, really—but I couldn't bear the thought of being parted from him, nor he from me. His sister had come from the island, and I'd moved into a little bungalow in the town, and Elthea came to keep house for me. She'd lost her husband, he drowned at sea, and we became friends. It was the happiest year of my life. I used to talk to her about Jesse; she knew, of course, that I loved him. I couldn't divorce Edward—it was unheard of. I was a Catholic, remember. Not only that, Edward was a serviceman, and patriots did not divorce the men overseas. Nor would Daddy Harleigh ever have countenanced such a thing.

"Then I got a letter saying that Edward had been gassed, and as soon as he had recuperated he was being brought home. So it came time for me to go back as well. By then I could walk and talk, and there was no reason to stay on, except for Jesse. He was heartbroken, but he'd never let me know it.

"Just before he came to drive me to the station, I had a visitor. It was Eotis Thorne. He said he knew who I was, and where I came from, and that he wanted money from me, or he would expose me and Jesse. He'd compiled a sort of dossier, a complete record of our times together, right down to the minute. I agreed that when I got home I would send him a thousand dollars. This seemed to satisfy him.

"So I went home again. Edward came back. I didn't want to face him at the station, but there was no help for it. The newspapers would be there, there were to be speeches—I didn't think my legs would support me when he got down off the train. I couldn't bear to look at him. No sooner were we back at the house than I realized there was no help for anything. He was worse than before, mean and sardonic, full of sly tricks and innuendo; and worse, Daddy Harleigh insisted we go away, a sort of second honeymoon, and he'd arranged a trip to Sea Island, Georgia.

"I could scarcely breathe when we went through Washington; Jesse seemed so near to me. I wrote him from Sea Island, saying I must see him again. On the way home we stopped off in Washington. I told Edward I wanted to see some Turner paintings at the National Gallery and he let me go. I'd arranged to meet Jesse in a drugstore around the corner. I told him how unhappy I was, and how much I needed him. He asked me to run away with him then and there, go back to his island, or somewhere in the Caribbean. I should have. But I couldn't. We had no money, nothing. I started to cry. Jesse leaned across the sugar bowl and took my hands, both my hands in his. There was a notions counter, with baby bottles and things. I saw Edward standing there, watching. He'd followed me."

He took her back to the hotel and got the truth from her. He said filthy things to her, beat her. She asked him to let her go. Enraged, he said he was taking her home and would do with her what such women should have done to them. He had always found her an object for his lust, and he would use her any way he chose. She realized he could never tell anyone; he would never besmirch his father's name. He brought her home and locked her up. This time it was to be for good. She was to be a prisoner in the house. He moved his things to another room, and while she stayed upstairs, he was down, drinking. He hardly went out. Once he told her if she really wanted to leave, she could kill him. He would enjoy that, he said.

She continued: "Daddy Harleigh died, leaving Edward his heir, as long as he remained in the house on the Green. That winter I came down with influenza. There was a terrible epidemic going around, and many people were dying. Miss Berry came to the rescue again. While I was sick, Edward took himself off to New York. I don't remember much of what happened then except I was terribly sick. I had a high fever and bad dreams, I was raging in my sleep. I talked a lot to Jesse, or about him; Miss Berry tried to calm me and brought in Dr. Brainard. She wouldn't have Dr. Forbes again. I went into crisis, and they didn't hold much hope. Then Edward came home again and—" She broke off, easing her eyelids with her fingertips, then went on.

"It was Edward who died. I got well, and he got sick. Dr. Forbes, who was still Edward's doctor, had Miss Berry giving him some sort of balsam treatments which didn't do any good. Edward's lungs were feeble after his gas attack in the Argonne Forest, and he had no resistance.

"He died. And I was free at last. I should have left Pequot then, there was nothing to keep me. When Mrs. Harleigh died, the family were all gone, but there was the money. Daddy Harleigh's will was valid, and as long as I stayed in the house I inherited everything. And that was that."

More or less. There had been the awful winter when she was in the house alone, when Mrs. Sparrow had gone to her and she had been polite but had adamantly refused any help. By March she knew what she was going to do. In April she announced she was looking for new help. Jesse and Elthea arrived at the end of the month, having replied to Lady's "advertisement," bringing "references from their former employer."

"I had no idea that Elthea would come, too, but she insisted. Said she'd gotten used to me, and it wouldn't do for her to look for another place, and besides Jesse was her brother. Out there, in the world, there would be race problems all the time. Here at home I was safe, we were all safe, from the world. Or so I thought.

"So I began a new life where I had ended the old one. Mama was dead by then, and I didn't have to worry about her finding out anything. It all seemed so simple. I had known I'd never be able to give up the money, the house—all the good things. Since the money depended on my staying there, it seemed simpler just to live where I was. It was Jesse's idea, really. I thought we would go to the island, but there had been a drought, with no crops for three years; there was no flour, the cattle died, his family was starving. Their sails wore out, there was no way to buy new canvas or to fix the boats. His brother's children had no clothes, the roof leaked during the rainy season, there were colds and illnesses. Jesse's father got worse, and needed medical attention. I was able to help them all, you see, with the Harleigh money.

"So Jesse and Elthea felt that they had come into my debt, and staying with me was their way of paying it off. I didn't want them to—just loving Jesse was enough. But we all stayed. And it worked, most of the time. I said Elthea must have a downstairs room, but no, she wanted to sleep up in the attic, said she was used to attics." (I recalled the bed with the sag in the middle; where Elthea had slept, alone.) "It became a kind of game, Jesse in his livery, driving me out in the Minerva. We'd talk back and forth through the tube, laughing and joking, and nobody suspecting a thing.

"Then there was the shrine, as Ruthie Sparrow always called it. You must know, it made Jesse very angry for me to put those things out on the table. I told him it was for show—for when people would come in, and I would appear the grieving widow. But what he didn't know then was that Edward had come back. At least I thought he had. I imagined I'd see him, watching us, laughing at us, waiting—all the time waiting. At first I tried not to let anybody know—I'd just go upstairs to our room and pull the shades, thinking I could get away from him that way, but he was there. He was everywhere. After a time it seemed as if I'd never come down again. I wanted to, but I couldn't make myself. Jesse never tried to persuade me, he seemed to understand about that part of it, and he'd just wait until I'd come out of it, but then there'd be whole patches I couldn't remember. It was like a form of amnesia. By that time I knew people were talking about me, so I just let them, thinking it might keep them from talking about something worse. And then, after a time, everything would be all right again, and when I felt safe, I would come down. And there Edward would be on the gate-leg table, and I kept him there to remind myself. It was foolish, I know, but I had it in my head and couldn't get it out. I hated myself for doing it—but it was a form of expiation, I suppose. Jesse kept telling me it was wrong, and to put the things away—but I couldn't. They stayed on the table until the party—my birthday party. Jesse just wouldn't stand for it any longer, he said I absolutely had to put the photographs away." (And finally I realized that I had been wrong in assuming that it was Colonel Blatchley who had insisted that the things be removed.) "So I did. Then we had that dreadful fight. I'd given in, finally, but somehow it all seemed too late. And so many years had gone by. I—I don't know what I thought, or why we even had a fight. I know I said terrible things to him.

"I was always afraid, you see. Afraid that—wanting Jesse, and having him, was too much to ask, that we'd paid too high a price. Sometimes I thought about what would happen if people found out the truth, and sometimes I didn't care at all—it just didn't seem important. There was a place at the seashore—remember the Manor House Inn?—and the man who owned the hotel came into Jesse's room, thinking no one was there. I'd been going over some accounts, and was lying on the bed resting. Jesse had his shirt off. You can imagine what Mr. Stevenson thought. It was easy enough to leave, but when I got home I was frightened again.

"Then I heard from Eotis Thorne. He wanted more money, so I sent it to him, but he wanted more, and then more. There was no end to what he wanted. I was deathly afraid Jesse would find out, and do something terrible. You've never seen Jesse's temper, but he had one, believe me. And it was Jesse, you see, who first brought it home to me that you must be told before you stumbled on the truth accidentally. He said I must prepare you for the truth, and when you'd heard it you would understand."

"But I didn't."

"Do you now?"

"Yes—I think so."

We talked it out, step by step, event by event, and I thought that I did understand. I could see, or thought I saw, it all. How happy she'd been to have Jesse go to the movies with us, she and he holding hands under her pocketbook in the dark while Rudy Vallee sang "Good Night, Sweetheart." The white hand and the black joining in secrecy, in longing.

"It was his ring that I wore, you see, not Edward's. A kind of wedding band. Except no one must know." I looked at her finger, strangely naked without its familiar circling of gold. "I had it buried with Jesse," she explained in answer to my unvoiced question.

Still, there were others.

"Did Jesse ever find out about—"

"Eotis Thorne? Yes. It wasn't just me he hated, but Jesse, too. Eotis was a Negro, you see, but with lots of white blood, which made him rejected by his own people. He could have passed for white, a sort of half-breed—very light skin and freckles, and as sometimes happens in blacks, red hair. You saw him several times when he came to threaten me."

"Eotis Thorne was the red-headed man?"

"Somehow I thought you knew. He never used the *E*, but called himself Otis Thompson Thorne. His initials were O.T.T. He was your Mr. Ott. Jesse shot him."

3

Through the rest of the summer the tale absorbed all my waking thoughts. I could think of nothing else. As the story had been related to me at Lamentation, my mind had run on parallel tracks, so to speak, and I realized how at variance with the true facts were those of Ruthie Sparrow's oft-repeated version. I went over it all again and again, sifting each kernel. But of the true facts there seemed only one important one. Lady and Jesse had loved each other. The simple truth was all that was required. She had loved him. He had loved her. It did not matter what others might have thought, whatever labels might have been attached to the relationship. All that really mattered was that they had loved each other.

Even I, who knew nothing of love—had scarcely experienced it —could see that it was this one simple fact that had sustained Lady through the time I had known her, and even before that. Listening to her speak of those years, I saw how difficult it had been from the beginning. And with what pains the whole charade, the hoax, had kept the town unaware. Even I could see that, after Edward's death, it was a prospect from which neither could retreat; yet how was it to be accomplished? Lady's weakness, if she had one, had been that she was unable to give up what she had attained to, the Harleigh money and property and the things it might provide. She wanted to be neither poor nor alone. But, the disposition of the property and money being so arranged, she was required to live in Pequot Landing, in the brick house on the Green. Jesse's coming there seemed the perfect answer. Why, we had wondered for so long, had a man like him been content with being a houseman? His content had come from elsewhere. Having wanted to be a doctor and take care of many, he had been happy taking care of one. Everything he'd had, he'd given to make that one person happy, and it had been enough for him.

The key, of course, had been Elthea, who, loving them both, had been willing to be a party to the deception. For under no circumstances could the two have lived alone in the house. They arranged all of it—but not without difficulty—not to be discovered; that was the thing, never to be discovered.

"It was not done simply," Lady had said. "We paid a terrible price. He did, and I did." Here her calm expression had slightly altered, her tone as well, and it seemed to me that perhaps there was something more than the apparent price that had been paid. Something to do with Edward? Her guilt? The shrine on the gate-leg table? I could not fathom it, yet it was there. In that final moment of revelation concerning Ott, she had spoken with such candor, and then vehemence. I believed her utterly, yet still I was left with the feeling she was withholding one last piece of the story, something that had gone unsaid.

"It's not easy to pretend," she had explained. "For a lifetime. It is a wearisome burden, pretending. Playing a game, acting a part —for others, not yourself. To make it easier for them, not you. It was all a masquerade."

I recalled our talk in the summerhouse, when she had spoken of the differences between things as they are and things as they seemed. "We all wear other faces, it's true. The good are not nearly so good, and as for the bad, I'm sure they're much worse than people think." And so she had thought of herself, for so many years. I would not have liked to carry such a burden. "Extraordinary," she had said, removing the Halloween child's disguise, "what a mask may do for one."

I wondered where she had gotten the strength to stand up to the rigors of leading a double life, and the danger of revelation in a small town such as Pequot Landing. Yet, until Dora had taken to spying in the carriage house, it had been accomplished. Poor Dumb Dora! If she could know what pain she'd caused.

But for me so much had become clear; now I comprehended Lady's guilt, her tears, her talking to herself, her vigils at the gravesite, at the living-room shrine. Small wonder she saw the ghost of Edward Harleigh wherever she looked, in whatever dark corner she might peer. A widow, living unmarried with another man, her black servant.

"It was the walks, mainly," she had said, her eyes growing misty. "That we could never go anywhere in public together, never be seen as a couple, except out driving. That was why you were always asked to take me around the Green, because he could not. I used to imagine what it would be like to be with him, walking, and that Mrs. Sparrow wouldn't pay any attention to us, that we could be just like other people, that what we had done with our happy lives wouldn't matter to people who had made their lives unhappy.

"He was all my hope, you see. In the nights I couldn't wait for the sun to come up, to see his face, and in the day I couldn't wait for it to be night, when I could hold him." She paused, then finished: "There was nothing I wouldn't have done for him. Nothing. Nothing I *didn't* do. Nothing."

And nothing he hadn't done for her. I thought again of Eotis Thorne, my Mr. Ott, who had threatened their existence, and whom Jesse had done away with. Lady had told me how he had removed the body to the cellar on that Halloween night, and then put on the coat and hat, and taken the streetcar, as a decoy, in case anyone—like me—had seen him arrive. Fear of discovery was what had prompted Lady's trip the following summer to Virginia Beach. They had gone to Memphis, where discreet inquiries were made to learn if Thorne's trips to Pequot were known. They were not, nor had he been even missed. But still Lady had not revealed to me of the final disposition of the *corpus delicti*.

I thought I understood the psychology behind the shrine on the gate-leg table. As Miss Berry had pointed out, the workings of Lady's mind were indeed elaborate, and for her the shrine was a form of self-punishment, some unfathomable need to be constantly reminded of what she was doing, and what would happen if discovery came.

But for my remaining weeks at home that autumn her earlier words seemed to hang in my inner memory: ". . . people who had made their lives unhappy . . ." That, and "our happy lives . . ."

Everything else seemed irrelevant.

Meanwhile, Hitler's panzers marched into Poland, and the world, our town, and all our lives became different. It was another beginning, or another ending; I could not tell which, for I was not—none of us were—aware of the vast changes that were coming. For me the measure of my life seemed only the distance across the Green from our house to Lady's, and it was there that it seemed the changes were most vividly drawn. As I grew in height, our dwelling, always crowded, seemed to shrink, until in fact I could reach to the ceiling when I stood on tiptoe, and inch by inch the yardstick marks on the kitchen door jamb crept swiftly upward toward the lintel.

And as its size diminished, the house emptied. Nonnie had already gone, and myself. Lew had graduated from high school the previous June and found a job in Mystic working for a lobster fisherman. Harry was now in senior high and employed nights at the Sunbeam.

This left only Aggie and Kerney at home. Ag was a junior at Thomas Hooker High when I was a sophomore at Blankenschip, and Kerney celebrated his tenth birthday that winter. Nancy began her sixth year with us, and she was the one constant factor on the premises, never changing, never different, never anything but Nancy. Ma might have retired, but she had been at the Sunbeam so long it had become a way of life for her, and she was reluctant to give up her position because we still needed the money. If Nonnie had never managed to lay by enough to put a cow in our shed, at least we now had a secondhand Studebaker in the garage, but there still were our college educations to be thought about.

During my sophomore year, I met a girl at a seminary near Blankenschip, and found I was spending more vacation time in New Hampshire. I believed myself in love, but this was short-lived after Dottie Frame moved to town. Dottie, beautiful, bewitching, auburn-haired, became the belle of Pequot Landing, and she had the boys falling all over themselves, myself included. I quickly switched affections and time schedules and now spent more holidays in Pequot than I had at school. None of this was lost on Lady, who watched my courting of the dazzling Dottie with no comment. It was a feverish four months, and there was a zealous exchange of letters (I labored over mine to her while my marks dropped; hers were bright and breezy, and I knew they had cost her no trouble) while I panted in expectation of the next holiday which would see me back on the Green again.

Across the way, I would notice each time I returned how strangely denuded Lady's house looked in its setting, with the old twin elms gone from in front, and two new trees providing little to make up for the damage from the hurricane. Between dates with Dottie Frame I managed to spend as much time as I could over at Lady's, but my periods away at school were sufficient to reveal the extent of the changes, in both the house and the mistress.

Two things were obvious. One, that for all those years it had been Jesse's and Elthea's hands who had kept up the luster of the house, and with their going that luster had dimmed. Two, Lady needed someone to replace them; but no amount of urging seemed to change her mind. It was as though, with the Griffins gone, she was unwilling to accept the presence of some stranger, nor would she suffer the adjustments this would have required her making.

She had another accident, one that, though we did not know it then, proved the beginning of her early decline into ill health, and eventually her death. She'd gone shopping upstreet and the heel of her rubber boot had caught in the escalator in a department store, and she fell. There were no fractures, but her old ankle injury kicked up and she was incapacitated, in addition to which she suffered painful bruises over a good deal of her body. When Dr. Brainard examined her—it had been some time since she had submitted to an examination of any kind—the good German Strasser blood was found to be lacking in red cells, and treatments were instituted to correct this deficiency. She got out the cane again. When X-rays were taken, it was discovered that the fall had put her lower back out of alignment, and she was required to wear a brace. When I went to her house, I would find her still cheerful, though she walked more slowly, and it required little effort for her to get out of breath; the slightest exertion tired her.

Worse was to come; a painful series of blood transfusions, a cast, hospitals, and the gradual wearing down of the entire machinery. Nobody knew at that time what lay ahead, but she already entered on the slow downward curve that would eventually see her buried in the churchyard beside Edward. Yet, until the time of Pearl Harbor, we felt she was managing well enough, except in the matter of household help.

While her ankle mended and she wore her back brace, it was necessary for her to be looked after. Rabbit Hornaday still made himself available doing odd chores for her, but more hands were needed. The parade began. For endless months the house on the Green saw a doleful succession of hired girls, maids, housekeepers, and practical nurses. None sufficed for Mrs. Adelaide Harleigh; one by one they arrived, and one by one they departed, with hard feelings on both sides, and the problem continued until Miss Berry once again came to the rescue. But Miss Berry was herself not in the best of health, and the search continued for someone to take over the heavier household work.

One apparent answer to the problem was the recalling of Elthea Griffin from Barbados. This, however, proved impossible. First, since her return to the island it had become her arduous task to take charge of her aged and sickly father, who required close and constant attention. Second, Lady adamantly refused even to hint in her letters that Elthea might be needed. It was not a matter of pride, but of consideration. Elthea, well advanced in years, had already performed a long term of service; it would be selfish to ask her now to take up her old duties. All of us were forbidden burdening her with tales of Lady's unfortunate turn of events. Against our better judgment the news remained undisclosed and Elthea continued caring for her father, while we cast about elsewhere for rescue.

The solution was, like most, a simple one, and I must confess it was not mine, but Ag's. This was in the late autumn of 1941, scant weeks before Pearl Harbor. Giving up serving tables at the Red Fox Café, Helen Zelinski came to the brick house across the Green, and she was the perfect answer.

It was as if she'd been waiting for years to step into her place at Lady's, and once finding it, she made the most of it. Lady called her a diamond in the rough, but nonetheless a gem. Helen had a rare strength, a primitive form that was at once knotty and smooth. Artless, often uncouth, she was louder and more rambunctious than our Nancy, as agreeable as Elthea, and as hard a worker as either. There seemed to be two distinct sides to her. She was both brusque and melting, and I soon discovered I could never know which to expect.

When I would enter Lady's house, she would look at me with a blaze of eagerness in her eyes; they shone with a willing kindliness that reminded me of photographs of the peasant immigrants arriving at Ellis Island—hopeful, desirous of good things, and full of strength. In all her looks and gestures there was appeal, a wish to please, and again I was struck by the vulnerability that she tried to hide behind her abrasive exterior. Life had not used her kindly; but Lady did, and the favor was returned, and once again things were running smoothly across the Green.

Coming home for the Thanksgiving holiday, I was, as usual, making the long trip down from New Hampshire by bus, since the train schedule was less convenient. I took a seat near the back by a window, alternately studying the worn copy of Bowditch's manual that had been Jesse's, and staring out the window, morosely thinking about Dottie Frame. Out of her sight, surely, in spite of her letters, I was also undoubtedly out of her mind.

When the bus got to Saltonville, a town in lower Massachusetts, we pulled in at the gas station that served as a stop on the route, and I got out to go to the bathroom. A pickup truck was parked at the pump, the driver squatting at a tire with the air hose. He looked vaguely familiar as I passed, and when I came out again, after calling the house to say I would be there in two hours, I discovered that the driver was Rabbit Hornaday. I hadn't seen him in some time and, like me, he had grown considerably. He offered me a ride to Pequot Landing in his truck, and though perhaps less comfortable, it was ultimately more convenient, because he would take me right to my door.

I was glad of his company. He wore new glasses, but the lenses were still thick and made him look more owlish than ever, enlarging his eyes as they did. But he could see well enough to drive, was in fact a good driver—"handy," as Jesse would have said—and I envied him his truck, jalopy that it was. A recent purchase, he had bought it with his mink money. I knew that he had been raising minks as a sideline, along with numerous other animals, and he said he'd driven up to Saltonville to buy a pair of beavers, which were in the back of the truck.

It was a strange situation between Rabbit and me. We were friends who weren't really friends—or the reverse, I wasn't sure. Uncomfortable silences opened between us which we both tried to fill with those topics we held in common, mainly local events and what we were going to do in the war when it came. Rabbit said that with his eyes they wouldn't take him. I knew he was disappointed. But he talked easily enough about his minks and beavers, explaining about the prices of the different pelts, nature habits, and so on, and I could tell he really had a feeling for animals. Far cry, I thought, from the scourge of Pequot Landing who'd massacred the Colonel's Belgian hares.

I asked about his sister Dora, who had been enrolled in a Quaker school near Philadelphia, where special cases like hers were treated carefully. Rabbit said she was getting along well; neither of us mentioned the events that had taken place that day at the railroad crossing. Several times I noticed that he'd bring Aggie's name into the conversation, but once he had it in, he didn't know what to do with it. He was, in fact, taking her to the movies that night. Ag and Rabbit Hornaday? I mentioned her name again, just to see his reaction, but he only suggested that I might like to come with them to the movies. Pequot Landing had recently acquired its own movie house, up on the Hooker Highway. I said I already had a date, having written Dottie Frame that I was coming home.

If Ag's name had produced no reaction, Dottie's did. Rabbit gave me a quick look, then began fiddling with the choke, but I knew he wasn't having motor trouble. I was having love trouble. I finally got it out of him; Dottie had been pinned to a college guy at the university and was going steady. So Rabbit and Aggie took me along to the movies that night.

The following afternoon I went to the library to return some of

Lady's books and get some others. As I put them on Miss Shedd's desk, I saw Cookie Bunder at a table in the corner with another girl I did not immediately recognize.

"How is school?" Miss Shedd inquired.

"Fine, Miss Shedd."

I don't suppose anyone ever gave much thought to Miss Shedd. She was just there, like Miss Berry, a local institution, and for uncounted years had supervised the reading habits of Pequot Landing. If any small fry ever thought they could sneak a volume of *Casanova's Memoirs* or *The Night Life of the Gods* past her eagle eyes, they were mistaken. "I don't think your mother would want you reading that," she would say. "Why don't you try *Northwest Passage*, it's very good," and she would put the other book aside.

After she had stamped the cards, I thanked her and went over to say hello to Cookie Bunder. The girl with her looked up and I realized it was Teresa Marini. What, I wondered, had happened to the Teresa Marini I had known? Had I been away that long, or had Dottie Frame merely blinded me?

Our whispering did not please Miss Shedd, and she obliged us with banishment. Cookie had to meet her mother, so I invited Teresa to the drugstore where we continued our conversation over sodas in the back booth. I couldn't get over the change in her. She was growing into a startlingly pretty young woman, with the dark glowing beauty of the Latins, deep shining eyes, and a smile that was broad and easy; I could tell right away that Teresa Marini loved to laugh—after my discovery about Dottie Frame I could use some cheering up.

While we were there, Porter Sprague came in, waiting impatiently while Mr. Keller filled a prescription for him. Spouse, he let those within earshot know, was not up to snuff. He glanced over at us without acknowledgment, but when he went out he said loudly to no one, "I don't know why these boys can't find some nice American girls to go around with."

I decided Teresa Marini was a nice American girl for someone to go around with—not me, however. I was still sunk over Dottie Frame. And shortly after I returned to school the Japanese bombed Pearl Harbor, President Roosevelt addressed the joint houses the next day, saying a state of war existed between the Axis powers and our country, and I buckled down to the books. I was to be graduated in June, and was hopeful of Officers' Training School, and a commission.

4

That Easter vacation, I went with Lady while she put the gazing-globe in its accustomed place atop the pedestal. We did not sit on the stone bench, however, for there was a chill in the air, and we came in to find that Helen had thoughtfully laid a fire. She brought sherry and biscuits and when she had gone I watched Lady in the lamplight; she didn't look well, I decided. With the outbreak of war, she had forced herself to come out of her self-imposed exile from the world, and joined in the home-front effort making itself felt across the country. She worked with the various Red Cross drives, and helped organize some of the local girls into student nursing units, and her kitchen was always open to welcome the air-raid wardens on their cold patrols around the blacked-out Green, when Helen would help her serve hot coffee and sandwiches. She even found it possible to go to church again.

When we had finished our sherries, Lady pointedly informed me that she was allowed two, so I refilled her glass, and stepped across Honey to poke up the fire. Helen came in and drew the chintz curtains, then the heavy blackout curtains that had been hung over them. Blackout curtains had become a mournful necessity in all our houses, and though one was used to them, still they had their funereal effect. Yet the room was as cozy and comfortable as ever, which I observed to Lady.

"Yes, perhaps," she replied, staring thoughtfully into the fire, "but who will have it when I die? The Historical Society? 'Josiah Webster House, Built 1702' and underneath 'Here lived Lady Harleigh for thirty years'? It's not much to leave, a house. I would like to leave something—but what? I wish I could have been an artist and leave a fine painting. Or have composed a piece of music that would be remembered. Or have written a book that would stay on Miss Shedd's library shelf. But I am not an artist, or even a mother, and when I die there will be only a stone in the cemetery."

She rested her eyes on me and smiled. "It's why I've loved you children so, hoping you would take some part of this house—and me—to remember. It's why I opened the house to you. It—hasn't been easy. I am a . . . private person. I have lived here and I shall die here and there are walls enough in this house. I have not wanted to build more of them around me. But sometimes it becomes necessary."

She seemed upset, and, leaving her sherry unfinished, she excused herself for her nap. I found Helen in the kitchen and asked her how Lady really was.

"She's well enough. She just needs people around. It's different now—she misses all you kids trooping in and out of here. And she misses . . ." Her glance went to the ceiling, and though I knew she meant Jesse I wondered why she gestured upward, then decided it was the notion of his having slept in Lady's bedroom for so long.

"You ought to write her, you know." Helen looked at me across the table where she sat leafing through a recipe book.

"I do, Helen."

"You ought to write more. She looks forward to your letters."

"But nothing ever happens at school. There's nothing to write about."

"Make something up. Make up a romance to interest her. You got a girl friend up there?"

I had several, over at the seminary, but since Dottie Frame I'd been keeping my nose to the grindstone—or, rather, in Jesse's copy of Bowditch's. Lew had already gone into the Army that winter, with Harry close behind, and I was itching to get into the Navy.

I graduated from Blankenschip that spring. Lady gave me a handsome wristwatch, and when I went to say goodbye to Miss Berry before I enlisted, she presented me with an onyx ring with a diamond chip in it, which had been in her father's stickpin. It was strange about Miss Berry—she seemed to look upon me with signal favor, saying she would be grateful if I would manage a letter to her sometimes, but I felt that it was not a relationship between her and me, but rather a mutual interest that we shared for Lady Harleigh and her welfare.

But Pequot Landing all seemed insignificant and far away when I went to boot camp at Great Lakes Naval Training Station, and thereafter to communications school where I became Signalman Third Class. I joined my ship at Bremerton, Washington, one of the first aircraft carriers to be floated since the Pacific Fleet was destroyed at Pearl Harbor, and when we made port after our shakedown cruise, I was granted a ten-day leave.

In the meantime Lady had had her accident in the department store, the tests had revealed her red-cell deficiency, and Dr. Brainard had discovered that the treatment he had instituted was not working. Nor did any medicine he prescribed seem to help. At last it was decided that Lady must go into the hospital for the first of her long series of transfusions.

She had become querulous and petulant by turns. She now seemed to regard the war as a personal inconvenience, and I heard from Aggie how she complained—about rationing, about the lack of gas, about having to keep the curtains drawn. She would not confront her illness as she had her life; she weakened, then succumbed to it. Nothing pleased her, she found every opportunity to complain, she refused to read the paper or listen to the radio, the news during those dark days upset her so much. It was as if she washed her hands of the whole business.

Her trips to the hospital and the transfusions proved more frequent, then ultimately became a regular part of her medical pattern. She had just been released when I returned home on leave, and as I came into her bedroom she gripped my hand, holding me and asking me to help her. She didn't want the doctor to send her back to the hospital again.

"I hate it so. If I have to do that to live, then I don't want to live. I don't—I don't." She began weeping, and seeing her cry was something I never could bear. To relieve her anxieties, I said I would talk to Dr. Brainard.

"It won't do any good. He says I must." She drew up the sleeve of her bed jacket and showed me her arms, covered with ugly bruises. "And they're going to get me a nurse. Why can't I have Miss Berry back again?"

"Miss Berry isn't up to it. Ma says she's been—" I didn't want to say that Miss Berry was also ill. I again reassured her that I would talk with the doctor and see what might be done.

Doctor Brainard spoke to me with candor, as if we were two adults together. Some of the hospital tests had revealed the fact, undiagnosed originally, that Lady, at the time of her influenza, had also been stricken with encephalitis, generally known as "brain fever." Though she had recovered on her own, she had suffered damage, which was now affecting her thinking processes and hastening the debilitation we were witnessing. The return to the hospital was absolutely necessary. Helen was not a trained nurse, and since Miss Berry's being put on the case was out of the question, other arrangements would have to be made. The transfusions could be administered at home, but they were a difficult process, since, because of a developing sclerotic condition, the arteries had contracted and it was a painful task getting the blood through them.

It was a long time before I saw her again. Our carrier was involved in a good deal of the South Pacific and mid-Pacific action. Off New Guinea, we suffered damage and fires, and during the action I was injured. Pieces of metal had to be removed from my back, and while I was in the hospital a letter from Helen reached me. I was due for leave again when my back had repaired, but the letter warned me of an altered Lady.

"She's as well as may be expected," her letter ran, "but she's been in and out of the hospital half a dozen times since May. And it's been so hot. Dr. Brainard says she is holding her own as best as can be hoped for. She seems so different to me. She talks a lot about her mother. I don't think she liked her very much. She don't seem to want to sit quiet or still for long. She keeps pulling at her dresses and puts on and takes off her bracelets all the time. Sometimes I don't understand her so good, but most of the time I do. Lots of times she sees a ghost—I think it's her dead husband. She don't want to pay attention to things like the war. The news about your brother upset her real bad, and she always asks when you are coming home."

The report of Lew's death at the Anzio beachhead had come to me through official channels. It had been a bitter blow to me, to all of us, and I knew how badly Lady would take it, but there had been no shielding her from it. It was Miss Berry who had gone and told her. Aggie had written that Miss Berry was up and around again, as well as ever.

When I came home that winter, I saw immediately the changes in Lady that Helen had mentioned. As I walked into her bedroom, she darted Helen a blank look, then put on a party smile. "Here's a nice young man come to see me." She regarded me brightly, but I realized she had no idea who I was. I came across the room and stood by her bed. "Yes, young man? You're in the Navy, is that it? Does your mother have a star in a window?"

"Yes." I bent and kissed her. She drew back with a sudden swift realization, her eyes brightening. "Is it you?"

She knew me then. Helen left the room, and I drew up the chair beside her bed. Honey lay on the rug, half under the dust ruffle of the bed, as if trying to get as close to her mistress as possible, and looked out at me with great, limpid eyes. Surely the dog knew that Lady would not be with us for long, surely she was as sorrowful as

I. Even with Helen's warning, I was not prepared for the change in Lady. While I had been in the Marianas, at Saipan and Tinian, she had aged considerably. Though her skin remained unlined, with hardly any wrinkles, it was drawn tight across the bone structure, and had the bluish glint of the long-ill. Her hair had gone completely gray, and though it was still looked after with care—Helen's work, I supposed—she was not the Lady I remembered. Her nose thrust out with beakier prominence, and I was more aware of the bump below the bridge.

"Well, what have you been reading?" I asked lightly, noting several books on the night table.

"Oh, those—it's something called *Forever*—something. I can't remember. It's about a trollop. I can't see the print. The girl doesn't read to me so well."

"Would you like me to?" The book was *Forever Amber*.

"Yes. But not that one. Take those back to—what's her name—Miss Shedd? and see what else she has."

"Did Miss Shedd pick these out for you?"

"Don't ask me things like that. I don't *know*. I only know they're unreadable."

"All right—'not to worry, not to fret.'"

"You." She pushed her hand weakly and playfully at me, and I made conversation as I might, telling her where I had been and how it had gone, and delving for whatever there might be amusing for her in it all. There was little. The war was in its third year, and though, since the battle of Leyte Gulf, they said the tide was slowly turning, for us it didn't turn fast or far enough.

Whatever talk she initiated on her own dealt either with her mother or with the wartime shortages, which she found a continuing nuisance.

"Imagine, Helen can't even bake—there's no chocolate, no sugar, no anything."

"Try it with honey. That's what Mother does. And you can still get coconut."

Helen came in with Lady's dinner. I started to get up, but she signaled me to stay seated.

"We've got meat tonight, Mrs. Harleigh," Helen said cheerfully, with a look at me. "Aren't we lucky? Mr. Andersen at the A. & P. got some beef, and he saved some for us."

"Meat? Meat? What sort of meat?" Lady lifted the silver warming lid and looked at the plate. "What on earth is *that*?"

"Rump roast! I can't eat rump roast."

"Of course you can. Woody will stay while you eat it. And don't you go feeding it to him; he gets plenty of beef in the Navy, isn't that so?" She fixed me with a look.

When Helen had gone, Lady picked at the carefully prepared food, but ate little. I didn't urge her.

After a while she went into a doze, and the tray tilted on her lap. I removed it, then stretched my back, which had been giving me trouble since Tulagi. I stood at the window, looking down across the Cove, at the yacht-club docks, empty of boats, the houses with their smoking chimneys, the barren trees, and, beyond, the bleak country roads, winding through white fields, snowy fields where foxes made their lairs, and the wind sang old songs.

Down in Lady's back yard I saw that someone had neglected to bring in the gazing-globe. In the frozen garden leaf blankets protected the unhardy perennials, shrubs were tented with stakes and burlap. What greens remained were shriveled, their leaves cringing against the cold. The icy walkway of brick, laid so carefully under Jesse's meticulous hand, still led precisely to the carefully laid-out circle of cemented brick, the vessel-shaped stone pedestal at its center, and, resting on its curved lip, the gazing-globe.

Dimly gleaming amid the frost-blue shadows, it seemed a small silver planet, orbitless, fixed, immutable, yet all-seeing, potent, and hypnotic, the harborer of secrets past and future. A fragile yet enduring sight, familiar and evocative, and I thought I could not remember a time when it had not been so.

Lady stirred, and asked what I had been looking at; I felt she had been observing me for some time. When I said it was the gazing-globe, she fretted, saying Rabbit was careless, didn't he know it could crack in the cold?

"Go," she commanded, "go and get it. Bring it here. I want it where I can see it. I never get to see my garden anymore. What's the sense of things if they can't be used!"

So I brought the gazing-globe in, and set the nub in a vase on her dressing table, where the globe shone before her mirror and among the glass perfume bottles and her ivory vanity set.

"There," I said, "is that better?" But she was crying, wringing her hands together and twisting her head on the pillow. I sat and tried to calm her. "What is it?" I asked, turning her troubled face to me.

"It's a terrible thing—me—alive. Why can't I die? How terrible that Lew should die, and I must go on living. God can be so cruel—"

I had hoped to avoid talking about Lew. I didn't know what to say, her tears upset me so. Her expression became fretful again as she turned her eyes back to the gazing-globe on the dressing table.

"It's the goblin's mirror, all of it, isn't it?" She closed her eyes and shook her head. "I didn't want to see things in the goblin's mirror. Ugly people doing ugly things. How ugly it all is—"

"What is?"

"Today. The world. The war. Ugly, ugly, ugly." She pounded her fists on her thighs. I tried to restrain her, but she thrust my hands from her, and threw her head back with a forlorn cry.

"Oh, I am a vain and foolish woman. Yes, foolish. I have wanted the esteem of the world, and why? Tell me, for what?"

She sobbed and would not be consoled. Then, face contorted, eyes streaming, she turned her head to me and groped for my hand.

"I have done terrible things in my life—dreadful things."

No, I said, and no again, but it was no use. I brought the nurse, who gave her a sedative, and at last she fell into an exhausted, murmuring doze.

We drew the blackout curtains, and while the nurse knitted in the chair, I sat on the foot of the wicker chaise, wondering at what Lady had said. In the curve of the gazing-globe I could see her distantly reflected, her head moving on the pillow and illuminated by the bedside lamp. Friend of my youth, not old even now, yet dying, but unable to die. Dying in the bed she had shared with Jesse Griffin, whose memory possessed her now as Edward Harleigh's had before. Guilt, and guilt. Ugly, and ugly. But "terrible, dreadful things"? Yes, she had been vain, perhaps even foolish, but, still seeing her reflection, I thought that it was as someone had written, "the best mirror is an old friend." Nothing she had done or could do would be terrible or dreadful to me.

It was her sad way of looking at her life, as the globe was a way of looking at images, at all of life, at the world. And again I saw what she had wanted me to see, that in the globe all continued in one unbroken line; there was continuance in time and space, and in existence. Infinity into eternity. And I thought perhaps that was why the Snow Queen in the story had set Kay his task, and why he could not do it; because "Eternity" could not be spelled from broken bits, but must come of its own accord and of one unbroken piece.

Later, I sat in the kitchen talking with Helen Zelinski. It was pleasant having a quiet moment, and it seemed to me, as we sat in the pool of light spreading over the old table, that the shadowy forms of Jesse and Elthea Griffin hovered somewhere around the edges, she coming from the pantry with a loaf of fresh-baked bread, he from the cellar in his slippers. It spoke to me of the years that had gone, and I thought I could sit there forever, content never to leave that friendly old room.

Just before suppertime Rabbit's truck pulled into the drive. Aggie was with him; they had been cleaning his mink cages and were cold and tired. Rabbit had brought two skinned hares to help his mother with the meat shortage.

"Oh, dear," Helen said doubtfully, "I doubt Mrs. Harleigh'd eat rabbit. Maybe I can fix it so she'll think it's chicken."

I could see that Rabbit was envious of my uniform, and he asked a lot of questions about shipboard life, and the fighting in the Pacific. I really didn't want to talk about the war. As I got up to leave, there was a hurried knocking on the back door, and when Helen opened it we found Porter Sprague blustering on the threshold.

"Someone left their lights going. That your truck out there?" he said sternly to Rabbit. He had on a tin hat and a Civil Defense band certifying him as an air-raid warden. Rabbit ran out to douse his lights while Mr. Sprague made official noises and jotted a note on a little pad.

"Just for the record. You home on leave?" he said to me. "That's some fruit salad you have there." He leaned to view my chest ribbons and I had to explain to him what each one was.

"I'd be out there myself, if they'd let me," he told the room at large. "I was with the 139th in France, y'know." Rabbit came back and resumed his chair without saying anything. "I wish all you boys could know," Mr. Sprague banged on, "that we're doing what we can right here on the home front. The Spouse is a spotter, y'know —plane-spotter. Every night, over there on the dike, don't matter what the weather. Too bad about those eyes," he said to Rabbit in a commiserating tone. He was as falsely hearty as ever; some people never change, I thought.

"How's Mrs. Harleigh doing?" he demanded of Helen.

"As well as can be expected," she replied mildly.

"Well, now, that's fine, just fine. You tell her Porter Sprague and Spouse send best regards. Hope she'll be up and around soon. Tell her we speak of her often, Spouse and I. How is your little girl, anyway? We never should have listened to that child." He polished the dome of his tin hat on the sleeve of his mackinaw, and replaced it. "Well, have to finish my rounds—two rounds a night, all around the Green. Amazing how old Miss Berry goes on, isn't it? Say—" He fumbled in his pocket, took out a bill, and pressed it into my hand. "You have a couple of beers on P. J. Sprague and Spouse when you get back to—well, wherever you're going. And slap that Jap, eh?"

Chuckling over his joke, he went out. Helen got up and closed the inner door.

"What did he mean about Dora? About listening to her?"

I looked at Rabbit and Ag, not knowing what to say. Rabbit said, "Who cares? You know how he is."

"No, I don't know how he is. What did he mean?"

"Forget it, Helen," I said, getting up and ostentatiously looking at the watch Lady had given me for graduation.

"I won't forget it—I want to know." Helen was trying to hold in her anger, and she was fearful at the same time, realizing that we were covering something up.

Ag spoke. "I think she has a right to know. It would be better for her."

I sat again, and told what I remembered of the poison-pen letters, of Dora's part in the affair, and of Jesse's death on the railroad tracks that day. When I finished, Helen was leaning her elbows on the table, crying.

"Dora did that? It's awful." She was aghast that it should have been her own child who had caused the misfortune. It was a terribly painful scene.

Undressing for bed that night, I looked at the money Mr. Sprague had pressed on me for "a couple of beers." It was a twenty-dollar bill. Well, I thought, it was a generous gesture, anyway. Maybe some people do change. Even so, it was difficult to think of him as anything but a cocky old blowhard, still trying to be a big frog in a small pond.

Years later, when I came home after the war, walking past their house on Main Street one evening, I saw a light in the living room. Impulsively I crept across the lawn and sneaked a look through the living-room window. He was sitting in a chair, while Mrs. Sprague sat on the sofa sewing. They were conversing quietly, but with animated interest. Then he got up and, passing the sofa to go into the hallway, he bent, kissed her on the cheek, and gave her hand a fond pat. They must have been in their seventies by then. Birds of a feather, I thought, but it was a nice thing for him to do.

5

Next day I took Lady's books back to the library and asked Miss Shedd (still Miss Shedd; she hadn't changed) to see if she couldn't find something amusing or interesting. She found me a Bennett Cerf humor anthology, and an H. Allen Smith, and before I left she leaned across her counter and kissed my cheek. There were tears in her eyes. Whoever thought old Miss Shedd was capable of that kind of emotion? "Keep safe," she said as I left.

I thought of the day I'd rediscovered Teresa Marini, over at the corner table, talking with Cookie Bunder. They were both away at college, Cookie at Swarthmore, Teresa in California. I had gone to the Marini farm and visited for an hour, while Mama Marini stuffed me with half of the dinner she was preparing. Teresa was living with her uncle, who had a vineyard outside of San Francisco, and she was studying to be a dental technician.

But there were other girls around. I found half a dozen of them at the drugstore. They were older, though, classmates of Harry's and Lew's, and most of them I knew only by name. But they looked pretty in their matching sweaters and cardigans, their bobbysocks and plaid skirts, with their hair parted and rolled in the pageboys that were currently fashionable. One I knew was Marge Harrelson, who'd been Lew's girl. She talked with me at the soda fountain. She didn't cry, but Ag had told me she'd had a tough time after Lew was killed. As we spoke, she kept touching the sleeve of my sweater, and I suddenly realized it must have been as familiar to her as it was to me, because it was one of Lew's. Leaving, I asked her if she'd like to have it. I took it to her the day I went to report for duty again.

When I'd taken the books to Helen to give to Lady, I went across the Green to call on Miss Berry. She felt, she said, right as rain, and she looked it. We sat in her sun porch, talking—the clusters of dogs moving around us, the canary in its cage, the sansevieria plant in the blue pot which had been in her window ever since I could remember. Her furniture looked the same: chairs well sat in, carpets heavily walked on, the plants tended, figurines of painted porcelain, no pictures to speak of. She had to explain the pedigree of the latest dogs, which had sired which, which had died. Like the Great Elm out the windows, like Miss Berry herself, it seemed the dogs would go on forever.

We spoke of Honey, Lady's dog that had been P. J. Sprague's. I said poor Honey must be seeing her last days, she moped around so, but certainly not from old age. We figured out that Honey must be almost ten, which wasn't old for a dog.

"What happened to the dog you gave Lady?" I asked her.

"That dog—that dog was a little Yorkie—Yorkshire terrier, don't you know. Pretty little thing. Adelaide was so fond of him."

Yes, I said, I knew that, but what happened to it? Something to do with Edward Harleigh . . .

"Yes, I s'pose," she remarked halfheartedly, and was in no way inclined to pursue the subject. "Adelaide's doing none too well, is she? Poor girl, poor dear girl." Her sigh was despondent; not like Miss Berry at all, I thought. "So young—so young to go. And to suffer so."

We spoke at length of our friend over in the brick house, but of the little dog not another word was mentioned until we stood at the door saying our goodbyes. As Miss Shedd had done earlier, she kissed my cheek, though her eyes did not tear. Miss Berry never allowed herself the luxury of tears. "When you come back, safe and sound, then we'll sit and have a nice long talk." I thought then there were things she wanted to tell me, but many years were to pass before Miss Berry and I had that talk.

The door closed, and as I stood looking at the Great Elm—that never seemed to change, either—a car shot from my left and careened into the drive, narrowly missing the phone pole. It was Gert Flagler, the car was a 1938 De Soto. She managed to more or less straighten it as she jerked to a stop and got out. She was wearing one of her round felt hats, and a butt-sprung tweed skirt with enough yardage for two, and the inevitable brogans, and she swung her great pocketbook with the same old gusto. But I detected a change in her attitude, a slight embarrassment as she ducked her head and put out her paw. "You're home. Glad to see you," she boomed, giving my hand a hefty shake. "Some war. Did you have a visit with Mary?"

I said I had, and was happy to see Miss Berry in good health again.

"I tell her she's immortal. Me, I'll kick off any day that comes around, but Mary, she's going to live forever." She plucked off her hat, blew out her cheeks, and rumpled her hair as she looked at her door front. "We've been living here almost forty years this spring. A long time. Poor Mary cooped up for forty years with an old thing like me. I dunno how she's put up with it." She turned and gave me a perplexed look, one of sudden discovery. "You think I'm just an old fool—all you kids thought Gert Flagler's just a fat, old fool." I started to protest, but her upraised hand silenced me. "I know, I know. I never was nice to you kids. Didn't know how to be. Scared hell out of me, you did. But I liked you all, honest, if you—"

She shook her head wonderingly, clasping her pocketbook against her chest.

"If what, Mrs. Flagler?"

"If you hadn't always been riding that damn cow. Made her milk go sour, y'know. Still, I liked havin' you kids around—I miss you now."

6

It was another twenty months before I came home again, in early August of 1945. The European war was finished, and by then people were saying it would soon be over in the Pacific as well, but our troops were bogged down on Okinawa, and predictions were that the Marines would have to take Tokyo on foot through the rice paddies.

I had been sent to Officers' Training School and been commissioned as an ensign, and assigned to a destroyer which was on "bird-dog" duty in the China Sea, in the Ryukyu Islands, patrolling the waters for downed fliers. Somehow, in that pocket of the globe, a letter reached me. It was from Helen Zelinski. She hoped I was safe, and that the war would be over soon. Then, without further preamble, she gave me the tragic news about her son.

For the past year Rabbit Hornaday had been working for a trucking company over in West Farms, running the route from Boston to Hartford. He was bringing down a load of canned goods from Crosse & Blackwell, and it being a cold night he turned on the heater in the truck. His glasses had steamed before he realized it and, missing a turn, the truck slipped from the road down an incline. He was pinned in the wreckage for eleven hours before he was found. They had had to amputate both legs.

The rest of Helen's letter held no better news. Honey, the setter dog, was dead; had been run over in the roadway by a speeding motorist. This was before Rabbit's accident, and he, being there at the time, had tried to save the animal, but had not succeeded. Lady was inconsolable. As might have been expected, she was much worse. The transfusions were being continued, but with no greater ease. She found little relief from her pain, and in the past year, to everyone's amazement, she had become a difficult patient. In the hospital she had actually slapped a nurse, and the nurse had quit the case. Another she threatened with her cane because the nurse "bustled and was too sunshiny." Dr. Brainard thought a nursing home might be the answer, but Helen, who had moved into a position of supreme authority in matters regarding Lady, had vetoed the proposal. If Mrs. Harleigh could come home again, Helen would take complete charge. Round-the-clock nurses had been hired.

"Half the time," Helen's letter continued, "she don't recognize anybody, of course. She often calls me 'Anna,' which was her mother's name. One morning she got away from the nurse and somehow got down to the kitchen. This was before Harold's accident and he was having a sandwich. Mrs. Harleigh shook her cane at him and we thought she was going to hit him. 'Don't you work?' she yelled at him, and when Rabbit said he was taking down the storm windows she got very red and said, 'Well, get on with it, then, and stop sitting around on your ——' (you know that word) 'Jesse never loafed around here.' It really was awful, Woody, it took three of us to get her back to bed again. Another time, when she rang her bell and the nurse didn't come, she threw a bottle at her dressing table. You know how she always keeps that gazing-globe on it. Well, the bottle just missed the gazing-globe, but it broke the mirror behind. And it upsets her that one of the nurses is a Negro. She says strange things about her, and I know if the nurse, Mrs. Johnson, hears them, she'll leave. And Mrs. Harleigh *needs* her. The doctor says she may go on like this for a long time, or that she could die any moment. And she's doing very strange things. I begged the nurses not to tell anyone out of the house about this, but because you're so close to her I think you ought to know.

"She keeps talking to her dead husband—you know, Edward? She still sees a ghost—I mean she really *sees* it. She talks to it all the time. It's awful strange. Then, sometimes she's perfectly herself and makes sense. She likes to have the gazing-globe put beside her bed and she stares into it, but she tries to cover the reflection of her face with her thumb.

"The nights are the worst, and Dr. Brainard has had to come over several times and give her a shot to quiet her. Once she found a shotgun in a closet and aimed it at the doctor when he came in. She kept saying he was Mr. Ott and she would kill him. Nobody could figure out who Mr. Ott is. When she's making sense, she asks about you and wants to know when you're coming home. I just hope she doesn't die before you get here. The doctor wants to put her back in the hospital again."

All of this I discussed with Teresa Marini when I found her, by accident, in San Francisco. Our ship returned to San Diego, and I was sent briefly to Treasure Island to have my back examined, and I came across Teresa in the De Young Museum. She had spent the early summer at her vintner uncle's, and was leaving at the end of the week for Pequot Landing. Since I was being granted leave, I arranged through friends to secure two priority plane seats, making sure they were side by side, and Teresa and I traveled to New York together, then took the train to Lamentation Mountain. A few days before we arrived, they dropped the bombs, first on Hiroshima, then on Nagasaki, and everyone was saying the war would end there and then.

If anything, Teresa had become more beautiful since I'd seen her last, and I planned on seeing a lot of her during my leave. She had other news of home. Dottie Frame had married an Air Corps pilot, and had gone with him to Georgia, then had left him four months later, and was now back in town. Jack and Phil Harrelson were due to return from Europe at any time, as was Teresa's brother Johnny. Rabbit Hornaday was bitter about his accident and wouldn't talk to anyone, except my sister, Agnes. Agnes was spending most of her time at Mrs. Hornaday's; he was recuperating there, going no farther than from his bed to the porch, where he watched the freights go by.

7

Agnes met us in Ma's car at Lamentation. She said Lady was having a bad day, and the nurse had asked that I come in the evening. We dropped Teresa at the Marini farm; then Ag and I drove to our house, where I had a happy reunion with Ma, Kerney, and Nancy.

Kerney had shot up, and his voice made me laugh, it had gotten so deep. He had cut himself shaving and had a Band-Aid on his neck. Nancy looked the same. Ma was so relieved to have me home that while we sat on the sofa she never let go of my hand. The telephone rang; it was Helen Zelinski calling to say that Lady Harleigh was awake, and that I might come over.

I scarcely recognized her, the change was so great. It is not a pleasant thing to see someone you love wither before your eyes, to alter little by little, or even greatly, as she had periodically from visit to visit, month to month, year to year. She was a diminished creature, and now there could be no doubt of it; she was dying.

But she knew me. I took her hand and held it in my two, then her other one came up and touched my cheek. She was crying.

"Have you come home?"

"Yes."

"For good? Are you safe?"

"Yes, I'm safe."

"Oh, my dear, my dear." Her hand felt soft and warm on my cheek. "I was afraid I wouldn't be here when you came." She made an effort to stop the trembling in her voice.

"How handsome you've grown. And an officer, too—all those ribbons. Your mother must be very glad. What is this bomb they've dropped on the Japs? Was it a big explosion?"

I told her what little I knew, assuring her again that I was all right and that the war would soon be over.

"It will be such a relief. I haven't been able to bake, you know, there's been no sugar."

I laughed and drew up the chair. "Yes, I know. No sugar." She closed her eyes wearily, and I patted her hand, though it provided her little comfort. The nurse and Helen had evidently fixed her up for the occasion. She wore a new bed jacket, and her hair was done up in a little pug on the top of her head. Patches of scalp showed through the gray fibers. Her cheeks were sunken; the skin around the eyes was drawn in wrinkles of pain, with pale blue pouches beneath. All of life seemed to have ebbed from her face; the passion, the ardor, even the smile had been absorbed, blotted up by the steady failing of her person. There was a deadly rasp in her throat, she was having obvious trouble breathing, but from time to time she murmured a few scarcely distinguishable words.

I stayed only fifteen minutes that evening. The nurse came in and signaled me to leave. Each day thereafter I would go and sit by Lady's bedside, and during her lucid moments I would try to amuse her, to occupy her thoughts, and divert them from whatever it was that troubled her so greatly. Sometimes she would recognize me, sometimes not. Once she insisted there was a tiger in the yard and I must get Edward's shotgun and shoot it. I made a show of doing this, and reported the tiger dead. She ordered the mythical creature skinned (Rabbit Hornaday could do this, she suggested); she would like a rug made of it, hoping for enough left over for a muff—winters were chilly, particularly sleigh riding. Another time she confided to me that the doctor (she couldn't remember his name) had recently taken her off liquor (she'd been off for more than two years), and would I sneak down to Elthea's pantry and mix her a martini? I did, unbeknownst to Helen or the nurses. Lady sipped it gratefully, between pejoratives for the doctor, that "dreadful Porter Sprague," and her own mother. At another time she insisted that Jesse must drive her to the beauty parlor to have her hair looked after.

One afternoon four of us—Teresa and I, Agnes and Rabbit—went on a picnic, driving through the old Connecticut River towns to a place we used to go to years before, where there was a waterfall and a shady pool for swimming. I'd brought along a portable radio, and so it was that we received the news of the Japanese surrender. We packed up our things and I kept the gas pedal down as we hurried back to Pequot Landing.

The town had gone wild with celebration. People were whooping it up in the street outside the fire station and the drugstore. Miss Jocelyn-Marie was applauding Porter Sprague, who was marching around with a Japanese flag and wearing his air-raid warden's helmet.

When we got to the Green, it seemed that all the doors were flung open and people were congregating as if by some recognizable signal under the branches of the Great Elm. The Sparrows were there, and the Harrelsons, and the Marinis—old Tony and his wife —and Teresa's younger brothers and sisters. And other neighbors, some of whom, newcomers, I didn't recognize. All those joyful, friendly faces, all the happiness of that momentous afternoon.

We stopped at Lady Harleigh's, where Helen said that Lady was being bathed by the nurse, and could we wait a bit. And if that racket out there didn't do Mrs. Harleigh in, nothing would. Cars were careening around the Green, some straight across it, including a spanking new squad car, siren going full blast, and someone was shooting off a gun. As though drawn to this most historic part of town, people were coming over from the Center, including P. J. Sprague, still with his Japanese flag, which he was flourishing like a matador's cape. Eamon Harmon and his wife were holding a sort of open house on their front porch, and the country-clubbers had already forgathered for a pitched and drawn-out celebration.

At dusk the streetlights came on, and though this had become common practice again since the danger of bombing from Europe had ended, still it was a happy sight. Drinks were being served at people's front doors, and rejoicing continued unabated. I wished Lew could have been there to see it. And Blue Ferguson.

Under the Great Elm the crowd grew more boisterous by the moment. Firecrackers were being exploded, car horns were blowing, one of the country-clubbers on the Harmons' porch had a jazz whistle, another a fish horn, another a cowbell, an orchestrated madness while more drinks were downed. Johnny Marini, Teresa's brother, appeared—had gotten into town that very moment—and there were tears and hugs among the many Marinis. I saw Helen waving from Lady's stoop, and while Teresa went home with her family I made my way across the Green, accepting backslaps and kisses as if I'd won the war single-handed.

"Is it over?" Lady asked weakly when I came into her room. "Is it really over?"

"It's all over."

"Thank God."

I made conversation, telling her about our picnic and the town's rejoicing out on the Green, and that Johnny Marini had come home.

"Oh, dear, oh, dear, you're all home. All?" She paused in fugitive recollection. "No—who's missing? Someone—" Her voice trembled more, and she began to cry.

"Lew—Lew won't be coming home," I said.

"Lew is dead?"

"Yes. Let's not talk about it, okay?"

"Oh, my dear, I've upset you—I'm so sorry." With difficulty she reached out and touched my face. I thought of the winter I'd fallen through the ice, and she had nursed me. Those hands, so loving and so willing. Now it was too much effort for her to even lift them.

She jumped slightly as more firecrackers exploded out on the Green. Sounds of merriment came from all directions; like the sounds of one giant party.

"You should be out there, with the others. Not here with me."

"Of course I should be here. I want to be. This is the best part."

"Oh, the best part—there isn't any best part anymore."

"It is for me."

"How dear you are. My l'il Ignatz—except you're my big Ignatz now. If I were younger, would you marry me?"

"In a minute. But I'm going to marry Teresa Marini, and I want you to come to our wedding. You know—larks and everything?"

"You're going to be married? To Teresa?"

"Not right away. Don't you approve?"

"Of course I do. Teresa is fine—a lovely girl. She'll give you lots of children. Lots of—" She trailed off, murmuring Teresa's name in a tone of vague speculation, as though wondering if she really did approve. Then she closed her eyes and was still.

Outside, the noise became even louder. I heard the bell of the fire truck, and it sounded as if there were people down on the lawn. I recognized Eamon Harmon's jovial bass voice, and Mr. Harrelson's. The 5:10-ers must be working their way down the Green, I decided. There were calls and shouts, and then they began singing, drunkenly, but happily. The nurse hurried in to shut the window, followed by Helen, who was bringing me a Tom Collins.

"What are they doing out there? Don't they know Mrs. Harleigh's—"

Lady opened her eyes and they caught mine as we listened to the singing. We had recognized it at the same instant.

"Wait," I told the nurse before she could slam the front window down. "Open it, she wants to hear."

She raised the sash again, and turned with a dismayed expression, but Lady was smiling. She knew the song was for her.

> "Good night, Lady, good night, Lady,
>   Good night, Lady, we're going to leave you now.
>   Merrily we roll along, roll along, roll along—"

She fumbled for a handkerchief, sniffled, and laughed wryly. "If that's Colonel Blatchley down there, you'd better tell him it's Lady that's going to leave him." The serenade ended and the voices quieted, though the revelry continued unabated at a distance. Helen and the nurse retired again, and I continued to sit by Lady's bedside. There was still the trace of a smile on her lips as I helped her straighten herself on her pillows. While she dozed, I wandered to the back window and looked out on the flowering garden, and thought of other times. I felt a bitter sorrow then, as ghosts from the past nudged me. I seemed to see myself on the carriage-house roof, with Lew below, watching as I flew into the cucumber frame. I saw Lady seated on the terrace wall while the boat parade went by. I saw us digging out the septic tank. Saw Dora spying from the loft window; saw myself in the wind, rescuing the gazing-globe. Saw Blue Ferguson's market truck parked at Mrs. Pierson's kitchen door. Saw Lady and Jesse making their spring garden. I thought with amusement how they had fooled us all, she playing the Merry Widow while they lived up here as man and wife. Absently, I ran the tips of my fingers along my chin: I needed a shave. How was that possible? I was still a boy, wasn't I? I hadn't been away, had I? Lew was still alive. Blue was driving for the Pilgrim Market, Jesse and Elthea were downstairs. . . . I raised my glass to absent friends.

" 'Ladybug, ladybug, fly away home—' "

Hearing her speak, I turned and saw her smiling, as if in that old and miraculous way of hers she were reading my thoughts. She broke off and lifted her brows, one of her minute signals I could still read.

" 'Your house is on fire, your children will burn. . . .' " I gave her back the line, and she asked me to take her to the chaise. I prepared it, then carried her in the bedcovers to it, where she lay back with a tiny sigh of contentment.

"Those tulips—did I put in bulbs this year?"

I explained that Papa Marini had come and done the work, which had restored her gardens to their former glory.

"Oh, Mr. Marini," she said, as if he were there with us, "thank you. Thank you." Her brow furrowed and she reached out toward the window. "But I don't see it—"

"See what?"

"The gazing-globe. Jesse's gazing-globe."

"It's there—in the vase on the dressing table."

"Why is it there?"

"You wanted it. You said you wanted it in the room."

This seemed to register, and to afford her some satisfaction. "Yes, that's nice."

"You said 'Jesse's gazing-globe'?"

"Jesse's, yes. He bought it for me, you know."

"No, I didn't."

Her eyes snapped briefly and her voice had an impatient edge.

"Well, he did. He said I could see the whole world in it, if I wanted. He said—" The effort of talking was costing her too much. I tried to calm her, but she was persistent. "He said, 'Broken mirrors can't be mended. Neither can people, sometimes.' Perhaps he wanted it as a reminder to me. I treated him so dreadfully that time. He always liked my hair long, he liked to sit there on the bed and watch me brush it. So I cut it. To spite him. To make him unhappy. Wasn't that a dreadful thing to do?"

I remembered it well, the day I'd overheard the argument about the shrine on the gate-leg table. I remembered her slamming the silver brush at the mirror and the shattering noise it made.

"I wonder . . ." she murmured.

"What?"

"Oh . . . nothing important . . ." She smiled reassuringly; then her expression altered slightly, became a little sly, a little knowing. "He's down there, you know."

"Who?"

"You know . . ." Again her brows indicated a secret understanding between us. "Our friend. Ott."

"Ott? The red-haired man?" On her deathbed, the conclusion, the dénouement, the final revelation . . . The room became still, and the silence of the room was broken by the bursts of laughter out on the Green. Someone was ringing the fire bell, and the country-clubbers were singing "Der Fuehrer's Face."

"Promise not to tell?" She said it like a little girl with a childish secret to be told.

"I promise."

"He's under the pedestal."

"The gazing-globe?"

"Yes. Under the brickwork."

"I thought he was in the sewer excavation."

"I know you did. I did, too. I was sure of it."

"First I thought he was in the coal bin."

"But he was. For a time. Then Jesse put him in a drift behind the carriage house. He was frozen all winter. By spring he had to be moved. Jesse wouldn't tell me where. I thought sure he'd done something to stop up the sewer line and that was why the Green was so wet. I was awfully frightened. But Jesse put him in the garden—it was the night of my birthday party—and next day he began laying the bricks over him. It was the last thing he told me—"

I recalled Jesse's disappearance at the party, and how he'd come in, cold and with muddy shoes, when Lady was singing. Recalled too the muffled words into Lady's shoulder that day at the freight station. "Yes. I see."

"No one will know, now. Will they?"

"No. No one will know."

"I'm glad."

A slight flutter of her fingers on the back of my hand, then she slid off to sleep again, or if not to sleep to that alien place she now spent so much of her time in. Her mouth opened and the rasp began in her throat again. The nurse would disapprove my having moved her, I was sure. I took her into my arms, returned her to the bed. She stirred uneasily, softly moaning, then uttering unintelligible sounds in a strident tone. When I had settled the covers around her again, she opened her eyes.

"Edward?"

"No. It's me."

All recognition was gone now. I said my name, got a glimmer. "Not Edward. No, I—wouldn't have supposed. He has been here enough, Edward."

"Has he?"

"Yes! Yes, he has!" The sound rang out, angry, defiant. She raised up on her pillow with an effort and fairly shouted the words at me, as though she found his presence in whatever form indefensible, heinous, not to be borne. She stared down at her pale, crabbed hand, clutching the top of the turned-down sheet. She held it up, inspected it. "I had pretty hands. What has happened? What have you done to me?"

"Nothing . . . nothing . . ."

"You have come for the end."

"It's not the end." In that reasoning yet hopeless tone that is self-defeating by its very intrusion.

"Yes. The end. Now. It is coming. Not quite now—but soon. He will come for me. He wants me buried beside him. He has told me so. So many times, he has told me. It will be his last revenge. I would a hundred times rather—no, no, it is fitting. Right and fitting." She laughed a wild, crazy laugh and I knew she hardly saw me. I reached to calm her, she flung my hand away, then fell exhausted on the pillow. Her torment was more painful to witness than anything that had preceded it. I groped for a glass and the bottle of sedative pills. She seemed to understand what I was doing, and she shook her head. "No. No pills. They make me sleep— If I sleep, you'll be gone. Bring—"

She was pointing at the globe. I took it from the bureau and placed it in her hands. She stared into it, looking like a gypsy fortune-teller, the hag-seeress. She spoke again: "All things, past and future are here. I can see them. The future—I will come back to you. I know you are waiting." I realized she was talking not to me but to Edward.

"Are you listening?"

Now she was looking at me; she seemed to have confused my physical being with his ghostly presence. I said yes, I was listening.

"Edward—he—" The name choked her, she couldn't get beyond it. I said she already had told me about Edward, reminding her of that day on Lamentation Mountain. She shook her head.

"No—more—more—"

But she could not. Using what little remained of her resources, she looked from me—or the imagined Edward—back to the globe. Her senses seemed briefly to right themselves, and her features relaxed slightly. Then, peering at her curved reflection in the globe, she began to cry softly.

"Do you love me?" she asked.

"Yes." I did not know if I spoke as myself or as Edward.

She said, "And Jesse loved me. That is enough for one lifetime. But I have done dreadful things—terrible things—"

"No—"

"I have! I have! I have lived in hell and I will go to hell. It's in the Bible! Dreadful, terrible things!" Her voice rose in a crescendo, drowning out the celebration on the Green. She did not continue, but lay panting from her exertions, staring intently into the globe resting on her chest. "But that is all in the past. We know the future. Now there is only the—"

She clamped her lips. The present would not do for her. Her fingers relaxed, the silver ball slipped from her grasp, and before I could catch it, it fell to the floor and smashed to pieces. Unperturbed, Lady glanced down with a faint smile.

"There," she said, as though in this dying moment she had solicited and won some small but signal victory. "Make 'Eternity' from those if you will."

She closed her eyes. I brought the wastebasket and one by one dropped the pieces into it, then brushed away the remaining bits of silver dust. The past, the present, and the future, exploded, gone.

I carried the basket to the door, then stopped as she murmured something.

"What did you say?"

"I said send for a priest. I want to confess."

"You mean the minister—Mr. Tuthill?"

"No. The priest. Father O'Brien."

Father O'Brien had been dead more than fifteen years. "You mean Father Huegenay."

"It doesn't matter. Any priest will do." And as I left her I heard her murmuring to herself. "I wonder what that fight was all about?"

She held on through the week, and though Dr. Brainard said she might go at any time, still she lingered. On Saturday Father Huegenay was sent for to administer extreme unction; afterward, he left with an awed expression, even as Father O'Brien had thirty years before.

She died on Sunday morning. I had gone to First Church with Teresa, and afterward we drove over to Lamentation Mountain. I don't know why I decided to go there, except I wanted Teresa to see it. I told her about the day Blue Ferguson had come home, and repeated parts of Lady's story to her. Parts only, for still there were pieces lacking, ones I was sure I would never have, and that the story would end there, unsatisfactorily. I repeated what I could remember, but the missing pieces were to elude me for another ten years, until I learned the last astonishing facts.

Gazing down at the river, I recalled my visit with Lady to Lamentation Mountain six years earlier. Had it really been six? Today, with Teresa, past, present, future seemed one together. Over toward Pequot, there were the roofs and chimneys at the Center, and the familiar steeple. First Church, that was the past; George Washington had worshiped there. The present was the oil-storage tanks out near the airfield; where there had been two, now there were half a dozen, with smoking barges moored at the dock pumps. The future? I thought I knew where that lay. I looked at Teresa's finger, and the ring I had given her two nights ago.

We spoke quietly of the town where we had lived, had discovered each other in the accidental way people can, and of how we planned on leaving together. We spoke again of Adelaide Harleigh, and at that moment it seemed to me that I could see the town with her eyes, she who had loved it. She had known it to its core, could recognize most of its citizens by face and name. She had been able to see their faults with humor, their virtues with pride, for though she was not born there, she was of Pequot Landing. Born a Strasser, raised on Knobb Street, she lived a Harleigh of Broad Street, on the Green. She would die a Lady. *There* was a past, and a present, and a future, and they, too, seemed all one.

Later, I was sure we had been speaking of her at the moment of her death. When we drove back to the Green, Mr. Foley was coming out the front door, and it was he who gave us the news.

"Well," he said, "she had a nice life, didn't she, Lady Harleigh?"

"Yes," I said, "she did."

PART FIVE

Recollected Songs

All roads may lead to Rome; they do not lead, however, to Pequot Landing. But I have lived to discover that as a road can carry one away, so again it can carry one back. Interstate 91 has brought me back so many times since I left. It cuts across the edge of town between the Great South Meadow and the village cemetery. Coming off the parkway, you can see the cemetery markers below the First Church steeple. When I die, my ashes will be scattered, but if truth were known I would rather be there, in that churchyard, by that church, in the shadow of that steeple. I like the notion of being buried near to where Lady Harleigh lies. We would be old friends yet, sharing that close green Connecticut acreage.

I find it easier going back now, though for a time I did not, and I remember my first visit after having been away for more than ten years. We came back, Teresa and I, to a family reunion, in October. We had been married when I graduated from college. We lived for a time in New York, where our oldest boy was born. We named him Lewis, after my brother. Our two daughters, Addie and Susan, were born in California. Addie, naturally, had been christened Adelaide. The occasion for the reunion was Papa Marini's eightieth birthday, and we brought the children back for it. I had mixed feelings about returning. Ma had died, Nonnie was married and living in Michigan, Kerney was studying languages in Europe, Harry worked for an oil refinery in New Orleans, Nancy was gone. The only one of us left was Ag. She had married Rabbit Hornaday, who ran a thriving practice as a veterinarian. Ag took care of the office for him.

Making the curve at River Road, I slowed the car and looked in through the cemetery gates. I could see Edward and Lady Harleigh's matching headstones, and I felt a strange sensation. Perhaps it was nothing more than just feeling that I was a stranger in my own hometown—perhaps it was more. But as we drove down Main Street, that glimpse into the graveyard made me feel alien, and everything seemed different to me. The Spragues had lived in that house—they were dead; who lived there now? I had no idea. Keller's drugstore was gone, and the Pilgrim was a supermarket. The Noble Patriot (its black proprietor, Andy Cleves—dead also?) was now a cute Colonial-type beauty parlor. The Academy Hall was now a museum. There was no more Academy Parliament, nor indeed any Town Meeting. Teresa's brother, Johnny, was the mayor of Pequot Landing, which was run by a town manager. The library was larger and elsewhere, likewise the post office. There was a modern steel and glass structure in place of that Gothic pile, the Chester Welles Grammer School. Miss Grimes was dead, Miss Bessie worked for an advertising firm in New York. Everywhere I sensed the cunning hand of Time at work. It was changed, all changed.

Still the same trees billowed (but haven't they grown, Teresa said. I, too, remembered them as much smaller), and still the houses along Broad Street (but don't they seem little? Teresa said. I, too, thought they had shrunk) presented their handsome fronts to us as we passed, boasting fresh coats of paint with carefully considered colors on shutters and doorways, where their owners had hung raffia baskets filled with straw flowers of seasonal colors, where they had polished their street numbers, manicured their lawns, and shined their windows. Yet who were they, these owners of the houses? No one knew. Strange faces, strange children, strange cars. Strange, all strange.

Before pulling in at the Marini farm I drove down the road so the kids could see where "Daddy used to live." Who lived there now? The house had twice been bought and sold. The Sparrows were dead, Gert Flagler was dead, Dr. Brainard had moved to Vermont. But Miss Berry, as we had heard, was still going. There was no sign of her as we passed; we made the turn at the old trolley stop, and then were in front of Lady's. Her estate had been divided between Elthea Griffin and me, with generous bequests to various town funds. The house, also left to me, I had sold to another of Teresa's brothers, Dr. Robert Marini, a dentist.

There was a bike on the lawn, other signs of playthings. The birch trees in front never looked so fine as the elms. Different, all different.

And the Great Elm was gone. Like Lady, it had died piecemeal, branch by branch, haggard, lopsided, grotesque, pathetic. It had been felled at last by the Dutch blight. I remembered a time when I had thought that, like life, it would go on forever. I told the kids how we used to stand, three, four, five of us, trying to measure our own growth against it, to girdle with our outstretched arms and clasped hands its immense girth, feeling the scrape of bark against our cheeks as we leaned against it. "Gee, Dad, that must have been some tree," they said—but after all it was only a tree.

Before dinner I took the kids out on the Cove. One of Teresa's cousins had a motor launch, and I suggested going downriver. I shouldn't have. Hermitage Island was gone. It simply wasn't there at all, and from my reckoning the river had taken a different course entirely where it used to flow by both sides of the island. It was as if it had never been.

Gone, all gone.

Back at the Marini farm, things were different, too. Most of the acreage had been sold off for building lots; what remained was untilled. Papa Marini was on easy street. Big, blustering Mama seemed smaller and quieter, though she cooked as much as ever. There were aunts and uncles and cousins and nephews and nieces and sisters and brothers, and I had trouble making out the faces I should have remembered. Ag came, and Rabbit, and it was good to see them. Rabbit got along very well with prosthetic devices, and Ag proudly showed off their boy and girl. Rabbit said that after we ate, he would take all the children to see the fat badger he'd recently gotten.

After dinner, on the excuse of going to the store for cigarettes, I went around the Green again, this time trying to scent out the strangenesses and differences. I went down to our old house and had another look. Poor old house, it was more ramshackle than ever. There appeared to be nobody home, so I walked down the drive, to see how Pa's fruit trees had grown. When I came around the side of the garage, I stopped and stared. The trees, four cherry, four pear, four quince, four plum, had been chopped down. The stumps remained, sticking up through the unmowed grass. I couldn't believe it. Who would cut down those trees, for what reason? I felt heartsick.

Gone. Changed.

Everything but—

Out on the street again, I saw Miss Berry sitting in her sun parlor. They said she was in her nineties. She saw me, adjusted her spectacles when I waved, but did not recognize me until I had rung her bell and she opened the door. I went in for a visit, and as the door closed behind me and she took me into the sun porch, the years seemed to gather me up and draw me backward. At Miss Berry's, nothing had changed. It was like a small time capsule of my childhood. Here were the same old pieces of furniture, the same rugs, the descendants of dogs I had known, even a canary in the cage—not the same canary but a canary all the same—even, as she herself pointed out, the same sansevieria in the blue pot.

Even Miss Berry herself seemed the same, her manner still brisk, her mind agile. She was humorous, kindly, interested. As we talked, I thought of all the years she had inhabited that sun parlor, that little piece of space leased for her lifetime, as if she had long ago staked it out for her old age.

We spoke of Gert Flagler, who had died during Truman's term, which Miss Berry regarded as a mercy; Gert had not seen the Republicans come to power again. We spoke of Eamon Harmon, who had once ridden a horse as Jared Ingersoll in the pageant, and who now rode a chair lift up and down stairs. Both he and his wife, Eva, had given up drinking and smoking. Thin Eva was now plump. We spoke of Colonel Blatchley, who had sold his house and was living in a retirement apartment down in Two Stone. We spoke of Mr. Keller, the druggist, who was dead, but whose son ran the business in a new store on the highway. We spoke of Lew, dead for twelve years, of Blue Ferguson, dead even longer, and of Elthea, who unfailingly sent a Christmas card each year, and at last we spoke of Lady. It was like leaving the best for last. The brick house, Miss Berry said, was very well maintained by Robert Marini. His wife, a pretty Polish girl, kept the gardens nicely and, having found the empty pedestal at the end of the brick walk, had replaced the gazing-globe with another one. Robert was amused by and friendly with the Old Guard, made his own wine, kept large dogs, and found the Great South Meadow good for hunting. Their four children were as bright and incorrigible as ever we had been. Of course, they hadn't *known* Lady Harleigh, but surely, she said, they had *heard* of her.

I suppose they must have. No one cares much now who are lovers, if they are black and white, mismatched by color, sex, age, or whatever one may miss by. Lady Harleigh loved her butler, was all that people said, not much more. Yet, if they knew it, there was more. Had been more, all along, the missing pieces. I got them now from Miss Berry, and if the pieces did not spell "Eternity," they furnished enough detail to complete the picture of a woman I had known as Lady Harleigh, friend of my youth.

As we reminisced about our old neighbor, Miss Berry slid effortlessly into her story. I did not have the feeling she was unburdening herself to me, but merely that close to the end of her long tenure she wanted to round out for me the story of Lady Harleigh's life. She was a comfortable old lady in her comfortable old parlor, telling me a tale. I listened.

"You have been fortunate in your friend. I should say *our* friend, for she was mine, too. She loved you very much, you know that— you were like a son to her. If she were still alive, I wouldn't say anything, she wouldn't want me to. Still, Lady Harleigh can't always have her own way." She gave a little laugh of amusement, frail sounds that fluttered soft as a butterfly's wings. "You're a grown man now, but who knows what the future holds, eh?"

"Yes," I agreed, "who knows?"

"You know she was living over there with her houseman, of course. The whole town does. No matter, it was what she wanted. People never know what it takes to make another person happy. In any case, she led a trapped life. Trapped by that dreadful mother, Frau Strasser, trapped by that dreadful father-in-law, Ellsworth Harleigh. I know—I was there."

I looked steadily at her and said nothing. She continued.

"Edward Harleigh was a ne'er-do-well from the beginning. If his father didn't hate him, he knew well enough what sort of son he was raising. There was one thing he wanted before he died: an heir. It was an obsession with him, to see the family name carried on. When the lawyers advised him to draw up his last will, he gave Edward two choices: either to go his own way and be cut off, or to marry and have a child, in which case he and the wife would inherit equally.

"It was Mr. Harleigh who decided Edward should marry Lady. He'd seen her when she came to the house to help her mother fit dresses for Mrs. Harleigh. Took a shine to her, as you might say. He liked what he saw: a sensible, realistic girl, who could hold Edward in check, and with plenty of robust life in her to assure an heir. He'd seen enough of those watered-down girls with names and money and no milk in their paps. So he decided Edward must have Adelaide Strasser of Knobb Street.

"Lady, of course, made the mistake so many women do. She was sure she could change Edward, which of course adds up to plenty of self-delusion, nothing more. The thing was, she didn't really like Edward. All the stories about him frightened her. Folks were surprised she didn't jump to the bait right away, and that she avoided

Edward every chance she got. So Mr. Harleigh had a talk with Mrs. Strasser, and those two got in cahoots. Oh, she was a tartar, I tell you. It didn't come out until after the old man was dead, but he'd settled a handsome trust fund on Mrs. Strasser for her getting Lady to marry Edward—and I guess she earned the money, because it wasn't an easy job. But little by little, between them, they wore the poor girl down. Edward was given orders to court her, and the old woman wheedled and cajoled and nagged until Lady started going about with him. Edward was charming and handsome, and could be a nice boy if he put his mind to it. And there was the promise of money in the air; poor Lady, she'd gotten so tired of scrubbing floors, and doing beadwork for her mother. So with Edward and the parents all pressing her, she said yes.

"So it's arranged that he takes her off on one of those overnight excursions, down to New York on a steamboat. But at Saybrook he got her off the boat and made them miss it. They stayed overnight at a hotel, and he managed to have his way with her, as the saying goes. And Lady wasn't one of those tramps from the River House, she had scruples. Why, he'd no sooner bring her home from a picnic, than there he'd be in the taproom with that Al Yager and Yonny Turpin from the feed store. There used to be a girl—Elsie Thatcher was her name—she worked the tables in the taproom. A nice girl, but not such a good one that she could resist Edward Harleigh. Old Mr. Harleigh got her run out of town for having a baby. Edward's baby. If Elsie'd been smart, she'd of fought for some money at least, but they sent the Constable with her to put her on the train at Lamentation, and that was the last anyone heard of Elsie.

"Edward had had a narrow escape, and the old man was furious, and if Edward didn't mend his ways, at least he darned them enough to fool Lady. They got married in a hurry. Went to Mexico on their honeymoon. When they got there, Edward informs Lady that she's pregnant. *Edward*, mind you. She'd been examined by that terrible Dr. Forbes, he was the Harleighs' doctor, and he didn't bother informing Lady, or even her mother, but told Mr. Harleigh instead. Now, there's a nice, small-town girl who doesn't know a lot about these matters, her mother's never told her about much, and here she is on her honeymoon, and she's already going to have a baby. They're to wait the birth out in Guadalajara and have the certificate date falsified, then pop up back home, showing the child all over Main Street as being just a reg'lar little fellow.

"Except the baby miscarried and died. Three days later Edward got her on a train back East, no one the wiser, but Mr. Harleigh's mad as a wet hen. They got back here and found that he'd picked out a house for them, the one across the Green; it's all furnished, and Lady never had a say in anything.

"But she was determined she was going to make Edward happy, and the old man, too. She had spirit, if nothing else. Naturally she didn't feel so well after losing the baby, and that's how I began looking after her. Mrs. Strasser came around a lot, kind of keeping her eye on the poor girl. Mr. Harleigh hadn't long to live, and he wanted that grandchild, preferably a boy, to have the name. Edward was more terrified of him than ever, but he went back to his wild ways soon enough, I can tell you, and Lady took the hindmost —she'd just have to put up with it. He began frittering away his time on cars, and horses, and what-all he could find to keep him away from the house. He'd found out about the plot between his father and Mrs. Strasser, and he decided Lady was in on it, too, and he felt *he*'d been trapped. He came to hate poor Lady, who was just trying to do everything right by him.

"She urged him to get out from under the old man's thumb, to go somewhere else and get a job, but Edward wouldn't have any of it. And you don't get out from under Ellsworth Harleigh's thumb that easy. So they stayed. Mr. Harleigh ruled Edward, Mrs. Strasser ruled Lady, and between them the young couple did just as they were told.

"There was Lady, seeing Edward off in his Pope-Hartford auto in the morning, just like any other wife seeing her husband off to work, but he didn't go to work; he went to the City Club or the country club, and back drunk for dinner. Finally, she got pregnant again, and I was hired to look after her full time. I was there when he came home, drunk as usual, and she told him. He only laughed, saying he knew he had it in him, and that would hold the old bastard, meaning his father, of course. All Lady had to do was stay quiet and let the baby come, while Edward lolled around the River House, or he'd parade her around the Green so's Ruthie Sparrow and the others could see that there was going to be an heir at last. And each Sunday she was required to make an appearance at the Harleighs', where the old lady would instruct her in being a dutiful daughter-in-law, dutiful wife, and certainly a dutiful mother.

"Lady told me around that time that she knew she'd made a terrible mistake. She being Catholic, there's no hope of a divorce, even if the Harleighs would have permitted it. And if she leaves him,

Edward knows he'll be cut off without a red cent. One afternoon she was waiting for him in the living room. He came home three sheets to the wind, as usual, and there was a terrible row. Edward was always angry in those days, but Lady had a temper, too—the German in her, I expect. He slammed out of the house, and when I went in Lady said she'd offered to go away after the baby was born. He came back and practically dragged her out of the house, and later she told me he'd taken her to the Harleighs', where he'd made her repeat what she'd said about leaving. I was given orders to keep her upstairs and not let her out of my sight.

"So I moved into the house full time until the baby came. I brought her one of my pups, a little Yorkie I thought she'd like for company. Lady named him Bert, after Bert Lytell, an actor she'd been sweet on when she was younger. And Bert was good company for Lady, but when Edward came home he'd always have that dog locked up down in the cellar, and he threatened me more than once, I can tell you, saying not to let it upstairs again.

"I wasn't afraid of him. Nor of any of them, if it came to that, Harleigh or no. My family'd been in this town longer than they had, anyway, and my father had dealings with the Harleighs—not to his profit, believe me. Even so, it wasn't hard to sympathize with Lady Harleigh, after what Edward did to that poor dog.

"One afternoon he surprised us—he'd come home early from the country club—we were upstairs, and little Bert was on the bed. He came in, weaving in the doorway, and he saw the dog. He grabbed me by the arm and pushed me from the room, then slammed the door. I thought he was going to murder poor Lady—but it was the dog he was after. There were dreadful sounds, and then a fearful smell. He'd picked that poor little thing up and thrown it in the fire, and held it there with the poker, until—oh, it's easy to hate a man who'll hurt a dumb animal like that, and I've hated even the thought of Edward Harleigh from that day.

"Pretty soon the door opens and he comes out. Lady comes after him with the same poker he'd used on the dog, and she caught him on the stairs. She hit him, and he struck her back, and she fell down to the bottom. Even then I might have been able to save the baby, but Edward wouldn't let me telephone for the doctor until he'd cleared the house of the burned smell and the evidence about the dog—he didn't want anyone to know what he'd done. I did everything I could to help Lady, but by the time Dr. Forbes got there the baby was already slipping.

"After that, there wasn't any use of her trying. She was hurt bad, she lost her powers of speech, and when Edward enlisted and went off to France, I got Lady sent down to a place in Virginia, to recuperate. When she came back, she was talking again, and walking well enough, and Edward came home a hero, and I hoped things might get straightened out. They went off down South, but when they came back it was worse than ever. No one saw Lady, and it turned out Edward was keeping her a prisoner over there, but I didn't find this out until later. He was drinking worse than ever, and giving her all kinds of abuse.

"Then Lady took sick and I was called in again. There was an epidemic of what was called Spanish Influenza going round, and she'd caught it. She was a sick child, and I thought she'd never pull through. The house was a sty. Edward was sleeping across the hall, wouldn't go into her room. I got things cleaned up as best I could, and asked Dr. Forbes to keep me on the case. Lady was raving and practically mad. I was waiting for her to go into the crisis. She got worse day by day, but Edward didn't care. He took himself off to New York, and I stayed by Lady's bed until she came through. Sat there for three days and nights until she opened her eyes and I knew she was going to be all right."

She paused, and I thought she was going to get up and fix tea or make another interlude in her story, but she merely eased her back into the chair and looked at me. When she spoke again, I supposed it was some slight digression, the feeble rambling of an elderly person. Shaking her head, she said, "Cain killed Abel; we murder where we will or must." I only returned her look, and she proceeded as if I had made an interjection after her last sentence. "We are only apes, after all," she said in an explanatory tone, "and which of us knows wrong from right?"

The question was obviously rhetorical; I made no answer.

Then Miss Berry said, "She killed him, you know."

Her look was even and candid, with a hint of wistfulness about it. I thought I had misunderstood something, and my wondering expression brought a rephrasing of the sentence.

"Lady killed Edward."

I was trying hard to understand, but was not succeeding. "She murdered him?"

"Yes. Adelaide Harleigh murdered her husband, Edward Harleigh." Thus it was put to me, and I had no reply. Miss Berry continued.

"It must have come out of the fever, the idea, for I'd caught mutterings of it in her delirium. When Edward got home, Lady's fever was broken, but she was still contagious. The afternoon Edward was due back, she was insistent about making all kinds of preparations, having me bathe her, having the mirror to fix her face, the brush to brush her hair, and she wanted the wrapper she'd worn on her wedding night, a sea-green wrapper with peacocks on it. That night when I got up for a glass of water, I saw her leaving her bedroom and going into Edward's. He did not put her out that night. He accepted her, and it was the death of him."

"How?"

"She made him make love to her."

"But Edward hated her, wouldn't have anything to do with her."

"Yes, but not that night. That night she managed him well enough."

I could see how it must have gone. Edward had always desired her, even though he hated her. He wanted that body. On the river-boat, on their honeymoon, after his return from France, even after Washington, he had used her. Edward coming back from New York, getting drunk downstairs, coming up, finding her—alluring, irresistible. She opening her wrapper, inviting him to bed. Taking advantage of his lust, seducing him into death with kisses, fondlings, caresses, her lips against his, the disease given, microbes the murder weapon, hatred the motive.

I heard again Lady's voice, saying the words "There was nothing I wouldn't have done to have Jesse. Nothing. And nothing I *didn't* do."

Nothing, not even short of murder.

"Even if he hated her," Miss Berry was saying, "he couldn't resist. She exposed him, and he knew she'd done it on purpose. He laughed and said he was glad. By then he had contracted a deadly lobar pneumonia. But still he took time to die. I couldn't keep her out of the sickroom. He kept watching her, and sometimes he'd laugh; he said he'd come back, and she lived in her hell. After he died, she got out all those things, medals and pictures and who knew what, and put them right where she could see them, every day. She wanted to be reminded of what she'd done. I told her it was wrong, but nothing could convince her. I told her I'd never come back into that house again, and I almost never have. It's not in the German character to feel guilt, but it is in the New Englander's, and Adelaide was always more New England than anything else.

But I don't think folks were put on earth to bear that sort of pain, no matter what they've done."

Nor did I. A sea-green wrapper with peacocks on it. I remembered the scene in the attic, Ag dressed in the wrapper, and Lady's look, a look of horror and of guilt. It must have been unbearable.

"Still," Miss Berry concluded, "she was nice, wasn't she? A very nice lady?"

Yes, I agreed, a very nice lady.

Together we shared her secret, but together we shared something else as well, for we knew that a woman may be weak or strong, commit folly, do dreadful and terrible things, be all or be nothing, and be—Lady Harleigh. And she herself had learned the greatest lesson of all: that we learn not through happiness but through suffering.

I did not go immediately back to the Marini farm, but cut across the Green, a familiar path, to the brick house over the way. I wanted to see the gazing-globe that Robert's wife had restored to the garden.

I had left Miss Berry's sun porch, where everything seemed the same. And now, seated in the garden that I could only think of as Lady's, on her stone bench, here, too, everything seemed the same. All my earlier feelings of disorientation fled as I looked around me. Though Lady was dead, at her place all seemed as I remembered it. The summerhouse was gone, destroyed in the hurricane, but the weathercock still spun on the carriage-house gable, and the brick walk still led to the little circle of cemented brick, last resting place of Ott, the *corpus delicti*. And within the circle, as of old, the gazing-globe. All the same: almost exactly as it had always been. I had changed; this had not.

A caul of cobweb stretched from the globe to the top of the pedestal. I wiped it away with my finger. A bug scuttled into the hole underneath. Putting my fingertip on the globe's "North Pole" as Lady had once done, I walked around it. And under the arc of my arm, as I moved, the globe reflected all those landmarks I had already noted for myself, flowing in one unbroken line, neither starting nor ending at any particular place, but infinitely continuing. And I thought if ever the word was to have been spelled from broken pieces, it had been spelled now. For the globe had been made whole again, a piece of magic made manifest not by esoteric powers but by the mere fact of a dentist's pretty Polish wife buying a new globe to replace the old one. Replacement, too, was continuity—perhaps even "Eternity."

Sitting there on Lady's stone bench, for no reason I could immediately perceive I remembered an incident that happened the summer Jesse had first put down the brick walkway, and the brick circle where I now was. The birdbath was still there then, and I had been filling it for Lady with the garden hose. I went in the kitchen, and she and I sat at the kitchen table eating sandwiches Elthea had made. There was a knock at the screen door, and a tentative voice called, " 'Day, Ma'am." It was a tramp, one of the hoboes who were everywhere in those Depression days. We'd often see them sitting in the open boxcars as the trains went by at Rose Rock.

"Good day to you, sir," Lady replied amiably, and asked what he wanted. Well, he said, he was looking for a handout. Could she spare him ten cents to see him along up to Hartford on the trolley? Lady invited him in to sit and have one of Elthea's sandwiches. I didn't like the tramp—he looked dirty and was unshaven—but he was a jovial sort of fellow, and soon gave us large chunks of his personal history. He'd held all sorts of jobs, had even been a barker on the midway at the Century of Progress.

"Did you see Sally Rand?" I asked.

"Sure, I seen Sally and her fans. Bubbles, too, but she's tricky, she don't let you see much else, 'cept all them feathers."

"Is that all?" Lady asked, "just feathers?"

"Well, at the finale there you get a peek at her behind—pardon, Ma'am."

"And you ride the trains, you say?"

"Trains, trains, trains, rode 'em all. But they're hard on a fellow's mouth, if you see what I mean."

"I should think it would be the other end it would be hard on."

"Train shakes up a fellow's teeth somethin' awful. Mine rattle around in there like dice." He was helping himself to his third sandwich. He said that mostly he stayed away from the cities, which had become fearful places, with nothing but breadlines and apple sellers on the corners. He had a wife and a mother at home, but he couldn't get work to support them. He kept to the small towns where good housewives like Lady helped him out.

"You're a lucky kid," the tramp told me, "having a mother like this."

Lady laughed. "I'm not his mother, I'm sort of a—distant relation."

"That a fact? You got a husband, Ma'am?"

"No, I don't."

"Too bad. A looker like you, too."

Lady hid a smile behind her coffee cup. When the tramp had had a piece of Elthea's lime pie and a glass of milk to wash it down, he got up to go, again asking for ten cents for the trolley. Lady took a bill from her pocket and put it in his hand. The tramp's eyes popped.

"Holy smoke--a twenty-dollar bill! I haven't seen one in I don't know how long." He stared at it, tugged it a time or two to hear it snap, then pocketed it. "That'll feed me for two weeks at least. God *bless* you—I didn't get your name."

"Just call me Lady."

"God bless you, lady. And, say—"

"Yes?"

"Could you just let me have the ten cents anyhow? I don't want to break the bill."

She gave him the dime.

And sitting in Lady's October garden, that was what I remembered, a tramp who'd seen Sally Rand, and was working the kitchen doors around Pequot Landing, and Lady, her eyebrows turned up in that way that told of her amusement, and the chuckle of appreciation that grew into the laugh that was hers alone.

God bless you, Lady, I thought.

From the stone bench beside the gazing-globe I saw someone standing in the driveway. Robert Marini's pretty Polish wife? No, my own pretty Italian one. I joined her, and arm in arm we walked down the drive. Worried, she had come searching for me.

"What have you been doing?"

"Looking, just looking."

"For what?"

"Something I lost."

"When?"

"A long time ago."

"Did you find it?" She looked at me so earnestly, with those great dark eyes, so fearful in their Latin gravity, that I laughed.

"Yes, I found it." She seemed relieved, and slid her cold fingers into my glove, and her lips were warm on my ear. "The kids all right?" I asked.

"They've just come back with Agnes and Harold from seeing the animals."

"Did Rabbit show them the fat badger?"

"Yes. Do you know what Lew said? He said it was 'gross.' Wasn't that a funny word?"

"For Lew or the badger?"

I kissed her cheek and we walked up the Green between the young trees that were replacing the old. People were keeping indoors on that bleak afternoon, and the Green was deserted. No dogs barked among the fallen leaves which flew in gusts, but as we walked along, Teresa and I, I thought I could hear the sound of summer voices under the Great Elm, where children played, and it seemed that the wind sang old songs.

As Miss Berry had said, it's good when one feels the affections of the past. They are among the lasting things—they will never leave us.

And as Lady had told me, never is a long, long time.